Painted

Ladies

Painted Ladies

SIOBHÁN PARKINSON

NEW
ISLAND

PAINTED LADIES
First published 2010
by New Island
2 Brookside
Dundrum Road
Dublin 14

www.newisland.ie

ISBN 978-1-84840-081-8

Cover design by Someday
Book design by Inka Hagen

Printed by CPI Antony Rowe, Chippenham, Wiltshire

New Island received financial assistance from
The Arts Council (An Comhairle Ealaíon), Dublin, Ireland

10 9 8 7 6 5 4 3 2 1

for Roger

ABOUT THE AUTHOR

Siobhán Parkinson is a well-known
novelist for children and young people,
and is currently Laureate na nÓg – the
Children's Laureate of Ireland. She has
won several awards for her writing and
is widely translated. She also works as
an editor and translator.

This is her second novel for adults.

AUTHOR'S NOTE

Although this novel is based on the lives of real people, it is a work of fiction and is not to be relied upon as an accurate account of these people's lives. Dates, names and events have been altered, elided, distorted and invented. In particular, the thoughts, emotions and motivations attributed to the characters are entirely imagined and no biographical weight whatsoever should be attached to them.

I am particularly indebted to Tonni Arnold's biography of Marie Krøyer, *Balladen om Marie* (Gyldendal 1999).

I have also drawn on the following sources: Poul Bernth, *Holger Drachmann* (Carl Andersen 1989); Emmy Drachmann, *Edith* (Sklovlaenge 1992); Maria Heilberg, *Martha, Marie og Anna: Martha Johansen, Marie Krøyer og Anna Ancher i Skagen* (L&R Fakta 1999); National Gallery of Ireland, *P.S. Krøyer and the Artists' Colony at Skagen* (exhibition catalogue, undated); Skagen's Museum, *Portraits of a Marriage* (1997); Lise Svanholm, *Malerne pa Skagen* (Gyldendal 2001; also published in English as *Northern Light*, Gyldendal 2004); Lise Svanholm (ed.), *Agnes og Marie: Breven meelem Agnes Slott-Moller og Marie Krøyer 1885–1937* (Gyldendal 1991).

Thanks to Roger Bennett, Valerie Coghlan, Paula Leyden, Deirdre Tinney, and most especially Tom O'Neill for comments on various drafts. Thanks also to The Tyrone Guthrie Centre, Annaghmakerrig, where part of this novel was written; to my brother Padraig Parkinson who lent me his apartment to write in and to Patricia Luz of Dublin and Skagen for her support.

Prologue

Hugo Alfvén fell in love with a painted lady that he saw one dark November afternoon in Copenhagen.

He always knew when he was falling in love because he heard a certain sound. It was a little faltering sopranino arpeggio, a tiny cascade of high, pianissimo notes. So soft that they floated away as soon as they were sounded, out of earshot. Tantalising. Then came a bar or two of . . . was it Grieg? – no, surely it must be Alfvén, his own music, as yet unwritten. It came echoing from some deep and distant lake high in the mountains, where melodies are tossed from height to snowy height and fade wistfully away, too beautiful to last.

Hugo sighed. That exquisite nape! A breathless sequence of quavers tiptoeing up and up and then tumbling delicately over each other on their way back down, and the knot of dark hair was the solid minim chord in which the rippling exhalation of the quavers ended. A tendril of hair escaped and floated about her sweet face, an appoggiatura.

Hugo spun away from the picture. 'Who is she?' he asked.

'Smitten, are you?' came the smirking reply.

'Who is she?' Hugo repeated, irritated at having to ask again.

'She is . . . our national beauty,' his friend said grandly.

'What nonsense! You can't have a national beauty; it is not like a flag or an anthem.'

'Nevertheless,' said his friend, spreading his hands, 'there it is.'

'She is almost beautiful enough to be Swedish,' said Hugo, half-mockingly. 'Well, I shall make her a Swede, you wait and see.' He tucked his muffler inside the lapels of his overcoat with a masterful movement.

'Make her a Swede?' asked his friend. 'Are you handing out free citizenship these days, in that forest of a country you come from? Let me guess – maybe you have left the Conservatory and landed yourself a job in the Ministry of the Interior so you can bestow Swedish passports on women you deem beautiful enough?'

'You do talk nonsense, my good fellow,' said Hugo, drawing on his gloves. 'Come along, it's late. We have to go. I feel a sonata coming on.'

'You're the one who's talking nonsense,' his friend said. 'What do you mean, make her a Swede? Explain yourself.'

'I mean I shall marry her,' said Hugo. He stood on the gallery floor and described a flourishing circle in the air with his walking cane, as if that clinched it. 'My goodness, have you no logical powers at all? Can you not follow a simple conversation?'

'Marry her! You're going to marry a woman in a picture! A painted lady.'

'She's not just a woman in a picture. She exists. You said so yourself, Dirk. That is quite the best thing you have said all afternoon, by the way. So, since she exists, it follows that I can find her and, having found her, that I can marry her, and if I marry her, she can become a Swede, can't she, you dunderhead?'

'Yes, but you can't marry her. She's married already. It was her husband who painted the picture.'

'Divorce, my dear fellow. Divorce. It is for cases like this that it exists. Now, come along!'

Hugo started to walk away from the picture, heading for the exit.

'You're mad,' said his friend, falling into step beside him, but he said it as if it were a compliment, as if it seemed to him that there was something admirable in becoming besotted with a woman in a painting. Then he added, with a bark of laughter, 'I do believe you've never experienced it before.'

'What?' asked Hugo.

'Love,' said Dirk.

'Love?' said Hugo, still striding briskly along. 'Of course I've experienced love before. What about Anke?' He named his last lover.

'And Karin,' his friend added, 'Ursula. Alice.'

'There, you see,' said Hugo triumphantly. 'I loved them all.'

'No, Hugo. No. They loved you. It's completely different.'

'Hmm,' said Hugo. He paused, then added, 'All the same, I envy him her. And you'll see, I shall have her.'

'It will end in tears, Hugo. Mark my words. They're a people apart, you know, that crowd of artists. They all live up in a kind of mad place in the north of Denmark . . .'

Hugo snorted. 'Denmark doesn't know the meaning of north!'

'Nevertheless. They're all married to each other.'

'That is usual,' snapped Hugo. 'One cannot be married to oneself.'

'No, no, I mean, they are all intermarried. They all married each other's sisters and cousins and they've all got each other's babies.'

Hugo sighed.

'I mean, they've all adopted each other's bastards. It's like a kind of *coven*, I'm telling you. The wives write and paint, if you don't mind. Like men, I mean. Not just watercolours. Actual paintings. You don't want to go anywhere near them.'

'You make it sound quite intriguing, my dear fellow,' said Hugo. 'I am more convinced than ever. And I can't leave this beauty trapped in a coven! I shall have to rescue her. Even if she has many bastards.'

'Oh, she hasn't got any of those,' said his companion. 'She's quite the most respectable of them, I believe. Doesn't paint. No madness in the family, no half-siblings in the house. German stock.' His voice fell on the last phrase.

Hugo snorted again. 'You can't scare me off with *that*. You'll see. I'll find her, I'll get her. You shall be my best man.'

Hugo's companion shrugged. By the time they reached the door of the gallery and looked out at the yellowy gloom of the November afternoon, the lights winking on one by one in the Tivoli gardens, Hugo seemed already to have forgotten the painted lady who, five minutes earlier, had absorbed his interest so completely.

Chapter 1

It was as big as a cathedral, that Hotel de Ville. *Two* cathedrals. Too flamboyant, perhaps, for such a heavy building, but impressive, oh yes, yes, it was that all right. Marie had been in a permanent state of being impressed since her arrival in Paris. She could never have imagined such grandeur. The Louvre – massive. The Palais Royal. The Invalides. The whole place made her feel about three years old, tiny and excited and oddly exhausted, but whirling – yes, *whirling!* – with the thrill of it all. It seemed to her now as if the flatness of the paving stones under her feet was an illusion, and she became suddenly aware of the earth as a spinning globe, like a huge children's ball, and herself barely perched on it, a minute figure in a sprigged cotton gown. She felt she had to make an effort to keep her footing on its curving surface, that she might fall off if she did not concentrate on maintaining her balance. And yet she looked up and vertiginously up, straining to see the mansard windows, the steeply sloping Parisian roofs, raisin-coloured and darkly gleaming above the pale stone.

By comparison with all this splendour, Marie's native Copenhagen was a homely sort of place, its gingerbread houses leaning companionably against each other. But no. She shook herself, as if giving herself a silent telling off. She must not even think . . . No. Allegiance to Denmark came before everything.

They spoke German at home, in Marie's family, but that was a secret. Nobody had ever told her this in so many words, but even as quite a young child she had known the protocol: she was to speak German to her family – even her dolls spoke German, or at least they listened in German – but Danish to everyone outside the family, and that included the servants. Of course, the servants would not have understood her anyhow if she had spoken to them in German, but that was not the main reason one used Danish when speaking to them. The main reason was that they must not be reminded that the family was German. Papa said it was because of 'that business over the annexation of Schleswig-Holstein'. It still rankled, he said. Whatever that meant.

She knew what it meant now that she was grown up – but only just. In any case, this *rankling* was supposed to explain why a German family in Denmark tried to be as inconspicuous as possible, and why she was required to try at all times to pass for Danish. Which was absurd, because she *was* Danish, born in Copenhagen, lived there all her life, never left it till now, on this trip to Paris.

Marie looked around and pinched herself. Silly, since pinching did nothing to reduce Paris to credible dimensions. And it was so *busy*, she could scarcely cross the street for omnibuses and phaetons and cabriolets and traps and, oh, landaus and . . . carriages she didn't even know the names of, and all jostling for space – pointless really, you might as well walk for all the speed you could get up in that mêlée, though goodness knows you would think those streets would be broad enough. Something to do with Napoleon, wasn't it, the *first* Napoleon, the way the streets in Paris were so broad? But Napoleon or no Napoleon, it was some challenge to fight one's way through the traffic now, not to mention what the horses left, brown and steaming, on the thoroughfares. Her nose crinkled unconsciously. *Ordure*, she should call it here – you had to call it something, after all, even if only to yourself. She straightened her back – well, well, that was not a thing to dwell on – and tightened her grip on her new green silk parasol, with its sleek ebony and silver handle, that Mama had given her for her trip. Not like Mama to be so hopeful, mind you. It must have been the green silk, fell for it probably. Couldn't resist. Mama fell in love with fabrics the way men fell in love with actresses, Papa always said, which was – and here he would enumerate on his fingers, one for each adverb – frequently, deeply, unwisely and expensively.

Marie carried the parasol for the style of it, furled like a walking stick, for it wasn't sunny today, not a bit; on the contrary, it was quite overcast. Warm, though, very warm, and close. Indian summer, you called it, when the weather was warm so late in the year. Of course, it was an umbrella she should have brought: those clouds, almost a blue grey, you'd have to mix a spot of cobalt in to get that colour. But she didn't have a stylish umbrella, and her parasol was so pretty, apart from the novelty of it.

Her mother always carried a preventative umbrella, even when the sun was splitting the paving stones. Single-handedly she kept the rain off herself and her family. A veritable rain marshal, she was. They all twitted her about it, pointing at skies wide and blue and innocent of clouds, how could it rain?

'It always rains,' Mama insisted, 'when you have no umbrella. So if you take an umbrella, it won't rain. It's quite simple. I don't see why you can't follow such a simple line of reasoning.'

'It is not we who don't follow, Mama,' Valdemar used to argue, 'it is your line of reasoning that doesn't follow. Look here, the way it works is that if you forget your umbrella and it rains, then you get wet, and then you remember how unwise you were to leave your umbrella at home, and your brain makes a link between forgetting your umbrella and getting wet. But it is not a causal link.'

'Of course it is causal,' said their mother stoutly. 'It is because you forgot your umbrella that you got wet.'

'Yes, but that is not why it *rains*!' Valdemar would be dancing with impatience at his mother's dimwittedness.

'I never said it was. But if you take your umbrella, you don't get wet and that is the main thing.'

⚶

'Mother, you are infuriating!' Valdemar barked.

'Take your umbrella, my dear,' said his mother mildly.

'But it is not going to rain, Mama, so it is an unnecessary encumbrance. Why can't you see that?'

'But you won't get wet, will you, if you have your umbrella?'

'I won't get wet because it is not going to rain.'

'If you leave it behind, it will rain,' predicted his mother implacably. 'Take it.'

And Valdemar would snatch the proffered umbrella from his mother's outstretched hand and stamp out of the front door, his teeth gritted in frustration.

'Another drowning averted,' Marie's father would say, winking slyly at his wife. 'If you go on like this, my treasure, the crops will fail.'

'Well, you never can tell,' Mama would reply. 'Better safe than sorry. And no doubt it rains where the crops are, since I am not there to prevent it.'

Marie laughed out loud, remembering, and a red-faced, rough-looking sort of man wearing a green baize apron and carrying a baguette winked at her. She started and, evidently pleased at getting a reaction, he motioned salaciously with the stick of bread. She flushed bright red – the scoundrel! – and turned back to the stream of traffic, sluggish but belligerent, that she was going to have to get the better of if she was to reach the other side of the street. She must remember not to laugh out loud on the streets. It gave the wrong impression. Honestly, the French!

Last night in her cheap room, she had lain stiffly on her narrow, lumpy mattress, the white coverlet drawn up to her chin, aware of a mousy odour, and felt the nearness of the walls and the low sloping ceiling and the bare and gritty floorboards. She was the centre point of a cuboid space of air defined by those mottled grey boundaries, and not a soul knew exactly where she was – though the landlady probably had a pretty good idea, but since the landlady didn't know *who* she was, it came to the same thing. It gave her, at the same time, a thrill of fear and a glorious sense of freedom. She'd sighed a deep and satisfied sigh and flung her arms out, imagining all the other cuboids of air containing people, all laid out in their beds, stacked one above the other like clothes in a chest of drawers, some of them in pairs, maybe entangled together. Perhaps not another being in the whole city was lying awake, imagining everyone else suspended in their boxes of air, separated from each other by walls and floors, but close, some of them close enough to touch without even leaving one's bed.

She was wearing her best cream dress today, in case after all she did need to open her parasol, for the blue did not look nearly so well with it, not nearly so well – blue and green should never be seen – and a large Italian straw hat, so summery. Much better to encourage the sun than to believe you could control the rain by carrying an umbrella.

There, she had finally spotted a gap in the traffic, and she darted into it and across the road. Now she fished in her pocket for that address Georg had given her. Some writer he insisted she should visit, an older man. She had no interest in visiting old Danish people in Paris; she wanted to meet young people, new people, artists. Writers were artists too, she conceded grudgingly, interesting enough in their way, but it was not the same. She wanted to visit studios, take drawing classes, painting classes, get herself the artistic education she could not get in Copenhagen – that was why she had come. Visiting some crumbling old writer was only going to be a distraction. Best get it over with, though.

She felt – no! – a single fat drop on her thumb. How could it rain on one's thumb? It felt too pointed, too personal. She looked all around, poking her hand tentatively in front of her, as if to test an imaginary tap. Nothing. The air was thick with heat, though it was not nearly noon. She must have imagined the drop, or it had splashed from some passing receptacle perhaps. She scrutinised the directions she had written down for herself and set off at a brisk pace.

A drop fell on her nose this time. A special shower aimed just at her? No sign of rain anywhere else. She hurried on. And then came three fat drops on the pavement in front of her, making spots as big as florins. There was no doubt about it now. A loud drumming on awnings. A quick smell of street was released by the moisture in the air. As she looked around for shelter, wet was suddenly everywhere as if it had been raining for hours. It rained so hard, the rain was splashing back off the pavement with the force of its own impact. Already Marie's feet were in puddles, her hat was streaming, her shoulders heavy with rain. She unfurled the parasol unthinkingly but it was porous and the silk became quickly sodden. It would be ruined, and what could she tell Mama? A headscarf – she had had a square of something, somewhere. She balanced the opened parasol upside down between her knees as she fished out the pointless headscarf and drew it clumsily over her straw hat, her fingers slippery with rain. It seemed to be getting heavier, if that was possible. Lightning blazed in front of her eyes, the whole street suddenly illuminated in its yellow-blue flash, and thunder rumbled almost immediately, all around her. The traffic seemed to come to a halt, the poor horses, drenched. People disappeared off the streets into shops and apartment houses and cafés. Only she was left on the pavement, brandishing her miserable green parasol, her fingers unable to fumble it closed, and with water streaming from her soaking hat, hair, cuffs, down her nose. Too late to take refuge in a café. She was so wet now she might as well go on. Down there and then right, across the *place* and the fourth on the left. She'd written it all out carefully before leaving her room.

Nobody answered at the Schillings' address. She stood shivering in the doorway. She must look like a drowned rat, though why rats should be particularly susceptible to drowning she did not know. Something to do with sewers, perhaps? What filthy things came to mind today!

Rain was falling off her as if she herself were somehow the source of it. She must get inside, out of this deluge. Her feet squelched in her boots. Why didn't they come? She was now as impatient to meet these people as she had been reluctant a quarter of an hour previously. She rang the doorbell a second time and a great gruff voice called out, '*J'arrive, j'arrive, soyez tranquille!*'

It was Mr Schilling himself who opened the door. She had expected there'd be a maid or at least a concierge, and she had to rearrange her face quickly to greet her host. He wasn't all that old after all.

'*Alors? Que voulez-vous, Madame . . . Mademoiselle?*'

'I'm Marie Triepke,' said Marie in French, stretching out her hand. Then she realised how foolish it was to speak French to a fellow-Dane – force of habit – and she lapsed gratefully into Danish. 'Dr Brandes sent me.' Marie held out a soggy envelope containing a letter of introduction from a professor at the university in Copenhagen, a man she had got to know some time ago when she had attended a series of public lectures, and who thought well of her mind, in spite of her looks. 'I'm an art student,' she added, trying to make herself sound something, 'from Copenhagen.'

'I see,' said Schilling. 'Well, well, come in, come in. Let's get a look at you.'

Marie stepped into the hallway and shook her parasol out onto the street. Now that she was out of the onslaught of the rain, her fingers came back to themselves and she managed to let the parasol down and roll it up, smiling apologetically at Mr Schilling as she did so.

'Not much of an umbrella,' he remarked.

'No,' she said, loosening the scarf she had tied over her hat. Then she took the hat off too, for it was still streaming water onto her shoulders. Her hair was coming down.

'Oh, my goodness me!' said Schilling, as he 'got a look at her', as he put it. 'It's an art student, dearest,' he called over his shoulder to his hidden wife. 'Female. Wet. And excessively beautiful.'

Marie blushed. She had never learned how to deal with it. She must have been about twelve when it started. She would come into a room with a message from her mother to a visitor, or she would be sent to the dairy for a pint of cream, or she would open the door to the postman, and it would happen. The Staring. She would put out her hand for the parcel or the cream or to hand over a note, and the other person would have forgotten whatever transaction was supposed to happen between them. At first, she had thought that perhaps her origins were revealed in her voice, some slight edge of pronunciation that she had picked up from her parents' quaint way of speaking. But then she realised that the Staring was happening even before she opened her mouth. She ought to have got used to it by now and in general she could ignore it but not everyone was as frank as Mr Schilling. Frankness is doubtless refreshing but just now she found it a little disconcerting.

Mrs Schilling called something to her husband. Marie didn't catch it.

'One that Georg has sent us,' Mr Schilling called back. 'Did we order an art student, my love? Can you remember?'

Marie hesitated. 'Oh, I'm sorry . . . I didn't . . . '

'Eh-heh! Eh-heh!' laughed Schilling. 'Joke, my dear young lady, just my rather hopeless idea of a little joke. "Order: one female art student, beautiful." Come in, I say, come in out of the rain!'

Though she was in already.

'Well, my goodness me,' said Mr Schilling again. 'Are you going to stay, or are you just coming to tea?'

'Oh, just . . . tea would be delightful.'

'Not staying, eh? Oh well, come in, come in.' He ushered her from the street door towards the door of a ground-floor apartment.

'It's a Miss Triepke,' he called to his wife. 'She has come for tea.'

He ushered her into the *salon* of the small apartment, and Mrs Schilling was now visible. She was reading the newspaper by the light of a tall, narrow window.

'Miss Triepke!' she called out, without looking up from her paper. *Enchantée*. I'll make the tea in just a moment, when I get to the end of this war in Africa. It's very gruelling, and I shall need tea after it. Do you take sugar?'

'One lump,' said Marie. Strange to be talking to the back of a person's head. 'But I could make the tea and you could get on with the war.'

Mrs Schilling looked up and laughed.

'She'll do, Schilling,' she said to her husband. 'Georg never fails us. Kitchen's that way.' She pointed towards the kitchen and went back to her newspaper.

Marie was thrilled with their eccentricity. To be sent to the kitchen without even having had a proper introduction! That would be appalling rudeness in anyone else, but these people made it feel like a privilege.

Mr Schilling followed her into the kitchen with a large bath towel and said, 'My wife, she forgets herself. You dry off; I'll make the tea. I know how she likes it. Get you warmed up in no time.'

'Good heavens, girl,' said Mrs Schilling, when Marie came back into the *salon*. She had put the newspaper aside and was able to concentrate on her visitor now. 'You can't sit around in those clothes. You are *saturated*. You'll get pneumonia, catch your death of it, and we shall be to blame. Come with me this instant and we'll find something for you to wear while your gown dries out.'

Marie murmured in protest, but she might as well have been a small damp hen giving peevish little clucks for all the notice Mrs Schilling took. She steered Marie by the elbows into another room, which was festooned with female attire, all too flouncy for Marie, and also, fortunately, too small. In the end, they found something to fit. It was a Japanese-style wrap. Mrs Schilling chafed and hurried Marie out of her dress, which was heavy still with rainwater, till she stood and shivered in her petticoat. The wrap was chill and flimsy and made her skin quiver.

'And your shoes,' said Mrs Schilling. 'Off with them. You'll have to go barefoot for the moment. I'll stuff them with newspaper to prevent them drying out like banana skins.'

Marie nodded. Now that she had taken off her outer layer of clothing, wet as it was, she was suddenly very cold and could hardly speak.

Back in the *salon*, Mr Schilling had opened the draught on the little shiny brown-tiled stove that was set into the chimney breast. He had pushed a chair close to it and pulled the other chairs and a small table away from it, for the day was too warm for sitting over a stove.

'Sit here, my dear,' he said, ushering her to an armchair. 'Oh, your pretty little feet!' he exclaimed, unselfconsciously.

For a moment, Marie thought he might pick her feet up and rub them for her. The thought filled her with dismay, and she curled her toes back in under her armchair, out of sight.

Mrs Schilling, meanwhile, was draping Marie's dress and sopping stockings, with shamefully stained feet, over the chair by the stove.

'So, you're here for the fair, I take it?' said Mrs Schilling when the tea was poured, as if the young woman opposite her was not barefoot and dressed in a morning gown.

'Lot of damn nonsense,' Mr Schilling cut in, before Marie could answer. 'Every mountebank and circus act in Christendom is here, every swindler and huckster and three-card-trick-man, every expensive whore and purveyor of cheap absinthe, every tawdry knick-knack-seller and every pimp, troubadour, dwarf, pedlar, liontamer, carpet-bagger and impresario, every fudge-maker and hoopla man and sausage-fryer, dancing girls from Bali, if you've ever heard of Bali, cocktails made from coconut and guavas, if you've ever heard of guavas, lamps fuelled by *electricity* that trap light in glass globes, steam engines for doing all sorts of chores that God gave people perfectly good faculties for doing themselves, fire-eaters, if you don't mind, small *black* boys dripping with jewels and waving ostrich feather fans. A human zoo! No, really, there *is* such a thing. Where you can see *Esquimaux*, and other freaks of nature. And all in the name of revolution, commemorating the fall of the Bastille. Prisons, prisons, all prisons, just different kinds, that's all. As for that monstrosity they have put on the Champs de Mars, that iron tower, like the skeleton of a building – all bones, no skin. Appalling. And the traffic is insupportable, *insuppor-table*.' He pronounced the second instance of the word in the French way, banging his fist on the arm of his chair with each syllable, and stopped for breath.

His wife laughed. 'Excellent, dear heart, you tell 'em!' She turned to Marie. 'He is not really a demagogue, my dear; he does not lecture us over tea every day. It's an article he is writing, you may count upon it; he's just trying it out on us.'

'I'm mainly here for the art exhibition,' Marie said cautiously.

'Ah yes,' said Mr Schilling. 'You're an art student. The Universal Art Exhibition, the grandest exhibition there has ever been on earth. Indeed, indeed. Well, it is like being invited to the birthday party of the world, is it not? There is nowhere it is better to be. This is where everyone *is*, my dear, this is the defining moment of history. Such gaiety! Such glamour! And Mr Eiffel's filigree tower, such a feat of engineering, and a work of art to boot! So elegant!'

Marie stared.

'Different article,' his wife explained, 'different journal. Pseudo-nym.'

'I see,' said Marie faintly.

'Well, we are so glad you came, my dear,' said Mrs Schilling. 'You will have to meet everyone. The Anchers are here, of course.'

'Oh!' said Marie, her eyes widening with delight. Georg had been right to send her here – how could she have doubted him? Such kind people these were, and they seemed to know just the people she wanted to meet. 'The Anchers! Good heavens!'

'Do you know them?' asked Mrs Schilling, but she did not wait for an answer. 'Mrs Ancher is such a dear person, we love her to death, don't we, Schilling?'

'Of course,' Marie murmured.

'Did you say you knew them?'

'No,' said Marie, 'but oh, I should love to meet them, simply love it.' She had to make an effort to prevent herself from squirm-ing with anticipation in her chair. 'I've never met them. I . . . I know their work of course.'

'And Krøyer. You must meet him too. He'll be here presently, I expect. Everyone says he is the best of the lot of them, best artist in Scandinavia, they say. That's the kind of person you will want to meet, Miss Triepke, since you are studying to be an artist.'

Marie drew in her breath and concentrated very hard on not blushing. She nodded. Of course, Krøyer, she would love to meet Mr Krøyer. Indeed, yes, she could venture to say it, she thought, yes. Actually, she *had* met him. She would not say they were ac-quainted, exactly. But they had been introduced. He had painted her, in fact, she added in a light tone. But it was only as one of a group, she was a sort of prop, really, background, he wouldn't re-member, she was only a student. Though he did also come to her studio from time to time, not her *own* studio, no, no, nothing as glamorous as that, a place where she painted with other women students.

'How do you mean, comes to your studio? You mean, he teaches you?'

Marie shook her head.

'Oh no, I wouldn't go so far as to say . . . We couldn't afford to have him teach us exactly. But he comes from time to time, and he looks at our work.'

'Just looks at it?'

'Well, yes, that is the idea. We ask him to come and give us the benefit . . . '

'I see. And you pay him? I mean, it is a commercial relationship? Like teaching?'

'Yes, of course we pay him. My goodness, we wouldn't expect him to do it just out of interest. Good heavens. But he does more than look. He grumbles.'

Mrs Schilling laughed and turned to her husband. 'There!' she said. 'I knew there must exist a vocation where you could be paid to grumble, dearest. An art teacher, that is what you should have been, dear heart. You look at paintings and you grumble about them and they pay you. What a splendid arrangement!'

'You forget, people already pay me to grumble. Haven't you heard my article about the World's Fair?'

'Oh, yes, but that is work, you spent the best part of a morning on that, I'll warrant. This sounds like more *impromptu* sort of grumbling. You come, you look, you grumble, you get the money, you go. A much superior formula.' She turned then to Marie. 'Tell me, my dear Miss Triepke, why precisely does he grumble? Is it that your work is not good? Or is it that it is *too* good?'

'Oh, I don't think we could be too good,' said Marie. 'I suppose it is that he has such high standards, you know.' She gave a nervous cough of laughter. 'He tells us what fools we all are, and then he storms off in a rage, sometimes, muttering about "dabbling women". We excuse him on the grounds of his genius, of course.'

'Well, I think that is too bad,' said Mrs Schilling. 'It is not very gallant of him to be so rude to artists.'

'Oh, but we are not really artists, you know. We are only students.'

'All the same,' said Mr Schilling. 'We shall have to tackle him on that.'

The colour drained from Marie's face. 'Don't, I beseech you, please don't. I would die of mortification.'

'Well, we don't want you dead, Miss Triepke, that would never do, so we won't quote you, but we shall have to take him in hand one way or another. We shall have to think of a more subtle approach, that's all. But don't worry. We'll keep your little secret.'

Marie's heart leaped. Her secret!

'What? What secret? I have no secret!'

'I mean that you accuse Mr Krøyer of disapproving of women who paint, that is all. What else could I possibly mean? I am sure you have no other secrets, Miss Triepke,' said Mr Schilling, but there was a rising, interrogative note to his voice.

Marie stood up to go. The rain had stopped, she said, and she wanted to get back quickly, before it started again. Mrs Schilling turned to where Marie's dress hung drying and patted the shoulders. 'Still damp,' she said.

'It's much better,' said Marie, testing the fabric with her fingers. 'If I hurry home, it will hardly have time to do me any harm, and I shall change as soon as I get there.'

She gathered up the gown as she spoke and moved back into the bedroom. The dress was still quite wet, and it clung to her limbs as she struggled into it, but she was warm now and she felt able to withstand its clammy grip on her shoulders. Her boots were starting to curl up, in spite of being stuffed, and getting her feet back into them was more of a challenge. She stood up at last, shod and dressed, though rather dishevelled. Never mind, she would treat herself to a bath when she got home; there was a hipbath, very economical.

When it was clear that Marie was set on leaving, Mrs Schilling handed her the battered parasol.

'Why, Miss Triepke, this is not an umbrella; it is a parasol.'

Mr Schilling gave a loud laugh and shook his head as if Marie were some dear but incorrigible child.

'Yes,' said Marie. 'I opened it automatically when the rain started. I never thought.'

'Oh, but that explains it!' said Mrs Schilling. 'You came out without an umbrella. What do you expect? Surely you know you must carry an umbrella if you want to keep the rain off.'

Mr Schilling threw his eyes up, as if this was a well-rehearsed argument.

'I know,' said Marie. 'That's exactly what my mother says.'

'Sensible lady; I shall look forward to making her acquaintance some day,' said Mrs Schilling, walking Marie to the door of the apartment.

She kissed Marie on both cheeks in the French manner. 'Come on Friday,' she said as she opened the door. 'Your shoulders are damp, dear, run away home now. And that hat — don't think of putting it on your head, you'll get, oh, I don't know, epilepsy or something. The Anchers are expected on Friday. Come to lunch.'

'Thank you,' said Marie. 'Friday lunch, without fail.'

Chapter 2

For the life of him, Marie's father could not see why she couldn't study at home like everyone else. But Marie had explained that art wasn't like engineering or business, much the same everywhere; that you needed particular teachers, who could teach particular skills, and that such teachers were rare, expensive and mostly in Paris. He didn't understand it, but he acquiesced. They couldn't really afford it, but the fact was that he and Marie's mother were desperate to remove her from Copenhagen, to get her away from reminders of 'that dreadful business' – as they called it in the family, though not in Marie's hearing – and if she had set her heart on Paris, then they would do their best to make it possible.

It all went back to Theo's death, that was the family view of it. A terrible time it had been, and her parents had been so grief-stricken to lose their darling boy that they hadn't noticed the effect it had had on Marie, who was at that awkward age.

Marie longed to paint him. He looked so beautiful as he lay there, his dark hair curling over the white linen pillow, his skin like marble, with a sort of blue sheen to it. If they'd only let her paint him, then she could be sure she'd remember him properly, and it was the fear of forgetting that bothered her more than anything. But she knew she couldn't do it without permission, and she couldn't ask, because she couldn't get to talk to them. Her parents had withdrawn into separate rooms as soon as the doctor and the undertaker had gone, and they'd left instructions that they were not to be disturbed until the morning of the funeral.

Someone gave Marie a rosebud to put on Theo's pillow, a red

rose from a hothouse in the Low Lands, but she thought it looked too red, like a blood clot staining the pillow. So when they weren't looking, she took it away again. She put it in a little cream jug full of water in the kitchen. If they noticed that the rose was gone, nobody said anything. Later, she wondered if she should have left it there with Theo. She worried that perhaps he might think she'd taken it away because she didn't want him to have it, that she wanted it for herself because it was so beautiful, but that wasn't the reason at all.

When she woke with cramps in the night, because all *that* had chosen to start at that very time, just when she couldn't even talk to Mama, she got up to change the strange lumpy bandage for a fresh one from the supply her mother had left for her. At least she was prepared. She'd heard stories of girls who were left in ignorance and to whom it all came as a terrible shock. She knew roughly what to expect, so it was only horrible, not terrifying, but it was bad enough and it made her want to cry. But since she hadn't cried for Theo, she would not allow herself to cry about *this*, so she cleaned herself up as best she could, made herself comfortable, and then went to get a glass of water.

She'd been too muzzy-headed to put on her slippers, and her feet made soft slapping sounds on the cold flags. She stood at the sink with her feet unnaturally close together, trying to warm one against the other and not wanting to put either of them down on a cold spot. In the eerie grey light that came in through the window over the sink – moonlight, perhaps, or dawn – she saw that the rose had opened in the warmth of the kitchen. It bloomed so prettily against the crockery that she threw it in the bin, because she couldn't bear to think that they would all come home from the graveyard tomorrow and Theo would be left all alone under the yew trees in the cold earth, and that the rose would still be alive in the cream jug on the kitchen dresser. She hadn't shed a tear for him, nothing would come, but at least she could kill off that stupid rose.

The next morning, when she looked, Dinah had thrown the coffee grounds from breakfast over the rose in the dustbin and it was all damp and curling and Marie was glad, glad, glad.

Oma and Opa didn't come to the funeral. They said it was too far, too expensive and besides, they said, they were too old and stiff for long journeys now. But Marie thought they just didn't like coming into Denmark; they preferred to stay in Germany where everyone understood them, not just the family. They said they would pray for them all instead.

They should have come, thought Marie, no matter how old, no matter how stiff. Mama would have gone to Germany if it had been one of them who had died. Or if Theo had been a grown-up, they'd have come. People came to grown-ups' funerals. It was expected.

Tante Ulla came, and she said Marie and Valdemar had to be good, and that they must spare Mama's feelings. That meant they mustn't talk about Theo. Tante Ulla didn't mention sparing Papa's feelings, so Marie thought she might talk to him about it all, but when she knocked on his study door he said, 'Go away, whoever it is, just go away.'

Clearly he didn't know it was Marie. He would never tell her to go away. He must have thought she was Tante Ulla. But she went away anyhow, and she went out into the garden and cut a yellow daffodil and put it in the cream jug and left it in Theo's room for him in case he wanted it, though he wasn't there any more; he was under the yew trees now, in the cemetery. It was the only thing she could think of to do for him, to make up for taking the other flower away. A daffodil is not the same as a rose, but it has a sweet scent and it's jolly. She hoped he would understand. Valdemar said he would. But Valdemar always said what he thought you'd like to hear; he was sweet like that. So she didn't know, and there was no one to ask, no one. Papa stayed in his study and Tante Ulla said Mama was 'distraught', which sounded terrible, and you couldn't ask Tante Ulla a question like that. Marie was the eldest now, Tante Ulla said before she left for Germany again, and she mustn't make trouble for the adults. She must keep Valdemar quiet and keep out of their way for the time being while they were so sad.

She wished keeping out of the way were not the best thing she could do for them. She wished she could do something consoling, like stroking their hair or reading to them from the Bible. Mama always said the Bible was such a comfort. Marie would very much like to be a comfort. When she was little, she was a comfort. Small children are like stuffed animal toys: good to cuddle. But a great girl like her, almost thirteen and already bleeding, it's not the same. She would only get in the way. So instead of finding someone to be a comfort to, Marie went and filled a hot water jar, a thing her mother had held out as a great treat to a girl with cramps. She wrapped it in a towel and went to bed with it resting on the lower part of her abdomen, great heavy thing, but it was soothing, as Mama had said it would be. She turned on her side, drew her legs up to cradle the jar in close to her and at last the tears came, hot and fast, dampening her pillow and growing quickly cold.

Chapter 3

It was years before Marie started to emerge from that chrysalis of grief, and suddenly announced that she and Oda, a school friend of hers from an arty family, were going to take drawing and painting lessons. Since women were not admitted to the Academy, she explained to her astonished parents, the girls were going to have to make their own arrangements. Oda had found an impecunious young artist who had agreed to teach them, but it was expensive to pay a teacher just to teach two of them and besides, Oda had said, they must try to make sure he was well paid, not just so that he would continue to teach them, but because it was important to support young artists. It had never occurred to Marie to think of herself as part of an economy that supported young artists, but Oda's father was a collector and a patron of the arts, and it came naturally to her to think like that. And so, in the interests of their art teacher as much as in their own, they had mustered a group of other young women who had agreed to share the costs.

Oda's father knew someone who owned a building in a run-down part of town, on the other side of the river, where people seemed to have enormous numbers of children and every second doorway was a huckster shop or some sort of workshop. Rents were low and, as a friend of the family, the landlord offered Oda a very attractive rate for an attic room with skylights facing north. It had been a milliner's workshop but was lying idle at that time, and the landlord said a low rent was better than no rent at all. Perhaps he thought these young women from respectable families would make a better class of tenant than he was used to.

Marie and Oda arrived on the day after the lease was signed

with bunches of mops and brooms and clusters of buckets and paintbrushes, and they trailed up and down the dingy staircase all morning, carrying buckets of clean water up from the pump in the yard and buckets of dirty water down.

'What's that smell?' Marie asked, as they trudged up past the closed doors of poor people's apartments.

'Calf's head,' said Oda authoritatively.

'It's disgusting,' said Marie.

'Well, be thankful you don't have to eat it,' said Oda. She could be relied upon to see the cheerful side of everything.

They scraped the floorboards clean of congealed dirt and swept away cobwebs and the long-since desiccated corpses of insects that were shrouded in their dry and sticky grasp. They cleaned the grimy windows with newspapers soaked in vinegar and gave the walls a fresh coat of limewash. By the end of the day, they were filthy and exhausted, but the new studio was bright and clean.

'Let's go home,' said Marie, gathering up the buckets and cleaning materials. 'If we touch a single grubby finger to all this glory, we'll smudge it.'

'All this glory!' scoffed Oda, but she was smiling. She pushed her hair away from her face with the back of a grimy wrist and sniffed. 'It smells so clean,' she said. 'But it makes me light-headed. Aren't you starving? I could eat a small animal.'

Together, they carried the stepladder they'd borrowed for reaching the highest corners and cleaning the skylights down all the stairs to the cellar, where it had come from, and then they tramped all the way back up again to fetch their buckets and mops.

'These are revolting,' said Marie, looking at the things that they had bought that morning, bright and shiny, from a hardware shop on their way to the studio. They were slimy now with dirt and wet. 'Hardly worth carrying home. Let's dump them in the first dustbin we see.'

'Such extravagance!' said Oda. 'There's one in the courtyard. But not the broom, Marie. We'll need to sweep the place. Leave it in a corner.'

Down the stairs they clattered again and out to the yard for the last time to dump their filthy utensils and wash their hands and faces at the pump.

The drawing classes started, and the group of students grew until there was no room for another easel in the bright little room under the roof. Other teachers were recruited, and most days there would be at least an hour or two of instruction. In the meantime, the young women painted together and consulted each other on their work. It was not exactly an art school, but it was much better than no art education at all.

Marie spent most evenings at Oda's house these days. Marie's mother had an eye for interiors, and their house was prettily decorated, but, after all, they only had tray-cloths and drapes and cushions and firescreens for decoration, and on the walls some ugly prints of mills and factories belonging to her father's firm; but Oda's father was a connoisseur and immensely rich, and their house was full of paintings by all the latest artists, even some by the great Søren Krøyer.

Krøyer was Marie's favourite painter – and man, she told Oda's brother Rex rather breathlessly one day, though in fact she hardly knew him. Why she should claim him as such a favourite she could not explain, even to herself.

Because of her father's connections, Oda had managed to get Krøyer to agree to visit the studio to look over their work and advise them. There was a flutter of excitement the first time he came. He was, after all, acknowledged as the leading painter in the country. They heard his foot on the stairs and scurried to their easels so they should be in an attitude of work when he came in.

He rapped on the door with his cane, and Oda's voice called out brightly for him to come in.

No one looked up except Oda, who went to him and spoke to him quietly, like a young nun receiving the bishop, indicating the painting girls, like rows of novices.

Marie ventured to look up and saw an unprepossessing man, neither tall nor short, narrowly built, with close-cropped red hair and a trim red beard, a freckled complexion and rather pale blue eyes. He was not attractive, without being exactly unattractive. His chin jutted as he spoke, and he wore pedantic little spectacles that glittered when he moved his head. He had a slightly fussy manner that betrayed a self-regarding streak. But for Marie, great artist that he was, he exuded a magic aura, around the edges of which she was content to bask.

He moved slowly up and down, stopping to look over each girl's shoulder and sighing from time to time. He came at last to Marie's easel and bent over to look. She froze. He was so close, in the narrow aisle, that she could hear his breath, and now, as he bent closer, she could feel the warmth of it on the side of her neck. Instinctively, she moved away from the heat of his body and then, as if to make up for this, she turned towards him and he drew in his breath sharply, and made a brief movement of greeting with his head.

Marie did not speak. She hardly dared to breathe. She turned back towards her work and stared at it as if she had never seen it before.

'Very good,' he murmured, but she could not be sure if he was talking about her painting or something else. He did not elucidate, just stood there for several moments. It was the Staring again, but it seemed to have a particular quality about it on this occasion, something she couldn't put her finger on. She knew she was supposed to go on painting, but she could not move. The air seemed to crackle.

'My dear,' he said at last, very quietly, as if he were addressing a beloved niece or an old friend.

Marie turned her head slightly towards him, expecting to hear some comment on her work.

'Will you sit for me?' he said softly.

She thought she must have imagined it, dreamed it up out of sheer desire.

'What?'

He repeated his request.

'Oh yes, of course.' Her voice was a whisper, not from the necessity for privacy, but because she hardly seemed to have the breath to speak.

Not a portrait, he explained. Nothing personal. He was planning a painting with a small group of people. He'd like her to be one of them. Just a few hours, nothing onerous.

Onerous. The word seemed alien. Nothing to do with this man could be onerous. To serve him in the smallest way would be a privilege. She was suffused with joy. As if in a dream, she put out a hand to take the little white card he was proffering. He pulled it back, before her fingers grasped it. He produced a small silver propelling pencil and wrote a time and date on the reverse of the card, and handed it to her.

This time, her hot damp fingers closed over it. It felt slithery. She propped it carefully on a narrow shelf at the front of her easel, intended for pencils and brushes, and stared at it. P. S. Krøyer, it said, in a flowing script, as if he had signed it himself. And then a printed address. 'Next week,' he said.

She nodded. 'Yes,' she said, 'oh yes.'

He withdrew, and she felt the chill of his departure as if the sun had gone behind a cloud. She rubbed the side of her arm, as if to warm it.

Brimming with excitement, she presented herself at the address on the card on the appointed day. She was going to meet the great man on his own territory. A manservant opened the door and ushered her into a roomful of people. Nobody introduced anyone. The others all seemed to know each other anyway, and they talked idly among themselves, like professionals — actors, perhaps, or dancers — on a break from work, tapping their yawns back with scant politeness, stretching their fingers, gazing at their shoelaces. Tea and coffee and dainty sandwiches were all laid out on a buffet, and one was expected to help oneself. She crumbled a sandwich on a plate and drank a cup of lukewarm tea. After a few moments, Krøyer came in and spoke affably, like the director of a play, giving his troupe an encouraging little talk before curtain-up. He indicated to her to sit here, to someone else to sit there, and all the time he kept up a cheerful chatter. Almost before they had settled in their chairs, around a grand piano, he was at work. She presumed he was sketching out the picture. She smiled when she caught his eye, but he did not seem to recognise her. After a short while, he bowed and left the room. That was all. It was over.

Feeling vaguely disappointed, and at the same time, embarrassed at her own disappointment — what, after all, had she expected? — she found herself at the door, and the manservant was asking if he should hail a cab for her. She took her shawl from him and shook her head.

The next time Mr Krøyer appeared at the studio, she sat in tense anticipation as he came to a stop at her easel. He leaned forward to inspect her work, and she arranged her face into a smile. But he just murmured, 'Very good,' again, in that non-committal, unhelpful voice, and moved on.

She had every reason to be disappointed, to feel abused, indeed, but his indifference provoked the opposite reaction in her. She excused it as a symptom of artistic distraction, something you did not only forgive an artist for but expected of him. When he came to the studio after that, she felt herself more and more apprehensive, until it came to a point where she could not bear to be in the room when he came in. She would excuse herself and hide behind the screen where the tea things were kept, or even leave the room altogether when he entered it, so agitated had she become at his presence. It had got to the point where her nerves tingled at the very sound of his name. It was like an illness, or an allergy perhaps. She could not bear to be near him, and yet she could not keep away either. She would stay in the room as long as she could bear the tension, but always there would come a point where she could stand it no longer, and she would have to make a bolt for it so that she could breathe again and bring her pulse back to a normal rate.

She tried to explain to Oda how it had been at the sitting, but she could not make her understand. Oda just said Marie was lucky to be so beautiful, to have eyes of such a pure, deep blue, which was not the point at issue at all, but Marie allowed herself to be distracted into discussing it. She tried to explain how her looks were a kind of liability, how it grieved her the way no one ever saw the real her.

'But what you look like *is* you,' Oda argued. 'That is how I recognise you when I see you on the street or when you call to the door.'

'No,' said Marie. 'If I were burned in a fire tomorrow, I should still be me, wouldn't I? Even though my face would be ruined.'

Rex joined in. 'But Marie,' he said, 'perhaps it really is your destiny to be looked at; maybe it is your role in life, and if you accept that that is so, you will be happier.'

Marie stared resentfully at him. He was an art student too, so perhaps he could not help thinking like that, but she did not really think that was a sufficient excuse. Anyway, she thought, you did not have to believe in destiny. Surely you could just be yourself. You did not have to be what someone – everyone, even – thought you ought to be.

'But I cannot exist only to be looked at,' Marie protested.

'You might.' Oda wriggled with amusement.

'Not *only*,' Rex conceded. 'But also.'

He tried to understand her objections, but nothing could convince him that she was not for looking at. He loved to watch her as she moved about his family's house, where she spent a good deal of time, sinking to the floor to tend a stove, turning to pass a plate of soup along at table, leaning forward to close a window or light a lamp, and there were times when he thought his heart would turn over at the way she tucked her hair behind her ear or leaned her cheek on her hand. Her beauty, he thought, was most expressed in movement, but not as a dancer moves, grandly, with emphasis. It was in the small, unconscious gestures of the everyday that she was most lovely, and that was part of her allure. You never knew when she was going to do something so exquisite that it made you ache, so you had to watch her all the time, to be sure of catching it.

'Pull a face, Marie,' Oda offered, 'and I'll see if your self is still there.'

But Marie wouldn't do it.

Rex was planning to be an art historian and critic, and he found a willing listener in Marie. Her interest in painting was insatiable, and he practised his insights on her. One day, in the midst of one of their discussions, she waved her hand in a particularly animated way in the direction of a painting, and Rex caught it. He hardly knew what he was doing. It was as if the excessive movement, like the flurry of a bird in flight, attracted his attention while disabling his normal social inhibitions. At any rate, he felt compelled to catch the flying fingers. He nestled them now in his own hand, to bring them back to earth.

She was startled, but not unpleasantly. She'd never had her hand held before, except as a small child. So pleasant, indeed, was the sensation, that she let her hand sink into his, and smiled when his eyes met hers. His face was pale and finely made, his eyes and hair dark. There was something in his look that reminded her of Theo.

He was relieved at her reaction, and surprised, and presently relief and surprise melted into pure delight.

'I thought it was going to fly away, into the picture,' he explained, turning her hand over in his. 'I thought I'd better stop it before it became detached from your wrist.'

Gently, he lowered her hand, still held in his, and let it go, by the side of her dress.

Nothing more was said, and Marie kept her hands behind her back when she discussed paintings with him after that, but only because she thought he might feel obliged to repeat the performance, and she thought that might be embarrassing for him; it was not that she didn't want him to. She thought about it often in the night, how he had caught her hand in mid-flight and about how it had felt, nestled in his, just for those few seconds. What if he had pressed the fleshy pad of her palm with his thumb! How would that have felt? Perhaps he had, and she hadn't registered it. Or perhaps she had, and she'd forgotten. Could you forget a thing like that? Would he ever do it again? How should she respond if he did? She couldn't decide, but her palms prickled at the thought. Was he more attractive than Mr Krøyer? He was younger. He was better looking. But was he more attractive? What did it mean, to be attractive?

Rex and Oda had a studio at home, but he used his part of it less and less these days, since he was now more engaged in academic studies. And Marie had nowhere to paint, apart from a small space in the crowded classroom studio. This struck him as unbalanced – that he should have a vast unused studio space, and she, who really needed to paint, had only the equivalent of dormitory accommodation. He invited Marie to use his part of the studio on days when there were no classes arranged at her own place, and she accepted with such obvious glee that he felt repaid already by her reaction.

Still, he thought she might feel she owed him something, and it would serve her sense of self-reliance if he were to exact some kind of payment. He thought about it quite carefully and, in the end, he came up with the idea that, in return for the use of the studio, she might occasionally sit for him.

'But I thought you said you had given up painting?'

'Yes,' he said. 'A painter needs a model to sit for him, but a critic needs an audience. What I am proposing is that you sit and listen when I talk and try out my ideas, and you react. Tell me if I am being stupid or pompous, or if I am missing the point. What do you think?'

'I would do that anyway,' said Marie. 'That is just conversation.'

'Well, I shall consider it a favour,' said Rex, 'and it will do nicely in lieu of rent.'

'All right,' she said, 'if you like.' But she was secretly thrilled to be asked to sit and listen rather than sit and be painted.

'And, of course, you can do the sitting while you are working,' Rex added.

'Oh!' said Marie. 'That's the best part: I owe you rent because I use your studio, and I pay my rent by using your studio.'

'Yes,' said Rex. 'That's the idea. Isn't it good? A new kind of economy.'

Marie laughed. 'It's all backwards,' she said. 'A woman sitting painting and a man sitting doing nothing. Except talking, of course.'

And looking, Rex thought, so not really backwards after all. He was pleased with his little scheme, and the element of deception was almost non-existent. She bent over her easel with a movement that made his breathing constrict, and he could watch the nape of her neck for hours while she worked. The intensity with which she painted gave her face a luminous quality that made him want to gather her right up into his arms until she disappeared. If Oda had not been there most of the time, he might have done it.

Sometimes Rex tried out his ideas on her, but oftentimes they just chattered idly about the picture she was painting or some other painting they had seen. From time to time, she remembered that she was under a sort of contractual obligation to join in these discussions, and she did her best to listen carefully and react appropriately. But most of the time she forgot about this duty of hers and those were the best conversations, when she just talked with him as a friend.

She longed to go to Paris, she told him one day when they were alone in the studio. Her family had recently removed to Augsburg, leaving Marie behind, and she had been happy with her studies and her friends for a while, but now she felt that she'd reached the end in Copenhagen. It was out of the question, of course. Her parents couldn't afford it, and she had no way of raising the money herself. It didn't occur to her that this was the sort of information one kept private.

'I'll take you to Paris, Marie,' Rex said immediately. 'We will take an apartment in Montmartre, one with lots and lots of stairs to run up and down, and we'll feed pigeons through the window and you will paint all day while I'm in the Louvre and, in the evenings, we'll take walks along the river in the moonlight and then we'll go home and read Byron to each other. What do you say?'

Marie laughed. 'It is a lovely idea, Rex. But I don't think it would do. Gentlemen do not accompany ladies on long journeys alone to foreign cities or stay with them when they get there. It is not done, my dear friend.'

'Oh, but of course, I should marry you first,' said Rex, as if it hardly needed explaining.

'I see,' said Marie, with a smile. 'Well, I suppose that would make a difference all right.'

'Marie, I mean it. That was a proposal.' Rex crossed the room and stood in front of her easel, so she would have to look at him.

Marie put down her brush. The man was serious. Her heart lifted. Her first thought was that if she accepted him, she could, as he'd said, go to Paris. Ignominious thought! Though those had been the terms in which he'd put it. Still, she revised the thought immediately. A better, worthier thought was this: she could marry this very sweet and kind-natured man who she wished most earnestly would press his thumb to her palm, and who shared her tastes and interests and plainly adored her, and they could go to Paris together and live in a room above Montmartre and feed pigeons and read Byron. He could hold her hand all he liked then, and she could hold his back. How delightful that would be! She thought for a moment of the unattainable Mr Krøyer. But what was the point of that? He hardly knew she existed. She could not turn down such a wonderful proposal on the grounds that she was attracted to an older man with whom she had no relationship.

'Rex!' she managed to say. 'My dear, my dearest . . .'

She gave him her hand, which he crushed in both of his, and then they kissed.

That was how they became engaged. Nothing more was said, but she knew he understood that she had accepted him. It was all surprisingly simple – all her wishes coming true at once, or most of them at any rate – you couldn't have everything, after all – and a fine, dear and astonishingly wealthy man for a husband, though his wealth was not, of course, the point. Still, it was a piece of luck.

There was no ring, not yet. They would have to talk to the parents, make an announcement. All in good time.

Marie danced home that evening. She was going to Paris. She

was getting married. Rex loved her. She adored him already, in a way, and love – in the romantic sense, as she thought of it – would come soon enough. He was going to be an important art critic, and she was going to be an artist, and they could spend all their time talking about art and looking at pictures and visiting galleries and making friends with other artists and everything was going to be perfect. She was going to have a perfect life. She felt as if she wore a magic substance on her feet that transported her effortlessly over the cobbled streets and wafted her up the stairs to the small room she had in the house of a friend of her mother's.

In her room, she dropped her shawl and purse, kicked off her boots, threw her arms in the air in an ecstatic arc and pirouetted around and around and around until her hairpins came undone and her breath grew puffy.

She wrote immediately, that very evening, to her parents in Germany, who were surprised and delighted when they received her letter. They knew the young man slightly; they knew him to be a serious person and of a good family. They had worried terribly about leaving Marie alone in Copenhagen when they moved back to Germany. What better outcome could there be than that she should marry the son of a merchant prince? Not that they were socially ambitious, but they valued security and they knew also that Marie thrived in the artistic atmosphere of her friend's family.

Mrs Triepke sat down there and then and wrote a note to Rex's mother, saying how thrilled they all were. It was the right thing to do. She always liked to do the right thing.

Chapter 4

'The great advantage of a ground-floor apartment, my dear Miss Triepke,' boomed Mr Schilling on Friday, 'is access to the garden. God bless the man who invented French doors, say I. Eh? He probably wasn't French at all, but we shall pretend he was, just for today, what do you say?'

'It might have been a woman,' said Marie.

It most probably hadn't been, but she hated the way everyone always assumed that everything good in the world could be put down to men. She gave a quick smile, though, to soften the impact of her sharp remark.

'Indeed, indeed,' said Mr Schilling gamely. 'Most likely. Very practical persons, the ladies.'

He led Marie through the apartment and out into a small oasis at the back of the house, all green and tumbling and scented with jasmine, into which the Schillings' dining table had been translated. So pretty, set with glasses and silver and porcelain plates, a cotton cloth embroidered in pale pink, very sweet. Around this festive board, as Mr Schilling would doubtless have called it, had he been required to describe the scene for one of his articles, sat a small party of guests. Marie couldn't hear the conversation from where she stood by the open doors, but she could tell it was in Danish.

She scanned the group quickly, her heart racing.

No sign of *him*. She was caught between disappointment and relief.

Mr Schilling ushered her out into the garden, and started to introduce her. A large, dark-haired woman who sat with her back to

Marie was talking animatedly to Mrs Schilling. She turned as her name was called. Anna Ancher's face was unbelievably plain – too long, and that nose! Large and hooked, it jutted out of her face like a gantry, giving her a witchlike appearance. Marie tried not to let her reaction show in her expression.

Anna was in mid-sentence, but she broke off as she turned to Marie. Her smile, warm and toothy, beamed like sunshine. Dark eyes, gleaming like healthy raisins, sallow complexion. And then, to Marie's horror, Anna tweaked her nose with her left hand as she gave her right to Marie.

'You get used to it,' she said merrily. 'After a bit, you don't see it at all, you just see me.'

Just see *me*!

'That's exactly what *I* . . .' Marie began, and then stopped herself. She couldn't say that. She would seem to be implying both her own beauty and the other woman's plainness. Oh, ground, swallow! she thought telegrammatically, hardly able to articulate, even mentally, so unbalanced was she by her own clumsiness – and the woman had been so good-natured too, and brave. How could she do it? To look like that, and to laugh at it. Marie was covered in a confusion occasioned by embarrassment at her own ingratitude. How could she complain about her looks when she might just as easily have grown up looking like *that*.

Anna sized up the situation at once, and she rushed in. 'Yes, I'm sure you find the same,' she said brightly, and patted Marie on the arm. 'More to us than meets the eye, eh?'

Mrs Schilling set a chair beside Mrs Ancher, and motioned to Marie to sit down.

Anna continued with her conversation but now included Marie in an enthusiastic invitation. 'We have found the most delightful lodgings. You must come and see, the dearest little house, awfully tiny, but fine, you know, perfectly comfortable, and cheap, you wouldn't believe it. But, anyway, yes, as I was saying, before that, when we first arrived, we put up at this terribly grand hotel. It was such fun. You know how the French are; they expect you to be so cultivated. We're not used to it, are we, Michael? I mean, we are country folk really, aren't we? My family keeps a hotel, Miss Triepke, my brother runs it now, in the middle of nowhere, at the tip of Europe, practically in the sea it is! We live a simple life. We consort with fishermen. Oh, I just couldn't get over this place, all swags and those absurd mirrors in their impossible gold frames, like something out of the palace of Versailles – have you been, Miss Triepke? You have to go, so sumptuous, sinful, no wonder they had a revolution – and the chandeliers! I enjoyed it hugely. I played at being royalty, didn't I, Michael?'

She tugged at her husband's sleeve.

'What?' he said vaguely. 'Where? At Versailles?'

Marie turned to look at the husband. So this was the artist who was so famous for his sea scenes and his heroic portraits of fisher-men. They reminded Marie of that opera about the pearl fishers, all sitting about on rocks looking romantic. He looked like a fisher-man himself, got up for church on a Sunday. His hair was badly cut and his jacket didn't seem to fit.

'No, no, not at Versailles. At the hotel, Michael, surely you re-member! I played at being royalty at that hotel we were in, the place we couldn't afford. I used to, oh, Miss Triepke, I used to come swooping down the elegant staircase and I would nod to the porter, so very graciously. I'm sure he was tickled to death. I'm sure it was perfectly clear to him that I wasn't royalty at all, that I spend my days with pigment under my fingernails, when I'm not helping my mother in the kitchen or pouring drinks for my brother's customers. Or mending my husband's socks by the stove.' She whooped with laughter at the mention of the socks. 'I do that too, really I do; I am most domesticated, aren't I, Michael?'

'Hmm,' said Michael.

'Oh, I am sure that's not true,' said Marie, 'not about the socks, about the porter, I mean. I am sure he was convinced you were a queen.'

'Will you take some lunch, Miss Triepke?' asked the host, waving a fork in Marie's face.

Marie looked at the food. It was mostly cold meats, salamis, studded with alarming lumps of lard. Some of it looked as if it was pure compressed blood. She'd heard they ate horse in France. Her stomach heaved. She shook her head. 'I had a late breakfast,' she said.

'Oh, do have some of the believed ham,' said Mr Schilling. 'Everyone has to have some of that.'

'I beg your pardon?'

'Believed ham. *Jambon cru,* don't you know. It is believed to be raw!' He spluttered with mirth at his own humour.

Marie hadn't the least idea what he was talking about.

'You do speak French, Miss Triepke, do you not?' he asked, in a tone that suggested it was impossible that she shouldn't.

Marie was flattered rather than alarmed that he should take her education so much for granted. But her French was hazy.

'Of course,' she murmured, 'but I am a little – rusty. If you don't mind, I will just take a cup of tea.'

'Tea? There isn't any. We can make some later, of course, but try this excellent wine, Miss Triepke.'

He shoved a glass of deep pink liquid in front of her, and obediently she took a small sip and wrinkled her nose.

'Aha!' pronounced Mr Schilling. 'I didn't like it either!' He beamed, as if serving his guest something she didn't like was a great achievement. 'But my wife claims it is famously good. Claret, it is called, something to do with the colour, I think. Tell me, my dear, and speak up so my wife can hear. What does it taste like?'

Marie sipped again and considered whether she should tell the truth. It seemed to be called for, so she put down the glass, folded her hands in her lap, and looked up at Mr Schilling earnestly.

'When I was young,' she said, 'my grandmother used to put a dollop of "regulating medicine"' – here she rolled her *r* exaggeratedly in the German way – 'into a glass of raspberry cordial, to disguise the flavour. That's what it tastes like, I am afraid: a combination of raspberry cordial and, um, medication for the *bowels*.'

Mr Schilling was delighted. He banged on the table with his whole forearm and laughed long and hard, though Marie had been trying to be accurate rather than amusing in her description of the wine. But if he thought she was a great wit, she would not try to set him right.

'A Prussian, your grandmother?' he asked as he wiped his face with a large handkerchief.

For the first time in her life, Marie admitted to her German ancestry without a trace of embarrassment. She had sensed it could be presented, in this company at least, as merely quaint. 'A Bavarian,' she said.

'A Bavarian!' howled Mr Schilling, as if she had made the most hilarious joke. 'Did you hear that, dear heart? Miss Triepke was fed regulating medicine by a Bavarian in her youth. *Pfui, Teufel!* No wonder the poor girl has no appetite. We shall have to take her in hand. She is far too thin.'

Mrs Schilling smiled.

'That reminds me,' said someone Marie hadn't been introduced to. 'You know Sarah Barr's grandmother is a gypsy. Or maybe it was her mother. Someone anyway, on the distaff side.'

People looked interested. Nobody looked shocked. It came to Marie that this was what it meant to be a bohemian. It wasn't about outrageous behaviour. It was about not caring who people's grandmothers had been.

'She reads the cards; in the blood, I suppose, and, wait till you hear this, this is good: she read Krøyer's cards last week, before he left Denmark.'

'And?' said Anna.

'And it seems' – he paused for dramatic effect – 'he is to meet the love of his life in Paris and be married by the spring!'

Marie's blood sang in her ears.

Anna roared with laughter.

'I would as soon expect that chair you are sitting on,' she said to the person who'd told the card-reading story, 'I'd as soon expect that chair to get up and dance the polka as Krøyer to marry! He hates the very idea. A cousin of mine has been trying to get him to marry her for years, and he won't hear of it. All the girls in my family marry artists, you know, the ones who marry at all, I mean. I started the fashion when I married my Michael, and they all thought it a great wheeze. But Krøyer! Married! That'll be the day!'

'Well,' said the unknown speaker, 'I am only telling you the story. We shall see.'

'Or not,' said Anna.

'Miss Triepke is a student of Krøyer's, you know,' Mrs Schilling boasted to Anna.

Marie let out a squeak of protest.

'All right, all right, an *occasional* student of Krøyer's, I should say,' said Mrs Schilling. 'She is here for the exhibition, of course, but I believe you are hoping to take lessons too, Miss Triepke, are you not?'

'Exactly like me!' said Anna. 'I am looking for a teacher too. We must look together.'

'But you are already . . . '

'What, an artist? Tra-la-la, yes, I've shown a few pictures, but I am only half-educated. I still have so much to learn, and especially about the French style. I'm so exhilarated by what I've seen here, these French painters, the ones people are calling the 'Impression-ists'. I'm planning to set up a studio, did I tell you? Our house is tiny, absolutely minute, but there is a room I can paint in. You can paint there too, Miss Triepke, I should adore it. It is awfully poky, but we could have such fun. Please say you'll come. Tomorrow. You must come to tea tomorrow and if you like it, we can set up shop on Monday. What do you say? And when we find Krøyer, we'll get him to recommend someone to teach us. Isn't that just the most perfect idea?'

Marie nodded. It *was* a perfect idea. She'd had a lot of perfect ideas herself, but they had never been practicable. Here was an idea, however, that was beyond perfect, since she could imagine it being implemented, and as soon as next week.

'Yes,' she said. 'Oh, yes, Mrs Ancher. Perfect. Thank you.'

Chapter 5

Anna Brøndum was only fifteen when she met Michael Ancher, but she was already over her nose. No one could have called her a pretty girl; not even when she was a child, when youth softens the contours of the face. 'Strong' is the sort of word people used to describe Anna's looks. It didn't bother her particularly, for looks were not much valued in her family. Indeed, all her sisters had 'strong' faces too. Once, though, when she went to church with her mother – she must have been about eleven at the time – Anna became aware that some of the other girls were nudging each other and giggling, and gradually it dawned on her that the source of their amusement was her nose. She knew her nose was large and hooked, but until that moment, having a large, hooked nose had seemed merely a fact, like having dark hair or being tall for one's age. Now, all at once, she realised it was something to be ashamed of. She held her prayer book up to her face, to hide her blushes as much as to hide her nose, and when she got home that lunchtime, she examined her face in the looking-glass in her bedroom as she had never examined it before.

The glass seemed to be full of nose. Anna turned her face to view her profile, and it seemed as if she was looking at a ship in full sail or a cliff with a huge rocky promontory. She lashed out at the glass and knocked it off the tallboy where it stood. It crashed to the ground and landed face-down on the floor. Gingerly, she picked it up by a corner of the frame, fully expecting it to have shivered into a million tiny shards that would tumble out of the frame as soon as she moved it and fall in a heap on the floor; but it hadn't broken, only cracked in a crazy line that roughly bisected the mirror. Relieved, she placed it back on its perch and looked in it again. Now her nose wobbled on her face and, after a little experimentation, she found that by standing at a particular angle she could make it disappear altogether and she could piece together an image of her face consisting of the two parts reflected on either side of the crack with a modest seam where her nose should be.

That's better, she thought. She would never have imagined how easy it was to amend her image.

Afterwards, she only ever used that mirror, and she quickly learned the knack of making her nose disappear as soon as she looked into it. That was the end of her embarrassment, and she soon forgot she had such a protuberance at all. She remembered from time to time, when she met a new person, and saw her nose mirrored in their eyes, but by then she had ceased to care.

The Brøndums were used to strangers – sailors, drunks, troubadours, men with secrets and bulging luggage and mysterious picturebooks from the West Indies – for their house was a hotel. Artists, too, had been coming for years, to paint the scenery and the local people, for seascapes and poor fisherfolk were fashionable in pictures at the time. To Anna, the fishermen and their families were neighbours, people she had known since childhood, but it appeared they had something about them that the grandees in Copenhagen liked to have in their paintings, though it was hard for the Brøndums to see why rich people who moved in large rooms under chandeliers would like to have on their walls reminders of poverty, wretchedness, cold, hardship, loss and deprivation. But it appeared that they did, and so the artists came, to experience closeness to nature, to live with the tide and the sands and the fishermen's comings and goings, their small triumphs and great sadnesses, good catches and poor, the ceaseless toil and effort that was the lot of those who lived subject to the sea's power.

Then there was the added drama of the lighthouse, the sound and the wrecks along the coast. Apparently it was all terribly romantic.

The children loved to see the artists coming with their easels and their paintboxes, their hats and capes and boots and picnic baskets. They piled into the hotel, they threw open the shutters, they sang in the mornings and drank beer and schnapps in the evenings and told stories by firelight. They were loud and tender, raucous and convivial, disputatious and amusing and they scared Anna half to death, partly because they were so loud and filled the small, still rooms so completely with their presence, but mainly because they stirred longings in her that she could not name. They were the first sign of spring and the last flurry of autumn, and when they were not there it was winter, the dark closing in about the little town and squeezing the daylight into narrower and narrower spaces, so that at last the days were only large gashes of light in the dark curtain of winter.

They could see that Anna was interested in what they were doing and, a few times, they invited her to join them, even though she was only a child, on those long summer days on the dunes, as they set up their easels and painted the sea and the sky. Mostly she refused, hanging back behind her mother when they were around, dropping her chin onto her chest so that her hair fell forward and hid her face. She was shy and, besides, she was needed in the kitchen to help with the chopping and peeling, the cleaning of sandy earth out of the layers of leeks, the gutting of fish, the seething of broth, the throwing out of slops, the feeding of the white hens that scratched about around the back door. There were so many mouths to feed in the height of summer when the hotel was full and, anyway, she liked to work with her mother.

But on one occasion, her mother said, 'Go, child.'

Anna looked up at her, surprised.

'You've been looking a little peaky lately, little one. You are too much about the house. Go down to the sea with the gentlemen, and be as helpful as you can. God will reward you.'

So Anna, rather dazed by her mother's order, went with the artists and sat beside them among the dunes, her legs sticking out in front of her, and her two feet dancing with excitement in their little black boots even though she was sitting down. She managed to sit quite still, and to smooth her skirt over her knees and tuck it in around her ankles to prevent ants from crawling up under her petticoats and stinging her calves, but her feet she couldn't control. They were like two little animals at the ends of her legs, quite in-dependent of the rest of her, and they lived their own jolly life, oblivious to her efforts to sit still. She'd pass the artists things as they worked and ask them nervous little questions about how they achieved their effects and she would answer their questions also, as best she could, about the village and the tower out on the dunes and the local people and their lives. All the while, Anna was longing to try her hand at this drawing and painting, but she was too scared to ask. She was not afraid that she would be refused, for she knew they liked her and would, in all likelihood, have indulged her child-ish request, but she was afraid because her longing was so great that she thought it must surely end in failure, and she felt it was eas-ier to live with the longing than to face that disaster.

Sometimes in the evenings, when the lamp was lit and artists drew around the fire and the family sat at the table, the girls with their needlework, their brother Degn with his accounts, the chil-dren would beg their mother for a story. It was always their mother who told the stories, for their father never said more than he had to. Sometimes he didn't even go that far, and they would have to work out what he would have said if he had spoken. They all be-came experts, in time, like people who work with deaf mutes, though old Mr Brøndum wasn't deaf, just taciturn.

On birthdays especially, the children would beg for their own birth stories, but as the years went by, the others came to concede that Anna's birth story was the best, and soon their stories got lost and forgotten, and only Anna's story went down in family history. *Tell about when Anna was born, Mama,* the children would say. *Tell about the night the Visitor came.*

The artists would light anticipatory pipes and the old-timers would nudge the newcomers, saying, *Wait till you hear, this is a good one, this is.*

There was nothing remarkable in the coming of a visitor, to be sure, but this was no ordinary visitor. He had heard how Skagen, even then, was a lodestone for artists who came looking for the wild beauty of the dunes and the quaintness of the local fisherfolk, and he had come to see for himself. He'd had a hard journey of it, especially the last stage on the post wagon, which came churning over the strand, and he was tired and cross when he arrived. He was often tired and cross, though, so perhaps it was not entirely the fault of the journey.

Although it was summer, Mrs Brøndum would begin, and the children would settle to listen. Although it was summer, the roofs of the houses and the chimneys seemed to be struggling up from under snowdrifts.

It was not snow that blanketed the place, however, the children would chant, for they had bits of this well-loved story by heart, *but sand*; and they would look at each other and smile, for they all knew very well how the sand drifted in the streets of this place.

Yes, their mother would say, not snow but drifts of white sand, and thrown down among the sand dunes, any place they could get purchase, were thatched yellow fishermen's cottages, sometimes half-ruinous, the straw or sod roofs falling in on the rooms.

The children nodded. They knew such houses. A poor old couple lived only next door in such a dwelling. Their own house was more prosperous. It had one of those typical Skagen red-tiled roofs, edged with lacy white scalloping, as if – so the great writer later remarked to his friends in Copenhagen – as if the people had taken huge needles to their rooftops and blanket-stitched the roof tiles to secure them against the wild winds that whipped over the seas, slicing the foamy tops off the very waves.

Say it again, Mama, the children would beg, when it came to the bit about the wind and the waves.

Slicing the foamy tops off the very waves, she would repeat, obligingly.

Off the very waves, the children would breathe, enchanted.

The wagon that carried the esteemed writer had rattled for hours over flat and desolate heath and moorland, purple and russet with heather and bogland vegetation and gashed with pools and ponds and water channels, silent under desolate grey skies except for the screams of water fowl in the air.

Now the wagon turned off the moor and onto the sands of a white beach which stretched for miles and miles in a wide fringe between blue-grassed sand-dunes and the sea. The horses were forced out to the sea's edge and, half the time, they had to splash through the water, for the beach was an obstacle course of up-turned fishing boats, some whole and to all appearances seaworthy, some just tarry skeletons, their greyed and jagged bones sticking out of the sand at awkward angles. Apart from the fishing boats, wrecked and battered or whole and buoyant, the beach was also scattered with odd beams and planks from long-dead vessels, ships which, in spite of the efforts of the locals to keep the fire basket burning on the light-tower, had foundered on the offshore sand-banks and whose broken remains drifted constantly ashore, furnishing the grateful local people with the timber that their hinterland lacked – a primitive and natural form of redistribution of wealth.

Occasionally, more precious goods came ashore too, chests full of fine blankets and fabrics – salt-damaged as often as not, but with the occasional length of untouched silk or damask buried so deep into the centre of the sodden piles that it remained dry in spite of its saltwater adventures – or stoutly caulked barrels of perfect red wine or sherry. The local people took their luxuries where they could. They sent out no orders, but they took the sea's deliveries as they came, and saw it as payment for the countless graves they dug for the perished sailors who washed up with the tide and the Christian burials they provided for all the dead who came their way, and no questions asked as to whether they really were Christians; Jews, Moslems, heathens – all got equal treatment here.

Ah, the children sighed. In truth, they had gathered many a piece of driftwood from the wrecks their mother mentioned, and occasionally there would be something interesting among the wreckage that the local scavengers would light upon, but they had yet to see a barrel of sherry or a chest of damask washed onto the beach. Poetic licence, their mother said once when they had challenged her on this.

The esteemed writer descended from the wagon at last outside a small but comfortable-looking hostelry. His legs felt weak and his head was light with a peculiar combination of motion sickness and hunger. His feet sank to his ankles in sand, though he could feel paved ground beneath his soles. The villagers regularly swept the sand from the streets, but they soon filled with it again, so that walking in this place was more like wading.

The children smiled again, for they all had experience of being sent out to clear a fruitless path to the front door when the sand drifted in the streets.

The smell of the sea was everywhere, overlaid with the affinitive smell of fish, from the lines of flounder that swung, drying in the wind, against the yellow or red walls of the houses.

The welcome inside the guesthouse was warm but rushed. The esteemed writer was glad of the warmth, but he did not appreciate the rush. He was shown to a room and simply left to his own devices . . .

The poor man, the children added with gusto.

The poor man, their mother agreed. No one came to tell him at what time supper was served. Nor indeed did supper seem to be served at all, for when he ventured downstairs, as he had arranged to meet a local dignitary in the dining room, he could find no one to ask where the dining room was, and there was no smell of cooking, only the all-pervasive outdoor smell of fish seeping indoors. He wandered disconsolately about for a bit, till at last he saw a large, domestic-looking woman rushing down the stairs.

You're not large, Mama, the children would protest loyally but with a giggle.

I was then, she would say with a little smile.

'Oh, sir,' she said, flapping her hands, 'I had quite forgotten you. You are not hungry, I hope.'

She had not, in fact, forgotten him, but the problem was that all she had in the house was a wonderful confection of choux pastry she had baked herself, for the great man's dessert; the girl she had sent to the next village to get the plumpest fresh fish she could find for his dinner had not returned, and she could hardly serve him his dessert before his main course.

'I am,' replied the esteemed writer drily.

'The fish will be cooked directly, sir. I hope you like fish?'

'Fish will do admirably,' said the esteemed writer, whom a sudden weariness had overcome, 'but I am parched as well as starved, so bring me a cup of tea first, while you are cooking the fish.'

'Tea? Oh! Yes, we can manage tea.'

'I am glad to hear it,' said the writer, bumbling into the dining room, which was filled with smoke, not from the fire, for it was August and hardly necessary, but from the pipe of a man who sat puffing in a corner.

The children giggled again. Their father was a notorious tobacco addict, and he created as much smoke with his pipe as a small chimney.

'Good evening,' said the writer, sitting down.

'Hmm,' said the man. 'Evening.'

Brøndum husbanded his words the way other men spared the wine or the coffee or the household's supply of soap. If he'd recognised his guest as the great writer, which is likely, he gave no indication of it.

The tea duly arrived, as did the gentleman the esteemed writer was due to meet, but the fish was a long time in coming, for when the girl got back with it, it had to be cleaned and prepared and baked. It was near eleven o'clock at night before it appeared. The writer's companion had long since departed in search of supper at home, and by now the writer was ravenously hungry as well as displeased.

'I will trouble you for some bread and cheese,' he said, as soon as the woman appeared with the fish, for it looked as if it wouldn't sustain him through the night, though when he tasted it he found that it was in fact delicious. 'And a small glass of red wine along with it.'

Cheese was apt to disagree with the esteemed writer's digestive system and keep him awake in the night, and he thought to counteract the effect with a little soporific alcohol. He was not a good sleeper at the best of times, being beset with anxieties in the dark of night.

Cheese! After all her trouble! Well, she could hardly tell him she'd spent all evening on the pastry.

'Red wine, sir?' she said with as much affability as she could muster. 'Certainly, sir. I believe there is a bottle in the cellar.'

'A bottle?'

'Or two, sir,' said the serving woman quickly. 'I am convinced, now you come to mention it, that there may be two or even three or more, sir.'

So saying, she bent over suddenly, and made a grimace, as if caught by a sudden cramp.

'I think I will forgo the wine after all,' said the esteemed writer, hurriedly, afraid now that the woman was going to collapse at his feet. 'And the cheese. Thank you. Good night.' And he stood up to leave the table.

It was too much for his hostess.

'Pray, wait, sir!' she begged, doubling over again in pain and grasping the back of a dining chair. 'I made you a special dessert.'

The esteemed writer loved desserts, and was mollified to hear that the woman had made one specially for him. Far better than cheese and wine.

'Why, that would be most fine,' he conceded, and sat down again. 'A very small portion, though, since it is so late.'

But even though he ate only a modest slice of the pastry, he lay awake much of the night, and he could have sworn, as he was finally about to drift off just before dawn, that he could hear the cry of a baby somewhere in the house. A very young baby, he thought, though he had not much discrimination in the matter of the age of babes.

And the baby who kept the esteemed and grumpy writer, Hans Christian Andersen, awake that night, the children chorused, *on his first night in Brøndums' hotel, was our Anna.*

Yes, their mother concurred. She was born, prematurely, after I had served the writer his dessert and hurried to bed with birth pangs brought on by the anxiety of it all.

The children clapped at the end, partly for the story and partly for themselves for remembering their own lines in it. The artists clapped too. The story had become a favourite with them, and they demanded it at least once every summer.

Mrs Brøndum always said that Mr Andersen was like the good fairy at the christening of a princess in one of his own stories – he brought gifts for the baby. He brought a sunny disposition, she said – though it's hard to see how that could be, for he was by all accounts a difficult man himself – and he brought artistic genius,

The others used to laugh at that idea and they would tease Anna about it, but it was true that the burning desire to paint had erupted in her, though they did not know it yet.

Chapter 6

O ne day, when the artists were out painting in the dunes or on the beach, Anna ventured into one of their rooms, on the pretext of tidying up, and indeed the room was a mess, bed linen and pillows in a heap on the bed, clothes strewn about, and a manly stench in the air. She hurried to open the casement. A large wooden blanket chest stood under the window, but the blankets had all been removed to make up extra beds, for the house was full, and the room's occupant, a young lad scarcely out of boyhood, had used the empty chest to store his sketches in. The high, padded lid was open, and papers spilled out onto the floorboards. She gathered up the scattered pages, in case they should blow away in the breeze that came through the open window, or so she told herself, but in reality she wanted to study the sketches. She found a tin of drawing pins among the debris on the floor, and she pinned the sketches all around the room, on the back of the door, on the walls, on the folded-back shutters, at about elbow height, and then she sat on the floor, in the midst of all the pungent chaos of this man's intimate life, and looked and looked until her eyes ached from looking.

No wonder her eyes ached, for it was already dusk when the artist came home and found her there, still looking. Anna leaped to her feet when she heard the door opening. 'Good evening,' she called out, brightly, as if it was the most expected thing in the world for a young girl to be in a guest's room, studying his work, while he was out about his business. But she was deadly embarrassed to be caught in a gentleman's room, and even more embarrassed to be caught looking at his pictures, for now the depths of her own longing to paint must be obvious, and she was either going to have to admit to it and give it up, or she was going to have to admit to it and do something about it.

The young man made the decision for her.

'Good evening, Miss Brøndum,' he said with a gravity she half-suspected might be mocking.

She tittered, for she was too young to be called Miss, and indeed he was not all that much older himself; he didn't join in her tentative amusement, however, but met and held her eye. Then he reached into the canvas bag of charcoal sticks and paints and brushes and pencils that he carried over his shoulder and pulled out a handful of pencils.

'Draw!' he said, thrusting a sheet of paper under her nose.

She shook her head.

'Paint, then,' he said, and flung open his paintbox, where the colours were still fresh and sticky on their palette, and he handed her a brush.

'I can't,' she whispered. 'I don't know how.'

'Come back tomorrow morning, after breakfast, and I will show you how,' he said. 'One hour, that's all. Goodbye for now. I will see you at supper.'

She found herself on the other side of the door with her heart pounding somewhere in the back of her head, it seemed to her. Her shoulders ached with tension, as if she had been hauling a boat ashore single-handedly.

The door opened again, and the artist stuck his head out.

'I forgot to say,' he added, 'that in return, I expect you to sit for me.'

'Sit?' she croaked.

'As a model. You will let me paint you. Or at least draw you.'

'Me? You want to draw me?' She put her hand to her face, and at once felt her nose, the one she knew she'd only pretended to be rid of. But now it was going to be in a picture, for everyone to see, her and her strong face and her ugly nose.

'I want to draw *everybody*,' the artist said, and closed the door again.

Excitement surged in her stomach, the feeling of anticipation she used to get on Christmas Eve. She was going to hold a paintbrush, mix the colours, swish paint around or dab it with precise little movements of her wrist and fingers, swirling colour out to the edges of the paper, or swirling it into little defined areas so that it created patterns and shapes that built up into glowing images. The idea that she was to be in a picture herself was alarming, but not alarming enough to dull her enthusiasm for this project, and she slept scarcely a wink that night, waiting for dawn and light and the promised hour with her artist mentor.

She took the proffered brush the next morning, and she looked and looked at the room about her with an intensity, so Karl told her later, that frightened him to see in one so young, and then suddenly she went at the page with a flourish and a small, low whine of concentration such as he had never heard before from a human throat, and then she turned, eyes shining, and said, 'There! That's how it looks. That's how I see it!'

He looked, prepared, he told her later, to be amused at her efforts and to say something mild and patronising, 'Good girl' or 'Well done', but when he looked, he was taken aback, flustered by what he saw. He was afraid, at first, he said, to attribute what she painted to talent, so he found other explanations: familiarity with the environment, youth, naïveté of vision, luck, even. But, he said, he knew he was only fooling himself when he saw her next attempt and her next, and, before long, he was presenting himself to her mother in the kitchen, to urge her to 'do something' about her daughter's talent.

Her mother was neither impressed nor surprised. 'I told you, Anna,' she said, matter-of-factly, 'that Mr Andersen blessed your birth with artistic genius. God knew how hard we worked to look after the poor man, and he wanted to repay us. At first, I thought you might be a writer, but when I saw how you learned your letters, I knew then that it was instead a painterly gift God had sent Mr Andersen to bestow on you.'

When the Brøndum children had been small, learning the alphabet, Anna had forgotten the names of the letters, and their sounds, but she had been able to remember the colours her mother had used when she chalked them for her. That is how she learned to read. A red one plus a green one plus a yellow one spelled 'door' or 'book' or 'cat' or whatever it might be. She did not so much read the words as perceive their glow. It was the same with things and people, objects and scenes, landscapes and interiors. She saw things not only as themselves, but as flickering pageants of light and colour. It seemed to her that everywhere she looked, life shone at her, even in its darkest corners – and there were plenty of dark corners to life in Skagen. Sometimes it seemed to her that it was light the world shone with, but at other times she knew it was really love. What could she do but shine back at it?

Her mother called this shining 'God'. Anna did not object, because she never would say anything to hurt her mother's feelings, but it didn't seem to her that the God she met in the local church on a Sunday morning had very much in common with the way the world shone expressly for her, Anna Brøndum. Even so, she dressed in Sabbath sober once a week and accompanied her family to church, and tried hard not to dance as she went, not to throw her arms out like butterfly wings and fling herself into the wind and speed along the streets with the unruly edges of her Sunday-wrapped shawl flapping with the joy of it all. She did her best to remember that her feet were in their Sunday clogs and to clump along in them as best she could and to hold her mother's hand and to look at the ground. But it was hard work, for even the ground was covered with jewels: here a pebble scoured perfectly smooth by the sea and bleached perfectly white by the sun so that it was a pearl at her feet; there a celandine flower beaming up at her from its nest in a stray clump of grass like gold from a treasure chest; somewhere else a driftwood fairy, a cleft stick for legs and tiny truncated twiggy arms, old and greyed and smoothed with voyaging over the waves and looking just like a little headless troll, which she found it almost impossible not to pluck off the road and stick in the folds of her shawl for a doll.

But now she had found a way to make the world shine all by herself. All she needed was paint.

Anna's mentor, Karl Madsen, came back to Skagen the following year, the year of Anna's fifteenth birthday, and this time he brought a friend with him. The two artists were one poorer than the other, and to save on costs, they shared a tiny room at Brøndum's, so small that they could not both stand up in it at the same time.

Anna took tea to them, as they were settling in, for she wanted to greet Karl. She had to stand outside the door and hand the tea tray in to them, so narrow was the room. Karl sat on the bed to allow the other artist, Michael Ancher, to stand and take the tray from her hands. Ancher was tall and skinny then, long-haired and unkempt. His face was fine and open but he seemed quiet in himself, not the ebullient, flamboyant type the Brøndums were used to among their artistic guests. Anna was immediately drawn to something reserved and melancholic in his disposition. Perhaps she sensed an agreeable challenge to her own equable nature.

He avoided her eyes as he took the tray from her, but he told her later that this was due not to rudeness but to his having been winded by love, which dealt him a blow as soon as he opened the door and saw her for the first time, a young girl with her dark hair about her shoulders and a gaze so clear he felt she could look right into his soul. Ancher was always a terror for romance, always in love with his own idea of love, and it was surely this, as much as the sight of Anna, nose and all, that knocked him sideways that day.

Anna took a more pragmatic view of things, but she was, after all, just shy of fifteen, and for her too the tea tray seemed to fizz in her hands as she passed it into his, so sharp and sudden was the current that was established between them at that first moment of meeting. As far as she was concerned, the feelings that raced through her body when she first laid eyes on Michael Ancher might have been the result of some obscure law of physics. She was barely out of childhood and she'd hardly heard of love. She'd come across the idea in poetry and songs, of course, but she'd never actually had as much as a conversation with anyone who had been in love – her parents' marriage seemed to be based on something much more mundane – and she'd certainly never experienced the feeling herself. Michael soon put her right. He explained all about love, and it was a revelation to her. He seemed to be some sort of expert on the matter, as well he might be at the advanced age, from her perspective, of twenty-five. That didn't happen quite then and there over the tea tray, of course. It took the whole summer long, and a glorious blossoming it was.

'Do you think old Jørgen is still in there?' Michael asked Anna one day. They were out on the dunes and she had told him Hans Christian Andersen's story of the besanded church, which he had written that summer that he came to Skagen and she had been born. The besanded church was no trope, though. It stood out there on the dunes, up to its neck in sand, only the tower rising into view.

'Definitely,' she said, with only half a smile, gazing towards the eerie church tower. 'Look, Michael,' she said then, 'the sand is blue today, look at it.'

'Blue?' Michael looked at the beach stretched out before them, miles and miles of it, and the sand was white, white.

'Yes, look, you see the way the sea and sky are a sort of . . . amethyst? Anyway, something jewel-like, I have never seen an amethyst, perhaps I mean something different, but it is a blue that is almost grey.'

'Yes,' said Michael, looking at the sea and the sky, which indeed seemed an almost mauve-grey in today's light.

'And now look, on the beach,' she said. 'Look at the footprints.'

There were no footprints. The sand was too soft and fine to hold the imprint of a foot for long. But there were dents, which might have been the shadows of footprints.

'Yes,' said Michael again, looking at the dents in the sand.

'Now, do you see blue?' she asked him, impatiently. 'Where the hollows cast shadows into themselves?'

'No,' said Michael, but he tried hard to see it all the same.

She shrugged. 'Well,' she said, 'perhaps men and women see colours differently.'

'Do you think that is possible?'

'No,' she said, 'but I see blue and you don't. Is that possible?'

'Anna,' said Michael, 'it is time you went to school.'

'School? I've been to school! Do you think I am not sufficiently educated?'

'Art school. You must go to Copenhagen and learn to paint.'

It was as if someone had spied on her in her sleep and infiltrated her most secret dream.

'They don't take women at the Academy, Michael,' she said quietly.

'To hell with the Academy! They know nothing in the Academy, old toffee-noses. We must find you a private teacher. There are plenty of studios where ladies may study art.'

'There are?' She felt her breath strangely constricted, as if her bodice were suddenly too tight.

'Surely,' said Michael. 'Do you think your parents would let you go?'

'Let me go? You make it sound as if I am enslaved! Of course they would "let me go".'

Michael smiled. 'Let a young girl like you loose on the streets of Copenhagen? I wouldn't be so sure of it, Annakin.'

'They trust me,' she said.

'It is not you they would need to trust. Copenhagen is a very long way away, and it is a big city, full of scoundrels and dangers.'

'If you think I should go, and you say it to my mother, then she will let me go. In fact, she will *send* me. You know how she is about my supposed special gift from Mr Andersen – I mean, from God, through Mr Andersen. It would be flying in the face of God's great plan for the universe if I were not to pursue this so-called vocation of mine.'

'Do you feel it is a vocation, Anna? Did you ever think to become a professional painter?'

'I have thought of nothing else since meeting you and the others who come here in the summer.'

'Very well,' said Michael. 'It is settled. I will help you to find a place. And unless I am very much mistaken, you have a bright future ahead of you, Miss Anna Brøndum.'

Michael was so smitten – though he didn't admit it at the time, or perhaps he hardly understood his own motives – that he stayed on in the fishing village way beyond the time when the other artists had hightailed it back to Copenhagen and civilisation and the snug warmth of small, stove-heated city apartments. In fact, so late did he leave his departure that he was caught out by a snowstorm on his return journey and had great difficulty guarding from the weather a large painting he was carrying with him to finish in the city over the winter months. Anna watched him go, crouched on the outside seat of the post wagon on the five-hour journey from Skagen to the railway station at Port Frederick. Already, she could see, he was numb with cold, snow settling all around the brim of his hat and trickling under his collar and icy sea spray whipping his face and sloshing around his feet, one hand permanently raised to steady the large, flat wooden box that housed his half-made picture and was lashed to the roof of the wagon and which he feared might slip free of its ropes at any moment and come crashing and slithering to the ground, where, if it did not instantly get soaked by sea water, it would surely be mangled under the wheels of the coach.

Chapter 7

'So *that's* how you met Mi – I mean, Mr Ancher?' Marie asked, her eyes shining. 'It's so romantic!'

They were clearing out the tiny room that Anna had designated as the studio in the little house she and Michael had rented in Paris, and trying to make two easels and stools fit into a space not a great deal bigger than a capacious cupboard.

'Yes. We were already engaged by the time he left that winter to go back to the city. Secretly, of course. We had to keep *stumm* about it because everyone was *scandalised*.'

'Oh! But why?'

'People,' said Anna with a grin, 'are, I find, easily scandalised. First they were scandalised about me and Karl. The pastor came to talk to my mother. Told her she had no business letting her daughter *sit* for an artist. Nobody quite knew what that was, but they were sure it was a sin all the same.'

'Surely not!'

'And when they discovered that not only was I shamefully *sitting*, I was actually participating in the devil's business . . . '

Marie drew in a sharp breath. She couldn't help herself.

Anna smiled. 'I hope *you're* not scandalised, Miss Triepke?'

Marie blushed. 'No, no, I . . . '

But Anna was already dashing on. 'What they found so objectionable, my dear Miss Triepke – Marie, may I call you Marie? – was simply that I was *painting*. They couldn't stand for that. Watercolours, they had the temerity to tell my mother, would have been acceptable. But oils – they drew the line at oils. Did you ever hear the like?'

'Oh, yes, of course,' said Marie.

Anna frowned.

'I mean, about my first name. Please do call me Marie. But how could people possibly think there is a moral difference between watercolours and oils?'

'I know. The most *ridiculous* thing I ever heard! My mother sent them away with a flea in their ear, I can tell you. Pious old meddlers.'

'I thought . . . ' Marie ventured. 'I mean, didn't you say your mother was religious?'

'Devout,' said Anna. 'If she were a papist, they'd have canonised her by now. But not an idiot. So *then*, you see, along came Michael and that was the most scandalous thing of all. Ten years older than me and an artist. He came to my confirmation. Can you imagine more diabolical behaviour?'

Marie laughed.

'And then they objected that I'd thrown over that "nice young man, Mr Madsen" – the one who'd been my partner in criminal painting activities the previous summer – in favour of this confirmation-attender! Oh, dear, you have to laugh, Miss Triepke, I mean, Marie, don't you find that?'

Marie nodded. You did. You had no choice around this woman.

'It wasn't true, of course. I mean, that I'd thrown Karl over. There was never anything between me and him – except a canvas and a palette. It was Martha he fancied in those days.'

'Martha. Your cousin? I thought she was . . .'

'That's right. My uncle had died, you see, and my aunt was left in – straitened circumstances, shall we say. So my father invited her and her two daughters, Martha and Henrietta, to move in with us. We were like sisters in those days, the three of us. Such times we had! Poor little Henrietta . . . Anyway, the next thing was, Karl discovered that Martha could draw, and he got terribly excited. Seemed he was fated to discover artistic talent in the female occupants of Brøndums' hotel. The villagers – oh, they were infuriated! The young men of the village weren't going to be able to find any wives at all, they argued, if these artist fellows, who had an unfair advantage, came and swept us all off our feet.'

'What was the unfair advantage?'

'Romantic appeal, I suppose. It certainly wasn't money, I can tell you. But how could a Skagen haberdasher compete with an artist from Copenhagen?'

'They wanted you to marry haberdashers?'

'Well, no, I suppose not exactly,' said Anna with a whoop of laughter. 'Librarians, perhaps, or harbour-masters. Persons of that calibre, don't you know.'

'Engineers,' Marie added, nodding. 'Magistrates. Upstanding fellows.'

'Exactly,' said Anna. 'Pillars of the community. Not these blow-ins with their fancy ways and their drinking habits and their loose morals.'

'But you were all mesmerised by the artists?'

'No. We fell in love with them. But quite decorously. We *married* them, Miss Trie – Marie. We didn't just set up house, you know. We were respectable girls, even if we did paint in oils. Except Helen, of course; poor Helen.'

'I thought you said Henrietta?'

'Oh, no. Henrietta was Martha's sister. *Helen* is her cousin – confusing, I know. But you won't meet Helen. She doesn't come to Paris, never leaves Skagen. Now, what would you say about a curtain on this window? It will be too bright at noon, we won't be able to see for sunshine, but we can't be doing with the shutters; we need to let the light in, but we have to try to filter it a little at midday. So I thought, a curtain in a light material. Maybe *half* a curtain, like they have in the cafés?'

'Good idea,' Marie said, wondering what Helen had done that had to have a curtain drawn over it. 'So go on about Martha. She didn't marry Karl, I know that, because she is married to Viggo Johansen, isn't she? Is she in Paris? I met him at the Schillings', but I don't think she was there. I didn't realise she was an artist too.'

'Oh, she gave up art when she married Viggo. She was too busy having babies. She's always having babies. It's like a vocation with her. I sometimes think —' Anna stopped suddenly. 'Anyway, as I said, Michael and I were the focus of village gossip that year, and Henrietta, Martha's younger sister, she thought it was a lark to be related to a girl – me! – who was officially being courted by a mysterious and talented stranger, and I really do believe she began to imagine how it would be if she could land one of the artists for herself . . .'

Martha spent all summer taking lessons from Karl Madsen, who had become terribly excited about her talent. When he went back to Copenhagen in the winter, he wrote voluminously to her, two or three letters a week. Henrietta was dying to know what was in the letters and, one day, when Martha was safely out of the house, she took a little peek. She knew Martha kept her letters in a wooden writing box with a brass clasp under her bed. The clasp didn't work; it never had, it was only for show. There was a bundle of letters tied with a satin ribbon. That posed a problem: she'd never be able to retie it properly. But there were three, recently received, which hadn't been added to the bundle. They lay loosely on top of the others. She opened each one, slipping the letters out of their envelopes, and unfolded them carefully, so as not to disturb the creases. Holding each letter in turn by the margins so her sweaty thumbs wouldn't smudge the ink, she read what Mr Madsen wrote.

Well! What a swizz! You couldn't call them love letters, that was for sure. Not that Henrietta had ever read a love letter, but surely to goodness they would contain at least some words of tenderness, maybe some descriptions of how distraught the writer was to be parted from his lady, something about the beauty of her person, that sort of thing. But these letters were all about *art*. Henrietta couldn't make head or tail of them. But, listen, maybe it wasn't *done* to write openly affectionate letters to your beloved; or perhaps Mr Madsen feared that Martha's mother might expect to read them. That must be it. The art was probably a sort of code, and if you knew how the code worked, you could read the love-making between the lines. Henrietta tried, but it was difficult.

Mr Madsen hugely admired Anna's eye for colour, he wrote. Anna! What was he talking about Anna for, in a letter to Martha? He really had not much tact. She was glad he was Martha's beau and not hers. He was hopeless. But, Henrietta read on, Anna would never make a draughtswoman. Henrietta laughed out loud at that. There you go, Miss Perfect Anna Brøndum, put that in your pipe and smoke it. You will never make a drau — what was it? A draught, a draughtswoman. She would give you a pain, she was so great at everything and a saint to boot, according to the adults.

She kept going, hoping to find out what Mr Madsen thought of Martha's own abilities, which Henrietta did not, herself, rate very highly. But not a word. Well, that proved it. If he had anything good to say, he would surely have said it. Henrietta considered briefly whether *she* might be able to draw, if it ran so famously in the family. Miss Hansen at school had always been very encouraging, but then Miss Hansen was like that, all sweetness to everyone, even the smelly children from the poorest houses.

Now, here was a rum thing. Henrietta lined the three letters up together and looked across the closing lines, and each one ended with greetings to the whole family, and always — this was the best bit — there was a tender thought for Henrietta. Would you credit it? Martha invariably passed on the family greetings, smugly, when she read Madsen's letters, but she had never once mentioned that Karl had sent a special thought to Henrietta. The mean-minded thing! It wouldn't hurt to say, *Karl says hello, Henrietta*. It wasn't as if he was sending her a love token or anything, nothing to be jealous of, for goodness' sake. It was Martha that got the letters, after all – and the drawing lessons. She might at least tell Henrietta that Karl wished to be remembered to her. That was Martha all over. Close. How vexatious that she couldn't tackle her about it without letting on how she knew what was in the letters. Squirming with irritation, Henrietta folded up the letters again and put them carefully back in their envelopes, closed the box and slid it back under the bed.

Now that she'd found out that the artist thought kindly of her, Henrietta began to feel tenderly towards him in return. Serve Martha right! If she'd passed on the greetings as the letters came, Henrietta would have taken them in her stride, water off a duck's back, conventional politeness. But now that she knew Martha had hidden Karl's kind feelings towards her, she began to regard his words as something illicit and precious.

The nuisance of it was that when she tried to imagine his face in the dark, in those moments between waking and sleeping when she needed something comforting to focus on, his features evaded her and his face dissolved as soon as she had managed to assemble it from the faulty mosaic memory. She was sorry now that she hadn't thought to study his face more closely when he was here. But maybe Martha had made a drawing of him. They were for ever sketching each other, these artists. She went carefully through Martha's drawings – worthless old scratchings, in her estimation – but she found none of him.

The artists returned, of course, in the following summer, like the swallows – every year, there seemed to be more of them – and there was more and more gaiety too in the village from May to September. The young people would make up parties to walk over to West Skagen to see the sunset late in the evening, or to go picnicking in the dunes on Sunday afternoons. Otherwise, the girls congregated to serve coffee and aquavit in the Brøndums' hotel for the men coming back from a day's painting out of doors. Henrietta got a chance to take several long looks at Karl Madsen, and found that she had remembered him quite well after all. She smiled at him when she caught his eye, even though she knew he was really Martha's beau and her sister had priority on him. But where was the harm in a little smile? Especially considering Martha's selfish behaviour over the letters.

One Sunday noon, after the family got home from church, there was something of a rumpus on the street. Martha opened the window to see what was going on, and the most glorious music came wafting in, accompanied by the sounds of scurrying feet. Henrietta rushed to join her sister at the window, and saw people streaming in the direction they had just come from, towards the church.

'It's the Pied Piper!' cried Henrietta delightedly, and she threw her shawl, which she had just discarded, back around her shoulders and scampered out to join the crowds.

'Wait!' called Martha, following her up the street.

It was coming from the church. Whoever it was had left the door open to let in some light, for the windows were shuttered after the service against the summer sun, and the music surged out into the streets and laneways. The townspeople thought the church organist had taken leave of her senses, for whatever that music was, it certainly wasn't hymns; nor was it a Bach cantata (though even that might have been a little ornate for Skagen). They crowded into the porch, until the porch became too densely populated, and then they pressed on into the aisles and nave, and soon there was a better congregation gathered than the minister had had at the service in the morning. They shook their heads and murmured to each other and wondered what demon was playing, but they stayed and listened all the same, and when it finally stopped, they clapped. In church! To clap in church! Henrietta looked ecstatically at Martha, who pursed her lips and looked away, without clapping.

Instantly, the people were ashamed of themselves, and the clapping died quickly away almost as soon as it started. The mysterious musician came clattering down the rickety organ-loft stairs and stood in the nave and took a bow.

Now, this was Henrietta's idea of handsome! Martha was welcome to her Karl Madsen. This one had a high sweep of forehead, flower-blue eyes and a noble nose, and he was wearing an immaculately pressed pale linen summer suit.

'What were you playing, sir?' asked some brave soul, as the young man started towards the door.

'Orpheus,' he answered in a fine, confident baritone.

'Orpheus? The . . . the *pagan* Orpheus?' asked the brave soul.

'No,' said the organist, 'I wouldn't put it like that. The opera Orpheus. *Orpheus in the Underworld.*'

After that the minister locked the church between services.

'Did you see him?' Henrietta asked excitedly, when they were well outside the church and out of the way of listening ears. 'Wasn't he splendid? That bow! Those eyes – so blue! And the music, oh, the music! Oh, Martha, did you ever think to hear such music in Skagen church? Opera; he said it was an opera. Oh, how I *long* to go to Copenhagen and see the opera! I am sure it is wonderful, all glittery, and if the music is like that . . . !'

'Get a hold of yourself, Etta,' said Martha, pulling Henrietta's shawl around her shoulders and marching her quickly homeward. 'You shall go to Copenhagen in due course, everyone does, and you can go to the opera if you like; I'll take you myself. But don't go spilling it out all over the streets of Skagen or the people will think you are getting above yourself. Talk of Copenhagen is for home, not for the village streets. The people don't understand. They'll think you are showing off.'

A few steps on, Henrietta piped up again, this time in a hoarse stage whisper, 'But he is splendid. Isn't he, Martha? Who is he, do you think? One of the artists, maybe? Though he dresses much more finely than they do.'

'Yes,' said Martha curtly. 'He is one of the artists. His name is Viggo Johansen. He is a friend of Ancher's and Madsen's. And yes, he is quite splendid.'

Henrietta thought it was terribly grown-up of Martha to call the men by their surnames like that, as they did themselves, but why she should be so sharp and short, she had no idea. Why should Martha care if Henrietta had fallen for the handsome organ-player? After all, Martha had that delightful Madsen running after her, sending her letters every second day when he was in Copenhagen. Surely she couldn't begrudge her sister a little love interest in her turn? Really, it was too bad. But that was Martha for you. Selfish to the core.

And then one morning, out of the blue, Karl Madsen proposed. Not to Martha. To Henrietta. *There* was a turn up for the books.

It was just after breakfast in the dining room of Brøndums' hotel, the very place where Hans Christian Andersen had sat with a rumbling stomach on the night Anna was born. The artists had gone off to get themselves ready for the day's painting – all but Mr Madsen, who lingered over an extra pot of coffee and read yesterday's newspaper, for today's hadn't arrived yet. Henrietta came in to clear the tables and saw him there.

'Good morning, Mr Madsen,' she said with professional good cheer. 'Are you not going to the dunes today?'

Madsen lowered the newspaper and said it. 'Miss Miller. Henrietta. Would you do me the honour of being my wife?'

Just like that, amongst the dirty dishes, plates streaked with egg yolk, slices of cheese quietly hardening and curling at the edges, with people clattering up and down the stairs – she could hear them clearly, calling out about lost palettes or damaged easels, speculating about the light, the tide, the wind.

'Do me the honour.' He might as well have been asking her to be mayor. And the door might come bursting open at any moment.

Henrietta bit her knuckles and stared at Mr Madsen. Then she put down the tray she was carrying and bolted.

A few moments later, she stuck her head around the door. Mr Madsen was still sitting there, disconsolately, pretending to read the paper.

'I'm too young,' she said from the doorway. 'But thank you anyway.'

Madsen looked over the paper and smiled. It was like the sun coming up. Funny how she'd never noticed that before about his smile. And he was quite good looking, in his way. A thin sort of way.

'That is easily remedied,' said Madsen. 'I can wait.'

How could she have been such a fool! Now she'd given the impression that it was just a matter of time. Well, she could hardly have said, 'Actually, I was rather hoping your friend Johansen . . .'

She didn't see him again for ages. He left that day for Copenhagen, and from there, she heard, he had gone to Paris. Paris! She had refused a man who might have taken her to Paris! What sort of a fool was she? Well, she was stuck here now for another year at least.

She tried to convince herself that she had sacrificed herself to her sister's chances, but it soon became clear – perfectly plain, like Anna Brøndum's face – that Martha was in love, not with Karl Madsen after all, but with that gloriously handsome young man who had dared to play Orpheus on the church organ, Viggo

Johansen. They were as good as engaged, it seemed, for Henrietta saw Viggo slip his arm around Martha's waist one afternoon when they were all walking over the dunes, and Martha certainly wouldn't let him do that unless they were practically married. They had moved away from the others, and Henrietta could see how he inclined his face towards hers. He was going to kiss her! Henrietta closed her eyes and turned her head away. She had never seen a man kiss a woman, and it made her queasy.

By the time she opened her eyes, the kiss was over. She'd missed it. What a little fool she was! She might have learned something.

But at least she'd found that she didn't mind too much that Viggo had chosen Martha rather than herself. She'd gone off Viggo, somehow, since Karl's proposal, though why that should be, she didn't know. Karl had started to seem more interesting, and she'd begun to long for him to come back from Paris. Oh, why hadn't she just said yes? It was his fault really, springing it on her like that. And couldn't he have chosen somewhere a bit more romantic than the dining room after breakfast? What self-respecting girl could be expected to accept a proposal offered in such inauspicious circumstances? Now she was going to have to get him to ask again, which was bound to be difficult – once bitten, twice shy, that sort of thing. But he'd said he would wait for her to grow up a bit. Oh, how she wished she hadn't mentioned that! Now it would be at least a year before he could reasonably ask again, and anything might happen in a year. What if he should meet a dancing girl in Paris? Or worse. Though men probably didn't marry dancing girls or painted ladies, did they?

'He never came back, though, did he?' asked Marie. 'I mean, he's not married. He's always alone, and he looks so ... preoccupied.'

A key clicked in a lock.

'It's Michael,' said Anna, bouncing to her feet. 'And I've forgotten to peel the potatoes. We're eating in tonight, trying to economise. We're always economising. It's a kind of secondary occupation, and it's more demanding than the primary one, I can tell you. Dear me. I'll have to get the water boiled quickly or he'll want to eat out again. Will you join us, Marie? We can all economise together – that way you don't notice so much. You don't need to help with the cooking or anything, it's only the potatoes. I've already made coq au vin – such an *extravagant* dish, full of *Burgundy*, but if you cook it yourself, you do save a lot, I must say. Say yes, won't you? You do eat fowl, I'm sure?'

'Another evening,' said Marie, gathering up her things. She'd stayed long enough. She couldn't be lingering like a poor lost soul waiting to be fed.

'Oh, I wish you'd stay,' cried Anna. 'Tell you what, I insist you come on Thursday. I'll give you the address of the restaurant, just a moment.'

'Thank you,' Marie murmured, taking the card Anna had produced. 'Thursday. Fine. I'll see you then. Good evening.'

Chapter 8

Marie's cramped room had two conditions: hot or noisy. Sometimes it contrived to be both, regardless of whether the window was closed or open. But she didn't care. It was her kingdom – queendom – and she was perfectly happy to perch at the small table beside the window, her French grammar propped open against the wall, and eat a forkful of potted herring or a chunk of cheese and a handful torn off a baguette rather than go out for expensive restaurant meals. Her idea of economising was rather more stringent than Anna Ancher's.

J'aime, she read dutifully as she chewed, *tu aimes, il aime* . . . The only person she ever spoke French to was Madame in the *boulangerie* at the end of the street, her and the cheesemonger. She did not much care for French cheeses – runny, rancid and smelling of cowsheds. She preferred cheese that was yellow and hard and sweet-tasting, like Jarlsberg. She'd found a single such cheese in the *crèmerie,* and she pointed it out dumbly on every visit, holding her breath against the sour smell of the place and nodding vigorously when it was identified by M'sieur. '*Bonjour*, M'sieur,' she might say to him tomorrow. '*J'aime. Aimez-vous? Alors, nous aimons.*' That would make an impression anyway. 'What excellent French you speak, Mademoiselle,' he would be obliged to reply. 'You surprise me. Do have this piece of cheese on the house. *Vous l'aimerez, bien sûr.*'

She smiled as she slapped the grammar closed, swept the crumbs into a fold of greaseproof paper and twisted it into a brittle rope. She must remember to take it downstairs to the dustbin before she went to bed. No point in encouraging the mice.

Mrs Ancher was always imploring Marie to join her and Mr Ancher at the Scandinavian Thursdays and, until now, she had resisted. It was far too extravagant, on her budget. But now that Anna had wrung that promise out of her to join them this week, she was going to have to go. She was not looking forward to it, though. A lot of Swedish jokes and too much to drink, and goodness knows how much it would cost. She'd prefer to hunch under the eaves with the mice and nibble modest pieces of her smooth Jarsberg-like cheese. Well, perhaps once wouldn't hurt, and besides . . . you never knew who might turn up.

So kind, Mrs Ancher. Practically forced Marie to share her studio. It wasn't just the use of the space. She was learning so much from her and the other painters who came by in the afternoons.

'You have a good eye for colour, Miss Triepke,' Margrit Ulsborg had said today, in the Swedish-accented proto-Nordic she spoke to Danes. It wasn't a language at all, but it worked: if you concentrated, you could understand it. Like listening to the announcements they made at railway stations, or when you were a child and you rolled up a newspaper to make a tube and bellowed into it. She was standing behind Marie, looking over her shoulder as she worked and smoking a cigarette from a long ivory cigarette holder. Margrit's smoking shocked Marie and made Anna hoot with laughter. Or maybe it was the fact that Marie was shocked by it that was so funny? Marie was going to have to start working at not seeming so shockable if she was going to be part of this group.

'Don't be afraid of the canvas,' Margrit said. 'Trust your eye to transmit to your hand, and it will come. You need to launch yourself into it, like swimming. Trust yourself to the paint and it will hold you up.'

Marie listened, but she never felt she got the swing of launching and trusting. She preferred to apply the paint with small, careful brushstrokes and bated breath.

'I can't swim,' she offered apologetically.

※

They'd all laughed. They were great ones for laughing. She didn't think it was so very amusing.

Thursday came, and Marie stood hesitantly on the pavement outside what she hoped was the right restaurant, squinting at the name over the doorway. It was written in a flowing script, difficult to decipher. She peered through the window glass, trying to spot familiar faces, Margrit with her cigarette-holder, or one of the Anchers, but it was all a blur, something to do with the lighting. She was just going to have to go in and make a fool of herself if it was, after all, the wrong place. She'd have enough French to ask, that wasn't the problem, but not enough, she imagined, to understand the answer, unless the waiter wanted to express his love for her. At this rate, she'd be accumulating unsuitable lovers all over the place: cheesemongers, waiters . . . She'd have to learn a few more verbs.

From inside the restaurant, Anna Ancher spotted Marie hovering on the pavement. She rapped on the window and beckoned to her. Marie smiled with relief. This was the place after all. She heaved the door open with her shoulder and stepped into the warmth and noise of the café interior.

'Move over, everyone,' Mrs Ancher ordered. 'Come along now, make room for Miss Triepke, look sharp about it. And be nice to her, she's new. I don't want any of those appalling jokes, either. Miss Triepke is a well-brought-up, unmarried lady; and I don't want her shocked to death by you lot, and no leering; I will not have leering. I suppose I can't stop you looking, but you must do it *respectfully*. Do I make myself clear?'

Marie blushed at this lecture. It would only make them worse if they were going to tease. *Aimez-vous?* Oh, yes, *ils aiment*, all right.

'This is Viggo,' said Mrs Ancher – Anna, she must remember to try to call her Anna – indicating a handsome blue-eyed man on the other side of Marie. 'I think you've met, and I know you know his paintings. Viggo Johansen.'

Viggo Johansen stood up and shook Marie's hand solemnly.

'He's married to my cousin, Martha; she's at the other end of the table.' Anna gestured towards a heavily pregnant woman, who raised her water glass unenthusiastically by way of greeting.

'And here are Mr and Mrs Tellman. He's a painter, too – perhaps you have met him in Copenhagen? And that's Holger Drachmann at the end, there, the disreputable-looking one with the curly hair, beside Martha. We call him the father of the house, because he's the oldest. It has been established beyond doubt, by the very latest calculus, that he is one hundred and five years old. Is that not so, Holger?'

Drachmann made a wide gesture with his arms from the other end of the table.

'He's a writer, though he also *thinks* he is a painter.'

'I shall put you in a novel, Anna,' cried Drachmann, 'and make you an evil art dealer with no taste, and then you will be sorry you insulted my seascapes.'

Marie was appalled at this threat, but Anna only laughed.

Marie took refuge in staring at the menu. It was in the same flowing script as the name over the door. It was like trying to read a letter.

'Have the *tournedos*,' Anna advised. 'It's always good here.'

Marie nodded, and let Mrs Ancher order for her.

She looked up from the menu and out through the large plate-glass window of the restaurant onto the street. It was dark by now, and the street was peopled by strange, bulky shadows, flitting from street lamp to street lamp. Funny how your mind could conjure up people just by *thinking*. She could have *sworn* . . . But yes, it *was*, wasn't it?

She touched Anna on the arm and cocked her head interrogatively towards one of the hurrying shadows. Her mouth formed a name, though she didn't speak it aloud.

It probably wasn't, Anna said, he wasn't expected, he didn't even know where they congregated. Nobody had seen him since his arrival – his rumoured arrival – in Paris; nobody knew where he was lodging or anything.

But even as she was saying all this to Marie, she stood up to get a better view and suddenly she was banging up a storm on the inside of the window and making wide beckoning gestures.

'Søren,' she called, though he couldn't possibly hear her through the glass. 'Søren! It's Søren,' she announced unnecessarily to everyone in earshot, with a delighted beam. 'You were right, Miss Triepke. Marie. How remarkable! Small world.'

'Not really,' said Michael. 'We're all in Paris. This is the area we always frequent. Stands to reason we will run across each other, as long as we don't all hole up in our bedrooms.'

Marie wondered briefly if this was a dig at her, but how could Mr Ancher know how she spent her evenings?

'Don't be such a spoilsport,' said Anna affectionately. She kissed Michael quickly on the upper arm, the nearest part of him to her.

Krøyer heard the rapping on the window as he went past the restaurant. He stopped and retraced a few steps. Anna! He broke into a smile and was just about to open the restaurant door when something caught the corner of his eye. Someone, rather. A dark-haired girl, sitting next to Anna. My God, she was lovely! Something almost unreal about her. Ethereal. She seemed to waver before his vision. Effect of seeing her through glass, perhaps. Something clicked in his memory. He'd seen her somewhere. But had she always been so . . . yes! It was that little German girl, wasn't it? She'd been pretty, he remembered that, the blue eyes, but a bit of a trial, he had thought her, setting up that ridiculous studio for women, all daubers. Thought painting was like embroidery or icing cakes. Something respectable to fill in the time between school and marriage. He couldn't abide that sort of thing, put him right off. She'd been the best of them, though, as far as he could remember. Good colourist, he'd thought. Yes. Nice use of light.

She turned her head slightly, to say something to the person on her other side – Viggo, if he wasn't mistaken – and he caught her profile, the fine, pure line of her jaw, softened by a light swathe of dark hair that fell forward across her cheek. My God! His breath seemed to catch in his throat as he stood with his hand on the door handle. How come he had never noticed her properly before? He'd . . . hadn't he put her in a painting? Yes, he had, he had, so he'd noticed something about her, but he hadn't . . . taken her in, somehow. She just hadn't registered properly. He must have been mightily distracted, probably stuck on a painting at the time. Extraordinary lapse all the same. Well, now was his opportunity to put that right.

She turned her head then, as if in response to something her neighbour had said, and looked straight at him. That wide blue stare. He looked in at her through the big glass café window as if she was in a picture.

A sensation as light-fingered and elusive as fever, only pleasant where fever was unpleasant, flitted over and through him, like a breeze. He felt his whole being, all his senses, his heartbeat and every pore of his skin suffused with a kind of radiant delight. He hadn't felt like this for . . .

What was her name? He was useless at names.

It wasn't simply that she was lovely. It was as if she gave forth loveliness, as if it were a quality that streamed from her.

As she watched Krøyer push against the door, the image of Rex Hirsch flickered through Marie's mind. That apartment they had been going to have in Montmartre with all the steps and the pigeons. It was a thought comprising one part nostalgia to two parts embarrassment. The whole delightful fantasy had collapsed almost before it had been constructed, leaving Marie disconsolate and shamefaced. She pushed the uncomfortable thought aside, and set about composing a smile.

Mrs Ancher made a space for Krøyer directly opposite Marie.

'You remember Miss Triepke?'

At the sound of her own name something rippled over Marie's skin, as if it were the surface of a lake wrinkling under a light breeze.

'Certainly I do,' said Krøyer, bowing slightly, in his finicky way. 'Certainly. Copenhagen. That studio with the . . . eh, the ladies. Yes. Indeed. It is very nice to see you again, Miss Trier, Triep.'

'*Triepke*,' said Anna, elbowing him. 'Helen always said you could never remember names. I think it's an affectation myself.'

Marie didn't trust herself to say anything. She just gave a tiny nod of recognition.

Krøyer threw his eyes up. 'Helen thinks she knows every last little thing about me,' he said wearily to Anna. 'It wears you down, that sort of thing.'

Anna patted his arm sympathetically.

'You haven't eaten your *tournedos*,' Anna said to Marie as the waiter came to clear the dishes away.

Marie looked guilty. 'I thought it would be a fish,' she said. 'I don't like beef. It sounded like fish.'

'I'll have it,' said Michael Ancher cheerfully. 'And you can fill up on the dessert. You're thinking of turbot, Miss . . . eh, Marie.'

Marie managed a little corner of a *tarte tatin* that Anna ordered. It felt as if she were eating rags.

'My dear child,' said Anna, 'are you aware of the connection between food and life? You have to eat to keep breathing. It is not just a story that your mother tells you to make you eat up.'

'I'll have the fish next time,' Marie said apologetically.

She had no recollection of telling Krøyer that she and Anna were looking for a teacher, but she found herself standing on the street afterwards, in the light of the café window, and he was saying he would come by in three days' time with the name of an art teacher he could recommend.

He seemed to be writing her address in a small notebook that he took out of his inside pocket.

'Three days?' she said faintly. A sentence. A promise. A promise wrapped in a sentence.

He busied himself with closing up the notebook, sliding it back into his inside pocket, not meeting her eyes. He did not want his pleasure at her disappointment to show.

'I am very busy just at the moment,' he said. 'I'm finishing a big painting, a commission, you know how these things are' – Marie did not know – 'there's a closing date by which I must deliver it. But I will be finished the day after tomorrow.' He smoothed the outside of his jacket, as if to check that the notebook was safely stowed, and then he let his eyes meet hers. 'After that I will speak to this teacher I have in mind about drawing lessons for you, and Mrs Ancher too, if she would like, and I will come by on the following day to give you the news. Will you be at home?'

Marie nodded. At home? She wouldn't leave her room for an instant on the appointed day.

'I tell a lie,' said Krøyer then, and put up a hand, palm outward, like a traffic policeman. 'It will be four days.'

'Four days?'

It sounded like an eternity.

'I can't make these arrangements on a Sunday, so shall we say Monday?'

'Yes,' said Marie. 'Monday. Yes.'

'In the afternoon. I will speak to this gentleman in the morning, and come to see you after lunch.'

Krøyer bowed briefly and left. She could hear his footsteps clicking precisely away into the Paris night. She listened until they had quite faded.

Chapter 9

'V ienna,' said Anna, and bit into a segment of orange. 'It was in Vienna.' The sharp, fruity smell filled Marie's tiny room.

Marie was hunched on her bed, her neck bent to prevent herself from banging her head off the sloping ceiling. Anna sat on an upright cane chair that looked as if it had been stolen from a café.

'I'm glad I didn't make Michael come,' Anna had said with a laugh, when she saw Marie's tiny attic room. 'One of us would have had to stand outside the door.'

'Go on about Vienna,' said Marie, shaking her head at the segment of orange Anna was offering her. She was going to have an awful job getting the smell out later.

Anna squelched the orange in her mouth and swallowed.

'Let me see.' She licked her fingers delicately, like a cat. 'It was ages ago. Ten years maybe? Makes me feel so old. Fancy being able to look back over a decade and still not see your childhood! Shocking, isn't it?'

'Vienna,' said Marie again. 'You were telling me . . . '

'All right, all right. Vienna. It's terribly grand, Vienna,' said Anna. 'Grander than Paris even, in a way, though on a smaller scale. It has – what shall I call it? – it has a sort of imperial bluster to it, Vienna. That's what it is. I tell you, those Austro-Hungarians know how to do splendour. Gold, you've never seen so much gold. But the coffee! You haven't tasted coffee till . . . '

'Anna, you were going to tell me how you'd met Mr Krøyer. I don't really need a guided tour of Vienna.'

Anna laughed good-naturedly. 'Very well. Let me see, we were there for an exhibition, Michael's painting, the big one, the one the king bought, *Will he round the point?*, it was being shown there. It was his first big success. We called it our honeymoon.'

Marie waited for her to come back to the matter in hand.

'Yes, well, oh, I remember, it was Viggo who introduced us to Krøyer. So handsome, Viggo, don't you think? Fits in very well in Vienna, does Viggo. He's the only man I know who can swagger while he is *sitting down*.'

Marie laughed, in spite of her impatience. 'Yes. He's the one who's married to your cousin Martha, who is always pregnant. And always cross, judging by the way she looked at me last night.'

Anna said nothing to that. Perhaps Marie had gone too far? But she had certainly sensed hostility from Martha, and she'd done absolutely nothing to deserve it, except be there.

Then Anna spoke. 'Well, Martha . . . she's had a hard life.'

'*Had* a hard life? She can't be more than twenty-five; whatever can you mean?'

'Well . . . '

'Something to do with her sister?' Marie pressed. 'The one you keep calling "poor Henrietta"? Did she marry Karl Madsen in the end?'

'She did,' said Anna. 'Three weddings we had that summer. Can you believe it! I married Michael, Viggo married Martha and Karl married Henrietta. It was like one long wedding; we'd only washed up after one banquet and it was time to start preparing the next one. My mother thought we should have had the same wedding dress, can you believe it, and pass it on from one to the other, save the expense. Actually, Martha might have agreed, she's very frugal, but I couldn't see Henrietta getting married in a third-hand wedding gown. Poor little scrap! She looked so lovely on her wedding day.'

Marie wriggled on the bed. She wanted to hear what had happened to Henrietta, but she wanted to hear about Krøyer more.

'Vienna?' she said again.

Anna laughed at her own delinquency in the matter of story-telling. 'Yes, Vienna, well, I was doing my royalty thing, you know how I love swooshing down those ornate staircases they have in swanky hotels – I remember it perfectly now, all elaborate balustrades and chandeliers. I had a new gown; it was too long, but I never took it up; I loved the way it trailed down that staircase behind me like a royal train. Of course the hem was ruined; I had to cut a big lump off it when I got it home. Martha came too, on that trip. She was pregnant, as usual. I don't think she was there that day, she must have been indisposed. She was never just pregnant. She was always sick too.'

The Anchers had been on their way out to dinner, Anna explained, when they heard Danish voices in the foyer of their hotel, and they'd turned to see what was going on. A small knot of people had gathered around, laughing and clapping and, at the centre of the group, sat this man Anna had never seen before. A lean sort of fellow, she said, russet colouring, spectacles. He looked like a gnome sitting there, hunched over an imaginary guitar.

Anna hunched and held her arms at a strange angle. 'This is my imaginary, imaginary guitar, Marie, if you see what I mean. You have to imagine that I am he, and that he is holding an imaginary guitar. Have you got that? It's a kind of double imagining, if you can manage such a feat.'

Marie laughed. 'Yes, I follow you.'

He was 'playing' this, according to Anna, with great flourishes and lots of twanging noises. She made some guttural sounds.

'And those are imaginary, imaginary twangings?' asked Marie.

'You are so quick on the uptake.'

In between the twangings, he'd been singing. It was some light-hearted thing, slightly bawdy – 'It's all right, I am not going to sing a rude song' – and his voice was high and nasal, making a mockery of the song.

'It's Krøyer!' Viggo had said. 'My! He's everywhere, that man. Come and meet him. He admires your work, Anna.'

Michael coughed.

'Sorry, Michael,' Viggo had said with a laugh. 'I'm sure he hasn't seen *Will he make it round the point?* yet. Otherwise, he would, of course, also be in love with *your* work.'

Michael had looked sheepish. 'He does a good sheepish,' Anna said affectionately.

Anna had fallen for Krøyer instantly, she didn't mind telling Marie. 'Well, there is something very attractive about him. It isn't his looks, it's his *way*. It wasn't only that he admired my work, though you can't help being well-disposed towards someone of such obvious good taste,' Anna said slyly. She had just liked the way he played the clown. He'd ripped a silk handkerchief from his breast pocket when he had finished singing and mopped imaginary perspiration from his brow. Here Anna mopped imaginary, imaginary perspiration from her own brow, with an imaginary handkerchief. Then he'd buried his face in the handkerchief, as if overcome with bashfulness. Anna followed suit. It had made her laugh, she said, her face buried in her hand. It made Marie laugh too. Michael had said it was all an act, self-promotion, and of course it was, but it had appealed to Anna's sense of humour.

'And you invited him to Skagen?'

'Yes,' said Anna, raising her head. 'But we don't *own* Skagen, as I have to keep reminding Michael. He could have gone anyway, on his own account. He probably would have in the end; his curiosity would have got the better of him.'

'And he caused havoc when he got there? That's what I've heard.'

'No!' said Anna, and sucked on another segment of orange. 'Not havoc precisely. But you know how it is with Søren. He fills places up. You notice it most in a room, but it happens on a larger scale too. He certainly filled Skagen up. People didn't like it much at first, but they got used to him. You couldn't imagine a summer in Skagen now without him.'

'By people, you mean the locals, the fishermen?' asked Marie.

'Good heavens, no, what do *they* care? One artist is much like another to them. All equally incomprehensible, I dare say, all irritating but good for a few quid if you play your cards right. Not me, though. I don't count as an artist because I am local. Isn't that a hoot! No, it was Martha, mostly, I suppose, who objected to Søren. Viggo did too, to a lesser extent. Michael, even, at the start.'

The problem was, Anna explained, that they all thought they had rights in Skagen. Michael had made his permanent home there, 'with me', said Anna, hugging herself – her delight at being married to Michael was unconcealed – and, in his own view, that gave him supreme rights. Besides, he understood the True Heroic Nature of the fishermen – Anna put on a deep, hollow voice at these words – and that gave him a different kind of claim on the place. Viggo felt the same; being married to a local girl too gave him pretty well equal rights with Michael, and since he was only there for part of the year, he felt all the more keenly the need to safeguard his patch. And then there was Holger Drachmann. 'You remember Drachmann, Marie. Writer who paints, but thinks he's a painter who writes.'

Marie nodded. Seascapes, she remembered.

He'd been going to Skagen longer than any of them, long before Ancher and Madsen and Johansen, and he believed that gave *him* some sort of special foothold; and he also claimed to appreciate the Heroic Nature of the fishermen – hollow voice again – just as well as Michael, if not better.

Then along came Søren Krøyer, no respecter of the tacit boundaries the others had set up.

'You can just imagine it, Marie. Recipe for disaster. Men and their territory, they are like cock robins.'

Michael came into the bar in Brøndums' hotel one stormy day when there was no fishing, and they were all standing around, the fishermen – *his* fishermen, and in a way, they *were* his, Anna said – he had spent ages training them up as models. Anyway, there they all were, drinking beer, and there was Krøyer, bold as you like, in the middle of it, with his easel up. Michael was furious.

'That's my subject,' he said angrily. 'You can't paint this picture. I've painted it already.'

Krøyer only laughed. He apologised for using Michael's models, he hadn't realised Michael had put so much effort into training them, but he said there was no danger they would ever paint the same picture.

'No,' said Michael sourly, 'because you can't paint fishermen. They look like professors in sou'westers, your fishermen.'

Krøyer took it in good part, bought another round of beer for the fishermen and a cognac for Michael.

'Michael,' he said, placatingly, 'let's not fall out over it. I won't paint in here again, since it offends you so much. I won't be stopped from painting the fishermen, though, and it shouldn't bother you if I do. We paint so differently. We could never paint the same picture, even if we paint the same subject. Ergo, we can share the subject; it need not pose a problem.'

Ergo? Ergo? What was ergo when it was at home? Michael was not convinced.

'He's – demanding, Søren is,' Anna said to Marie. 'Well, *you* know how demanding he is as a teacher, but I mean, as a person, as a friend. You can't go half measures with Søren. Either you are with him or you are against him.'

'Like Jesus!' said Marie.

Anna stuffed her knuckles into her mouth like a schoolgirl caught saying a rude word. 'My mother would kill me,' she said and giggled. 'She loves Søren half to death but, even so, I don't think she would put up with anyone comparing him to Jesus!'

There was a lull in the street sounds coming through the window. The afternoon had reached that low point, when everything seems to dip into sleep. The voices of children from the courtyard were stilled, and even the endless sawing of the pigeons seemed to have stopped.

Anna's chair creaked as she stood up. 'Swap?' she said, indicating the chair to Marie. 'Getting stiff sitting in the same position.'

Marie leaped up and Anna took a turn hunching on the bed.

'Tell me more,' said Marie, creaking into the chair.

'More of what? What do you want to know?'

'I don't know,' Marie said. 'Tell me about Skagen, the artistic life.'

'"The artistic life",' said Anna mockingly. 'No such thing!'

Marie knew better. Anna just didn't appreciate what she had, that was all.

When Anna got married, her art teacher from Copenhagen had sent her a wedding present of a set of copper saucepans, and a message of congratulation that ended by advising her to throw her paintbox into the sea, and settle down now to being a wife. Marie gasped, but Anna thought it the most splendid joke.

'Copper saucepans!' she snorted. 'Can you imagine! Of what earthly use are saucepans to a person whose family runs a hotel? A present that lacked imagination, I have to say.'

'It is not the saucepans that bother me,' said Marie. 'It's the idea that you should throw away your paintbox. Does he not know the fine artist you are?'

'Well, teachers see their pupils' worst work, Marie. Maybe they are the only people to see it. That gives them a different perspective. And it always drove him mad that I couldn't draw.'

'You can draw well enough,' said Marie loyally.

'Mr King took a more *robust* view of my talent than you, my dear. Said I painted like a cow! He meant that I sloshed colour about as if my brush were a cow's tail dipped in paint. I think that was a little unkind.'

She laughed.

'I'm glad you stopped working with him. He didn't deserve you. A cow!'

'Oh, I was always fond of him,' said Anna forgivingly, 'and I am sure the saucepans cost a small fortune. He is an old man, you know, you can't expect him to have modern ideas about women artists.'

'I would have thrown the saucepans into the sea sooner than the paintbox,' said Marie.

'Oh, no. They are too beautiful for that. I did a much better thing. I gave them to Viggo. He is so fond of domestic interiors. They look just splendid, my saucepans, in those paintings of his, gleaming away merrily over Martha's head. He complains about how difficult he finds coppery glints, but it doesn't show; they look wonderful to me. Though it does take him forever to finish a painting. I can't understand how he makes any income at all. That's the artistic life for you now, Marie – it is dogged by poverty. If he does a picture or two in a year, that is the extent of it. They are always broke; it wears poor Martha down, that and the constant flitting between Skagen and Copenhagen.'

When they were in Skagen, Viggo complained of finding no inspiration there and he longed for Copenhagen, Anna said, but when they were in Copenhagen, Martha hankered after home. And so, every few months, the growing family bundled its life – clothes, music, toys, books, easels, paints, shotgun, workbox, boots, capes, kittens, bed linen and Martha's favourite cooking pot – into trunks and boxes, and made the increasingly burdensome train trip up or down through flat and windswept bogscape, and settled, like migrating birds, on a convenient perch, until the season changed, or

Viggo did, and they upped sticks and made the journey all over again in reverse.

'It will be easier when the train comes all the way to Skagen,' she said. 'For now, it's a day's trip to Port Frederick, and then another five hours by wagon to Skagen.'

Anna sighed. Marie could see that the whole harum-scarum thing had a kind of eccentric romance to it, the idea of trailing up and down the country after one's artist husband. But, in practice, maybe it would be a strain. And Viggo didn't sound like the most amenable of husbands. One shouldn't trust a man who swaggers.

'And he paints Martha?' That part sounded wonderful. A kind of loving.

'Endlessly. And the children. They are so paintable, children, aren't they? Like puppies. They all do it; Michael paints Helga too. We all paint each other. We have a regular rogues' gallery in the dining room at home, pictures of all of us by others of us. Michael says it will be an heirloom or something of the sort. A pictorial history, I think he calls it. Lah-di-dah, men have such notions!'

'Who is Helga?'

'Our daughter. Have I not told you about Helga? How could I have neglected to tell you about my darling? Oh, she is my golden girl.'

Anna paused, an orange segment halfway to her mouth, while she dwelled for a moment on her darling girl. She was thinking of a time when she'd done the most shocking thing. She'd gone with one of the Skagen artists and his wife as far as Port Frederick. They were going on a trip to London, and Anna had just gone along to wave them goodbye. Standing on the docks, Rike had said suddenly, 'Anna, why don't you come with us?'

Anna laughed. 'Don't be silly. I have no money, no trunk, nothing but the clothes I stand up in.'

'You can borrow some of Rike's,' Laurence said. 'She always brings enough for a small female army.'

'And I can lend you money,' Rike added. 'Enough to see you through. It's only for a couple of weeks. Why don't you come? The carter will take a message back to Michael. He won't mind, will he?'

Anna hadn't really wanted to go to London. But the idea of absconding tickled her. She had just finished a painting, and she needed a break before starting another. She'd always got restless in these interludes between paintings. She'd thought quickly. Michael was at home, he had no plans to be away for the next few weeks. Helga would be looked after. And if Michael found he was busy, one or other of Anna's sisters would look after her, or her mother would do it. Anna wouldn't be missed. And since she hadn't a painting to work on, she might as well be away as at home.

'Very well! I'll go!'

Martha would have been appalled, but the Telmans had thought it a great laugh. They had sent word back to Skagen that Anna was off on a jaunt to London and would be home in a fortnight.

When the boat docked in England, a constable had boarded before the passengers were allowed to disembark. Nobody knew what was going on. People stood impatiently on deck, with their trunks at their feet, and handbags and hat boxes piled up.

'They've probably been alerted by the Danish authorities,' Laurence said. 'Warned that there's a wanton wife and negligent mother on board. Maybe they won't let you into the country, Anna. They probably don't want that sort of person here. You could be deported, I suppose. Would you like us to go back with you, or will you be all right on your own?'

For a moment, Anna's heart had stopped. Deported! And she couldn't very well ask the others to go back with her and ruin their holiday.

Then she realised it was a joke, and the constable was just carrying out some everyday customs business. It had shaken her more than she admitted, though, even to herself.

Helga had not thought it such a great laugh. She'd cried for three nights, or so Michael said when Anna got home, and would not be comforted. Anna was stricken with remorse when Michael described the child's desolation at her mother's absence. She had brought Helga an English doll, with real hair and the rosiest china cheeks, but the little girl threw it aside and sulked. Anna could not blame her; though, privately, she'd thought Michael might have made more of an effort to put the child at ease. Surely to God he had known she'd be back; it was only a moment of innocent madness, there had never been any question that she'd abandoned them.

That first night home she had had a nightmare. It wasn't the fear that woke her, but the eruption in her body that it had occasioned. Swimming up out of terror, she had felt as if her genitals had been stabbed with a blunt instrument. Lying in a knot of sweaty sheets, the aftershocks rippling through her abdomen, she forced her dry tongue between her dry lips, imagining it flickering like the tongue of a dry creature, a basilisk, perhaps, and she told herself, as her mouth began to moisten, 'It was only a dream, only a dream, you haven't been arrested for maternal negligence; you haven't been abandoned on a strange shore with no money, no papers, no baggage, no companions, wearing carpet slippers.' Slowly, luxuriously, she had turned onto her side, smoothed the bunched-up fabric of her nightgown over her legs and settled to listen to the echo in her pillow of her heart returning to its usual rhythm, feeling the softened plumstone in her groin wedging back into its moist and fleshy lodging place. She moved her damp thighs and the slip and catch of flesh on flesh released more unexpected darts, and the dull tick of blood receding.

She had reached out sleep-heavy limbs for Michael in the dark, but instead she encountered her daughter's sturdy back and she remembered, pressing her cooling face against Helga's spine, spooning her body protectively around her daughter. She'd remembered that she was a mother now. Her husband slept alone these days. The child moved and grunted in her sleep and suddenly kicked out, her small round heel catching Anna in the abdomen. Anna smiled in the dark, thinking about how naughty she'd been, abandoning her responsibilities, leaving Michael to cope, scaring poor little Helga. She shouldn't be laughing, it wasn't funny, but the more she thought this, the more the laughter welled up inside her. She'd tried to swallow it, not to waken the child, but the more she pushed it back, the more the laughter seeped out, and eventually, flinging her body back onto her own side of the bed, she had given herself up to it and laughed and laughed and laughed. She'd laughed till Helga woke, waving her rounded limbs in surprise. Anna rolled back to hold the child close, and as she gathered the small body to her own, she felt under her palm the hard, inflexible hand of the cast-out English doll, rehabilitated by night-time, and she laughed softly again.

'So pretty, so sweet-natured,' she said to Marie now. 'I miss her. But she has three other mamas at home; she won't miss me at all. I explained to her that I was going away and that I would be back, and she gave me her solemn permission, little princess that she is. They all dote on her, my sisters and my mother; she is a lucky child to be so loved. Not to mention me and Michael. If there is any truth to the idea that you can spoil a child with too much attention, she will surely grow up a criminal. But she is the best child. She sits so patiently for Michael. You will just have to come, Marie. If you can come all the way to Paris for an exhibition, you can come to Skagen for a summer. You will love it, my dear. We are all there, all of us you see in the group here, and more. And we have such parties! Say you will come.'

Marie nodded. It all sounded wonderful – but also rather terrifying.

'The poor fishermen, they didn't know what hit them,' Anna was saying now, as she stripped another gleeful segment from her orange. She was back in storytelling mode. 'First it was just painters all over the beach, the harbour, the village, the bar, asking them to "hold that pose, my good fellow", slipping them a few rigsdaler. Then it was Michael with his elaborate *mises-en-scène*, they could be hanging about on the beach for days, just holding their nets or gazing out to sea. Next thing the artists were inviting them to parties in the hotel, asking them to sing shanties, if you don't mind, and half of them without a note in their heads, feeding them beer. Drachmann the same – you remember you met him the other night? – prising stories out of them, romanticising them to Hades and back, not that they care, can't read anyway, most of them, poor fellows, haven't a clue what he writes about them. It ended up with them fishing champagne bottles out of their boats at dawn, after our all-night beach parties. That was the last straw. Sent a delegation up to my brother about that, said they were not a rubbish-removal service. Quite right too.'

'All-night beach parties!' said Marie, mildly shocked. 'Champagne!'

'Well, my dear, you wanted to know about "the artistic life". But not every night, you know. Just now and again, when Søren finishes a big painting, for example. Or when it's someone's birthday. And it's mostly Sekt, not real champagne, but what do we care? It bubbles and it foams and it makes a bang.'

When he discovered Skagen, Søren had told her once, it was as if he had come home. He had found a place that suited him, and where he could feel at ease. That was why he came back, summer after summer, and why he painted, as he put it, exuberance and the endlessness of days. Michael was different. He lined up his careful choruses of fishermen and painted each face with meticulous care – it would do your heart good, Anna said, to see the care, the love, with which Michael painted his blessed fishermen, so that every wrinkle and freckle showed and everything was all trim at the edges. You might almost walk into the picture, so perfectly did it mirror village life. But Søren – he simply set up his easel, took a good long look around, thought for a moment, and began to paint. It was not that he painted casually, but he did it with such ease and grace that it appeared spontaneous.

Marie wriggled her toes.

He painted the light and the landscape incessantly, Anna said. 'And us! We are his favourite subject.'

'You?' asked Marie. 'You and Michael?'

'No, no. All of us. Company, that is what you might call it. He loves to paint company. And he makes mythical creatures of us, angels in human form. It's a funny thing; we look exactly like ourselves, and yet we are scarcely recognisable, so luminous do we appear. His favourite thing is when we are gathered at table, having a meal, in the dining room, or out of doors. There is something about the way he paints, he makes a lunch party under a tree look like something from a grove of enchantment – the trees filtering the sunshine, a kind of sparkling weather. I don't know, Marie, somehow, everything Søren paints *glows*. It is a gift.

'When Michael and I moved into our new house, what a party we had that day! It was summer, we'd brought the table out into the garden, put it under a tree, and everyone came. Oh, it was wonderful, all sunshine and singing and shifting light and glinting wine and celebration. *Skål*! That's what he called the painting he made of it.'

'I know it,' said Marie.

'The day after the party, Krøyer turned up, bright and early, with his easel. When Michael opened our front door to let the dog out and the morning sunshine in, there was Krøyer, busily sketching the background for his painting.'

'Good morning, Michael!' he'd called, all full of good cheer, as if he were the owner of the garden and Ancher a passing neighbour.

'By God, Krøyer!' shouted Michael. 'Can you not leave a man in peace at least in his own home!'

'It's only the garden,' said Krøyer equably, as if gardens were public rights-of-way. 'Splendid morning, great light. I just had to come. Would you stand there for me for a minute, just there?'

He consulted a photograph that had been taken at the champagne party and that he was using as a reference for his painting. Michael flew into a fury. The fellow was like a toxic pest, the way he wormed his way into your life and stole all your best ideas. Why hadn't Ancher thought to make this painting? Damn Krøyer. He was always a step ahead.

'That's you, there, in the middle, Michael, at the head of the table,' said Krøyer, half to himself. 'So if you would stand just there, and raise your right arm for me? Just for a minute, just so I have a point to hang the composition on.'

'I certainly will not!' Michael practically snarled. 'Get out of my sight, Krøyer, before I call the constable.'

'The constable!' said Anna, doubled over with giggles. 'Can you imagine?'

'Ooh, touchy, are we, this morning?' said Krøyer, undaunted.

'Listen, Krøyer, damn your eyes! I will not have my garden turned into a studio for you. Go and paint somewhere else. You don't pay rent here, and you won't use my property for your damned enterprise.'

'We have musical evenings, too,' Anna was saying now. 'Viggo plays – he's tremendous – and Søren, of course, and he sings, Søren, the sweetest tenor you ever heard. But mostly it's Helen who plays. She's my cousin, did I say, or at least my cousin's cousin. She is just out of this world on the piano. She knows every tune ever invented, and if she doesn't know it, you only have to hum it once, and she can play it. She plays the way the rest of us talk. Or breathe. She hardly bothers with sheet music; it just comes in at her ears and out at her fingers, all in one motion. She plays and plays and plays and the rest of us dance and dance and dance.'

Anna leaped up from the bed and did a twirl in Marie's tiny room that knocked the jug – tin jug, luckily – off the washstand. It made a tremendous clatter, and immediately someone in the room below let a stream of swear words and hammered on the ceiling.

Anna ignored it.

'We roll up the rugs . . . ' She made a rolling motion with her arms, like a teacher explaining the verb 'to roll' to a small child. 'And we rollick . . . ' Here she made a comical motion with her body that was like dancing only standing on the spot. 'All night long sometimes. Mazurkas . . . and polkas and waltzes.' As she named each dance, she mimed its characteristic movements, but without moving her feet, and pointing down towards the room below with a mortified look on her face, until Marie thought she would get a stitch from laughing.

'Oh, it is so splendid!' said Anna, falling back onto the bed. 'Say you will come, Marie. Say you will come.'

'What happened to Henrietta?' Marie asked, by way of answer.

Anna looked suddenly serious.

'What makes you ask?'

'You keep calling her "poor little Henrietta", and then – well, Mr Madsen, Karl, is always alone, so . . . '

'Very well,' said Anna. 'I'll tell you.'

Chapter 10

Little Henrietta, who had dithered between two men and vied with her sister for both of them and finally plumped for the one who had asked her – Henrietta had had to wait out her year after turning Karl Madsen down the first time he had proposed to her that summer's morning in the dining room of the Brøndums' hotel. But he came back for her, as promised, and this time she accepted with alacrity. They were married as soon as the banns were read – *All three girls married in that same summer. So romantic!* everyone said.

They had a whirlwind honeymoon and then moved to Copenhagen for the winter, and for Henrietta's confinement, for she had fallen pregnant almost as soon as Karl held her in the night for the first time, and her baby was due in the spring. Her sister Martha was pregnant with her first child also, and she was due a few months later. Henrietta was overjoyed to be ahead of Martha for once, the senior sister in motherhood.

The sisters strolled together in the King's Gardens on wintry afternoons, their dresses swinging in an unfamiliar rhythm as the fall of the fabric accommodated their swelling bodies. Henrietta wore her pregnancy lightly whereas Martha was sick and lumbered from the start, but she did her best to keep cheerful, and Henrietta made her laugh, the way she chirped and burbled and laid plans. In the mornings, when the light was strongest, they sat at the tall, narrow windows and sewed their layettes. It was a sweet, heavy time, and the sisters had never been so close. Good wives, they were, sewing quietly together and planning how they would share their baby things, and help each other out when the babies came, taking turns to mind both children while the other mother took a rest. The rocking cradle Karl had made for his child was promised to Martha in due course, with the proviso that she must keep it in good condition for Henrietta's next.

Henrietta's mother, Mrs Miller, came from Skagen for the birth of her grandchild, and put up at Henrietta's on a small trundle bed Karl had borrowed from a friend. She came for the birth, and she stayed for the funeral, for poor little Henrietta, that sweet young girl, bubbling with the excitement of new love and pending motherhood, did not survive the birth. That awful fate that women most dreaded befell her, and she died in childbirth before she was twenty years old.

Marie gasped. She'd known it all along, but still she gasped to hear it.

In a desperate attempt to staunch the haemorrhaging, the doctor had suggested setting the child to suckle, but, like all the other measures he had tried – ice packs, raising her ankles higher than her head, a herbal concoction – it didn't work, and to her mother's and her sister's consternation, Henrietta's young life had seeped slowly away into the mattress before their very eyes, her baby at her breast.

The doctor sat with his head in his hands, tears streaming between his fingers. The bereaved mother had to rouse him and send him on his way to the next woman who needed him. She forgave him, with swimming eyes. She said it could not be helped. 'The Lord giveth,' she said, 'and the Lord taketh away.'

While her mother made peace with God and the physician, Martha took the newborn orphan and wrapped him in a layer of soft, warm lint. She drew a little cap over his tender fontanelle, a cap that Henrietta had sewn only two days ago – she'd been so taken with petticoats and shawls and broderie anglaise for best, she'd almost forgotten to make caps. Martha tucked the cap down over the tiny whorls that were his ears, and kissed him. She was the first to kiss him, and she was conscious of the privilege. Her heart broke as she kissed him, but she went on kissing him, every finger, every toe. Her own baby was not due for three months, but she knew at that moment that she held her first-born in her arms.

'Henry, we must call him Henry, mother,' she said, suddenly sobbing. 'Henry, for Henrietta.'

'Yes, Martha,' said her mother, who was already about the business of washing her dead child's body, tears streaming down her face, 'that is a good thought. Henry. Karl will hardly object. Poor Karl.'

'Poor you, mother,' said Martha. 'Poor us.'

They laid her out in her wedding dress, little Henrietta. People said she looked like a doll.

Bitterness entered Martha's soul that day, Anna claimed, and nothing was ever sweet to her taste again. She took a dim view of things from then on. Everything in life seemed dark and threatening to her, and laughter was banished from her house.

Chapter 11

The cheesemonger's bell tinkled as Marie opened the door to the street. She was putting her purse away, tucking it down into her basket, under her groceries, so that it would be safe from pickpockets. Her father had told her that Paris was full of pickpockets. She'd been in the city for more than a month, and she hadn't heard of anyone having their pockets picked but, all the same, you couldn't be too careful. It was because her head was down, concentrating on the purse and the basket and the wedge of cheese, that she didn't realise someone was coming in the door that she was going out of.

'Miss Triepke!' boomed a Danish voice.

She looked up. A large and ebullient man wearing a wide-brimmed hat was smiling down at her, his arms open in greeting.

'Why, Mr Drachmann! I didn't know you lived in this area.'

'I don't,' he said. 'I come for the cheese. It is excellent, is it not? My wife – my *third* wife – adores it.'

His third wife! What a peculiar way to refer to her!

Drachmann was watching for her reaction, but she kept her face bland.

'You have met Emmy? But of course you must agree – about the cheese, I mean. That's why you are here, is it not? Do you live near by? Can I see you home? What is your favourite kind?'

Marie considered which question to answer first. The simplest, perhaps.

'Gruyère,' she said.

'Ah, delicious!' he agreed. 'Emmy loves it. I tell you what, I'll just make my few modest purchases, and then I'll see you home. Or coffee. We could have a cup of coffee. Now, that would be an adventure, would it not, Miss Triepke?'

'Well . . . '

'Good, good,' he said, as if she had agreed to his suggestion. A man used to getting his own way.

'You will be wondering what happened to the other two wives,' he said, when they had settled into a café Marie had often lingered outside but never ventured into, for it looked too expensive, with its marble pillars and its domed ceiling and its plush furniture.

'I . . . wouldn't *dream* . . . '

'Oh, yes, you would. You take me for a regular Bluebeard. I can tell by your nervous glances.'

Marie sat up. She would not be spoken to like this, even if he was a famous poet or seascape artist or whatever it was that he was so revered for.

'If I am nervous, Mr Drachmann,' she said sharply, 'it is because I feel a little uncomfortable in such a grandiose establishment. I am used to more modest surroundings. It has nothing to do with – '

'My multiplicity of wives,' he cut in, slapping his thigh at the good of it. 'Quite right. I am far too vain. Emmy tells me so, Anna tells me so, Mrs Brøndum of Skagen, my very favourite living saint, tells me so. So I conclude it must be true.'

'I wouldn't . . . ' Marie was about to say that she wouldn't *dream*, again, but she stopped. She didn't like to repeat herself.

'*Café au lait*,' she said to a waiter who had suddenly materialised by their table, flourishing a pencil and an enormous notepad, as if he expected guests to order immense quantities of items. She would be a disappointment to him. '*S'il vous plaît*,' she added, as if to soften the blow.

Drachmann ordered a *café noir* (as he *would*, thought Marie) and a *religieuse*. 'Two *religieuses*,' he amended, when she asked what that was. 'You'll see,' he said. 'It means a nun, but you can eat it. No cannibalism involved whatsoever, I do assure you.'

Well, maybe she could eat it, but she had no intention of doing so. He could find that out for himself, though. She wasn't going to argue in front of the waiter.

'But if you don't mind, I'm going to tell you anyway,' he said. 'About my plethora of wives. Partly because I like to talk about myself. I am my own very favourite topic of conversation. It is the same with most people, of course, but other people don't usually admit it. Not everyone is as frank as I, Miss Triepke.'

Marie laughed in spite of her mild irritation.

'When I was young . . . and yes, that was a very long time ago, before you were even born, I eloped with a lovely girl. We shall call her Velma. It didn't last. She ran off before our daughter was even born. I never got to see the child. Is that not sad, Miss Triepke?'

Marie inclined her head. He could interpret it as a nod if he chose to.

'Well, I thought it very sad. I have got over it by now, in case you are concerned, but, at the time, I was overcome by melancholy. I went into quite a *decline*, my dear.'

'Indeed?' said Marie, doing nothing to disguise her insincerity.

'Alas, Miss Triepke, you are not as soft-hearted as you look.'

This remark did not merit a reply, in Marie's view, so she said nothing.

'It cost me a fortune.'

'What did?'

'The divorce. From Velma. It doesn't seem fair, Miss Triepke. I should have listened to my parents. They did warn me. They said it would turn out like that. They were simple folk, but wise. Even all these years later, I still get quite choked up about it. She ran off with my baby, and then she turned around and demanded a king's ransom of me.'

Marie clucked in mock sympathy.

'I see you are unimpressed. But consider this: if I hadn't married her, she couldn't have insisted on all that money by way of settlement. It seems unfair. I did the right thing. I stuck by her and married her when I found there was an infant on the way, and that is how she repaid me.'

Marie threw her eyes up.

'You would think once bitten, twice shy, wouldn't you?'

'I would think once bitten, twice bankrupt,' said Marie. 'If indeed your first wife did demand a fortune by way of a divorce settlement.'

Drachmann laughed. 'Well, well, I am not a rich man, Miss Triepke, but . . . In any case, let me proceed. I went to a party, you see, in this rather splendid house. No idea how I got invited. Lost in the mists.'

'I thought you were a martyr to melancholy, Mr Drachmann, at this point. But not so bad that you didn't go to parties?'

'Oh, yes, I was. I had been. But I was frightfully young, and you know how the young are? Resilient. Even in the face of tragedy. So by this time I was back in circulation, you might say. And whom should I meet at this party only the sister of my very first love.'

'Your sister-in-law? Ex-sister-in-law, I mean.'

'No, no, the sister of my first sweetheart. I had known her before I met Velma.'

Marie digested this piece of information. 'I see. You had a sweetheart before you were a child bridegroom. And she had a sister.'

'Fortunately for me, Miss Triepke, she had more than one. But I anticipate. I'm lucky with the ladies, you see. I seem to run across pretty girls all the time. Like this morning, for instance.'

She could not help smiling at this last piece of automatic gallantry.

'So you went to a party and you met the sister of an old flame. A pretty girl.'

'Polly was her name. Appropriate, that, isn't it?'

Marie smiled again. In spite of herself, she was starting to enjoy the entertainment he was laying on for her.

'Well, I fell for her, hook, line and sinker, Miss Triepke. It was love at second sight, so to speak.'

And the most tremendous piece of luck, he assured her. There he had been, feeling disconsolate about his failed marriage, his lost child, his poverty, his lack of prospects and the failure of the world (so far) to recognise his great and special talents. And now here he was in this illustrious company, and there was old Polly – he remembered her well, and damn him if she hadn't turned out far prettier than her sister had been – smiling up at him and introducing him to her husband.

'*Husband*!' Marie exclaimed.

'A complication,' Drachmann conceded. 'But there you are. Must be a rich bugger to own this pile, I thought. He was the host, you see. No other earthly reason why Polly would have married him, for he was as dim as he was kindly.' A combination Holger clearly found irksome in a man.

This good-natured fool invited Holger to visit them the following week at their house in the country.

'Visit you?' Holger had said, disingenuously, running a finger around the inside of his glass to scoop out the last delicious smear of port, and managing surreptitiously to catch Polly's eye as he did so. Polly stood at her husband's side and smiled her agreement up at him. Seeing her smile, her husband expanded his invitation.

'Yes, come to lunch, why don't you? On Thursday.'

'Lunch?'

Polly's smile broadened. Her husband loved to see her smile.

'Or dinner,' he amended. 'Yes, dinner, may as well make it

dinner, better grub. Well, if you're coming to dinner, you might as well stay over. Bring your valise. Stay a day or two.'

'Hmm, stay a day or two? Hmm.'

Still Polly grinned broadly. She added a charming little nod to her repertoire of enthusiastic assent.

'A week! Stay a week! We have a fine property by the lake, you'll enjoy it. The views! The shooting! My good fellow, you're welcome to move in for a little holiday with us, since you're' coming all the way. Rum, that you knew Polly before – I bet you would have snaffled her for yourself, if I hadn't beaten you to it! Pretty girl. Never think she'd had two children, would you?'

'Two children!' Marie breathed. 'Oh, Mr Drachmann!'

He put his hands up. 'I know, I know. I should have seen it all coming. Anyway, I went home and I packed my valise. Then I thought better of it. I unpacked it and packed a trunk instead. That was better: enough for a week or two's sojourn in the house by the lake. What good fortune! I thought to myself. Just what I needed after that business with the settlement. It wears a man down, that sort of thing. Women are so emotional at times like that. An idyll by a lake was just what I needed. Peace. Sunshine. Lapping wavelets. That sort of thing. And hadn't Polly turned out well!'

He had omitted to tell anyone where he was going, Holger explained sheepishly. Just packed up and left, gave his friends a right fright. He hadn't been well – divorce takes it out of a man – and they imagined him collapsed in the woods, dead or, worse, dying and unable to call out for help. They wondered if they should inform the police, or at least the forestry authorities. But something held them back. They had an inkling Holger was able to watch out for Holger.

They judged well, for far from lying dead under a tree, at that very moment when his friends were discussing his possible untimely demise, Holger was lying stretched out at full length on the floor of a rowing boat in the middle of the lake, taking the sun on his face. The middle seat of the boat was loose and easily removed, though whether it had just worked its way loose through age and rot or whether it was expressly prised loose to allow just such full-length idling is not known. All was still. The boat drifted; there was no perceptible swell. Even the birds were silenced by distance from land and perches. The voice of the lake-water was softness itself, barely plashing against the side of the boat.

Holger moved his head slightly, seeking a more comfortable position on the cushion. Polly settled the cushion, which was on her lap, and shaded his eyes with her hand.

'All right?' she murmured.

He could feel the thoughtful shade her hand made over his eyes, and he risked opening one.

'Mmm,' he answered, and raised his forefinger to her face, her charming face. He traced the line of her jawbone, brought his finger around under her chin and rested it to the side of her mouth.

'And you a married lady,' he said, with mock disapproval, and tapped his finger playfully against her face.

She took the tapping finger lightly in her own fingers and moved it between her lips. Tobacco and liquorice. She let it rest on her lower row of teeth for a moment; then, cupping his hand in both of hers, she bit gently into the finger, nail and pad and all.

'My God!' he said, and the boat lurched, swung back, steadied, lurched again, and settled then into a rocking motion. Holger was an experienced boatsman; he knew what he was about. The boat rocked and rocked, but it never lurched violently again, as it had with that first sudden surge.

You can stay all afternoon in a gently rocking boat, as long as the boatsman knows what he's about; all afternoon, and never feel the slightest need to pick up an oar or steer a course in any partic-ular direction or sit up and stretch your limbs, or even look up at the sky, never the slightest need. The afternoon can pass very pleasantly indeed, though nothing seems to happen at all, except that the boat rocks and rocks and rocks.

Holger never did go home. There was plenty of room, a cottage on the grounds. It had been a gatehouse or a gamekeeper's lodge, something of the sort. Of course, it needed a bit of cleaning up. Polly organised that – good at that sort of thing was Polly.

'Great girl,' said her husband. 'Rum you two knowing each other all that time ago. Delighted you're able to stay, must get a spot of shooting in soon, one of these days, eh?'

Cobwebs were shaken out of the rafters, a fire lit in the stove, a cat locked in for a day or two with no food to solve the rodent problem, the windows opened for a day or two to solve the cat-piss problem, a bucket of whitewash lashed over the walls, a few rugs and blankets sent down from the house, a rocking chair, an oil-lamp, candles and candlesticks – things a poet needs – *et voilà*!

'My very own hermitage,' Polly's husband boasted. 'My very own folly, eh, that's good. Not that you're the fool, Drachmann, no, no, it's just a manner of speaking, don't you know. Like they had in the grand houses in England, you know, hermits in the grounds. A poet's just as good, I reckon.'

'Indubitably,' said Holger. 'Would you by any chance have a cigar about you?'

'Certainly, certainly.'

The only blot on the landscape was Polly's husband's exceedingly good nature. Holger really could not tolerate so much unwarranted kindness in the long term. Guilt set in. He had to get away. Travel was the answer. Get clean away, Germany, the Alps, England, anywhere.

But by now – these things happen, and they happened especially to Holger – Polly was expecting Holger's child. This was more than he had bargained for; but, dammit, the child was his and he would own it. He'd mislaid a child already – no, dammit, he'd been *robbed* – and he didn't want that happening again. Nothing for it, in that case, but for Polly to make a clean breast – a clean breast, that was the only thing. While Holger was still abroad, of course. Then, when she had secured a divorce from her obliging husband – capital fellow, top notch – she would meet Holger. He would go to Paris to wait for her – Karl Madsen was there, the painter, you know, poor young widower, had a large apartment by all accounts, perfect. They could marry, as soon as Polly's divorce came through. Yes, marriage was the answer, since there was a child involved. The decent thing. Stop the wagging tongues. Holger had been in this position before, of course, and he hadn't planned on remarrying, but then, he hadn't planned on begetting a child either. Planning, to be frank about it, was not Holger's strong suit.

In the meantime, there was the little obstacle that Holger's divorce from his first wife had never been quite finalised. Morally, they were divorced, and he'd followed the paperwork through, up to a point, but since he hadn't had another marriage in view, he'd let the whole thing lapse when things had started to get complicated. By complicated, he meant the money angle. She had insisted that Holger should pay her a stipend to bring up the child. Dammit, he couldn't guarantee that. He had no income, for Christ's sake. And she'd taken the child from him. She couldn't have it both ways, in his view. If she was going to run off with the child, well, then, surely it was her responsibility to bring it up.

But he was going to have to settle it all up now, that was clear, so that he would be free to marry Polly. He made a clean breast too, wrote it all down in a letter to Velma's solicitor. He'd been a bad boy, he admitted it; there'd been infidelity, even before the separation. He was no good to her, no possible prospect of a reconciliation. She was a free woman, as far as he was concerned. It was all his fault, good heavens, he even had a child by another woman.

He accepted full responsibility for the failure of the marriage, though he felt in his heart that there was fault on the other side too, but now wasn't the time to argue the toss. And he could offer a small sum.

Karl Madsen's apartment was, unusually for Paris, large and airy and reasonably cheap. There was plenty of room for Holger, Karl wrote magnanimously to his friend, when he heard he was coming to Paris. Holger accepted the implied invitation with alacrity, taking the precaution of not mentioning Polly. Karl was perhaps just a little disconcerted when she arrived shortly after Holger with a new-born baby in her arms, but he could hardly turn them out.

It was a girl, Gerda. Holger liked girls. His first-born, the one he never saw, had been a girl too.

They made a strange ménage. A woman with a new baby and two men, neither of whom she was married to. Karl took a touching interest in the infant, often getting up at night to tend to it when its parents were too sleepy to bother. Staggering to the latrine at night, Holger would sometimes stumble across them in the *salon*, Karl asleep in an armchair, the baby asleep on his chest.

Poor Karl. Missed his own little one. Terrible story, that. Terrible.

Polly's divorce came through quickly and easily. Her husband's decency faltered at the child, but he saw sense in the end. Holger's came through too, at last. She probably wanted shut of him at that stage. There were no more obstacles: the marriage between Holger and Polly could go ahead as planned. Relief settled on the happy couple.

Then, with only weeks to go till the wedding day, Polly fell ill: a fever. Holger was distraught, especially since it turned out that he had to go to Oslo after all. Apparently something still had to be signed, something that could not be entrusted to the post. Fortunately, Madsen had been in Paris long enough to know a Danish doctor. It was settled that this good doctor would attend

Polly, and Drachmann could go on his business trip with a light heart. The fever was nothing life-threatening. The doctor had seen several cases of it already. She would pull through, no need to panic.

And so Holger left his beloved in the hands of this medic, and went as swiftly as he could into Norway. He would be back within ten days, he assured them. It was only a question of signing some papers, making a down payment.

It took a bit longer than ten days. When Holger got back to Paris a month later, he found Karl pacing up and down with a screaming child in his arms.

'She's teething, I think,' he said, handing the red-faced, reeking bundle of noise to its father. 'I'm glad to see you. I need some sleep.'

'Where's Polly?' asked Holger. 'Out choosing her trousseau no doubt. Fully recovered, then. Good, good.'

'No,' said Karl. 'I mean, yes, she made a good recovery, but, oh, Holger, she's gone, I'm afraid. She eloped with that Danish doctor.'

Holger put the child down on a sofa, where she promptly, blessedly, fell asleep.

'Eloped? But she was eloping with *me*. You can't elope from an elopement.'

'Seems you can,' said Karl. 'Or Polly can.'

'So you hadn't actually married her?' Marie interrupted.

'Not actually. But, dammit, Miss Triepke, she had my child. As far as I am concerned, we were as good as married. I am an honourable man.'

'Let me get this straight. Wife number two ran away before you could marry her.'

'Technically. But I still count her as a wife. As I say, I am an honourable man.'

'I see. Proceed.'

'Well, she'd left the child with some friends, but they had had to go to London, couldn't take her, obviously, so Madsen had taken her back. Fond of her, you know, by this stage. Lovely child, I have to say, my little Gerda.'

Marie's mouth was open.

Polly had left instructions that Holger should have her if he wanted. She wasn't looking for any money, she said.

'Money!' exclaimed Marie.

'No, no money, she didn't want any. Just as well, considering my first wife had already bled me within an inch of my life, Miss Triepke.'

'That's shocking, Mr Drachmann. Really shocking.'

'Yes, I have to say, I was shocked. Reeling, in fact. I suppose a woman who walked out on two children already is not the most reliable of mothers. I should have known, I suppose. But there you are, love is blind. All the same, even for Polly, six weeks seemed a bit young. It could have been some childbed madness, I suppose. That's the only thing I can think of. Or possibly the fever had inflamed her brain.'

'Isn't six weeks a bit young for teething?'

'Is it? I don't know. Maybe it wasn't teething. It could have been colic, I suppose. I don't know a great deal about babies. Do you?'

'Certainly not,' said Marie.

'So you can see my predicament, Miss Triepke. No sooner had I divested myself of one wife than the next one disappeared. At least this one had left me the babe. Dear little thing, but what was a man to do with a motherless girl-child? Poor little mite. Not her fault.'

'So what did you do? Did you have any sisters you could call on?'

'Not personally. But you will remember that Polly had sisters. I hired a nursemaid for the time being, and I sent for Polly's sister.

Holger had gone over all the women of his acquaintance in his mind, but he couldn't think of a single one who was good enough to look after his daughter. That was not quite true: he could think of a few, but none of them met the other requirements of the position, for, after all, he'd have to marry her. He couldn't think of any other way of making a stepmother of a woman, or at least not one who would last the course.

Enter Emily Cumin, Polly's younger sister. Apparently Polly had written to her and had made a clean breast, and Emily had rushed to Paris to comfort Holger, denounce her sister's disgraceful behaviour, and help with the poor abandoned child. Holger had been overcome with gratitude. Karl had had his doubts, but what could he say? He just went on paying the rent. Holger never thought to offer to share it.

As luck would have it, and luck had ever been Holger's friend, Emily – Emmy, they called her; call me Emmy, she had said – had been passionately in love with Holger Drachmann for years, since her early teens, when he first came courting that other older sister of hers, his first sweetheart. Emmy never thought she'd get him. Strangely, it never in her wildest dreams occurred to her that Holger would, years later – having married, fathered a daughter and left his wife – have an affair with *another* sister of hers, that she in turn would leave him with a child, and that he would be looking for a suitable wife to be a stepmother to it. Amazing how things turn out.

Holger was less surprised than Emmy by this extraordinary turn of events. He took it as his due that things worked out in his favour in the end, and it was the most suitable possible arrangement, in his view. Next best thing to a child's mother, her maternal aunt. That had been Karl's advice. She was attractive too, Emmy, fetching little thing, quite like Polly in some ways. He didn't in the least mind marrying her, and she was thrilled to marry him. Amazing how things turn out.

And he had the most terrific idea for the honeymoon. A fishing village he'd discovered, at the tip of Jutland. Skagen. Completely isolated. Sea, dunes, sand. Wonderful. And what could be better for the little one than a spot of sea air.

'Amazing how things turn out, Miss Triepke, don't you agree?'

'Why are you telling me all this, Mr Drachmann? It's quite a story, I agree, but I don't believe you have been honest about your motivation for telling it. It can't be vanity, Mr Drachmann, because . . . well, frankly, you don't come out of it all that terribly well, do you?'

'I like you, Miss Triepke.'

'You can't like me. You hardly know me.'

'But I do. If I get to know you better, which I very much hope to do, then I may get to understand you, and to respect and admire you, to empathise with you. But for the moment, I am content just to like you. Let's say I have taken a shine to you.'

'And that is why you feel the need to bare your soul to me?'

'No. One reason I like you, Miss Triepke – could I call you Marie?'

She nodded.

'One reason is that I can see what fine stuff you are made of. We artists, we claim to be sensitive, but we're as tough as nails really, you know. Have to be. Art is a demanding way of life. You're more fragile than the others. I'll put it this way: I can't see you running off with random gentlemen, leaving litters of abandoned children in your wake.'

'I should hope not!' said Marie.

'So let's call it a cautionary tale. If you are going to get mixed up with us, Marie, you'll find it's not all champagne parties and walks on the beach. That's all, my dear. Be warned. Take an old man's advice. Søren Krøyer is a wonderful artist, but he is not . . . husband material, shall we say?'

Husband material! Marie felt herself blushing.

'I wasn't . . . I didn't . . . I am not on the lookout for a husband, thank you very much.'

'No doubt. But I saw what I saw in your eyes the other night, and I just thought you should be warned. I couldn't break any of Søren's confidences, of course, so I thought the best course was to tell you what a scoundrel I am myself, and let you draw your own analogies.'

Marie was frozen to her chair with embarrassment. Was it so easy to read her?

'Now, let's see. You haven't eaten your *religieuse*, Miss . . . Marie.'

Marie regarded the dumpy confection smothered in chocolate.

'It looks too filling.'

'It's full of custard, but the pastry is as light as air. Try a forkful at least.'

Marie dutifully scraped a little of the pastry, with some of the butterscotch-coloured custard clinging to it, onto her pastry-fork and ate it.

'Too sweet,' she said. 'Sorry. Take it home to Mrs Drachmann, why don't you?'

'The third Mrs Drachmann prefers cheese,' said Holger, standing up to go. 'And the third Mrs Drachmann prefers her husband to be home in time for lunch. Let me take you to your apartment, Marie, and then I must be getting along.'

Chapter 12

Krøyer was putting the final touches to his large canvas when a knock came at the door.

'*Entrez*,' he called loudly and stood back from the painting, his brush dripping colour onto the studio floor.

'Special delivery, M'sieur.'

He looked around. A youngster in a peaked cap held out a letter with a large blue cross on it and several daubs of red sealing wax.

'You have to sign for it, M'sieur,' said the boy, taking a small ledger, as it seemed, out of his satchel. 'Here.'

'What, what?' Krøyer grumbled. 'Give it here.'

He raised the brush to sign his name.

'*Mais non*, M'sieur!' shouted the boy in alarm.

Krøyer laughed. 'It'd be worth something, that.'

He signed not the boy's ledger, but the bottom right-hand corner of the painting. It could be drying while he dealt with the boy and his bureaucratic little book.

'Now for you. I have a pen somewhere, you will be relieved to hear.'

But as the gentleman had spoken in Danish, the boy had no idea what he was saying. He grinned awkwardly.

Krøyer rumbled his fingers about in a jar that used to contain *cornichons* and now contained a selection of pencils and crayons, and found his fountain pen among them.

Danish stamps. Hmm.

He handed the boy a few sous and waved him away.

As soon as the door closed behind the lad, Krøyer remembered his painting. He opened the door and called the boy back.

'I have to deliver this painting to the *mairie*,' he said. 'But it is too large to carry on my own, and I am damned if I am going to trust it to some carter. For fifty centimes, will you lift it with me and we can take it over there together? It's not heavy, just awkward.'

'Fifty sous?' said the boy. 'Naw. My back gives me terrible trouble. I wouldn't risk it for that.'

'A franc then. That is daylight robbery,' said Krøyer. 'Twice what the carter would charge, but I'd rather have you, you seem a nice boy.'

The youngster coloured up, but he nodded. 'I have to finish my deliveries first, though.'

'Good God, boy! For this kind of money you can take an hour off.'

'No,' said the boy. 'It is all special deliveries. They are urgent. If they come late, I will lose my job, and a franc won't see me very far in that case.'

'Go, then,' said Krøyer. 'But be back within the hour or you can forget it.'

'I won't forget,' said the boy cheerfully, and went off like a shot off a shovel.

'*Dedans une heure!*' Krøyer called after him.

'*Une heure,*' came the echo back along the hallway. Then the front door banged.

Krøyer tested the surface of the picture with his finger. Better give it a bit longer.

He sat down at a dusty table and picked up the letter. He didn't like the look of it. Too thin to be money, but why else would anyone register a letter?

He turned it over in his hand, leaving two large, painty smudges on the envelope. He dropped the letter and wiped his fingers with a turpentine-soaked rag, and waved them in the air to dry them off. Then he tore the envelope open, since he had no paper knife to hand, and slipped out the letter, two closely written sheets of thin paper.

He looked first at the signature. One Christian Christensen. Never heard of him. A double Christian, sounded too godly for anyone's good. Might be some sort of relative of Helen's. Not a brother; he didn't think she had a brother.

He sighed. This did not bode well.

They never corresponded. That was part of their understanding. While he was in Skagen, in the summer time, she could depend upon his loyalty. Once he left on his travels in the autumn, though, he was a free man. Mind you, he was starting to chafe at it all at this stage. She had begun to presume, and the affair was beginning to develop something of the character of marriage. He had not bargained for marriage. He had made that clear to her from the outset – he was scrupulous about that; he had specifically ruled it out – and she had accepted his terms.

It surprised people that he bothered with her at all, a fine gentleman like him. She was nothing much to look at, and she had a halting step – the effect of some childhood illness – but in a way, that had been the attraction. She was innocent of the airs a prettier woman might have given herself, and she was grateful for his attentions. A much undervalued aphrodisiac, gratitude.

And besides, he had liked her. He saw a kind of secret, rough-edged sweetness in her that was related to her vulnerability. She'd been a tough nut to crack, all the same. God-fearing. God was some opponent, much more difficult to wear down than a mortal rival, but in the end she had come to see things his way.

It had been one of those long, light nights, dancing and champagne at the hotel, Helen queening it at the piano all evening, everyone flinging compliments at her to fuel her playing. She thought she was doing them a favour, playing for hours like that, but it worked both ways; they were providing her with an audience, and she craved that. *Look at me, look, see what I can do, and look how obliging I can be.*

She loved the way she could make the room ring with her music and the thuds and taps and shuffles and trick-tracks and gasps and squeals and whinnies of the dancers as their feet flew and their breath grew shorter and they could barely laugh, they were so puffed.

'Do you know 'Roses from the South', Helen?' someone called out. 'It's *divine* to waltz to.'

Helen's fingers would ripple into Strauss.

'Can't you play one we all know?' came some cavilling voice.

She laughed and lilted into an Offenbach tune they'd all been humming the previous year.

'Why doesn't Søren sing for us?' someone suggested in a break in the dancing.

'You know I will sing,' he'd said. 'But it must be Schubert.'

'Oh, not Schubert,' wailed Emmy Drachmann. 'Too serious. Schubert doesn't go with champagne. Viggo will play Mozart. Could you manage a little Mozart, Søren?'

Søren shrugged. If they wanted Mozart, he would not insist on Schubert. He had a quick conference with Viggo and then he stood by the piano.

'*Ein Mädchen oder Weibchen wünscht Pappageno sich,*' he sang, and Anna snatched up a tambourine belonging to her daughter and shook it where the bells should ring. 'Doodly doo,' she sang between the main lines of the song, laughter bubbling through her voice, 'Doodly doo. I'm the xylophone!'

He walked Helen home that night, as usual, under stars that were barely visible in the northern summer sky.

'Helen?' he said, as they jostled along, in a tone she had come to recognise as an enquiry about 'the physical side' of things, which had been under discussion between them for some time. He had explained to her all the modern thinking about this, what an old-fashioned idea keeping one's virginity was, how freely-given love between a man and a woman was something that transcended bourgeois convention. She'd never heard of bourgeois convention, she said, but he said she knew all about it even if she didn't know the name of it. It was what people like her parents would call common decency. He gave a short laugh.

There was nothing wrong with common decency, in her view, until Søren pointed out its narrow-mindedness, well-meaning narrow-mindedness, of course – he wouldn't like to suggest that people like her parents were deficient in any way. No, they were not deficient, just limited in their experience. Whereas he was a man of the world. He knew about these things.

That was just the problem, Helen sighed. That was why she should not . . .

But tonight, something had changed. Tonight she did not explain her scruples to him. She did not tell him how a girl like her, brought up as she had been brought up, could not, simply could not, behave like the ladies he knew in Paris or Vienna or Prague or wherever it was that he had got all his clever ideas. Tonight, when he said 'Helen?' in that tone, she nodded.

He could scarcely believe it. She'd seen the sense of his argument. She had shaken off her damned moral objections.

She had, of course, done no such thing. She had made a pragmatic decision. She knew that if she held out much longer, he would lose interest and, besides, she saw it as a kind of grand pagan ritual that transcended marriage, but was also a *form* of marriage, don't you see, which would bind them together in a way that no piece of paper could. A plighting of troths, that was what you called it.

She had reasoned her way to this position, and now all she had to do was see it through. The consequences would be grave, she knew that, but she did not want to end up like Anna Brøndum's unmarried sisters, shrivelled virgins, dividing their time between domestic drudgery and religious observance. She was made for finer things. Look at her musical gifts, for a start. That proved it.

She knew she was relinquishing a bargaining chip, but it was a chip whose worth was diminishing with every passing year, and she had calculated that she could get the full value for it, or more, even, while it was still worth something.

She nodded, and bit her lip and looked up at him with a brave little smile and raised her head for a kiss.

He was suddenly flooded with tenderness for her. She was a damaged little thing, and she trusted him. He would be careful. He would be so careful.

She could feel his breath on her hair, warm and urgent.

'Where?' she whispered, half expecting that he would want to take her in the open air, on the beach, perhaps, or in the dunes, to make it all more *natural*.

'My studio,' he said. 'Come on.'

His studio was near the hotel, where they'd just come from.

'If they see us going back . . . '

'We've forgotten something. You've left your music behind. No, better, I need to fetch something from the studio. Oh, Helen!' His voice was suddenly breathy and urgent.

They started to run, back the way they had come, he with his long-legged stride, she skittering unevenly beside him.

He turned to her after a moment and suddenly swept her up and ran the last few hundred yards with her in his arms. She laughed like a child. A light mist started to fall, so light they couldn't feel the drops, but when they touched each other's faces, their fingers were smeared with damp. She put her fingertips to her lips and tasted rain and something slightly salty, the taste of his skin mixed with the taste of champagne and the summer-sea air.

'Shh,' he said, setting her down at the door and fumbling for his key in the eerie blue night. 'Shh, your honour is at stake.'

She giggled nervously. He turned to her and saw how her hair was netted with mist. It glittered with refracting moisture, like tiny diamonds in the moonlight.

He shouldered open the door into the studio. There was that warm, sweet smell of paint and linseed. She expected it to darken suddenly, when they closed the door, but she'd forgotten the rooflight. Blue dusk poured in on them and silvered their skin.

He took off his hat. Awkwardly, before he'd even kissed her, she raised her skirts, not knowing what to do, not knowing that this was the gesture of a whore, not of a beloved. What did she know?

The innocent lewdness of her gesture filled him with tenderness again, and for a moment he could not move, he could not speak, he could not respond, but then he felt a new rush through his veins and he pushed her skirts higher, higher, and pulled her down onto the sandy floor.

It was not a friendly letter. It took some deciphering, for this Christensen apparently did not want to commit to paper exactly how the situation stood; he wrote of calamity, dishonour, shame, misfortune, duty, family, honour – how did he get from dishonour to honour in the space of a paragraph? Nevertheless, after several close readings, Krøyer could not avoid the conclusion that Helen Christensen was pregnant.

How could she have let this happen? His heart raced as he re-read the letter, the thin sheets of paper fluttering in his shaking hand. She *knew* how he felt about this sort of thing! They had discussed their relationship half to death; they had an agreement, they had an understanding. She knew the limits as well as he did. She was a wicked, deceitful woman. Michael Ancher had been right, absolutely right. How could he have doubted his friend's advice? Michael had said from the start that she was no good for him. When Søren pointed out how vulnerable she was, how much in need of protection, Michael had fizzed with anger. 'Fragile as a lump hammer', he had said; those had been his very words. She was going to grind him to a pulp and ruin him as a man and as an artist.

Yes, he had been right. They were all out to get him, those Skageneres, jealous to a man – and woman. That was the truth of it. They resented him. He was more talented than they were, and they didn't like it. It was as simple as that. Could he help it that he painted with ease in two hours what it took them three weeks to cobble together? Three months in Viggo's case.

So this was her first swing of the lump hammer. She was out to entrap him, by the ugliest of means. To use a helpless child . . . despicable. *His* child, to use his child to get her own way. She was a small-minded and miserable woman, hysterical too, and weak in the head. That childhood illness that had left her lame, clearly it had inflamed her brain as well. The conniving *bitch*!

Krøyer shocked himself. He had never thought a word like that about a woman before, any sort of woman; but then, no woman had ever played such a filthy trick on him before. He had to have a drink to get over the shock of it. He poured himself a little pastis and swirled it quickly in the glass before knocking it back.

It hit him like a blow to the nose, numbing his face and then slowly un-numbing it, the blood returning exquisitely to his features as the alcohol worked its way down through his system till it warmed his very toes. Ah!

He took another heady slug.

There was a knock on the door. Devil take it! At a time like this! Angrily he stood up and lurched to the door, glass in hand.

'The picture, M'sieur?' said the boy uncertainly. 'I'm back. To help you with the picture.'

The picture.

'Yes, yes, of course, the picture. Come in, come in, don't stand there shuffling.'

He hunkered down and found the scraps of wood he kept under the table, measured them expertly with his eye against the canvas, and quickly nailed them together into four triangular structures. These he fitted over the corners of the painting, as protection against the journey, and then stuffed newspapers in between the wood and the canvas.

'Here, boy,' he said. 'Help me with this.'

He was shaking out some jute sacking. Together, he and the lad wrapped the picture in two thicknesses of the sacking and secured it with stout twine. He raised one side of the large rectangular parcel to test its weight. It was light by comparison with its bulk. That was the advantage of letting them frame it themselves. All the same, he wished he had asked the boy to bring a friend with him. It was time he stopped being his own porter.

'Right,' he said. 'Now, you go first, backwards, out the door. I'll take the other end and direct you.'

It was nearly an hour before he got back, and his muscles ached, but he had been paid on delivery, and he was feeling expansive.

He poured himself another pastis and took up the wretched letter again. Perhaps it wasn't true. Perhaps he'd misunderstood this idiot's fumbling prose. He unfolded it, reread it. It was so obscurely expressed, it might have been alluding to bankruptcy or an outbreak of tuberculosis. But no. He had to admit that although other constructions might reasonably be put upon what was actually written on the page, there would be no earthly point in this man's writing to him about such alternative calamities. Obviously, this calamity was his fault, and there was only one calamity that could befall Helen that could be his fault. Yes, yes, the message was clear all right.

He spent the day tidying up the studio. He'd been painting for days, and it was full of half-eaten meals, scrunched up papers, paint-spattered cloths. He bundled it all into a sack, careful to fill it loosely for fear of spontaneous combustion – turpentine was the devil for that. Then he opened the door of the stove and fed the contents of the sack slowly into it. There was an instant whoosh of oily smoke and a small shower of greasy soot, but he kept on feeding the stuff in till it was all consumed. Then he closed the stove door and stamped out the few sparks that had fallen to the floor, grinding them under his heel.

He turned back to the room and read the letter yet again. Nothing had changed.

He sat up all night. He went into the small sleeping cubicle off the studio, and took off his boots, but he did not undress. He paced the room in his stockinged feet till dawn. He drank a little more pastis, then he drank a little more. Next time, he added a shot of water and watched the clear amber liquid turn a cloudy yellow.

He blamed Emmy Drachmann for this. She'd driven Helen to distraction with the way she flirted with him. It had tipped her over into despair, and now look where the whole miserable business was going.

Emmy was only two years married, three at most, though she seemed to have more children than it was possible to have acquired in that time. Someone said one of them had come as part of the dowry, whatever that was supposed to mean. There might be twins, of course. She had a twin herself; these things ran in families, he understood. Anyway, she was permanently pregnant, or nursing some wailing creature. She had no shame. Thought nothing of joining in their conversations over the head of a snivelling brat. Whipped it out, even, he'd seen her do it at least once, and stuck it in the infant's mouth to shut it up, and just went on talking as if it was a sugar stick she'd given the child. Extraordinary behaviour. You could *hear* it, sucking away like a young calf, and swallowing. Gallons of it, there seemed to be.

And there she sat with her infant at the breast, talking nineteen to the dozen about some Viennese psychiatrist, some theory Brandes had about sex, if you don't mind – *sex*! She didn't even blush! – and he swore she *winked* at him.

She was lovely, he had to admit it. In spite of being festooned with children, milky with maternity. The knotty blue veins of those swollen breasts that she had no qualms about exposing to all and sundry – they were repugnant; yet even as he formed the thought, he felt a fascinated desire to trace their translucent blue outline with his finger, to take the weight of those laden breasts in his hands, and to gently pinch the extended nipples. He groaned even now at the thought. He'd fallen for her, hook, line and sinker, no denying that. No wonder Helen had panicked. You couldn't blame her.

And then Emmy had tried to palm her twin sister off on him. He'd never been so insulted. As if it were Emmy's *looks* that were the point, though of course, she was awfully pretty. And there was no doubt that Veronica looked like her all right, damn fine lookers the pair of them, he wouldn't have minded in the least – if it hadn't all been so *complicated*. Couldn't deny a certain level of smittenness in the direction of Veronica also. She did it on purpose, Emmy, playing with him, she was, toying with him. It was unforgivable really. And it wasn't fair on Helen.

They sent Veronica packing soon enough. Probably started making eyes at Drachmann, he wouldn't wonder, couldn't have *that*. So she disappeared, off back to Copenhagen no doubt, or Stockholm, someplace sophisticated enough for her. She had an older sister somewhere, he remembered. Polly, her name was, stuck in his mind for some reason. She was probably pretty too, if she was related to that pair of sirens.

Emmy kept up her teasing ways with him. He didn't know where to look. Did it even with Holger in the room. Could be some thing they had going, of course, the pair of them, involve a third party, nothing like a little jealousy to spice things up. Appalling.

There'd been that night on the boat. They'd gone out, the three of them, Emmy and Drachmann and Krøyer, on a trip to the lightship. Just for the lark of it, and for once Emmy had left her children behind. Søren had taken a canvas with him, which made Emmy laugh.

'You can't paint on a *rowing boat*, Søren, surely to God.'

'Well, no, not with you two great galumphing idiots filling it up. But when we get to the lightship, there might be a spot where I could set up. You never know. An hour or two would do it. All I need is an hour of calm seas. And think of the seascape you could paint if you were actually out in the middle of it. Worth a try.'

Drachmann had bridled at the word 'seascape'. Thought he had a monopoly on the sea, the way Ancher thought he had a monopoly on the fishermen. Drachmann should stick to literature, in Krøyer's view. His seascapes were dreadful, murky things, but the kind of thing they liked at the Academy. Typical of Drachmann, that. Supposed to be this great exponent of the Modern Breakthrough, all new ideas and so on, hobnobbing with Brandes and the rest of them, and yet he went on churning out this mediocre stuff because the Academy liked it. Riding two horses.

Not a chance he could have painted that day, though. A storm had blown up out of nowhere, making it impossible to row back to shore. Luckily they had already reached the lightship, and they were able to clamber on board before the storm had really peaked. They had been trapped aboard all night, and a wretched night it was.

Holger found he could just about hold himself together with dignity by sitting very, very still. He had looked like a bearded Buddha, sitting bolt upright, sat like that all night, counting his breaths and not moving a muscle. Emmy hadn't discovered the knack, or she hadn't the patience, or stillness didn't work for her, or she nodded off, or something. In any case, she'd jumped up several times and rushed out of the cabin, letting in gusts of cold, oily, fishy, spray-wet air. Must have been a trial, that, to Drachmann, but somehow he had managed not to move, just given a reproach-ful groan. Emmy made the most dreadful honking noises, and then she would come back, stumbling and sobbing. Drachmann did not so much as look at her, poor girl. What could Krøyer do? He could hardly have put a comforting arm around her with their good friend the Buddha keeping watch all night.

He didn't suffer from seasickness himself, and had slept most of the night, stretched out on a narrow bunk.

'I don't suppose they have any coffee?' he'd muttered in the morning, as he was putting on his boots.

'Don't!' moaned Emmy.

Krøyer stood up, banging his head off the low ceiling.

'Ouch!'

He ran his fingers through his hair and beard, by way of brush-ing them, smacked his face a few times to bring a bit of life to it, and took in a few deep breaths.

'God, it stinks in here!'

'Don't!' said Drachmann.

'Don't what?'

'Don't . . . anything. Go away!'

Krøyer laughed, but obligingly left the cabin.

Dawn had broken over the swilling deck. The swell had less-ened, the captain said. He'd put them in a rowing boat directly, and take them ashore himself.

Krøyer returned to his companions with the glad news.

'Get in another boat?' Emmy was appalled. 'A *smaller* one than this?'

But they had consented to it in the end, because the alter-native was worse.

Emmy was actually green. Krøyer pointed this out to her as they came ashore. 'Could I paint you, do you think? When we get ashore, I mean, while we're drying out. Since I have the canvas with me in any case.'

'You want to paint me green?'

She must have been too ill to argue. She was fighting, she told him, to keep her stomach where it belonged in her abdomen. How could Krøyer possibly think of anything other than the heave and swell of the waves and the necessity to ride them?

'You can sit very still,' he said. 'You won't have to move. You can use the time to recover yourself.'

'Søren, you would paint in hell,' Emmy said.

But she had let him. They had to wait anyway for the cart the boatman had promised he'd send to collect them and drive them home. She huddled on a bench on the beach, hugging herself to keep the damp air out. She said she felt as if her skin might crawl off her flesh and slither away unless she concentrated on keeping it pressed to her body. That made Søren laugh, and she said he was cruel.

'You should write, Emmy,' Krøyer said. 'You have a way with words.'

He did the picture in no time. She hated it. It made her look half-dead.

'You *were* half-dead,' Krøyer said. 'You're starting to brighten up a bit now.' He leaned over and touched her cheek, which was starting to flush with the slightest pink. 'It's not quite finished,' he added, 'but I can do the rest in the studio. I'll remember. Your face – it lives in my heart, Emmy. I could paint you with my eyes shut.' He'd whispered that last bit, of course, though Drachmann was striding up and down the beach at this stage, well out of earshot.

Emmy shook her head, but a smile crept over her face all the same.

Holger liked the painting. He liked anything to do with Emmy. He was besotted with her. Explained all the children, Søren supposed.

'It's beautiful,' he said, coming over and wrapping Emmy in his cloak.

'Helen will be worrying,' she said pointedly to Krøyer.

Krøyer didn't answer, just packed up his paints. He had to carry the picture gingerly, by the edges, all the way back to the village.

The painting had created a sort of bond between them, a bond that Emmy presumed upon at every opportunity.

One evening, when they were all partying together as usual in the hotel dining room, after the light had got too weak to paint by, Søren had asked Emmy to show him a piece of music she had brought along. He hummed a few bars, and then he said, 'Oh, Emmy, this is lovely, do play it, will you? I'll sing if you'll play.'

Emmy took the score and sat to the piano. Krøyer huddled beside her on the piano stool, so that he could read the words while she played. After a few false starts, they got the rhythm of it, and the tune took off. She played away with much laughter when she hit a false note, he pausing to let her catch up from time to time.

'Hurrah!' he called at the end. 'That was terrible! You play so badly.'

'You sing too fast,' Emmy retorted and they laughed into each other's faces.

'Let's try it again!' Krøyer said. 'We'll do better next time.'

'Søren, please don't!' Helen called. She was sitting by the fire drinking tea in an interval in the dancing. 'It's too painful to listen to. If you really must sing it, I'll play for you.'

'It's all right, Littlest,' Søren said. 'Emmy will get it right this time and, if she doesn't, I'll play it myself. No need to bother you, dear.'

'Søren! I *said* not to!' Helen screeched like a fishwife. 'Why can't you ever do as I say?'

Silence had fallen over the room, like a blanket. All eyes turned on Krøyer.

'Well,' he said, 'well, well.' He pushed his spectacles up his nose. Then he turned to Emmy, his cheeks flaming.

Emmy smiled. 'Shall I play, Søren?' she asked, provocatively.

'I think . . . I think you'd better not, Emmy,' Søren said lightly. 'Helen, dear, would you like to try?' he called.

Helen glared at him. She hated having to cross a room in public, with nobody's arm to hold. He knew that.

'No,' she said. 'I've changed my mind. But not about you not singing. Leave it. Come here.'

'Thank you, Emmy,' Søren said, standing up from the shared piano stool.

'Not at all,' Emmy said, with exaggerated graciousness. '*Enchantée.*'

Søren went to Helen's side, and she'd practically boxed his ears for him, so severe was the tongue-wagging she'd given him. He sat quietly at her side, not answering.

'Sorry, Littlest,' he said, when she paused for breath. 'I didn't think. Forgive me.'

But she'd left early, went off with Anna who'd had to go to see to a sick child.

It was that evening that Michael had advised him to end it with Helen, while he could still make his exit with some dignity. Søren hadn't wanted to listen to Michael. He was fond of Helen, he'd said, very fond of her, and that was true. She was a defenceless little thing, fragile, and he felt he owed her his loyalty. He might not have felt so indebted to her if he had not been nursing a secret guilt about Emmy, but to Michael he simply said that she'd sacrificed a lot for him.

'Sacrifice?' Michael had said. 'Calculated risk, I'd call it.'

Krøyer had been shocked.

'She will grind you down, Søren. She will ruin you. It's happening already. She has cowed you.'

Cowed! Him!

'Yes,' Michael said. 'Look how she treated you tonight. Jealous as a she-devil, and with no justification, none. To abuse you like that in front of everyone, in public. You can't allow it, Søren. You have to stand up to her. I say, end it now, and keep your self-respect.'

He should have taken Michael's advice, he saw it now. They'd made it up within a few days, but he knew the damage had been profound. It hadn't been just that row about Emmy and the music, of course. There'd been constant naggings lately, endless demands. She'd started – he had to admit, Michael was right – to behave like a wife, the worst sort of wife. The Emmy row had just been the last straw. He'd tried to patch it up, he'd tried to feel the old tenderness for her, but their bond had been stretched beyond its capacity and now it hung slack and lifeless between them, linking them loosely rather than binding them together. It was going to have to end, he knew it.

She must have known it too, and now here was this last-ditch effort to pull him back to her side. Damn her! Damn her to hell!

What guarantee had he that it was true? It could all be a ruse to bring him running back. As soon as he would arrive in Skagen, sure as eggs was eggs, she'd be all tear-stained. Miscarriage, she'd say, looking for sympathy, throwing herself into his arms.

And yet, it might be true. It *must* be true. If it had been a ruse, she would have written herself. She would not have involved some cousin. No, she could not humiliate herself like that unless it was true.

It was true.

He poured another drink.

Well, he was a man of . . . he was a man of something. Honour. Yes. He was a man of honour. His duty was clear. He would have to marry thewretchedwoman. After all, he had been hasty in his first reaction. She would hardly have gone this far just to entrap him. The idea was . . . fanciful. He mustn't be fanciful, it wasn't good, it led to . . . well. He shook his head to clear it, and took another gulp of pastis. Ah!

That was it, yes, clarity. It all came clear now, like the pastis with the water added, no, before, yes, *before* the water . . .

The risk was too great, see? It had all been an unfortunate accident, most . . . mostunfort . . . And even if she had been playing a desperate game – poor thing, she must have felt driven to it. Well, it was his child, nodoubtaboutit. She was no slut. She'd loved him, poor creature. Misguided little fool. What did these people teach their daughters?

He'd have to dothedecentthing, there was no way out of it, nowayout, or he'd have no reputation at all. But of course, it was just a . . . formula? A formality, yes, that's the word, a formality. Give the child a name, poor little bastard. No, not a bastard, that was the point. Afterwards, he would divorce her, cut her off altogether, havenomoredealings. He'd make a settlement, of course, both on her and the child. He was an honourable man. Beshiiiides, this was his child, possibly his son, yes, his little boy.

Perhaps he could get custody, as part of the divorce settlement. Hadn't Drachmann done something of the sort? He'd have a talk with him. Man to man. That'd be the thing. Prise the boy out of her grasp, bring him up among decent people. Yes, that's what he'd do. Money wasn't the issue. He could make money, if necessary. He'd paint the crowned heads of Europe if he had to. He wasn't proud. That is to say, he was, but he could keep his sense of perspective all the same.

He took another gulp of pastis to swallow the thought. This time his head really did clarify, oddly. It was as if he had put on a pair of mental spectacles.

There was that enchanting girl to think of, too: young Miss Triepke. There was no doubt in his mind about her: one, he wanted her; and two, if he was going to have her, he'd have to marry her. She was that lavender-water-clean sort they bred in Germany. She would not be seduced. She could hang around with artists all she liked, but her essentially bourgeois nature shone out of her, bless her pretty little Lutheran nose.

He wanted nothing to do with marriage – horrible, suffocating institution, death to art – but even if he could bring himself to contemplate it, he was stymied now by this latest development. He could hardly expect Marie to wait while he married and then divorced Helen. And anyway, if she would not be seduced, it was not very likely that she would be prepared to marry a divorced man with a child.

How had it come to this? Two days ago he had not been the marrying type. Now here he was, considering not one but *two* marriages. He gave a bitter laugh. He needed more time, to think it through. He poured one last pastis to clear his head again and paced the room one more time.

Perhaps he'd been overhasty. Perhaps he didn't need to go quite so far, in the matter of Helen. In fact . . .

A solution began to form in his mind. A solution demanding iron resolve and quick, firm action on his part, but a solution none the less. Just a little more of this excellent pastis, he thought to himself, and all would be quite clear.

Of course he would – must – see her right, no question, absolutely no question. Poor thing must be in a panic. Settlement, no problem. But there was no point in acting in bad faith, that only compounded the wrong. They would have to sit down together and discuss this properly like two adults.

Later, when he had made his own arrangements, they would come to an agreement that would suit everyone. He was a reasonable man. And after all, it was not as though she was some innocent young girl. Everyone already knew she was his mistress. Different situation entirely. Fresh start the best thing all round, most likely. No problem about that. Yes. Much the best. Yes. He just needed time to put the arrangements in place, that was all. Just time.

He lay down, fully dressed, on the bed, and slept quickly and deeply. After an hour or so, his own snores woke him up and he lifted his head, expecting a thunk of pain to knock him back, but his head was remarkably light, not in the least weighed down by anxiety or alcohol. He got up slowly and put his boots back on.

As dawn seeped through the crack between the shutters, he sat down and wrote to Christensen, a most civil letter, he thought, in the circumstances. He explained that he would be detained in Paris for some time, but that he fully intended to be back in Denmark in the spring, as usual. He trusted that it would not be too late to address the situation at that point. He was as delicate in his own phrasing as Christensen had been in his; the lady would not be compromised, should the letter fall into the wrong hands. Certainly, he said, he would meet his obligations towards Miss Christensen; he was careful not to mention exactly how. Since financial considerations would surely be part of whatever arrangement seemed appropriate, he went on with delicious refinement, it was best if he stayed in Paris for the moment where he could attend to business matters and accumulate the required funds. He liked that phrase, *the required funds*. It was delightfully ambiguous, while at the same time serious-seeming and manly. He took another sip of pastis. He scratched out the bit about 'whatever arrangement seemed appropriate'. It sounded evasive, as if he might be trying to wriggle out of it. That was not the impression he wished to convey. It was essential that his letter gave Christensen to understand that he would take the honourable course, without actually committing himself to anything in particular. He wrote instead, 'since financial considerations are of paramount importance'. That was better. Then he changed 'paramount' to 'great'. He didn't want it to seem as if he thought money more important than the other aspects of the case – honour, decency, that sort of thing.

He wondered about the timing. Would the spring be soon

enough? Well, if not, Christensen would surely insist on an earlier return; for the moment, he'd hold out for the spring, give himself time to make his own arrangements. He ended by assuring Christensen that there was no question of his evading his responsibilities, and requesting him to convey his sincere wishes for her continuing good health to Miss Christensen, yours, etc.

He added a postscript mentioning an enclosure and saying how important he considered it that she was attended by a good physician.

He reread the letter, then copied it out in a fair hand and sealed it in an envelope with a couple of large notes. Next, he laced up his boots, called the concierge for a postage stamp and went out into the wakening street to post the letter. When he came home he lay, still dressed, on his bed and slept again, this time for fully six hours.

On waking, he called the concierge again and demanded hot water.

After his bath, he left his room and went out into the streets of Paris in broad daylight, looking for a whore.

Chapter 13

For four nights, Marie had lain tensely awake until dawn. Winter was almost upon them and the days were already perceptibly cooler, but it was still hot and stuffy in her attic room, and she daren't open the window at night for fear of bats. She'd seen them one evening at dusk, flitting eerily over the courtyard. It was the clattering of the house and the cries of children going to school that woke her from the unhealthy morning slumber that follows a sleepless night. She rolled, heavy-limbed and gummy-eyed, off her mattress and yawned.

As for food, she couldn't face it. She lived these days on bouillon that she could buy from the *traiteur* in the next street. He must have thought she had a sick person to tend, but it was only her own self.

The Monday morning was the worst. She woke earlier than usual, and there was a lump of tension in her chest. She washed and dressed mechanically, putting on her best gown, and then sat stiffly on her bed, waiting. Her fingertips were slippery with perspiration. She couldn't have drawn a line, even if she had had the heart for it. The pencil would have slithered from her grip.

She counted the hours as they were tolled from a nearby church tower. Ding dong *ding* dong. And then again, Ding dong *ding* dong, ding dong *ding* dong. And so around the quarters till it came to the hour, when the dinging and the donging were followed by a solemn series of bongs, each one falling like a guillotine. Then came at last the solitary bong that announced the first hour after noon. And the second. When a person said 'afternoon', what did they mean?

Technically it could be any time between noon and about six in the evening. But they usually meant between about half past two and five o'clock, and mostly they meant about three or four. She would not start to fret, she promised herself, until the half-hour had sounded after two.

The time for fretting came. And remained. It was now four o'clock, and still he hadn't come. If he did not put in an appearance by five, she would give up on him. And then she would have to start her life all over again, and where would she get the energy for such an enterprise?

But before the quarter hour sounded after four, she heard a creak on the stairs. She leaped up from her bed and patted her hair, cast about for a shawl. Why hadn't she done these things earlier? She'd had all day. Where were her boots?

Then came a knock on the door. He was using his walking stick to make a firm, rapping sound. It seemed to knock on her heart. She held her breath, wanting the moment to last, him outside the door, she inside it, close enough to touch, if the door had not been stoutly closed between them.

She slipped her feet into a pair of light shoes. No time to lace up boots.

Then she opened the door, and tried to look surprised.

'Oh, Mr Krøyer. It's you.'

He bowed and smiled. 'We had an arrangement,' he said, as if he needed to explain his presence. 'You had not forgotten? I hope I am not disturbing you?'

'Not at all,' she said coolly, conventionally. 'There's a café at the end of the street. We will be more comfortable there.'

She could hardly let him hunch on the bed as Anna had done. Apart from the impropriety of it, he was too old for that sort of thing. He must be getting on for forty.

She slipped out of the door and locked it swiftly.

'Do you know,' said Krøyer, 'there are one hundred and two steps and now you want me to go back down all those steps again? I call that most uncivil.'

For a moment, she froze. He was offended. Or he was going to force his way in.

Then she saw his smile, and realised he was joking.

'Oh, I think you will find Café L'Artiste more to your taste than a dingy little room like mine,' she said, with an attempt at gaiety.

'*L'Artiste!*'

'I know,' she said, drawing on her shawl. 'What Mrs Ancher would call a hoot.'

Down the wooden stairs they clattered, all one hundred and two of them. The landlady was standing in her doorway at the bottom. She lived in an enormous apartment on the ground floor, with no walls or doors, everything all jumbled in together: sink, sofas, birdcages, bed, stove and three raggedy-looking Pekingese dogs, one of whom was in her arms at that moment.

'No gentlemen, Mademoiselle' she snapped. 'That is the house rule.'

'*D'accord*, Madame,' said Krøyer brightly. 'That is why we are going out. *Bonne journée* to you also.'

Krøyer tipped his hat and bowed. Madame looked unimpressed.

'What a *coiffure!*' he said. 'Like something from the court of Louis *Quinze*.'

'Yes, you could house a whole menagerie of small rodents in it, couldn't you? Eats her dinner off a newspaper.'

'And this is a bad thing?' asked Krøyer.

Marie nodded. 'Artists may be excused if they are extremely busy. But for regular folk, it is not done.'

He looked at her, to see if she was joking. Was her seriousness real or assumed for comic effect? He couldn't be sure. That was the thing about Germans.

She said she would have a hot chocolate. He had a beer. They sat side by side, looking out onto the street, like a courting couple.

The teacher he recommended was willing, Mr Krøyer said. If she would call to this address – he handed her a neatly folded square of paper – within the next day or two, Monsieur would be delighted. And if Mrs Ancher cared to join in the lessons, they could also share the costs. That was quite in order, he had taken the liberty of establishing that.

Marie concentrated on listening, because she knew she would have to make some sort of a sensible reply, but her heart kept bursting into song, and that made it difficult for her ears. There was no reason for it. He had not said anything that suggested he had more than an artist's passing interest in an art student. Perhaps it was just his physical proximity that filled her with euphoria. But she thought not. No. There was something indefinable about his manner that transmitted itself to her. She knew, she just *knew*, he had not come only to give her the address. He could have posted it to her, if that had been all. He wanted to be here, sitting next to her, talking to her.

As he stood up to go, he asked if he might call on her again.

She hesitated. Appeared to hesitate.

It might be better if they arranged to meet here, she said, at the café. Avoid ruffling Madame's feathers. What she was thinking was, he hasn't said why. He hasn't offered any excuse for why we should meet again. He just wants to see me. She wanted to hug herself with delight, but she managed to comport herself with passable dignity.

After that, he never offered an excuse for coming to call on her. He simply asked if he might come, and she said that of course he might.

They started to go about together. He took her to the opera, to the theatre, to art exhibitions. He told her all about the pictures. He gave her his opinions on every artist – Monet he pointed out as particularly wonderful. She agreed, a little breathlessly. Everything suddenly seemed so urgent with Mr Krøyer these days. He explained all these ideas the French painters had about colour, about how you could put colours side by side on the canvas, and the colours mixed *themselves* in the viewer's eye. She found that hard to believe, until he pointed out examples to her. She could hardly keep up with him. He showed her Japanese prints, which he told her were probably the finest art in the world. To her they looked rather strange and static, but she listened and she tried to see what he saw in them. There seemed to be a lot of moonlight, and ladies with strangely triangular chins dressing their hair. He talked to her about light and space and the balance between overall composition and detail. He talked about photography with an excitement she found hard to understand, for surely it was only going to rob painters of their livelihood, especially portrait painters. He came to Anna's 'studio' and looked at Marie's work and made some helpful comments, much kinder than the things he had said in Copenhagen the previous spring.

She felt as if she were living in some other air, an air that bore her up as she walked so that she never felt the cold press of the pavement under her feet, an air that fed her with exquisite delicacies without her having to pause to eat, an air that sang into her body and was exhaled as dancing. She was like a daisy, small and pretty and fringed, dipped in the pink of enchantment. She was like a dandelion seed, floating high over the world and homing in on some grassy patch, only to lift again over the treetops and the horizon and sail to some foreign shore to a new home abroad. She was like a flag, flying in ecstasy from a height that would have made her dizzy, only that she knew she was anchored and safe. She was like a ballerina, twirling endlessly in the arms of her beloved. She was like a swan, sailing home over the lake to her nesting place.

She was like the Snow Queen skimming over her icy kingdom on a magic sledge, but a good Snow Queen, with no chip of ice in her heart, only warmth and laughter and joy. She was a fairy princess, swooping down from the tip of the Christmas tree, dispensing stardust from her wand which scattered all over the world and landed as laughter in children's bedrooms and playrooms and schoolrooms. She was the modest maiden in the story who is discovered by a prince of the realm as he rides by on his milk-white steed and who is swept from her earthly abode into her true magical home in the clouds. Nothing could spoil it. Everything was charged with delight. It was a dream; it was a cloud of glory; it was heaven.

Christmas came, and he invited her to dinner on Christmas Eve with the Schillings and some other friends of his. She hardly knew what they ate, only supposed it must have been some game bird, with glazed vegetables and fruit sauces or compotes, because that was Christmas fare. She tasted nothing. She gave and received gifts, and could not remember, ten minutes after, what they had been. There was chocolate and there were figs. There were crystallised fruits. There was port and sherry and brandy and gin and something very sweet and sticky that she had rather too much of and that tasted of burned apricots. There was definitely a shining tree, huge and sparkling, and children, dancing around it, singing Christmas songs. There had been a Nativity pageant, but the baby had cried so much they'd had to put him to bed and use a doll instead, but the other children kept complaining that the doll was a girl in street clothes and not suitable for the Christ Child at all, which made the adults laugh – and the adults' laughter made the children crosser still. She remembered the laughter and the tears, but what she mostly remembered was how Krøyer had walked her home through the dark and icy Parisian streets and waited on her doorstep while she fished out her key in the blue and fizzing gaslight, and insisted on waiting on the pavement till she got to her room and lit her candle and opened the shutters to wave to him, so he knew she was safe.

She imagined how she looked to him, the square of soft yellow light appearing as if cut into the roof when the shutters were opened, her form, still in her street clothes and her winter bonnet, silhouetted within it. Then the muffled clatter as she pushed out the right-hand casement of the window and bent the top half of her body out, leaning towards him from a height. He wouldn't be able to make out her features but he'd know her voice, calling, 'Good night, Mr Krøyer. Thank you for a lovely evening! Sleep well.'

She could see him, his lean figure and his pointy beard on his long, pointy chin, outlined by the eerie light of the gas streetlamp. He waved his hat at her.

'Happy Christmas,' she added. Sleet was starting to slant through the air. She could see tiny, half-melting snowflakes, moving in the uncertain light of her window, flickering and wafting. 'Put your hat back on! Or your ears will freeze!' She could make out the driving sleet around his head, haloed by gaslight.

It was probably the best moment in their whole relationship, him there on the pavement, her up at the window, each with eyes only for the other.

'Happy Christmas,' he called back, and waved again, and then she saw him ram his hat down on his head and watched the angular shadow that was his figure moving away and blending into the darkness.

He invited her on an outing to a village outside Paris on the day after Christmas. They hired a cab and they ate fresh white cheese like curd out of a pot and little wrinkled red apples and thick brown bread and drank rough red wine and laughed at a family of geese they saw huddled under a disused cart, and then they came back by barge to Paris, sailing down the Seine. It was cold, and they had to huddle delightedly together to protect each other from the wind that whipped around their faces; so close they huddled that once, when they turned to face each other, they kissed, almost by accident, she thought, just by the proximity of their lips. But the second kiss left her in no doubt. It wasn't an accident. It was an articulation of endless love.

Marie was no Helen Christensen. She had not had her head turned by long summer evenings in Skagen and champagne parties under trees. If a man kissed her, that meant one thing, and one thing only. She had learned nothing, it seemed, from the Rex incident, about the necessity of establishing the facts before making assumptions. But fortunately for her, Krøyer needed to be quite sure she understood, and so he proposed in so many words, there and then, on the boat on the Seine, in the piercing wind.

Marie answered by kissing him back, and then again, and again, and again.

'You haven't said yes, Miss Tr – Marie,' he said, drawing back from a kiss.

'Haven't I?' she said, flinging the words on the wind. 'I thought I had.'

'So that is a yes, then?'

'Yes,' she said, 'yes, yes, yes.'

He smiled. His favourite word from a girl. It was unbelievable. The unassailable, unattainable Søren Krøyer had become engaged to a slip of a girl, an unknown art student with nothing more to recommend her than an honest disposition and a pretty face.

Chapter 14

P*aris, Tuesday*

Dear Mama, Dear Papa,

How have you all been? Did you have a good Christmas? Of course, I missed you all terribly, never been away from you all at Christmas before. Thank you so much for the parcel, everyone. The *Weihnachtsgebäck* in particular were much appreciated, Mama. It was lovely to have something special to share, especially since people have been so good to me, so kind to a waif abroad, so to speak. They're all abroad too, of course, but somehow I seem to be more so. Wonder why that is? I suppose because most of them have proper homes here, the artists – the other artists, I have to start saying, though I feel so silly, calling myself an artist at my age, considering I have never shown a picture, much less sold one, so I know I am still just a student, but they all say you have to call yourself an artist, and if you don't respect your own art, you can't expect that anyone else will. I suppose they have a point.

My dears, I have some tremendous news. Now, listen, I know I have done this before, but I was much younger then, fully six months (!) and this time it is all much clearer, much cleaner somehow, no wretched family to interfere. Yes, you've guessed it! I've got myself engaged. And this time, I promise, promise, promise it is for real – a ring and everything, a beautiful antique sapphire. He is a little older, Mama, and I know you will approve of that; you always say I need someone to steady me.

You will be wondering who I can possibly mean, and you are going to be astonished when you hear, because it is someone Very

Famous. Can you contain yourselves? It is Mr Søren Krøyer, the 'greatest Danish artist of his generation', they call him in the newspapers. Can you believe it, your little Marie engaged to the greatest anything? You may remember that I knew him slightly before, in Copenhagen, so it is not just some crazy whirlwind thing, I have admired him most awfully for years, absolutely years. You remember that painting I appeared in last year, where I was part of a group in a parlour scene? You remember how excited I was to be painted by this wonderful painter – you've got it. That's him!

Now, I promise you, you are going to like him excessively. And of course we are coming to you for the wedding. I did wonder about Copenhagen – St Thomas's would be so nice, Theo and everything – but Søren says we should not put you to the trouble of coming all the way; it is much easier for us to go to you. He is thoughtful like that, as you will find out soon enough for yourselves. He says we must go to you anyway, as he wants to have a word with Papa, ask for my hand sort of thing, though I have told him that we are not an old-fashioned family, except in the best sense, that of course you will both be very happy to welcome him as a son-in-law, none of that old marriage settlement nonsense and so on, that you both just want me to be happy. But I should say at this point, as I know Papa is always a little anxious about 'matters financial', that Mr Krøyer is very comfortably off – for an artist, that is, and of course it is a more precarious life than most, but really he is most dreadfully famous and people pay enormous sums for him to paint their chambers of commerce and so on, so we shall have no worries on that score; we shall be able to afford a nice house, in due course, or a very stylish apartment at any rate.

I know you will be delighted for me, and will welcome Søren into the family. He is so looking forward to meeting you, practising his German like mad, though I have told him there is no need, that you both have excellent Danish, and Valdemar, like me, is a native, but he says it is only your due that he should make the effort, and he is most frightfully good at languages – you should hear how he natters away in French, and it is such an unforgiving language, French, isn't it? I am really struggling with it, and especially the wretched numbers. Søren says they have inherited some ancient counting method based on sixty rather than one hundred, and that in consequence of that they have had to make up the numbers in between. I suppose he is right, but really and truly, calling ninety-nine 'four twenties nineteen' – that is not counting; I call that mental arithmetic! But Søren says, look at an hour: sixty minutes, and a minute: sixty seconds, that is supposed to prove about the old method of reckoning, and I suppose it does make some kind of sense.

Well, I must stop blathering on, I am sure you are not in the least bit interested in French numbers, and are only dying to know more about our plans. Our plans are, as previously indicated, to come straight to you as soon as we can get away from here, and to marry in Augsburg as soon as it can be arranged. We are in a dreadful hurry because we are so much in love, and also, Søren says, because he is terribly ancient (joke! – he is in his late thirties, not exactly ready for the chair by the hob yet!) and does not want to waste a single day longer than necessary of those remaining to him in not being married to me. Is that not most deliciously gallant of him? Anyway, we hope to leave here within the week, ten days at the outside, and to be with you all directly. I do hope you will be able to put us both up, Mama, at such short notice, though Søren can easily take a room locally if there is not a bed for him.

So excited to be coming home, and bringing 'my young man' for you to meet. Do drop a line by return, so we get it before we depart Paris, and say all well.

Your ever so thrilled and deliriously happy daughter,

Marie

P.S. You remember that couple I told you about, the Schillings, who have been looking after me so well since I have been here? They send you both their kindest regards and say to tell you that since they are self-appointed *in loco parentis* here, they have given us their blessing and they wish you to know that Mr K. is one of their oldest friends and you can be very happy to have him for a son-in-law. It's the strangest thing – when I met them first, I had no idea they even knew him, and it turns out they are the best of friends for years!

P.P.S. Yes, Mama, I am being very careful to eat regularly; that is the great thing about Paris: you can buy food so easily, already cooked if you like (and I do like), so you can eat well without having a cooking stove. And these days, since I am going about so much with Søren, we eat out a tremendous amount – he is such a sociable person, loves to entertain and to party. Valdemar will love him too. He will be able to take him around the *Bierhallen* and show him what proper beer is like!

P.P.P.S. (Definitely the last addendum, as I have to catch the post now in a moment.) We are going to Italy on our honeymoon. Just think – a trip to Italy and it's a honeymoon! How can one girl bear so much happiness? I think I shall burst.

And I know I said positively no more addenda, but of course I must add, Happy New Year. The year you will become parents-in-law to the most delightful man on earth!

Chapter 15

Helen had that puffy look about the jaws. Martha recognised it immediately, and her heart sank. Other people's troubles had a knack of turning up on her doorstep. Only days back from Paris, and here came trouble. She was turning into that kind of person. There was one in every family, the one people turned to.

She didn't know why it had to be her. She was not particularly kind – once your heart has been broken, you forget how to be kind – and she most certainly wasn't rich. It was as much as she could do to pay the bills – not on time (that'd be the day), but in rotation, so that none of them was outstanding long enough for the creditors to pursue them. She was capable, though, and she was resourceful – had to be, all those children and Viggo as much a child as the rest of them. That's what it was, she suspected, that was what brought people to her when they were in trouble. Let's ask Martha. Martha will know what to do. Why couldn't they learn to be resourceful for themselves? She hadn't been born resourceful. She'd had to learn. Why couldn't they?

Martha sighed.

She wore mourning gloves, Helen, which Martha thought a little over-dramatic, and that squashed hat that made her look like a flower-seller, and a loose coat. Well, she would.

'And what brings you to Copenhagen, Helen?' Martha asked innocently. She could have said something right off to let Helen know she'd already guessed her banal and dreadful news. It would save Helen having to find the words for it. But why should she? Let her stew for a bit. Interesting to see how she would put it, what euphemism she would choose, what excuses she would offer.

'Oh, I . . . I needed to see . . . '

A child yelled somewhere, and Martha stood up to go to it with an exaggerated sigh.

'I'll be back in a moment,' she said. 'Children,' she added cruelly, 'you know what they're like. There's always something. You never get a moment to yourself.'

'I'm sorry to barge in on you like this,' Helen said as Martha went to the door. 'Only, it's a bit of an emergency.'

She had a letter in her lap. She picked it up now and passed it from hand to hand. The gloves were the fingerless kind. Her fingers were red and puckered, as if she'd been doing laundry.

Martha didn't react. She was weary of emergencies. She just nodded and said again, 'I'll be back.'

Helen was still hunched in the same chair when Martha returned. She looked up at Martha. There were black sacks under her eyes, which were gummy with lack of sleep.

'So, what is this emergency?' Martha asked, sitting opposite her cousin.

Helen put a panicked hand on her stomach and waved the letter she was clutching in her half-lace fist in Martha's direction.

Martha took the letter, noting the Paris postmark.

'Krøyer?' she said, though she'd promised herself she wouldn't prompt Helen, she'd make her spit it out.

Helen nodded. A tear squeezed out of one eye and trickled fatly down her cheek. Martha wondered how you could weep out of only one eye.

She looked at the address. She didn't recognise the name, only the Christensen part.

She opened the letter and read it quickly. She almost laughed. A lot of reassuring nothings. She checked the date. Four months had elapsed since it was written.

'He didn't come?' she asked, looking at Helen over the letter.

'No,' said Helen. Her voice was tiny.

Martha waited.

Helen said nothing.

Martha got impatient. Suddenly she couldn't be bothered making Helen say it.

'How far gone are you?' she asked.

Helen gasped at the directness of the question.

'Six months?'

'More,' Helen whispered.

'Must be small,' said Martha, relentlessly. 'Or are you over-corseted? That's not a good idea; you'll make yourself ill. And it will harm the child. Though perhaps you don't care about that.'

Helen gasped again. 'It's a boy,' she said. 'I feel sure it's a boy, it kicks so hard, I can't sleep at night, he's so athletic!' In spite of everything, there was pride in her voice. She'd never had those conversations expectant mothers have – hopeful, speculative. She'd only had tears and a hard, humiliating exchange with her cousin Christian. He was a pastor. It was his line of work.

'That means nothing,' said Martha. 'Girls kick just as hard. What do you want to do?'

'I . . . I don't know,' said Helen. 'I thought, maybe you . . .'

Martha snorted. She finished Helen's sentence for her, 'You thought I might think of something? Oh, I can think of several things, but none of them seems very attractive. What do you want to do?'

'I want to die,' whispered Helen, and she snivelled.

Martha would not be lured down that road.

'Well, perhaps you will,' she said bitterly, thinking of Henrietta. 'It does happen. But I wouldn't count on it and, besides, it's terribly final, death, Helen. You wouldn't like it, really. Anyway, I would say it is out of your hands.'

Martha had never recovered from Henrietta's death. It was not just being saddled with her sister's baby – she loved Henry, she would never use a word like 'saddled' about him – it was everything: the sadness, the loss, the pointlessness, the unfairness, the fear. And it was the way she was expected to cope. She dated that expectation to Henrietta's death. It had embittered her, and she knew it, but she couldn't really do anything about it, or wouldn't. If she were honest, perhaps she had grown a little fond of her bitterness. It saw her through difficulties, gave her an excuse not to join in other people's follies.

'So, short of dying, what do you want?' she asked Helen now.

'I want him to marry me, of course.'

'Oh, for heaven's sake,' said Martha, picking up the letter. 'Will you have some sense? I suppose he'll send money. That's something.'

'Money? What good is money to me? I'm ruined, Martha.'

'It's much better than no money,' said Martha, practically, 'and you were ruined anyway, Helen, don't be so melodramatic.'

Helen sobbed uncontrollably now, her washerwoman's hands clawing at her face in their ludicrous lacy gloves.

Martha waited for the worst of the sobbing to abate. There was no point in trying to talk over the racket.

'Maybe you could go away. If you had money, you could go away. A lot to be said for that. Anonymity.'

'Where should I go? I only speak Danish.'

'Oh, Helen,' said Martha snappishly, 'stop creating problems. You can learn things. You are not too old to start a new life for yourself. You could be a widow, for example. You have the gloves,' she added spitefully.

'Oh, these . . . ' Helen wiggled her fingers. 'They were all I could find.'

Martha didn't believe it. She was sure they had been worn for pathetic effect.

When Henrietta was a child, she had had a wooden doll, a marionette, in a crinoline. You could turn the doll upside down and her dress turned inside out, right over her head, revealing voluminous bloomers. Henrietta had found this very funny, especially the way the doll's legs ended in a scrawny wooden arse, like two thick pencils side by side inside their glued-on bloomers. She would wiggle the legs to make the wooden buttocks move, and she would fall about laughing at the effect. Martha was mortified. For some reason, the thought of Helen and Krøyer in that studio of his in Skagen always made her think of that pathetic wooden doll with its dress over its head. The image came before her now, and it unsettled her.

'Perhaps he'll come yet,' said Helen. 'It's not too late.'

It was, in fact, too late, but they didn't know that then. The news of Krøyer's hurried marriage in Germany had not yet reached Copenhagen.

'No,' said Martha. 'Don't delude yourself. If he has not come by now, he is not coming. Oh, Helen, how did you let yourself get into this mess?'

Helen said in a flat tone, 'I loved him.'

It had the air of self-defence about it. It sounded as if it had been trotted out before.

Martha wanted to say that love was all very well. She wanted to say that Helen should have thought of the consequences before she did what she did in that studio. She wanted to say, that's what you get, you stupid woman.

What she actually said was, 'The swine.'

Helen nodded.

'Who knows?' Martha asked. A stupid question. Everyone must know. She was like a ship in full sail – a small, ungainly cargo ship.

'No one,' Helen whispered. 'Only you. And Christian, of course.' She indicated the letter.

'Have you been dismissed from your job?' Martha asked.

Helen taught music in a girls' school. It was a live-in position.

'Not yet. I told you, they don't know.'

'Well, then,' said Martha, putting on a cheerful, bustling, let's-make-the-best-of-it-shall-we? voice. (Who was this matron? Where had she come from?) 'Well, then, that's good, very good. You must resign. Better that you leave rather than that you are pushed out. Health problems, you can say.'

'But . . . '

'We'll keep it in the family,' Martha said. 'That's all there is to be done.'

'How?' asked Helen, hope oozing through the carefully neutral word.

'You'll have to come to us, of course,' Martha said.

She'd never even liked this girl. She was bossy, overbearing, and her voice, sharp and irritating. Her waddling gait. She certainly didn't want her in her house. But what else could she say? She could not leave her to be thrown out onto the streets when the school finally decided it had to take action.

'I can't,' Helen wailed. 'Where should I sleep? How should I live?'

Martha ignored the question about where she should sleep. What did she expect, that Martha was going to turn her children out of their beds so Helen could have a room? She could bed down with the girls and be glad of it. She could put the youngest on the pot in the night, stop her eternal bed-wetting. She should be grateful not to be thrown back on her parents, who were sure to make her life a misery, if they had not already disowned her. Martha couldn't be bothered to ask.

'You can help out with the children,' she said firmly. 'You're a teacher after all. You can pay your way in lessons.'

Helen put her hand to her mouth. A governess in her own cousin's home. Teaching times tables and history to the little Johansens. Well, it might be worse, and it was only until . . . afterwards, and then, then she would see. Anything might happen. Krøyer might even come, he'd have to turn up at some point. He might fall in love with the child; that could happen; he'd want to own it; they could still be married, even after the birth. And once it was done, well, people forget. Within a year or two, they would just be another married couple with a child. Maybe they could have another. After all, it was not hopeless.

'And you can help about the nursery,' Martha was saying. 'God knows, I could do with a hand.'

Worse than a governess. A children's nurse. A semi-servant. Wiping noses and bottoms, helping out on bath night.

But Helen nodded.

'What about Viggo?' she asked.

'Leave Viggo to me,' said Martha heavily.

'Thank you, Martha. I can . . . I can never thank you enough.'

'Nonsense,' said Martha, coolly. 'Go and fetch your things, hand in your resignation, and I'll see if I can find a quilt for your bed. You'd better come immediately. I'd say they are close to asking you to leave the school, so you should get out while you can do it with dignity. Afterwards, you can look for another position, pay your way. Supper's at seven. If you could manage to stop by the green-grocer's, I need some cabbage.'

'Cabbage?' Helen stared. It was starting already, this earning of her keep.

'Onions, too,' said Martha,

'Very well,' Helen said. 'Cabbage and onions. Right.'

'Leeks, if they have them,' added Martha.

'Leeks,' said Helen quietly. She got the idea.

'Oh, and beer. Viggo likes a bottle of beer with his supper. Could you manage that? Can you carry it all? Mr Bang, two doors down, he sells beer. Have you change?'

'That's all right,' Helen said. 'Just the one bottle?'

'Unless you want one yourself.'

'No,' said Helen. 'No.'

Chapter 16

R*ome, 23 July*

My dearest Anna,

Well, as predicted, the wedding went off splendidly. There is no point whatsoever in describing it, because all weddings are much the same, aren't they? But it was very sweet, and Søren made such a wonderful impression on my family. I *knew* they would take him to their hearts, but still, it is a relief to know that I was right about that. We stayed on for just a few days, and then we left on our honeymoon! Oh, Anna, I do love to say that. 'We are on our honeymoon,' I tell everyone who cares to listen, though I am perfectly sure it is quite clear. You can tell it from the spring in my step and the way I just *glow* all the time.

We arrived in Rome at last on Sunday. It was such a journey! Søren, I have discovered, does not like trains. He sits scowling for hours, huddled against the dusty upholstery, and he refuses even to look out of the window. He complains that the coffee tastes like mud and the tea tastes like boiled weeds – and I have to say he is absolutely spot on in both cases, but I don't mind; I was just so thrilled to be travelling through all that wonderful landscape. The first part was spectacular, from Munich to Bozen – Bolzano, the Italians call it – and then to hear Italian being spoken! It is so delightful; I much prefer it to French. These water vendors, they look for all the world like Germans, with their alpine hats and leather knickerbockers, but they're Italians all right; they are striding up and down the platform shouting something that it took me some time to decipher. It sounded like *ehhquehhmorali*. I finally deciphered it as *aqua minerale*! They sold it in seltzer jars, and you lean out of the train window to buy it from their carts. Søren complained that it was overpriced, which of course it was, but at least it didn't taste of elements of the landscape, I pointed out to him, which he had the good grace to smile about.

Our hotel is in a little alleyway, which is a good thing, because it's shady. As soon as you go out into the squares, you are walloped by the heat of the summer sun. I am glad I have my trusty green silk parasol that Mama gave me. Do you remember, I had it in Paris, and Mr Schilling made such fun of me for using it as an umbrella? It's surprising how well it survived, I have to say, because you really are not supposed to let silk get wet. You can't beat quality, Mama says. In any case, it creates the loveliest soft green shade, though of course it is still terribly hot, parasol or no parasol. I am so glad of all the muslin frocks Mama made me bring. She said muslin was much the coolest thing and it is true, apart from linen, but you can't travel with linen.

We haven't run across any Danes so far. No Scandinavians of any kind, but my dear Anna, there are more English in Rome than you would need to meet in a lifetime, all hurrying about with wicker baskets and enormous tartan rugs. What could they want with rugs in weather like this?

'For sitting on,' Søren maintained. 'They like sitting on the ground, the English, like children. Never did understand what they have against tables and chairs.'

That couldn't be true, I thought, a whole nation couldn't have a preference for sitting on blankets. But do you know, he was quite right! I noticed it myself, once he pointed it out.

'Coo-eee! Charlotte!' they call to each other. They're all called that, or Bella or Edna or Hester.

I couldn't believe people would picnic, actually picnic, on the stones of the Forum Romanum. No sense of the sacred, the

English. Mind you, I have to admit I was a little disappointed in the Forum myself. I had been so looking forward to it. There were these wonderful engravings of ancient Rome in a book of Papa's at home; I used to pore over it on endless wet childhood afternoons, but it didn't look a bit like the pictures in the book. 'It's just a heap of old stones, dear,' I heard an English matron muttering to her friend. 'Very *hot* stones, Mabel,' her friend replied with a sniff. I thought I should die of the longing to laugh! As if 'hot' was a *moral* quality.

The place was crawling with artists, as you'd expect, students mainly, all drawing away feverishly, but Søren and I didn't find it interesting as a subject, so we didn't set our easels up. We'd rather paint the peeling yellow facades of modern Rome, with their dark green shutters.

Of course, it was terribly interesting to see the Forum, terribly interesting. My guidebook really wasn't of much help, though, I have to say. I'm dashed if I could distinguish an ancient *via* from a rutted track or tell one temple from another.

'I see where they got the idea for the Arc de Triomphe, though,' I said to Søren, pointing to one reasonably intact arch – one that did not look like part of the entrance to a temple. I must say, I felt terribly well travelled as I said that. 'It's just like that one over there, isn't it?'

He didn't really seem to know much more about it than I did. Dear me, I hope I am not being disloyal. I should hate that. To turn into one of those *managing* wives we see at breakfast in the *pensione* (that's what they call a small hotel here), telling their husbands not to wear that collar again, dear – *frayed*, they whisper, as if it was something shameful that clothing wore out – or demanding money with menaces, as Søren calls it, listing all the things they have to buy in their high, excited voices, as if all the guests wish to know about their headache powders or their eau de cologne requirements or a dressmaker who simply has to be paid, my dear, or she will never run up another thing.

We really are having the most wonderful time, Anna, and I'm so happy. It is amazing, really, how many things we agree upon, Søren and I, and in the end, that's what counts in a marriage, isn't it? Sharing the same tastes and opinions, so that talking to your spouse is like talking to a more interesting version of yourself.

We both loved the Sistine chapel. We came out clutching each other with delight, our heads swimming with colour. 'So blue,' Søren kept saying, though of course there are thousands of colours, thousands, but Søren relates especially to blue. We've been back twice already, in spite of the suffocating heat, just to drink in all that heady colour.

St Peter's itself, I have to say, we did not like so very much. Just too vast, Anna, and so empty, and with that vast, empty square in front of it. I asked Søren if he thought it was our Protestant souls, making us baulk at all this Catholic conceit. But Søren claims he hasn't got a Protestant soul. I thought he was being a bit literal. It's a question of upbringing, isn't it, not of religion per se, so I said so. Well, would you credit it, we nearly came to blows about it! I was just arguing for the sake of it; I found it interesting. In my family, everyone argues all the time; it's a way of making conversation. But he suddenly announced that we must not argue. 'I never quarrel,' he said. 'I don't allow it.' I thought that was absurd. In fact, you might say it's just a way of winning all the arguments – refusing to let the other person express their opinion. He really got awfully rattled when I pointed this out. 'Marie, I said, no quarrelling. And I mean, no quarrelling.'

That put me in my place! I have to say, I was a little sore about it. It's not terribly fair, is it? But he's right, I suppose. There is no point in spending one's energies on arguments when there are so many much more pleasant kinds of conversation one could be having. So, I did the wifely thing. (You see, Anna, I am learning fast!) I changed the subject, and pointed out that the waiter looked exactly like a hedgehog. And so he did! A short, round, dapper man in a morning coat, and slightly hunched, and his hair – black shot through with grey – was brushed back off his face, like a headful of quills.

Søren ordered me a thing called ravioli. I don't like the spaghetti, I have to say, all slimy. I cannot eat slimy things. Søren says that is absurd, that sauces have to be *damp* – as he calls it. It's in their nature to be so, he says. The ravioli is not so bad; it's made with the same flour paste as spaghetti, but it's in squares, and they're stuffed with spinach, which I like, and the trick is to smother it with this very dry grated cheese that they have. I was just sprinkling some on my lunch when Søren said it was like sawdust on a butcher's floor, soaking up the blood. I nearly got sick! But I suppose I shall get used to the food.

I hear Søren's step on the stair, so must finish up now. It's almost time to go for our *aperitivo* and watch the Romans taking their evening walk. It's so entertaining. So I'll stop here and hope to hear from you shortly.

Much love, also to Michael. And a kiss to Helga. I am dying to meet her when we finally come home.

Your loving friend
Marie Krøyer

Copenhagen, 25 July

Dear Anna,

Well, Helen's child was a boy. I delivered him myself. (I shall qualify as a midwife if I do much more of this.) He did not live long. Viggo says he was premature, but I think there was more to it. He was the most peculiar little monkey you ever saw, one eye bulging open, the other gummed shut, haggard as a gargoyle. I made Viggo wrap it up in newspaper and get rid of it. Helen never asked what we did with it. Sometimes I wonder if she thinks we did away with it, but then again, I wonder if she didn't, accidentally, like, roll over on him in the night. He was dead by morning in any case. I fished him out of the sheets before she woke up. I couldn't help feeling sad – you don't want to see any young thing die – but I have to say it's for the best. At least she is not encumbered. If we can get her away quietly, she may live it down yet, and be grateful to us in the future. She is not very grateful at present, but I try to make allowances.

I do think there may have been a question of *disease*. You know what S. was like. V. says this is a disgraceful idea, but Anna, if you had seen it, it scarcely looked human. And look at the father. Curvature of the spine. V. says that is from bending over easels, but I think it can be a symptom. I knew a nurse once who told me all about it, horrible things.

To think of them, Søren and Madame Marie, gadding about all over Italy, painting and sunning themselves and God knows what all, with not a thought in the world for Helen or her child. Damn Søren to hell for a filthy scoundrel. God knows how many bastards he has spawned over Europe that we've never even heard of.

Never sent another øre either, as far as I know, after that first letter. Blotted it out completely, as if it had never happened, very convenient.

I would like, Anna, to tie Søren Krøyer and Holger Drachmann together and drop the pair of them over the harbour wall in Copenhagen, see if they could find the little mermaid; that'd keep them busy for a while, a woman with a fishtail. To *think* that I have sat at that man's table, drunk his champagne, appeared, damn it all, in his *paintings*.

And she is as bad. How her parents can have swanned off to Germany and left her to her own devices in Copenhagen I will never understand – it's not Christian – and then not to raise any objections when she wanted to go flaunting herself unchaperoned in *Paris*, of all places. Asking for trouble. Nothing but the purest of luck that she ran across Søren, which solved her problems very nicely for her, I have to say.

In any case, we are getting together a collection for Helen. Viggo has some connection in New England, thinks he can get her a position out there, if we can raise her passage. Between us all, I am sure we can manage it.

Your loving cousin,
Martha

Skagen, 4 August

Dear Marie,

No time for a long letter today, my dear, so this is just a very quick note in response to yours. Very glad to hear all your news, and glad you are enjoying Italy. We are all well and Skagen is sparkling in the sunshine.

Would you pass a message to Søren, my dear. I am sure he will like to know. Michael would have written himself, but he is from home, hence this rather roundabout way of letting S. know. It is sad news, about a family he knows well in Copenhagen. Hirsch is the name; he's a collector and immensely rich. He has several of Søren's paintings. It's not him; it's their boy, Rex. He died the other day. He was known to be a consumptive, but . . . well, there is *talk*. The poor boy had gone into quite a decline about some fly-by-night girlfriend. He may have been . . . of unsound mind, I think is the phrase they use. In any case, there you are. No point in speculating. One way or another the poor lad is gone from them, and they are grief-stricken. Michael and Viggo are already on their way to Copenhagen to the funeral, hence this note from me. They thought Søren would wish to be represented by his friends.

Life is so sad, Marie, it makes me glad to hear of your happiness.

I will write again soon, if I get a chance.

Your loving Anna

Rome, 20 August

Dear Anna,

I nearly died when I got your letter. I know the family. Oda is a friend of mine since childhood. And I knew the boy who died. We were quite close at one time. I am distraught. I long to discuss it all with you, but cannot do so by letter. Søren is very upset too, of course, and he is writing to the parents.

We are on our way to Naples. Søren wants to see the bay.

In haste, Marie

Copenhagen, 21 August

Dear Anna,

Just a few lines to say that Helen has left. Viggo says to thank Michael for his help on that score. We'll let you know when we hear from her that she has landed in Boston and is set up in her new position.

Have you heard the latest about the Hirsch boy? By his own hand, as you know, over 'some girl'. But it is not 'some girl' – I have it on the best authority – the girl in question was none other than our friend, Marie Triepke. I *told* you she was up to no good. In any case, the family soon put a stop to her gallop. Insisted on annulling the engagement, quite right too. They paid her off, apparently – and that's how she could afford to go to Paris, and as soon as she landed there, as we know, she set her cap at Søren. Horrid little gold-digger. I always said she was too sweet to be wholesome, and now you see. If she hadn't appeared when she did, we might have prevailed upon Søren to do the right thing by Helen.

I am glad they are out of sight and out of mind for the moment. I could not be responsible for my actions if they were anywhere near me.

Martha

Skagen, Wednesday

Dear Martha,

That is sad news; it made me quite downcast, and I do not like to think you think it was 'all for the best'. I am sure there is no question of what you suggest. The child was premature, that would explain it, not fully developed. Even if you think such things, dear, you ought not to write them down.

God bless you for the help you have given the poor woman, and I am glad she is to leave Europe altogether. Much the best arrangement for her, though I am sure she will be lonely.

I hope you will be able to come to Skagen now that it is all over, even if only for a few short weeks. Let me know if I should air the cottage and light a fire.

Affectionately,

Anna

Capri, 22 September

Dearest Anna,

You will think we have been swallowed up by an earthquake or a volcano or some such Italian disaster, it is so long since you have heard from me, and in truth we have had something of a (fortunately more minor) Italian disaster. We were in Naples in August, and I fell most horribly ill.

The Bay of Naples is very beautiful, but I cannot recommend the city, as it is a filthy place, and full of typhoid fever, which is what I succumbed to. I was in bed for weeks, rolling about in greying sheets, with the most appalling fevers, couldn't eat, couldn't sleep and yet was permanently in a kind of twilight dream world. Søren quite expected every moment that I was going to die. And I *wanted* to die, Anna, I really did not have the slightest desire to go on living. Apparently it is the water that is contaminated, though some people say it is a sort of miasma from the swamps. I don't know, but whatever it is, it's a dreadful illness.

You will, I hope, be glad to hear that I have regained the will to live (!), and I am much better, but to tell you the truth, I am still not quite recovered. It can take months, the doctors say, even years, and the way I am feeling, I can hardly even imagine being fully well again. Ordinary good health seems to me some exotic and unattainable condition that I have hardly the energy even to aspire to. I can barely pick up a paintbrush, Anna, much less paint.

When I was well enough, we removed here to Capri. The doctor recommended it. He is a Swede, a delightful man, and we were so lucky – not only did he recommend Capri as a place to recuperate, away from the foetid airs of Naples, but he actually gave us the key to his own villa at Anacapri, and it is from there that I write.

I would not go so far as to say it was worth being ill to have found such a wonderful spot to recover in, but very nearly! We live like lizards, basking all day in the sun. We eat olives and goat's cheese and bread – all food I can manage – and the local wine suits us very well; they say it is safer to drink the wine than the water! We get up with the sun, which suits me, because I do not sleep all night and lie awake sometimes for hours, and then, when the heat gets unbearable in the afternoons we sleep behind slatted shutters. And the evenings – pure gold! We bathe our feet and ankles in the sea – it is amethyst, turquoise – and then we eat something light and sleep again till sunrise. You just can't imagine it. It is so completely different from anything Danish!

We shall stay on here through the winter, I think, and then come home in the spring or early summer. Italy has been wonderful, but I can hardly wait to get home.

Your loving friend,
Marie

Wednesday

Dear Emmy,

The children all have the scarlet fever and we are quarantined. Do not dream of coming near us. I will let you know when we emerge and it is safe for you to visit. I was so glad to see the back of Helen, but now I am sorry she is not here. I could do with another pair of hands at the moment, even if they had to be Helen's.

I've had to let the maid go. Can't pay her as well as the doctor.

Speaking of whom, he is due at any moment, I will ask him to post this. Hoping all well with you and your brood. Battening down the hatches now and won't appear again till we've weathered it, could be weeks, maybe months. Think of me!

Martha

I have no time to write to Anna before the doctor arrives. Will you send her a note on my behalf? Thank you.

M

The children went down like ninepins, following one another onto the ottoman at the foot of their parents' bed, where sick children were put to be tended to in the night. In all that time, Martha never left the apartment. Viggo brought food and medicines in and took the waste out. He lit the stoves and did the accounts. Martha managed the laundry herself while the sickest child was sleeping, stamping on the clothes in the bathtub till the skin between her toes started to peel. Then she slept, in the soapy, steamy atmosphere of washing hanging to dry on a clothes-horse in the kitchen and on the backs of chairs placed around the living-room stove. She did most of her sleeping in daylight hours, when the sick children slept and she could snatch time, because the fever always seemed to be worst in the small hours and she spent her nights sponging down small bodies, forcing medicine into children, begging them to drink just a little of this delicious cooled fennel tea with honey in it, to keep their strength up.

When Viggo went out for food he wore a mask soaked in carbolic and made signs to the woman in the shop two doors down. He placed a list on the counter, which she did not pick up, just read from a distance, and she packed everything quickly into a crate for him to take away. He put the money on the counter, beside the list. He never knew what she did with it. Did she wash it? Or fumigate it? Some days later, when he was preparing to go again for food, he found a crate with similar supplies already packed in the hallway, with a crudely written label addressed to themselves. Evidently, the shopkeeper preferred to wait for his money than to have contamination stalking his premises. Sensible man.

One by one, the little ones recovered. Martha was weary. Viggo was like a bear. But they had survived. It was as if they'd been away for a long time, on some sort of vile retreat for penitents. When the quarantine was lifted, it felt like emerging from hibernation. Martha opened the shutters to let the air and sunshine in, and caught sight of herself for the first time in months in a mirror. She had aged three years, she thought, in as many months. She desperately needed fresh air and exercise. She would wash and dress the children and go and see Emmy.

Emmy was expecting again; she must be close to her time. Other people were shocked at Emmy and Martha, that they had so many children, but what could you do? Their husbands brought home a variety of devices and washes that were supposed to prevent conception, each one more depressing than the one before, and none of them effective. And so the babies kept coming, and what could their mothers do only love them?

When Martha got to Emmy's, she found much the same conditions as she had recently left at home. They'd had the fever also, and had been quarantined. The children had all recovered by now, except Anders, Emily's six-year-old, and the bonniest child. He was still very ill. The baby was due any day, and Emmy was exhausted from broken nights and the weight of the pregnancy. Martha put her to bed immediately and whooshed the other children into the living room. They'd grown used to living almost permanently in their parents' bedroom over the weeks since they'd been ill, and they didn't want to leave.

'Out!' said Martha sharply. She'd had enough of squalling children. Her tolerance was at an end.

The children trooped out, shocked at Martha's tone. Martha closed the shutters so Emmy could sleep and then she sat on the sofa with Anders, and held him for three long hours, while Emmy slept for the first time in days.

The child was burning in her arms. He was delirious with fever, and at times yelled in terror. Martha covered his mouth when he cried out, to give Emmy peace, and rocked him back into a semi-coma. When at last he settled, she fetched lukewarm water, to bathe him. His golden curls were dank and spiked with sweat. She laid cool flannels to his skin while he slept uneasily, flinching from the damp cloths. She dabbed away the sweat that trickled over his little freckled nose and kissed his clammy forehead.

When Emmy woke, Martha went to make broth in the kitchen. Drachmann was nowhere to be seen. Out somewhere, breaking quarantine. The kitchen was cold and filthy. She wished she could send the children out to play. Instead, she told them to draw. Solemnly, they took out paper and pencils and drew.

There was nothing to make broth from in the kitchen. She boiled some water to scrub away the worst of the scum of three months' worth of Holger being in charge. Then she boiled some fresh water to make tea, which she brought to Emmy in the bedroom. Anders was awake and crying. Martha gave him some tea, but he spat it out. Emmy looked terrible.

'Has the doctor been?' Martha asked.

Emmy nodded. 'Yesterday. He looks in every other day. He wanted to put them in isolation, but I said it would kill me; I begged him to let me keep them with me. They're all better anyway, except poor Anders. He has to be better before the new one comes, or it'll catch it too, and probably die on me. I don't know how I should bear that, Martha.'

Martha came every day after that. Drachmann was never there. She brought two small chickens, plucked and prepared, and boiled them up in the kitchen. She served the children the meat with potatoes and barley, and she gave them apples afterwards. They hadn't had a proper meal in days, just bread and cheese and pickles that their father brought home in the mornings. The broth she took in to Emmy and Anders. Anders was worse – his heart was racing – but Emmy took the broth.

On the fourth day, Anders died. Mercifully, the other children were so exhausted from broken sleep and poor food and lack of fresh air that they just sat listlessly wherever Martha told them to; they never opened the door to the bedroom, where Emmy sat kneading Anders' white knuckles with the pad of her thumb, unable to weep. Martha knelt on the floor behind her and brushed her hair. It was the only thing she could think of to do for her.

After a while, Martha went to make bread and milk for the others and keep them distracted for a little longer. She asked Emmy if they might come in, but Emmy didn't answer. She hadn't said a word for hours. She still held Anders's hand in hers and stroked it from time to time.

Martha said, 'Emmy, I have to tell them.'

Emmy took no notice.

Martha came out of the bedroom and told the children that their brother had gone to heaven, but that they must not mind too much, because he was going to send them another little brother or sister very soon.

'I don't want another little brother,' said Axel, matter-of-factly. 'It's my train set. Anders is always losing the coal pieces out of the stoker's wagon.'

'Hush, Axel,' said Martha. 'Don't speak like that of your brother. You will miss him.'

'I won't!' said Axel defiantly, and then he started to cry. 'How come he gets to go to heaven!' he sobbed. 'I never get to go anywhere nice.'

Martha took out her handkerchief and wiped Axel's face with it. 'You'll go there one day,' she promised him.

Still Axel sobbed.

'There'll be better train sets there,' Martha said, 'one for everyone, no sharing.'

Martha waited until Holger came home. He was mildly drunk. She went out onto the landing when she heard his footsteps, so the children wouldn't have to see their father's reaction to the news that his child had died while he was out carousing.

He fell to his knees on the landing and sobbed.

Martha told him to pull himself together for Emmy's sake. 'Wash your mouth out before you go to her,' she said. 'You stink of wine.'

Then she went home.

She cried all night into Viggo's chest. She kept seeing Emmy's vacant face, her thin fingers working over Anders's dead hand.

When Holger went in to Emmy, she had laid Anders in the bed beside her, and would not let Holger near her. Two nights she slept with her dead child cold in her arms; two nights Holger slept in the outer room, wrapped in his cloak.

On the third day, she let him take the child and have him measured for his coffin. When he was laid in it, in his Sunday sailor suit, she filled his arms with lilies and would not let them put the lid on till Martha came and talked her into it.

Drachmann had been with a girl when Anders died. There were always girls. Martha never understood how Emmy put up with it. Emmy said it was his nature, he couldn't help himself. Martha said that was nonsense. He always came home, though, Emmy said, as if that were some sort of victory.

He stayed home all week until Anders was buried and quarantine was officially lifted. He wept over the coffin, which was more than Emmy could do. He locked himself in his study and wrote poems about the angel of death. He read Goethe. He came late to meals. He burst into tears every time he looked at the other children. They took to hiding behind the furniture so he wouldn't see them.

Emmy was almost glad when he started to go out again in the evenings. She would take the children in turn on her knee, even the older ones, when their father left, and promise them that they were not going to die. She would dream with them about the new baby they were going to have soon. She drew pictures for them of Anders with wings, and of the new baby in its cradle; the new baby playing with the wooden bricks that Lili had decided she was too old for now; the new baby listening to a story, with its thumb in its mouth. The children watched, wide-eyed. They didn't ask any questions. It was as if they were afraid of the answers.

Drachmann was out again when the baby came. Emmy had to send the eldest, Gerda – Polly's child – who was only ten, to call Martha. Martha sent Viggo for the midwife and hurried over to Emmy's herself.

'Did you bring a chicken?' asked Axel, when Martha appeared.

'Go and play,' Martha said. 'You take them to the park, Gerda. Be back by six. I'll have something for you to eat. I'm sorry, no chicken today, Axel. You'll have to settle for bread and milk, but I've brought something special – toffee squares for afterwards.'

The midwife had been and gone by the time the children got back from the park. The baby had slipped out ten minutes before she had arrived, into Martha's hands.

'Look, Emmy, isn't he lovely?' Martha kept saying. 'Oh, Emmy, he has a look of Anders. Look at him, please look.'

The children stood behind each other at the bedroom door and peered in. Martha came out and fed them, and then they sat in the living-room and waited. Nothing happened for the longest time. In the end, Gerda knocked on the bedroom door.

'Did the baby die?' Gerda whispered when Martha opened the door.

'No,' said Martha. 'He's fine.'

'Did Mama die?'

'No. She's asleep.'

'Why can't we come in?'

Martha hesitated.

'I told you, your mother's asleep. I tell you what, though, I'll bring the baby out to you in a moment.'

She brought the baby to the other children, and she unwrapped him so they could see. They all crowded round and she opened up his little fist to show them the baby's handprint: the perfect pink palm with its strong little lifeline cutting across it, how his fingers were divided into three by the inner folds of the knuckles.

'Did Anders send him?' the little ones wanted to know.

'Yes,' said Martha. 'He asked God to send him, so you wouldn't be one short.'

'He's smaller than Anders,' Lili said. She laid her own pudgy palm next to the baby's, amazed at how huge even she was by comparison.

'He'll grow,' Martha assured her.

All night, Martha walked the floor of the Drachmanns' apartment with the baby on her shoulder. Emmy wouldn't look at him. She couldn't, she said. She said she wanted to die. She said she'd kill the baby as soon as look at him. It frightened Martha, who had never seen Emmy like this before.

Emmy said it wasn't fair that the baby was alive and Anders was dead. Martha tried to reason with her. She told her that the baby needed her, that Anders was beyond her care now, but this child needed mothering. Emmy turned her face to the wall.

'Where were you?' Martha asked Drachmann when he turned in, drunk with something more than drink. It was five o'clock in the morning. Martha had been waiting, with the newborn in her arms. The other children were asleep.

'With Rita,' he said, as if Rita were his younger sister or his aged aunt.

'Who's that? Your chorus girl?'

Drachmann winced. 'She's not a chorus girl. She's a musician.'

'Maybe you would ask Rita to come and mind your children,

since she is so fond of you,' said Martha. 'Or does she know of their existence?'

'She knows.' His voice was low.

'Yes, I expect you have put them in a poem and showed it to her. Nymphs, no doubt, sprites, who can live on air and water and don't need any looking after.'

'Stop, Martha,' said Drachmann. 'Why are you tormenting me like this?'

'Me, tormenting you! That's rich, Holger. That's very rich. I delivered your son this afternoon – yesterday afternoon, it is by now. Look at him, here he is. Is that a form of torment to you? Delivering your child? Well, I'm sorry if that is the case. Go to Emmy and see if you can lift her out of the dark hole she has sunk into, will you, please? God knows, it is you who have pushed her into it. Maybe she cares enough about you to rise up out of it for your sake, though I don't see why she should. I wouldn't. It's a boy, did I say? And if Emmy does not come round, Holger, he will starve to death.'

Holger wept. Martha ignored his tears and thrust the child into his arms.

'I have to go home now. I have children of my own to see to, and I need some sleep. Good morning.'

Martha returned before noon. Holger was pacing the room with the child. Emmy still would not look at the baby.

'Emmy, dearest,' said Martha. 'I will make a bargain with you. Will you listen?'

Emmy turned her back.

'Emmy, I will take him, I will look after him until you are ready, but I can't feed him. It is months since Anke was weaned. You will have to feed him yourself. I will bring him to you for feeding, and, in between, you can rest and recover. I will do everything else. Can you do that, Emmy? You don't have to look at him, and I will stay with you while you do it. Emmy? Please. Do it for me, if you can't bring yourself to do it for him.'

For months, Martha reared Emmy's child. She took him four times a day to his mother for feeding, and when he cried in the night, she fed him sugar water. As he got older, she gave him cow's milk. In this way, they staggered to four months, and then they weaned him on stewed rice and mashed fruit. Emmy always said he was half Martha's.

Martha was so exhausted by this time that she could hardly function, but Emmy had recovered. She got out of bed in the mornings without needing to be cajoled, and she had started to look after her children again. But the hole that Anders's death had torn in her life was raw and bleeding and poor little Paul could never mend it, however darling a child he might be.

Chapter 18

'M*ilan, 21 May*

Dear Anna,

We are on our way at last, as you can see from the postmark! We hope to be in Copenhagen within the week, and thus to escape the heat of the summer here. It depends on the journey and the train connections et cetera, and especially on my health, for I cannot travel for more than a few hours a day; I feel quite weary and fancy I am going to expire for lack of air.

I am so looking forward to being at home. Søren wants me to meet the mothers! I am sure you know, Anna, about his two mothers: his actual mother, who by all accounts is mad as a hatter, and his aunt, who brought him up and is in every way except the most fundamental, his 'real' mother. He says she's dafter than the officially mad one – but I am sure he is just pulling my leg about that; he is making fun of the situation because it is so very peculiar. And then next summer we plan to spend in Skagen. Do you remember, Anna, how we used to fantasise, in Paris, about my coming to Skagen, and how you used to tell me about the fun you all had there? Neither of us dreamed at the time, did we, that I would be coming to Skagen as Mrs Krøyer?

Your very excited friend,
Marie

Chapter 19

It was a perfectly ordinary house on a perfectly ordinary street, Marie was glad to see. It was not that she had been expecting anything dramatic; it was more that she hadn't known what to expect at all, and it was reassuring to see that it was all very ordinary.

Søren's mother's apartment was on the second floor. She greeted them civilly, offered them tea.

'I'll make it,' said Søren.

'Chamomile for me, dear,' she said, sitting opposite Marie. 'Since I am wearing my yellow gown today. I like things to match,' she said to Marie conspiratorially.

'Yes,' said Marie. 'I see.'

'Now, where were we?' asked Søren's mother.

'Nowhere in particular,' said Marie. 'We have just arrived, and Søren is making tea.'

'They call it The Dolls' House,' Søren's mother said in a whisper, leaning towards Marie. Marie was prepared. Søren had warned her that she would want to talk about this.

'Yes,' said Marie, 'so I believe.' She caught Søren's eye as he came in with the tea.

'The lawns are neatly trimmed,' said Søren's mother, in a high voice, as if she were reading from a script, or as if she had entered a trance, like a medium. 'And the trees know how to behave themselves, because if they don't they'll get the chop, and it has those flat white walls, and the windows, the windows, millions of them there seem to be, the windows glitter and glitter. They watch you, those glittering windows, as you come up that long, long driveway, your skirts muddying as you go. You can't help it, it's not your fault, the mud, but they twitter and they grumble all the same when they see that your hemline is spattered and your boots are clogged with it and they blame you, though they don't say so outright. You get muddy walking out of the real world and into Toyland. That's just the way it is.

'We look like people. We have the right number of arms and legs (most of us) and real hair that hurts if you pull it, but we're toys, dolls. We walk about jerkily from time to time, at the permitted hours, and our glazed eyes open and shut and we say only the things we've been programmed to say, *Yes Herr Doctor, Thank you Herr Director, I love you*, that sort of thing.

'They take away the muddy dresses. I don't know if it's because they're muddy or if it's because they're ours. I suspect the latter. But it doesn't matter. We don't mind. Our dresses are stiff and uncomfortable anyway; it's quite a relief to be rid of them. They give us white gowns to wear, like angels, and they make us wear our hair down, too. Something to do with hairpins, the evils thereof. So we are just like angels, you see, with our hair flowing down our backs and our loose white gowns. Angel dolls. We don't have to wear corsets either; we just flop around inside our white gowns; it's like being permanently prepared for a bath, only the bath never comes.

'I tell a lie. Of course they do allow us to bathe. Did you really think they would be so cruel as not to give us baths? No, no, not at all, that is quite the wrong impression. I can't think why I would have wanted to give that impression. Forgive me. Yes, yes, we are allowed to bathe. We have a bath once a week, and they change the water after every third person, so really it's quite hygienic. Of course it is better, undoubtedly it is better to be first, especially if one of the others has, you know, her time, and it does get a trifle cool and slithery by the third person's turn. But then the good thing is that if you are third this week, it will be your turn to be first next week. There always is a good thing, I find. It's just that here in The Doll's House it's sometimes a little harder to find the good things, but then that's a challenge for us, and that's a good thing too, being challenged. It makes you a stronger and a better person and God will love you all the more. He loves us all. I do understand that principle. I know we are all His children and that He loves us all, but He loves the good ones better. He must. Otherwise there would be no point in being good, would there?'

Here she paused and clawed Marie's knee interrogatively. Marie gave a tentative smile to show she was not afraid. She looked at Søren, who was tilting back in his chair, like a schoolboy.

The old lady had lost interest in having her question answered, and was off again.

'We wash our hair also,' the old lady said. 'Not in the bath. That wouldn't do. Matron disapproves of hairs in the bath. They bring us basins to wash our hair, once a month we do that, as more often is too much trouble, and they are right you know, drying one's hair is so troublesome, I do find that. They get the fires going on hair day and it's really quite warm all over, and the smell of clean hair drying, it's delightful. They brush it for us, too, and that is most pleasant. We are not allowed brushes ourselves, of course, so they have to do the brushing. It is quite the nicest day in the month, when they dry the hair and do the brushing. Mine is an unusual colour, would you not agree?' She wound a strand of yellow grey hair about her fingers, and watched delightedly as the light fell through it.

'It's not that common, flat, flaxen blonde, is it? It is more a cop-pery blond, almost pink in a certain light, and everyone remarks on it, how beautiful it is, and I must say, I know it is vain of me and I shouldn't have this reaction, but I must say it is most gratifying to hear the things they say about it, how rich it is, how it glows when it is washed as if with some sort of inner fire. I've got plenty of inner fire, but it's not in my hair.

'I mustn't be crude, however, because it upsets the other girls, who apparently are innocent. So they tell me, and I wouldn't want to upset them, so I keep my mouth shut most of the time. When I think of it, anyway.

'The food is good. Well, not good exactly, but then we mustn't have knives or forks, and they do pretty well given that constraint. So it's mainly puddings, rice pudding, mashed potato, hashed beef or mutton stewed to a sort of a thick saucy consistency, which is quite tasty with the mashed potato, sago pudding, macaroni – that's Italian, though you'd never guess it; it doesn't remind me of Italy at all, not the least hint of the Mediterranean about it. They worry about our intake of green stuffs. Honestly, it would make you laugh the way they worry about that. Anyone would think we were butterflies, I often think, you know, cabbage whites, flitting about in our loose white gowns, needing to ingest lots of green stuff. They ladle it out, the green. They tell us it's spinach, but I don't believe them; I think it's a special sort of moss they grow just to make sure we get the right amount of chlorophyll into our bloodstreams.

'You didn't think I knew about chlorophyll, did you? Oh, you don't know much about me, then, no you don't. We have a scientist in the family, you know. Not a blood relation, you understand, just a brother by marriage, but still, you get to learn things from family members whether or not you are actually related to them by blood. I think people set too much store by blood, myself. There is no necessity at all to be physically related to a person in order to talk to them over the breakfast table. There has to be some connection, I understand that. One doesn't meet just anybody at the breakfast table. Oh no, don't misunderstand me. I do not mean to imply that one might meet the postman, for example, at breakfast, or even the clergyman. The circle of people one is likely to breakfast with is quite narrow, when you come to think about it, and by and large it does consist mainly of persons related to one.

'Where was I? I have no idea, do excuse me, no idea at all how I came to be talking about breakfast. Dear me. Yes, the breakfasts here, well, to be honest they are a little disappointing. Porridge, they call it, but it's much thinner than the porridge we have at home and there's never any honey with it, not even on Sundays. To be fair, there is syrup on occasion. Not golden syrup – the black stuff, treacle. It does make a nice change. Of course there are all the days in between, when there is no treacle, and those breakfasts are, to be frank, a little daunting, a little dull, but then you see there wouldn't be the same pleasure in the treacle days if we had treacle every day, now would there? So you see, there is some sense in only having the treacle from time to time.

'I said that to the Herr Director only the other day and, do you know, he quite agreed with me. He is such an agreeable man, you know. That is to say, we agree on almost everything, he and I. I find in the long run that is quite the best policy. Life is so much more pleasant when the Herr Director is being agreeable, and, as he puts it himself, "If you are agreeable, Cecily, then I am agreeable and we are agreeable and no one gets hurt."

'He's not quite right about no one getting hurt. I do find it hurts, from time to time. At the beginning it hurt horribly, but then one gets used to it, I suppose one loosens up or something, but even lately I find that it can be painful, especially if he is in a hurry, as he often is, since he can't be away from his other duties for too long.

'And then there was the other painful experience. However, I have resolved not to dwell on it, because if I do I only get upset and the Herr Director has advised me that I should not upset myself. "Do not dwell on it, Cecily," he has said, and I am sure that is good advice. If I dwell on it I am sure to become very upset, very upset indeed, because then I remember how excruciating the pain was and that is unhelpful, most unhelpful to my recovery, everyone tells me so. Even still it's a little painful, when I remember it, and my breasts become tender all over again. They bandaged them up for me, to ease the tenderness. I said, "But if you let him suckle, surely that would ease the pain, it's just that they are full, my breasts, full of milk." But they shook their heads and they said, "No, Cecily, no, no, you don't understand. If you suckle him you will ease the pain now, but then there will come more milk and more," and I said, "But that's good, it means the little one will not go hungry," but still they said, "No, that's not a good idea, it will only bring you too close." I said, "But we are close. I'm his mother." And they said, "Hush, Cecily, don't say that. You are a young girl. You must put this dreadful experience behind you, you must forget."

'I think, I think when they say "this dreadful experience", they mean you, dear,' Søren's mother said, only she called him by his proper name, Severin. That was Norwegian. She was Norwegian. He'd told Marie to expect that. 'They don't mean all the other things: the Herr Director and his breathing and the days without treacle and being third for the bath and the poor tortured trees in the grounds and the way they cluck about the mud on your dress. They mean the baby.

"'He's dead, isn't he?" I said then. That's what I thought at the time, dear, I don't wish to alarm you, it's just that that's how it seemed at the time. "He must be dead or you'd let me see him." "No, no, he's quite alive," they said. "He's not a very healthy baby," they said, "he needs special looking after, but he's not dead or any- where near death. He will be perfectly all right."

"'Bring him to me," I said. "Bring him to me, bring him to me, bring him to me, bring him to me, bring him to me."

"'Hush, Cecily," they said, and they clustered about the bed, and someone put a cloth over my face, that sweet-smelling stuff they used during the pain, and I tried to scream, but the smell over-powered me and I couldn't scream, screaming only seemed to bring the smell right into my bloodstream, into my brain, and I thought I should suffocate, so I stopped screaming and I let my body go limp and they tiptoed away from me.

'And then I screamed. I screamed and screamed and screamed. I screamed for my baby and I screamed that I would tell the world who the father was and I screamed that I would run away and that I would set fire to this place and that I would go to the newspapers and that . . . I screamed every threat I could think of, and they came at me with the cloth again and I bit the orderly and then she started screaming, she said I was rabid and that she would be in-fected and she ran from the room – she's new, poor girl, and not used to how things work here. I am sorry I bit her. I would not have bitten her if I'd had any choice in the matter, but it was her arm that was closest when they tried to put the cloth over my face, and so I just bit; I did not think, "Whose arm is this?"

'Then they brought the coat. I knew they would. They always do if you bite. The coat is a monster; I hate it. They put it on and you can't breathe, or you can, but only if you concentrate, and you have to try so hard to breathe, you have no breath and no thought for anything else. Your arms are pinned and your legs, I don't know what they do with your legs, but they seem to go numb, and all you can do is roll, and they gag you too. That is probably why you can't breathe. You must go very still, very, very still, for they won't take the coat off unless you are quiet, but as soon as they take it off and ungag me, I start the screaming again.

'In the end – several days, it must have taken; I know because the milk in my breasts had dried up by then – they gave in. They said, "Give her the child." And so they brought him to me – you, I mean, dear,' said Søren's mother. '"How old is he?" I asked, but they wouldn't tell me. They said I should know. Two weeks, I would reckon, maybe three, no more. They had a bottle for feeding him, with a teat, cow's milk. "What a waste," I said, "all that milk I had." But they didn't listen to that. They said, "You feed him, in that case, if you insist on having him with you." And so I took the bottle and I fed it to him and he looked up at me as he took the milk and his eyes were dark, dark navy blue and very, very deep and I knew I was not a doll and I drowned, I drowned in his eyes. Your eyes, Severin. "I will never let you go," I said. "Never, never, never."'

Tears were rolling down her cheeks, now, and she was rocking back and forth in her chair, but she made no sound.

Marie shifted uncomfortably and looked again at Søren. He was staring at the floor.

'Do you know Mr Darwin, dear?' Søren's mother asked suddenly.

'No,' said Søren, 'I don't know Mr Darwin.'

'I thought you were famous. People tell me you are famous. I would have imagined all you famous people know each other. Well, that is a pity, a great pity, because I would like to meet Mr Darwin; he seems such an interesting man, quite fiery too, I like a man with a bit of fire. I read that book, you know, about the species, and I have a question for him. I have been thinking about flies, you see.'

'Flies, mother?'

'Yes, well, you see, sometimes I sit here in this room, a very nice room it is too, my son pays for it – oh, yes, you know that, that's you, Severin, isn't it? Well, I'd like you to know that I am happy here in this room, that I manage very well, and that absurd little maid you send is awfully good, cooks and everything, and quite good-natured, though stupid, you wouldn't believe it, refused point blank to read Mr Darwin's book. But anyway, this is the thing. Nice as this room is, I do sometimes get a trifle bored, and then I think I am going to climb the walls, climb the walls, that is what people say, is it not? People are so poetic, are they not? Wonderful people, people are. Anyway, climb the walls, sometimes I feel I could climb the walls, and then, you see, I started to think, it is only the impossibility of it that has prevented me, for, in spite of what they say, I am not mad enough to think that I can shin up the smooth-plastered walls of a room. I could manage a stone wall or a brick wall easily enough, I have always been agile, but the walls of a room present an unscaleable plane to all but those possessed of suction pads on their feet, like flies. At least, I believe that is how flies manage to walk up perfectly smooth walls, though why they should want to, or what evolutionary advantage it is to them I cannot imagine. And that is where Mr Darwin comes in, dear, you see, I hope you have been following? I should like to know what evolutionary advantage it is to them to be able to walk up walls. When you consider that flies have been around, so one presumes, for countless thousands of millions of fly-generations, only a relatively few thousand of which can have overlapped in time with the smooth interior house wall, it is indeed mysterious that they should have developed this apparently useless capacity for wall climbing. So if you should happen to meet Mr Darwin, dear, do you think you could remember to ask him? I should count it a special favour.

'And now you must go away. That is the drill. You come, we have tea, sometimes there is cake, and we have a little talk and then I get quite worn out, and so you go. Thank you for bringing the lady doctor with you. She is very beautiful.'

'She is not a doctor, mother. She is my wife.'

'So you say, so you say. Well, goodbye, goodbye, you will come again, and you will bring me the news about the flies, will you not? You could ask my son, he is famous. He will know.'

She turned to Marie then and asked, 'You've heard of housemaid's knee? But of course, I was forgetting, you are a doctor, you will know all about it.'

'Housemaid's knee?' said Marie, wonderingly. 'Yes, I have heard of it . . .'

'Aha, there, you see. Everyone has heard of it. But they don't know about housemaid's mind. That is a closely guarded secret; very few of us know about it.' Here she tapped the side of her head comically. 'My sister suffers from it. Severin's aunt, that would be. Married a professor, no less, but eats in the kitchen all the same. See? Housemaid's mind.'

'Goodbye, mother,' said Søren, kissing her papery cheek.

'Goodbye,' she said cheerfully.

On the street outside, Marie said, 'Oh, Søren!'

'She's not so bad, really,' he said. 'Is she?'

'But she's wonderful!' said Marie.

'Wonderful?' This was not an idea that had occurred to him before.

'Flies!' said Marie. 'I loved it.'

'But the hospital, the chloroform, the straitjacket, all that.'

'Yes, but that has been her experience. What else should she talk about?'

'I suppose so,' he said. 'Yes. But wait till you meet the sane one!'

Chapter 20

C*openhagen, 30 May*

Dear Anna,

I am speechless! I cannot believe it! After all I have *done*, this is the thanks I get. I know it won't seem very serious to you, Anna, and by comparison with other things, it is trivial enough. But it's all very well for you. You *live* in Skagen. Your husband doesn't insist on keeping an apartment in Copenhagen. For me, the summer is the only time I get at home, and it is very precious to me. And now I hear that Her Ladyship is not only planning to be there *all summer long*, though they know perfectly well that it will put us out no end if they are around – but to add insult to injury, they have gone so far as to take the house that we always rent, summer after summer. I don't blame the landlady: they offered her twice the money we usually give her, which is already more than we can afford. I call that ungallant, Anna, I really do.

And after the winter we've had of it, Helen with her wretched confinement, then all the children so ill, and the cold, and the bills and then poor, sweet, little Anders, and Drachmann carrying on with that chorus girl while Emmy lay in childbed, and those months I spent nursing Emmy's baby that she couldn't bear to look at – after all that, my house in Skagen is being rented by this pair of interlopers from Paris, Rome, wherever they call home these days.

Really, it is insufferable. Our funny, poky little house, with its low roof and its rickety doors that don't meet the jambs and its smoky stoves. That dear little house where the children had measles that year – you remember – oh, it is too bad, and the cat had kittens under the sink and nobody could run water for weeks till she had weaned them. To think of the Krøyers sitting in deck chairs – nice spanking new ones, no doubt, from some store in Copenhagen – by that glorious white rose bush in the garden, the one I have lavished so much care on for *years*, since it was a failing little sapling. I can just see them, reading their modern novels, or books Georg Brandes recommends about the rights of women and the evils of marriage and how Christianity is misguided nonsense and we are all descended from apes.

They'll be drifting through those sweet grasses grown high in the quick summer sun, going from the house to the little outhouse at the bottom of the garden that smells of last year's apples, or sitting on the worn sill of the door to take their boots off and pour out the sand that fills them, before entering the house. They – not us, they – will hear the larks twittering foolishly, precipitously, all day and the song of the blackbird rippling out at dusk. The tomcat from next door but two, the big smelly white one, you know him, Anna, he'll come nosing in the gate, sniffing the bins with his pink, rabbitty nose, looking for scraps. They'll get to know the names of the children in the gardens nearby and learn to time their long summer days by the screeches from their swings and the mealtime silences. They'll lay tables out of doors – I can just see them, like in those idyllic paintings of Søren's – when the weather is good and they'll invite you all to coffee-and-cake, and they'll have friends to stay in the little attic room that smells of sunshine and limewash, with the landlady's bright crocheted blanket pulled over the worn and patched linen, and they'll linger over breakfast among teapots and eggshells and discuss world affairs and the latest news from the salons in Paris with writers and artists from Copenhagen.

It isn't fair. It just isn't fair. We'll be stuck in the heat of summer in the city, and they'll have everything. They have everything already, and now they're taking my birthright from me, my home place.

Infuriated,
Martha

Skagen, 4 June

Dear Martha,

I do sympathise, my dear, but Marie is my friend and I cannot be unhappy that she is coming to be near me for the summer. Would you like me to look out for another house for you to rent? Maybe on the other side of the dunes, where you would not have to see the Krøyers every day if you do not want to?

My advice to you, my dear, is to cheer up and write a novel. You're wasting your talents on letter writing.

Your loving cousin,
Anna

8 June

Dear Anna,

Thank you, no. Do not think of looking for another house for us. I can hardly bear the thought of it all, and I could not stand to spend a summer trying to avoid those people.

Viggo's wretched Christmas tree is still not finished. It is too bad. It was such a delightful idea in December, with all of us in our winter clothes and the candles all alight and everyone holding hands and singing, but it has been going on for *six months* now, and still the living room is full of this damnable tree *and* the easel, and there are pine needles everywhere – in the children's shoes, among the cushions, I even found one in the soup yesterday. And then the candles burned down, and Viggo had me running around all the hardware shops, looking for Christmas tree candles in June! I suppose it will sell, because it is certainly a very attractive painting, but who is going to want to buy it at this time of year? And what shall we live on between now and next Christmas? I can't imagine Viggo ever painting anything else, he is so obsessed with this one.

Perhaps it is just as well that we are not coming to Skagen, because I do not see how we could afford it this year.

Martha

Chapter 21

Mrs Professor Krøyer was delighted to receive her daughter-in-law, absolutely delighted. Would they mind just slipping their shoes off? She'd spent all morning on the parquet, back-breaking, but there was no point in leaving it to the servant; if you want something done properly, do it yourself, that's what she always said. Normally she could have offered them cotton over-shoes, save them the trouble of unlacing, but they were all in the wash this morning, they got so dirty, you wouldn't believe it. Well, now, delighted indeed. *Enchantée*, she should say, since they had so lately come from France, or was it Italy? Ah, Italy; well, she knew no Italian, goodness me, Italy. Papist country, she believed. Couldn't be doing with that sort of thing herself, but it takes all kinds, doesn't it? Mustn't grumble.

Well, well, well, it was quite a thing to see her Severin married. She never thought she'd see the day, to be perfectly honest. She thought he would be her boy for ever, just for ever, that they would go on living here in this nice house – it is a nice house, isn't it? – just the two of them until they took her out in a box. In a box!

Of course, she'd always known Severin would *amount* to something. Such a talented little boy he'd been. But shy, oh so shy, hard to believe it now, of course, he was quite the man about town, droves of friends, positively droves of them. But he hadn't always been so outgoing, so *gregarious*.

'Do your remember, Severin, how you used to crouch under the dining table? You said it was your den in there, but it was just that he didn't want to have to shake hands with the guests, Mrs

Krøyer. Oh, it is funny to call someone else by that name; good heavens, who'd ever have thought it? What a job we had getting you to sit up to table, Severin, and hold your knife and fork. Villem was always so nicely mannered, put you to shame; I used to be mortified. I always wanted him to outshine Villem, you see, Mrs Krøyer, he being the father's favourite. The father always thought Villem would be the one to shine, thought he showed promise, just because he was good at his letters, so I felt I had to take Severin's part, you see, stand up for the little man, he couldn't help it if . . . Well, well, I am proud of both my boys, of course. Very proud.'

'Of course I was shy,' said Søren now, irritably. 'How could I have been otherwise? I was so overprotected, never allowed any contact with other children. It is a wonder . . . '

'Oh, Severin, that's not true. Of course I didn't allow you to roam the streets. You might have fallen into a canal, or anything. You went to *school*.'

'Not until I was ten.'

'Well, you were delicate, your health . . . '

Søren sighed loudly and crossed his legs, pulling irritably at the fabric of his trousers around the knee, and describing a series of quick circles with his swinging foot.

'And you went out to play. I never held with that idea the poor people have, Mrs Krøyer, keeping their children all cooped up indoors. They know nothing of the benefits of fresh air and exercise. That's what children need, I always said. You used to go over the street to explore that lumberyard opposite, don't you remember? We lived in a more . . . modest area then, Mrs Krøyer.'

He remembered all right, but those forays had been so fraught, because he knew his mother was watching his every move. He was supposed to play in full view of the window at all times, so she could reassure herself that he was safe. But it was hard to remember or even to gauge which parts of the lumberyard were clearly visible from the drawing-room window and which not, so he felt himself much confined in his play, and he could never venture into the little hut where the lumber workers brewed up their morning coffee, although they often invited him to join them, forlorn little chap he must have seemed. They clearly felt sorry for him, playing alone, balancing on the logs and climbing over the woodpiles, wrapped up like a small parcel with legs, in his stout little overcoat and his muffler and mittens and his felt hat with earflaps.

'I bought him his first paintbox, Mrs Krøyer,' said Søren's mother.

'Yes,' he said, 'you did, you did,' and his manner noticeably softened.

It was a shameful thing to be met at the school gate by your mother, when all the other boys could have really good fights on their way home, or climb trees and shoot catapults, but, even so, he had to admit that those afternoon walks home – once they were out of earshot of his schoolmates' jeers – were often the best part of the day. He and his mother would walk through the city streets and stop for a little treat. Sometimes they'd go into the bakery and Severin would get a Viennese pastry filled with cherry jam and dotted with slices of sugary toasted almonds. And sometimes they would call into the toy shop, which was filled with all sorts of delights: wooden trains and lead soldiers and brightly painted spinning tops and balls of every size and colour and puzzles and dolls with wooden limbs and china faces and wonderfully elaborate doll's houses with tiled roofs and walls that opened to reveal perfectly furnished little rooms. They never bought anything in the toy shop, for toys were much more expensive than jam pastries, but just to visit was a treat in itself. 'You can be planning what you would like to have in your Christmas slipper, Severin,' his mother would say, but Severin didn't need to plan because he had known since the very first visit they paid to the toy shop what it was that he hoped to find at the foot of his bed on Christmas morning, and that was a paintbox.

'A paintbox?' asked his mother. 'Are you sure?'

He was quite sure. It was what he wanted more than anything in the whole world. 'More than anything,' he said, and he added slyly, 'mother.'

'Call me "mother",' she begged him, but when his other mother was around *she* said the same thing. The two mothers fought a continuous silent battle for Severin's affections. The little boy looked from one to the other and he called his foster mother 'aunt' to the other mother, and called the other mother 'aunt' when the foster mother was in earshot.

The foster-mother-aunt's fatty heart did not often have adventures in her chest cavity, but on that Christmas morning, she could have sworn it actually somersaulted. She could feel it behind her ribs, the way it jolted, like some squat and meaty and vigorous young bird, an immature guinea-fowl, perhaps, trapped in a fleshy cage and eager to burst out of it. Sometimes it worried her that she had thoughts like this. Most of the time, she tried not to have thoughts at all. That was the safest plan. If she thought too much, she might go mad. These things were known to 'run' in families, and who knows when she might be stricken down, if she allowed herself for one moment to give in to weakness. Not giving in to weakness was what had got Bertha where she was today, a respectable married lady with a husband who had a big job at the university, and just because she had started out as a servant in the house, that was nothing to be ashamed of; indeed, it was an indication of her own sterling worth, that she had been able to overcome such an unfortunate start in life.

Of course, the fact that both her children were really her sisters' illegitimate offspring – Villem was the son of another sister, who had lived with them briefly and had had an affair with Bertha's husband, not a nice situation, but then, a sister makes such a poor rival; no one ever has the least sympathy for a woman who seduces her own brother-in-law under her sister's roof – well, she had to own that that meant a certain stigma attached to her little family. But on the other hand, it meant she had two fine boys, blood relations if not actual sons, and without the necessity for her to endure either the pain and risk of childbirth or the messy and appalling conjunction of bodies necessary for conception. So after all, it was, by and large, a good arrangement, as good as it was possible to imagine, in fact, and as for the stigma, that was just in other people's eyes, people who didn't understand, and besides, it could be kept at bay, she had decided, by a regime of extreme domestic hygiene. She was proud to say, the very mites in the carpets would starve to death in her house, so vigilant was she in her crusade against dirt.

The thing about Severin was that he had had an unfortunate start in life, too, and it was up to her to see that it did not come between him and his glorious future. He was to be a scientific draughtsman and illustrator; it was all planned. Those whatever-they-were – molluscs, did they call them? Disgusting word, disgusting things – that he drew for his father, everyone said they were exquisite, the best molluscs they'd ever seen, *made* that paper of his father's, and he'd only been nine years old. So what if Villem could read? – any fool could learn to read and frequently did. But the way Severin could draw, and in a trice too, with scarcely an effort – that was a special gift, not given to many.

And now it seemed he wanted to paint. Painting was perhaps not an inclination to be encouraged, however, for who ever heard of anyone who made a respectable living from painting? She wasn't having her son a common tradesman, out in all weathers painting the shutters of people too lazy to paint their own. And another thing: where there were paintboxes, there were undoubtedly paints, and paints had a tendency to spill, to smear, to stain, to create a cleansing nightmare, in fact. On the other hand, the boy did not often ask for anything, and it was not good always to deny children their heart's desire. It might lead to an inflammation of the brain. And there was also the fact that a paintbox was an attractively inexpensive Christmas gift. Besides, Bertha felt it was healthy to go against one's own impulses, at times, for such denial was sure to be bracing for the soul and invigorating to one's moral and spiritual health. And so she thought she might, perhaps, allow the paintbox.

She knew that Severin had wanted it, but she was not prepared for the delight with which he fell upon it on Christmas morning, jumping for joy, literally jumping, hugging it to his chest as if it were a puppy or some animate thing, kissing it, actually kissing it. This last Bertha thought a little distasteful. But what truly constricted the young guinea-fowl in her chest was the way he turned such shining eyes to her and rushed into her arms, burying his grateful head in her large, soft bosom. She did not care to be touched – as a matter of fact, it made her come over all queer – but on this occasion, she owned it was a more than pleasant sensation, and she responded awkwardly but sincerely, by patting him repeatedly on the back and saying, 'there' and 'yes' and 'good', over and over again.

All was changed, now, of course. She knew now that a painter could make a living without having to paint other people's shutters; indeed, she would hardly believe it if someone had told her that's what she'd thought in the past. She'd seen Severin's paintings of important people, wealthy families, powerful committees, and she'd been astounded at what he had been paid for them, but she took it in her stride all the same – she'd always known he would be someone.

And now here he was, married. That wiped everything out, she thought. Marriage was an excellent simple against all sorts of contamination. It blotted out the past, created a new beginning. She wished them very well. Very well indeed. How charming of them to call. So sorry about the overshoes. Would they mind not putting on their shoes again until they were on the doorstep? Goodbye, dear boy. And to you too, Mrs Krøyer. Goodbye. Goodbye.

Chapter 22

The door to the Anchers' low red house in Skagen stood wide
open to the summer sun. A large white cat lay curled in a
square of sunlight in the tiny hallway. Marie could have sworn
she'd seen that very beast nosing about her own garden.

'Anna!' she called, from the doorstep. 'It's me!'

Anna appeared, wearing an enormous blue apron, which en-
veloped her body.

'My dear, you are so welcome!' she exclaimed, stepping over
the cat and taking Marie in her arms in an enthusiastic embrace.
'To see you at last in Skagen – well, well, this is quite a day, come
in, come in! Is Søren well? He is painting, no doubt, or he would
have come with you; he is always painting, Søren – Emmy Drachmann says he would paint in hell! I have made you a cake! Come
and admire it. It is not beautiful, I have to say, but it is made with
love. Oh, drat this cat, he is everywhere, thinks he owns the place.'
She toed the cat and he opened one eye and stretched but didn't
move. 'Just lift your skirt and leap,' Anna advised Marie.

'You left the hall door open,' Marie said, by way of explaining
the cat.

'It is never closed in summer time, except when we go to bed,
and even then – oh, dear, I have to admit, we sometimes forget. It's
easier to leave it open, means we don't have to keep jumping up
when people call. They can drop whatever it is in, without disturbing us, or if they want to see us, they can come straight through
into the studio. And what do you think of our darling house?'
Anna was whooshing Marie into the kitchen, where the welcoming

cake was. 'Of course, it is not new any more, but I still congratulate myself on it every morning when I wake up and find myself here.'

'Very fine kitchen,' said Marie, looking around her.

'Fiddlesticks,' said Anna. 'A kitchen is a kitchen, it is not the kitchen I expect you to admire. Let's make some coffee, and then you can come through into the sitting room – no, Michael's working there, won't be disturbed under any circumstances. Are you a circumstance, dear? I suppose you are. The dining room then, we have the most charming dining room. Imagine, a sitting room *and* a dining room! Frightfully grand, isn't it? But that is mainly because the sitting room is also Michael's studio. Or rather, the other way around: Michael's studio turns into a sitting room in the evening.'

Marie spotted the cake. It looked like a heap of crumbs precariously moulded together.

'My poor cake!' Anna said, following Marie's gaze. 'It is not a happy cake, is it? Lemon Collapse, I think we should call it. I believe it will taste quite good, though, in spite of its lack of external beauty. Can you reach down the cups, Marie, they are there over your head. Best china today, since we have company.'

Anna smoothed a linen napkin over a small tea tray as a tray cloth, and anchored it with the cups and saucers, which were almost too pretty to be real.

'Wedding present,' said Anna, as if reading Marie's thoughts. 'People do have the strangest ideas about what one might need.' But she was smiling delightedly, like a child playing house.

Anna poured hot water over the coffee grounds, and plonked the battered old kitchen coffee pot down on the tray with the delicate Limoges ware, and the rickety cake, sliced now into awkward chunks.

'There is a silver coffee pot someplace,' she said. 'But I really can't remember where. I didn't ice it,' she continued, indicating the cake. 'I don't like icing. Hope you don't mind. It is your cake after all.'

Marie had not eaten cake since she was twelve.

'Without icing is perfect,' she said.

'Now, let's get a look at you,' Anna said, as she put the coffee tray down on the dining table. 'Marie, you are so thin! You were always thin, but this is shocking! And you do not look well.'

Marie looked away. 'I told you I had been ill, Anna, it was all in my letters.'

'Yes, but that was months ago, last summer. My dear Marie, I am quite distraught at the figure you cut. You have no colour in your face at all, unless you count the dark circles under your eyes; and your poor thin little arms – like sticks! Søren doesn't notice what you eat, I dare say, or rather, what you don't eat. You will eat some of this cake, Marie, if it kills you. Which it will not, I assure you.'

But before she sat down, Anna said, Marie simply must come and see her studio. She had a proper little studio now, separate from Michael's. It was not very large, but it had lots of windows.

'Doesn't Paris seem so long ago already?' Anna asked, as they wandered through the house. 'Of course, for you, Marie, so much has happened, getting married and everything, going to Italy. Did you go to Florence? The Uffizi? How I *long* to see the Uffizi! And the Sistine, of course. I *must* get to Rome.'

As for herself, she'd come *bounding* back from Paris, Anna declared. 'Everyone said so, that is the verb they used, *bounding*, makes me sound like a greyhound, doesn't it!' Anna laughed loudly.

It was seeing all those French paintings, she reckoned, the way they used light and colour – gave her new heart.

'The very first thing I did when I got home – Marie, you simply *have* to see it, it's the best thing I've ever painted, at least I think so, though it is so hard to judge one's own work, is it not, Marie?'

Marie looked longingly around the studio, but Anna was urging her to look at a particular painting. It was of a blue room, with a child sitting by the window, bent over a piece of needlework.

'That's Helga,' said Anna. 'In my mother's parlour. I'm so proud of this one, Marie.'

The girl was perched like a bird, only half-settled on the edge of a chair, her blonde hair a fuzz of lemony light, the sunshine making a window-square on the wall beyond.

It was such a joy to paint, didn't Marie find? Anna painted endless rooms, doors, windows – she indicated canvases all around the room, leaning against the walls – all netting sunbeams. In some there were people, going about their business – Marie hunkered down delightedly to examine them – people sewing, taking off their boots, eating their breakfast. But this was Anna's favourite, Helga captured for ever in that blue room, sunshine streaming around her 'like love', Anna said. 'To paint sunshine – it's the hardest thing. I had been working all year at it, and I think in this painting, I finally got it, don't you think?'

And what about Marie, what was she working on these days? Anna was leading the way back to the charming dining room and the little feast. The coffee would have brewed by now.

Marie shrugged. 'Not much,' she said.

'Oh, Marie, what a shame! It's all the travelling, is it? Upsets your routine?'

'It's more the illness. I haven't got the energy.'

'I shall make it my mission to fatten you up, Marie, so that you get your energy back, and then I'll thrust a brush into your hand, and we shall paint together, as we did in Paris. It was such fun, was it not? You loved it. I know you did.'

'Yes, Anna,' said Marie mildly, vaguely.

'Marie, I know how dispiriting it is not to paint. I have days like that. I go to bed restless. But when I am really stuck into a painting, those are the best times. Helga doesn't get any lunch, poor love! What a terrible mother I am!' Anna beamed at her own maternal negligence. 'On days like that, I send her over to the hotel for a bowl of soup as soon as she comes home from school. I don't even dress on those days, I just sit and paint and paint in my nightgown – I am a disgrace, quite a disgrace! – with my robe around me and my feet in the most disreputable pair of old carpet slippers you can imagine, I would be ashamed to let you see.' But she seemed delighted at her own wretchedness all the same. 'I paint until the light fades, and then I stand up and stretch, like the old tomcat out there, and I quite shock myself to discover that I am still in my nightgown, and ravenous, I am absolutely ravenous! Because I probably have forgotten breakfast, not to mind lunch – as bad as you, my dear! And cold, even in summer, I am cold, from sitting still all day; I believe my blood congeals in my veins, can't be healthy. But there it is. Then what I do is, I butter myself a piece of bread and, oh, this is so delicious, I step, still chewing it, into my bath, quite the lady, and I thaw out in the hot water. Come and see, the best room in the house!'

She pulled Marie by the wrist and flung open the door to a modern bathroom, with a plumbed bath.

'Can you believe it? Have you ever seen such luxury!'

The bath and basin and WC were all blue and white, like crockery, with motifs of flowers and leaves. Marie made the appropriate exclamations.

'Then I get dressed quickly,' Anna said, leading Marie back to the dining room, 'and I put my hair up and I pretend to be a proper person. I cook the dinner, just like anyone's wife, and set the table and I call Michael and Helga and we all sit around and eat and talk and behave like a family. Glorious, don't you think?' Anna folded her hands contentedly in her lap.

Marie nodded. Glorious. Yes, a real family.

'I will choose the smallest slice for you, dear,' Anna said as she poured the coffee. 'And you will tell me all your news while you crumble it so that I will think you have eaten it.'

Marie laughed softly. Anna was such a tonic, and so sharp!

'Italy was beautiful, wonderful,' she began. She hesitated. 'But you are right, I am not very well, and . . . oh, Anna, I have been so worried!' She let her fork clatter onto her cake plate and took out a lawn handkerchief.

Anna stopped her prattle and sat still, waiting for Marie to speak in her own time.

'It is partly the typhoid, you see,' said Marie. 'I am much recovered, but it has left me . . . winded, I suppose. I tire easily. And I cry easily. I never did before. I was stronger before; now I am a quivering jelly, ready to burst into tears at any moment.'

'How you do mix your metaphors, dear,' said Anna, not unsympathetically 'Jellies quiver, but they never, in my experience, burst into tears.'

Marie smiled. 'Anna, you do me good,' she said.

'Well, I am glad of it. So now, tell me. What are you so worried about? Your health?'

'No. Yes. Not only.'

'Well, then, we are making progress.'

Marie smiled again, in spite of herself. 'I don't know where to start. Anna, you know that story you wrote to me about last summer, the boy who . . . died?'

Anna nodded.

'People are saying the most dreadful things!'

'I know.'

'You've heard? Way up here in Skagen?'

'Gossip travels fast.'

'Martha?'

'Martha.' Anna nodded again.

'What does she say?'

'That you . . . well, that you had a romantic entanglement with the lad. I take it that is true?'

'We were, I mean, I *thought* we were engaged to be married. And then the family suddenly closed ranks and turned me out. Oh, Anna, it was dreadful. So humiliating. I couldn't think what the problem was.'

'But the poor boy was very ill, Marie, sick to death. I suppose they did not think he was fit to marry.'

'I didn't *know*! I should have known. I thought he had a look of Theo. In fact, that was partly why I fell for him, I realise now. I did-n't make the connection. I didn't realise it was the illness that cre-ated the resemblance.'

'Theo?'

'My brother. Died young. I don't want to talk about it, Anna, because if I do I shall weep.'

'Poor Marie.' Anna patted the back of her friend's hand.

'So, well, anyway . . . the thing was, as soon as his parents found out – I loved his parents, they are charming people, Anna – but they suddenly showed me the door. I thought it was because I was poor, or German, or . . . Christian!'

'Whereas *they* thought *you* had spotted an opportunity to marry into wealth and be left a rich widow.'

'Oh, Anna! I don't, I *can't* believe they would have had such a poor opinion of me. To marry with a view to becoming a widow, what a wicked idea! What do people take me for?'

'That's Martha's opinion, my dear, you may as well know. In the same way that Søren . . . '

'What about Søren? What has this got to do with *Søren*?'

'Nothing, nothing. Let's just say, people marry for all kinds of motives, Marie.'

'People marry for *love*, Anna!' Marie wailed and stood up, pacing the room. 'Is that a naive idea? I thought it just a good, honest, pure idea, not a stupid one! You married for love, Anna, did you not?'

'Yes, yes, of course. And it is not a stupid idea, it is a fine one, you are right, do not distress yourself, Marie. Sit down, can't you? Sit down.'

'But I must know – are you saying Søren did not marry me for love?'

'Of course he married for love, Marie. Anyone can see how he loves . . . *adores* you.'

'I don't want to be adored.'

Anna was flummoxed.

'Loved, yes,' Marie went on earnestly, 'but not *adored*.'

'You do make fine distinctions, Marie,' said Anna faintly.

Marie flounced back into her chair. 'Adored is for muses, models, *mistresses*. Adored is silly frippery. Adored is Holger Drachmann and his chorus girls. Loved is what I want to be, Anna. Cherished.'

'Of course you do, of course. I am sure Søren cherishes you, Marie.'

'But you seem to be saying he married me for some other motive.' Marie was weeping openly now.

'I did not say so. I said that Martha thinks so, but Martha's views are warped, Marie. You have to take that into account.'

'So what is Martha's warped view of my husband's motivation in marrying me?' asked Marie sourly.

Anna sighed. 'He had a girlfriend before you.'

'Anna, he was nearly forty when he married me. Of course he had girlfriends before me. I may be naive but I am not stupid.'

'Martha thinks his marriage to you was a little . . . convenient.'

'How?'

'It was, she thinks, *partly*, a way of breaking off a relationship that had become a bit overpowering.'

'I see.' Marie sat very still and composed herself. 'Well, that is not so very bad. People do . . . '

'No. It's not bad at all.'

A pause. The clock ticked. Marie could hear Michael moving about in the next room.

'Is there anything else that is grieving you, Marie?'

'Many things grieve me.'

'Let me guess. You have met the mothers? They sound a daunting prospect, I have to say.'

'Well, yes. The sane one I did not much like, the one who brought him up. But the mad one, the one who gave birth to him, I rather liked her.'

'Søren half-suspects she puts it on, you know, the madness.'

'Well, it's true that she is as sharp as a razor about some things, but I suppose that is not incompatible with madness.'

'A mad person who pretends to be sane is pathetic,' said Anna, 'and a sane person who pretends to be mad is dangerous, but a mad person who pretends to be mad, maybe . . . '

'You think she pretends to be mad?'

'Marie, I have never met the woman, I couldn't possibly judge. But pretending to be mad – well, it could be the closest she can get to sanity.'

'But that's daft,' said Marie.

'No,' said Anna. 'Listen. It does make a kind of sense to pretend to be madder than you are. It puts you outside the conventions, beyond people's reasonable expectations: it must be quite liberating. And it gives you a role. The mad aunt. The mad mother. I can see a lot of advantages.'

'But only if you are mad to start with,' Marie said. 'I am sure it is torture to be mad.'

'Sometimes it is torture to be sane.'

'That's it,' cried Marie, and she leaped up again and paced the room swiftly. 'That's exactly it! That's how I feel, sane and tortured.'

'My poor Marie – tortured! What is the problem? Can you explain it? Do you want to?'

'I grew up in a family like yours, Anna,' said Marie, sitting down again. 'Parents and children. No step-parents or half-siblings or cousins or babies abandoned and taken in by aunts or any of those things.'

'That is most unusual, Marie. And you are forgetting my cousins Martha and Henrietta – we took them in when their father died. It's the natural thing.'

'That's different,' Marie argued, unconvincingly. 'But, you see, since I have met Søren, it is nothing but babies who don't belong to their mothers and husbands who have affairs and wives who run off with sailors.'

'Nobody ran off with a sailor!' said Anna.

'Oh, for goodness' sake, I'm speaking figuratively, but you see what I mean? Everything is so *irregular*, somehow. Look at Søren's own family: his mother is really his aunt and his aunt is really his mother and his brother is really his half-cousin, and his mother's children are really her two sisters' children and his father is not his father but he is his brother's father, only, of course, his brother is, as previously noted, his cousin! And besides, the ones who have babies are not married, and the ones who are married do not have babies.'

Anna could not suppress a giggle. Marie looked daggers at her.

'I'm sorry,' Anna said, 'but you make it sound like Gilbert and Sullivan, Marie! I feel I could sing it.'

'It's not funny, Anna!'

'I'm sorry. I . . . '

'And then, look at Emmy's children, look at Martha's, even. Does nobody bring up their own children in Skagen?'

'Emmy and Martha are both bringing up their own children, Marie,' said Anna, a little stiffly.

'Yes, but you know what I mean. They each have children whom someone abandoned.'

'I hardly think Henrietta . . . '

'I'm sorry, Anna. You're right, I beg your pardon. But you do see what I mean. It just all seems so *strange* to me.'

'But, Marie, that's nothing to be ashamed of. Is it not, indeed, a noble thing? I have my differences with Martha, my dear, but I think she can be proud of herself for bringing up Henry, and likewise Emmy for bringing up Gerda. And it's the same with Søren's foster-mother-aunt, whether you like her or not, she did bring him up out of the kindness of her heart. Would you prefer if she had left him in the asylum with the mad mother?'

Marie gulped. 'Of course not. I am just saying . . .'

'Marie, my dear, I can understand that you find our ways strange, as you put it, but if you go on thinking like that, you will *make* yourself unhappy. How can you be happy if you fret about such things?'

'I like things to be clear. I like to know what's what. I don't like fuzziness.'

'Things are never clear, Marie. In my experience, clarity only happens in pictures. Stay there.'

Anna leaped up and ran out to her studio. She came back with a picture. 'Not one of mine. Michael painted it,' she said, placing it on the mantelpiece so that Marie could view it. 'It's Helga's christening.'

Marie looked at the painting.

'I see,' she said, but all she saw was a picture.

'A perfect family grouping, the kind of thing you like, Marie. A babe, its two parents, and a clutch of friends and supporters, gathered at the font. What could be more representative of Christian marriage and familial devotion?'

Marie could not imagine what Anna could mean, so she just listened.

'It is a pretty fair representation of Helga's christening,' said Anna, tracing the outline of herself, holding the child in its flounce of christening lace.

Marie nodded, and went on studying the picture.

'But, in fact,' said Anna, 'the painting took weeks – months – to paint.'

'Yes?' said Marie.

'Not everyone paints with Søren's alacrity. And Helga was very young. You do not think I was going to stand around in a chilly church for days and days and weeks and months while Michael painted the scene, do you? Besides, she'd have been toddling by the time the picture was finished, not a babe in arms at all any more!'

'I see.' Marie still saw only the picture.

'So what happened was, Michael sketched the scene at the actual christening. And then he got people to pose, different people on different days, while he painted them in. I posed maybe on two occasions, but I did not have Helga in my arms. That dear little babe you see – that was a doll of Henrietta's that I found on top of the wardrobe after she died. Poor little scrap. She'd laid all her dolls in tissue paper and stacked them in twos and threes 'so they won't be lonely' – I remember her saying it – and packed them in shoeboxes, and she put them on top of the wardrobe, behind her mother's hatboxes. She found she'd grown out of dolls. That was only a few years before she married Karl.' Anna pushed away a stray tear with the back of her hand.

Marie was still staring at the picture.

'So you see,' said Anna, 'the baby is a doll. And as to the mother, well, I was not going to stand around in the cold either. I had a small child to mind. So I lent my best dress to a friend of mine and I asked her to stand in for me.'

'But it's you in the picture, Anna.'

'From the neck up, it's me. I sat for Michael at home in the evenings and he painted the head – onto the body of my friend, who was wearing my best dress.'

Marie laughed. 'I'd never have guessed.'

'No,' said Anna. 'But you see my point. That kind of perfection – that kind of *clarity*, if you like – only happens in pictures. In real life, people ask their friends to do favours. They lend them dresses and they borrow dolls and they make do with what they've got. And when it comes to it, they bring up each other's children, and that is a fine thing, in my view. Life is imperfect, and the best we can do is help each other out and muddle through as well as we can. You could see it as hypocrisy or you could think it strange, or you could interpret it in any number of ways, but it's just getting on with what life deals out, do you see?'

Marie stared at the painting and said nothing. At last she gave a tiny, almost imperceptible nod. 'I see,' she said. 'I wasn't . . . at least, I don't think I was . . . '

'No, I am sure you weren't being critical. You are just trying to understand.'

'I have to go,' Marie said. 'Søren will be fretting.'

She stood up and drew her shawl around her.

'Take this,' said Anna, thrusting a plate into her hands.

It was a slice of Lemon Collapse, 'for Sørens's tea', Anna said.

Chapter 23

M arie gave grave little lunch parties. The company of painters
in Skagen was not well disposed towards lunch parties, for
they broke up the day and used precious sunlight hours. They preferred to paint till dusk and then gather for food and drink and
partying. They came to her parties, however, for Søren's sake, but
they found her ways townish, and they had their own methods of
letting her know it. They made catty remarks about how her
eggcups matched – as if matching tableware was an indicator of
a petty soul – and they affected to be shocked that she kept her
front door closed until somebody knocked upon it.

Marie tried to ignore their jibes, but she felt them all the same,
and she felt their unfairness too. It was jealousy, Søren said – they
were just as unkind about his linen waistcoats and his silver pocket
watch, sneering at the way he dressed as if his dapper sartorial
choices were some sort of threat to the artistic integrity of the
community. It was lack of charity, Anna said, and an indication
that people had 'little to be doing'. But Marie knew it was plain
bad-mindedness, and she could not see what she had done to at-
tract such odium. It couldn't be just her style of reform dress that
people objected to – what should artists care about such things? –
or her polite ways. It might, of course, have been her looks.

Skagen itself was not the problem. Skagen was wonderful, quite
as charming as Anna had depicted it in Paris – the endless silvery
blue sands, the two blue crazy seas washing over each other in
front of your eyes, the fishermen and their boats, the dunes,
the lighthouse, the spire of the silted-up church rising eerily out
of the sands.

Søren took a childish delight in how well Marie took to the place. They had acquired a large brown dog, and she went for long salty walks with it along the shore and threw sticks for it into the vast, vast blue of the vaulted sky. It stopped, panting, with ears comically pricked up in two flabby triangles, waiting to hear the sound of the stick as it fell onto the surface of the sea, and then off it bounded into the water, all silvery splashes and excited barks, in pursuit of its prey.

Marie could stand on the sea's edge and let her mind soar into sheer blue, feel herself almost dissolve in the light, but when she turned to go home, to sit for Søren or to busy herself about the house, she found that the exhilaration of moving through the summer air frittered under her fingertips as she turned the handle of her own front door.

It was not Søren's fault. It had nothing to do with him. It was that as she closed the door behind her, and the pulsing roar of the waves was muffled by the fabric of the house, she felt closed in and . . . here was the thing: pointless.

She tried to describe the feeling to Anna. 'Futile' was one word she used. 'Fraud' was another. Anna listened intently, but she could not seem to pick up what Marie tried to communicate.

'You can't be a fraud, Marie,' she said. 'You are authentic as the day is long. You are honest and clear-sighted and open-hearted. What is fraudulent about that?'

Marie sighed and said something about how trying it was to live with such a great artist. This had nothing to do with her feeling of being a fraud, but it was an idea that Anna understood, and that was something.

'If you would only paint, Marie, you would feel better. It is this eternal not-painting that is debilitating you.'

Marie said she could not remember how to paint. Her fingers had forgotten. Or she didn't see the point of it any more.

'The point is that there is no point. You just do it. If you would only do it, Marie, you would remember how to do it, and the point would suddenly be clear to you.'

'But you have just said there is no point.'

'Well, of course there is a point. What I mean is that the point is not amenable to discussion. It is not something you can explain. It is about as sensible as eating with your feet to try to explain why one paints or what it means to paint or what the value of it is. You just have to do it, and then it is as obvious as eating with your fingers. I mean, your mouth.'

Marie's throat rippled with laughter. 'Anna Ancher, if you were not a painter, you would have to be a writer. An essayist, I think, or one of those people who writes ruminative things in the papers.'

'That's what I say to Martha,' said Anna. 'I wish she would write more. It would draw the poison out of her.'

'If that is the point of writing,' said Marie desolately, 'then maybe I should try it myself.'

Chapter 24

Holger Drachmann always held that his infatuations were personally meaningless but necessary to his art. This was an argument that left Emmy cold, but she had come to a grudging accommodation with his philanderings, and even secretly agreed that they were necessary — not to his art, that was self-justifying nonsense — but to his fidelity to her. Because he was faithful in a way, not as fidelity is generally understood, but in the sense that he always came back to her, and for weeks, then, months, they would live off the double sweetness of his contrition and her forgiveness.

Until Rita.

What Emmy could not bear about the Rita situation was not that Holger loved this girl as he had not loved any of the others, but that he was foolish enough to believe this. Surely he must have sufficient familiarity with the workings of his own emotional life to know by now that this was just another temporary passion and that it would pass as the others had. Rita was different from the others in one respect only: she was clever, where the others had all been bovine in their stupidity, as far as Emmy could make out. And being clever, she made demands, and she made them early on, before the grip she had on his heart lost its power. Instead of warning him off, these demands had the opposite effect: they made his passion seem all the more urgent, his love all the more real, and his attachment to her all the more necessary. Having established her power over him, Rita, sensible girl that she was, went for the prize: she demanded that he leave Emmy.

'My dear girl,' Holger had begun that Sunday afternoon when he went to take his leave of his wife.

They were in the kitchen. It was the servant's day off, and Emmy was buttering bread for the children's supper. The day was mild, but the kitchen was cool, and she could feel a chill breeze around her ankles. Her feet always felt the cold first. She fancied a faintly rancid odour rose from the butter, though it had been stored on a marble slab in a cool spot in the larder, and it was quite hard and resistant to the knife.

She wouldn't look at him. She wouldn't make it easier for him.

She went on buttering and replied softly, 'I am not a girl, Holger, which may well be the problem.'

Holger was obsessed with youth. He regarded it as a quality whose properties he could share by virtue of proximity. If only he could be around young people – young women – he would somehow himself be suffused with the zest and vigour he believed he needed to inspire his poetry.

'And I am quite clearly not your dear,' Emmy went on, 'so don't condescend to me, please. It's bad enough what you do to me and the children without pretending that we are dear to you. Please pass me that ham.'

'My dear Emmy,' he insisted, grasping her hand, ignoring her request for the ham. 'You are most dear to me, dear as my own soul.'

'That's not true, Holger,' she said, disengaging her hand as coolly as she could manage. 'If it were, you wouldn't be going to say what I know you have come to me to say.'

'My dear, it pains me . . . '

'I hope it pains you, Holger. I hope it wounds you and that the wound is deep and raw.'

Emmy had laid down the buttering knife and picked up a sharp, thin-bladed one, with which she proposed to slice the ham. It was all she could do: live up to the situation. She made a thrusting movement with the knife towards Holger's body, as if inserting it between his ribs. Then she twisted it sharply in the air and let it fall with a sudden clatter.

Holger jumped.

'You are not blameless,' he said, as if goaded into it. 'You've had your own affairs.'

'What!'

'Krøyer – you were in love with him; don't think I didn't notice. Broke Helen's heart.'

'Krøyer! I was never in love with him, not for a moment. *He* was in love with *me*.'

'You encouraged him.'

Emmy shook her head. 'I sang a song or two with him. I laughed at a joke or two with him. That is the sum total of my "affair", as you call it. I did not leave my marriage for him. Do not even think to make a comparison!

'I have put up with so *much*,' she went on, her voice high and strained. She reached out for the ham herself, as if the moment with the knife hadn't happened.

'I know,' he began contritely, 'but I –'

'I have put up with it,' she continued, ignoring his intervention, as if she were delivering a prepared speech, 'because always I knew that your heart belonged to me.'

She scuffed at her eyes with the back of her hand and bent to retrieve the sharp knife she had dropped. She stood up, then wiped the knife perfunctorily on a corner of her apron and started to slice the ham forcefully, the knife juddering against the meat.

Holger's voice came in a strangled whisper. 'It did . . . it does.'

'No, Holger. You have done the worst thing. You have lost your heart, and it wasn't yours to lose. You have given to another what rightly belongs to me. That is irretrievable, and because it is irretrievable, it is unforgivable.'

'Unforgivable, Emmy? Don't say that!'

'I can only forgive where there is a purpose of amendment. Even the Lord God himself requires that much. Don't ask me to out-divine the divinity, Holger.'

She stopped her slicing and looked up at him, tears streaming silently down her face.

'I wish . . . Emmy, I feel as if my heart has broken in two. Can you not take your half of it and be content with that?'

'No, I can't, because it will not bring you back to me.'

'Emmy, I will, I will come back to you. I promise you. I must go to her now, because I cannot live without her. But I will come back to you. I always do.'

'Then why must you go?'

'Because . . . she . . . insists. She won't put up with my living with you any longer. Those are her terms.'

'Those are her *terms*! My God, Holger, you allow her to set terms? It is for me to set terms. I am your *wife*.'

Holger would not meet her eye.

'She . . . she says you are like a shadow that follows her, that she cannot live in the shadow of another woman.'

'I am the one who has lived with the shadow.' Emmy waved her knife in the air again. 'I have lived for months with a shadow marriage going along side by side with our marriage. *I* am the one to complain of shadows.'

'She insists that I free myself of you,' Holger said with despair in his voice.

'You cannot free yourself of me,' Emmy said. 'We are married.' She said it with more conviction than she felt. Their marriage was based on real esteem, but it had always felt temporary, an edifice that was at once sturdy in itself but ever in danger of crumbling at any moment, like a well-built house in an earthquake zone.

'I know, I know; I will send you money, of course, for yourself, the children. I don't mean to cut you off.'

'Why, thank you!' Her outrage shrieked through her sarcastic reply.

'Emmy, don't! Please, don't make this so hard for me.'

'I will not take responsibility for how hard it is for you, Holger.' Emmy's voice was edgy now, cold. Her tears had stopped. 'This is your own doing, your own choice. I may have to let you go, but I do not have to make it easy for you.'

'Please understand, Emmy. You've always understood before. She is my muse. She is my source of inspiration. How can I work without my muse?'

He raised his arms dramatically, in a gesture she had seen so often that it had acquired the status of caricature.

'And if I can't work,' he went on emphatically, like an advocate in a courtroom ramming home his point, 'how can I live? How can I keep you and the children?'

They'd had this argument about inspiration before, on countless occasions. She was weary of it. She wasn't going to enter it again.

'So you choose her?' she said, relentlessly.

'Emmy, Emmy, be reasonable.'

'I am being reasonable. If I were unreasonable, I should pick up this saucepan . . . ' Emmy picked it up. 'And I should beat you about the head with it.' She raised the saucepan above her shoulder, as if she were indeed about to bring it down upon his pate.

Holger put up his arms to protect himself.

She lowered the pan. 'But since I am being reasonable, Holger, I will not beat you about the head with a saucepan, since that might very well end with my arrest. Also, it would be unreasonable, and by all means, let us be reasonable.' She gave a gruff laugh, like a dog coughing. 'Now, can I ask you please to leave with the least possible fuss? Take your things, and just go, quietly. And do not go near the children. I cannot bear to have them upset. Just disappear, do you hear me? Go!'

He went to pack, and then he looked in on the children, but only from the doorway, as they played at a complicated board game of their own devising. Their shining heads bent over the table, concentration etched into the way they hunched forward, unspeaking, giving only occasional squawks of surprise or irritation when one of the others made a move.

He closed the door on his family and left for Rita's small apartment.

Copenhagen erupted. Holger always said the Copenhageners were more provincial than villagers. It might be a capital city, but the people had peasant souls. They wouldn't countenance Drachmann living with his singing girl. The singing seemed to be part of the problem, which was absurd, in his view. If she'd been a seamstress or a governess, would that have been more acceptable? It seemed that it would. Certainly it would have been quite different if she'd been a countess. There was something about the fact that she earned her living from her voice that made her somehow unworthy. To him, this meant she was an artist, like himself. In the eyes of the world, or at least of the burghers of Copenhagen, it seemed it made her practically a prostitute.

They were eventually forced out. Nobody would speak to them; they couldn't even get credit at the grocer's. To be judged by a grocer! It was too humiliating. Drachmann would not tolerate such impudence. They'd have to leave this small-minded city, get out of this narrow little country altogether, escape into the broad landmass of Europe, find a place where the locals didn't care who they were or what their legal situation was, where they could be accepted for themselves rather than their marital status.

He felt deeply misunderstood, first by his wife, then by his fellow-citizens. A poet's lot. He ought to be glad of it, he supposed, but he was getting too old for this sort of caper. He'd rather have his own fireside. The irony of this desire did not occur to him.

They settled on Hamburg, since Rita knew people there who might be able to put her in the way of work. She went ahead of him, and once she'd established herself, she sent for him to join her.

It wasn't all that very far away, which was another advantage. Drachmann could come home in an emergency, he assured Emmy, when he went to take his final leave of her. It was several months since he'd left their shared home, but now he'd come to say good-bye altogether to her and the children.

All she had to do was get word to him, he said. He'd come flying to her side to assist her in any way he could.

She stared at him, her eyes brimming with tears. She couldn't speak, though she wanted to say that he was here now, and she needed him now, so why must she wait till he was abroad before sending word to him that he was needed at home? She couldn't say it. The logic was perfect, but he'd have an answer, and she was weary of logic. Arguing with him was like trying to prove theological theorems using mathematical formulae. It made her head ache and it didn't work. So she remained silent.

He thought his heart must stop. He took her in his arms, and she fell against his shoulder.

'Come with me, Emmy,' he whispered.

She stiffened, then moved sharply out of his embrace.

'Are you mad? How can I go with you, up sticks, move the children, to follow you into Germany, so you can be with your mistress? It's ridiculous, Holger. I don't see how you can even suggest it. Besides, you've said, she won't allow me in your life. Those are her *terms*, as you put it.'

'I mean to the station, Emmy, to see me off.'

Emmy laughed a sharp, mirthless laugh. She despised herself for a pathetic creature, grasping at straws, thinking even for a second that he wanted her with him. He hadn't been inviting her back into his life. He'd only wanted a moment of drama on the platform.

'I can see you off from here,' she said. 'There's the door. Open it, and leave. Goodbye.'

He opened his arms to her again, but she refused the embrace. She couldn't bear to stand so close to him, encircled by his arms, knowing that within hours another woman would take her place, rest her head on his shoulder, while Emmy was left with longing in her heart and a cold place beside her in her bed.

'Please, Emmy. Don't make me go without your blessing.'

She stood her ground.

'You ask too much, Holger! You are my husband. You are the father of my children, including my dear, dead son. And you can leave us all, and still protest that you love us.'

'I do, Emmy. I do.'

'But you choose to go.'

'I have no choice.'

'No, Holger. It is I who have no choice. I thought I had. It wore me down, you know, always choosing you, in spite of everything but, now, you have chosen, and you have not chosen me. I cannot bear it, Holger. I have not the strength. I grow too old.'

'Come to the station with me, Emmy. The carriage is ready.' Drachmann opened the door, and sure enough, a large cabriolet, piled with luggage, stood waiting. The horses stepped delicately at the sound of the door.

Emmy allowed herself to be led out onto the pavement. She looked around her, in a daze. Everywhere horses, carriages, people, movement, life being lived. It occurred to her that she might rush into the street and throw herself under a horse, and end it all, her body crushed by the wheels of a coach as her soul had been crushed by Holger's betrayal. But she couldn't do it. She felt as if she were made of stone, dead already. She turned to go back into the safety of the house.

Gerda, their eldest daughter, Polly's little girl, came running out of the house with a cloak in her arms. She threw the cloak over Emmy's shoulders. 'Go with him, Mama,' she whispered. 'Do as he asks.'

'I can't,' Emmy said.

'You are making a memory, Mama. You won't be able to forget this day, so you may as well remember it as well as can be. Shall I come with you?'

Emmy nodded.

Gerda held her hand all the way to the station and Emmy squeezed the child's hand so hard that she had a row of little quarter-moon marks on her hands for hours afterwards, where her mother's nails had bitten into the flesh of her palm.

At the station, Gerda nudged her mother forward to embrace her father one last time before he climbed up into the train. The train puffed and squealed and snorted its filthy way out of the station, and Gerda braced her body against Emmy's to prevent her mother from falling under the train. Then she gathered her mother, who suddenly seemed little and fragile, in her strong young arms, and, still with both arms about her, walked her out of the station and up the long, wide street, past the winking lights and the tinny music of the pleasure gardens, to where the other children gathered at the window, waiting for them, their sleek heads all clustered around the window frame, their large round eyes wide with anxiety.

Chapter 25

One day, in Marie's second or third summer in Skagen, Anna came wobbling out to Marie's house – by now they had built their own, but Martha still did not come to the old coastguard cottage she had considered 'hers' before Marie Krøyer usurped it that first summer – on a new-fangled thing called a bicycle, to bring her news of Holger's pending arrival.

'It is an instrument of the devil,' Anna assured Marie, as she came to an uncertain halt outside her friend's gate. 'If God had intended people to ride, he would have given us wheels instead of feet. And to put two wheels one behind the other, when any cartwright could tell you that is an inherently unstable configuration, is to fly in the face of science as well as God.'

'If you are so opposed to it, why do you use it?' asked Marie, bewildered.

'Opposed, fiddlesticks,' shrieked Anna. 'I am merely quoting the butcher, the grocer and the cobbler, all of whom I met in the village this morning. And the parson. He furnished the information about the inherently whatsit. You'll have to try it Marie, it's like sailing, only not so cold!'

Marie viewed the velocipede doubtfully.

'But you'll be too busy sitting for Søren,' said Anna, 'eternally sitting for Søren. You won't have time to learn.'

She didn't mean it critically. Anna had not a critical bone in her body, but it stung all the same.

'I can't help it that Søren likes to paint me. And I am his wife. Do you think I should let him run off like Holger and find alternative models, so that I can learn to *cycle*?'

'Holger doesn't use models.'

'You know what I mean.'

'But who would paint just anybody when they could paint you, Marie?'

'I sometimes think that you suspect that it is why he married me, to secure me as a model.'

'Marie, why are you always looking for reasons that Søren married you?' asked Anna, suddenly serious. 'I keep telling you, you are responsible for your own unhappiness if you insist on thinking like that.'

'In the first place, Anna Ancher, I am not unhappy, just thoughtful. And in the second place, I am not looking for reasons for Søren to have married me; I am looking for reasons *you* think Søren married me.'

'I am glad to hear you are not unhappy, Marie, though you do a good imitation of it, I must say. But I assure you that I never speculate why Søren married you. Why should I? I see the most beautiful woman in the country and I see the best painter in the country, and I think, as anyone would, *marriage made in heaven*. And I also know that you love each other, and that you are as sweet-natured and kind-hearted as you are beautiful, so why on earth should I ever even wonder why your husband married you? It is you who mull over that question incessantly, my dear. Something is bothering you, and it has been bothering you ever since you came back from Italy, and I think you are going to fester with worry and unhappiness and inability to paint unless you face up to whatever it is.'

Marie's face crumpled and a sound that might have been a sob escaped her, as she stood there in front of the house, by Anna's new bicycle.

'Come inside,' said Anna, taking her arm, as if she were the host and Marie the guest.

'Chamomile tea,' said Anna, when they were ensconced in

Marie's sunny sitting room. 'I shall only be a moment, and you, my dear, will compose yourself while I am making it, and then you are going to disburden yourself to your very best friend on earth, after which, we shall consider the situation. All right?'

Marie sat kneading a handkerchief and staring out of the window. She neither spoke nor nodded.

Anna came back quickly with the herbal infusion and gave Marie a cup, which she drank obediently.

'Now, Marie, out with it. Whatever it is, it is eating you up, and I do not want you to be devoured from the inside out.'

'One evening in Paris,' Marie began, 'shortly after we became engaged, we went to the opera. I'd never been to an opera. I was open-mouthed with the grandeur of it all.'

'Hate opera,' muttered Anna. 'Fat women screeching and fellows leaping about with swords. Can't see the point.'

'I was talking to someone in the foyer, at the interval. I'd lost contact with Søren for a moment. When I looked for him, he was being approached by a creature in a violet gown with a parasol to match.'

If Marie heard Anna's sharp intake of breath, she gave no indication, but went on with her story. 'She was dressed like everyone else, no more gaudy than the rest, though perhaps that shade of mauve was a little loud. She didn't wear too much rouge; she might have been asking where she could buy a programme, but I knew instantly what she was.'

'Marie!'

'Søren turned his shoulder to her, but she walked around him and faced him again, saying something to him, pleading with him. Poor creature, I thought. She must be desperate, to approach a gentleman like that, in a public place. Perhaps she had a child to feed. So I went quickly over to Søren and I whispered to him that he should give her some money. He was shocked at the idea.

'I assumed, Anna, I just took it for granted, that he was horrified at the thought of speaking to a member of that vile profession. I thought he was afraid of being contaminated by her filthy trade.'

Anna made a sound like air being expelled under pressure from her nose.

'I felt so sorry for her, Anna, to see her being publicly shunned like that, so when Søren turned to go back into the auditorium, I ran after the girl.'

'Marie, you never . . . I can't believe it!'

'Actually, when I reached her, under a streetlamp, I saw that she was no girl, and that she was, after all, wearing rather a lot of rouge, but cleverly applied, you know. I suppose they learn to do that. So anyway, I pressed a coin into her hand. Afterwards – oh, Anna, you will see the funny side – I realised it was a krone. Not of much use to a Parisian streetwalker.'

Anna allowed herself a low chuckle, and Marie cracked a small smile herself.

'Anyway – this bit is frightful. The woman laughed, and her mouth opened onto a forest of brown teeth. I was horror-struck. I fled back to the theatre, and I never mentioned a thing about it to Søren.'

Anna waited to see if Marie had finished. She was staring into space.

'So, Marie?'

'Well, at the time, I didn't allow myself to think it, but now I realise, she wasn't just, you know, soliciting – isn't that what they call it? – in that theatre foyer. She *knew* Søren. She was certainly looking for money, but it was because she felt he owed her something. When I look back on the way she spoke to him, of course it was the way a woman speaks to a man who has let her down in some way. That was why he was so agitated.'

'How can you know that, Marie?'

'That is just by way of prologue, Anna; there is more.'

'More? My Lord. Go on.'

'Not about her, about Søren. Well, then. When I was so ill in Italy, we got the doctor, of course. Søren was terribly kind. He held the glass for me to drink from at night, because if I held it myself, I bit into it and cut my lips. He sponged me down. He changed my sheets and clothes, brought me warm milk to drink. He counted out the pills the doctor left for me. He sat for hours by my bedside and held my hand and talked to me, to cheer me up. He sang to me; I didn't even know at that stage that he could sing! If I hadn't been so sick, it would have been delightful, like being courted all over again.

'But then, one day the doctor came and he and Søren had a long talk. I could hear them from the next room. The doctor raised his voice, and the last words he said before he left the house were, "If you do not tell her, my good man, I will do so myself."'

'What did he mean by that?'

'I'm coming to that. Søren came into my room and told me the doctor said it was typhoid fever that I had, but that he had another health concern also, and he felt I ought to know that I might have been exposed to a certain kind of disease.'

Anna's hand flew to her mouth.

'I'd never even heard of it, Anna! I couldn't believe such a thing existed, and that a man could catch it from . . . a person such as that woman in violet in the theatre foyer, and bring it home to his wife.'

'Oh, Marie, Marie, Marie!' Anna was holding Marie in her arms now, and she rocked her gently.

'I haven't got it, Anna. The doctor checked me over thoroughly and said he saw no reason to believe . . .'

'But you worry about catching it?'

'No. I mean, I did, for a long time, but now, no. That's not it.

What I really worry about, Anna, is whether I can safely have a child. And that is what is eating me up on the inside, as you put it. The fear of that.'

'Poor Marie,' Anna whispered. 'Poor, poor Marie.'

'So what do you think I should do?' Marie asked after a few moments.

Anna shook her head and thought for a while. Then she said, 'I suppose, Marie, the best you can do is to inform yourself. I know, it's distasteful, but you have to find out all you can about this disease. You can't make a decision until you are armed with the facts.'

Marie concurred. It wasn't much of a plan, but it was something, and it gave her something to concentrate on.

Marie took researching syphilis seriously. She was well over the initial shock and disgust by now – though she thought ruefully of Rex with his honourable tuberculosis – and she had decided on a rational approach. To Søren's silent dismay, she sent to Oslo and London for the latest medical textbooks on the subject and studied them avidly, taking notes and looking up unfamiliar terms in a medical dictionary she had bought for the purpose. She had a careless habit of leaving these dread tomes lying around where anyone might see them; he had to run around in the evenings, after she had gone to bed, hiding them in drawers.

Armed with science, Marie prescribed a precautionary course of treatment for her husband before they embarked on parenthood.

'But I am clean, Marie,' he said.

She thought of the purple-gowned woman with the brown teeth beneath the steps of the opera in Paris and shuddered.

'You don't think I would have married you if there was the least danger . . . '

She raised an eloquent eyebrow.

'I promise you,' he said, drawing his hand wearily over his forehead, 'I swear to you, I haven't had a symptom for years. I have been treated by the best doctors in Europe. I spent a whole summer in the Alps. I've had mercury till I thought it would seep out of my pores and trickle down in fat, weighty tears from my eyes. Nineteen pills a day I ate for weeks. And powders too. I've had baths and beatings, purgings and flushings, leeches, even, revolting things. I've drunk goat's milk fresh from the udder, I've eaten herbs and potages, I've drunk vile tea made of seaweed. I even visited an old woman in the Black Forest, Marie, who touched me all over with a charm – a relic, some mediaeval saint. I have been fumigated, salivated . . . I swear to you, there is not a vestige of that damned disease in as much as my little toe, in the smallest vein, in a hair of my head. I am cleansed.'

She listened patiently to his litany, right to the biblical proclamation with which it closed. She'd heard it dozens of times before. 'All the same,' she said, when he finished his little speech, 'we have to be really sure.'

Chapter 26

Whatever chance Marie had of breaking into Skagen society, Rita was never going to be accepted by the Skagen crowd. They were loyal to Emmy. Emmy was good fun, she had adorable children, she was pretty and witty, she gave great parties, she read interesting books, she had good conversation, she played and sang, she was writing a novel, she was game for anything. Everyone loved Emmy. Except Holger, apparently.

He claimed otherwise. He said he would always love Emmy, in spite of everything.

This didn't go down well. He made it sound as if it was her fault, people said, with his 'in spite of everything'. He didn't say even this much, though, when Rita was within earshot. She wouldn't hear of it. She wouldn't have Emmy's name mentioned in front of her. You'd think she was the wronged wife, people said, and Emmy the predatory mistress, instead of the other way around.

Drachmann couldn't believe it, the way they gave him the cold shoulder. He was an artist, after all, an artist among artists. Surely they couldn't have the same petty attitudes as the narrow-minded Copenhageners? But it seemed they had. Without Emmy, and especially with Emmy's rival, he was not welcome. They were not as bohemian as they pretended, the Skagen artists, when it came down to it. He was the only free spirit among them, it seemed. They kept reasonable hours these days; they had curtains on their windows; no doubt they went to church, the wives at least; they ran up accounts with the local merchants. They sold their paintings to the highest bidders. He'd seen Martha Johansen at work in that respect. He'd seen the account books she kept, the way she set one buyer up against another, organised auctions to keep the prices up. They had become merchants, dealers in their own productions. Ancher did it too, churning out painting after fisherman painting to meet orders from the art-dealers of Copenhagen. They'd become trapped by their own popularity, the lot of them. They had left behind the lofty ideas of art as the communication of the gods and artists as the messengers of the heavens, and had developed the souls of shopkeepers.

The Krøyers were the only exception, even if they had at-home times. Krøyer was a man of the world: he didn't seem to mind about Rita, though he had always been very fond of Emmy. And Marie had never really known Emmy, so there was no residue of loyalty there to cloud her vision. She had no objection to inviting Rita, though when she found out that Rita was a sobriquet, she insisted on calling her Amanda, a name Drachmann couldn't stand.

'The least you could do for a person was call her by her name,' Marie said. Rita was supposed to sound more becoming, but to Marie's ears it made her sound like someone's aunt. Amanda was a pretty name, and it had to do with love. What was wrong with that? But it seemed that Holger thought it 'showy' – an objection Marie found amusing, in view of the way Rita dressed (rather more frills and flounces than were proper), and the way Rita talked (not what you would call an educated voice) and the way Rita behaved (poured tea into her saucer and made conversation with the servants in front of guests). None of these solecisms offended Marie, but, at the same time, she couldn't see that a girl like this needed to be protected from the supposed frivolity of a name like Amanda.

The curious thing was the open view of marriage Marie took. Drachmann found that surprising.

'I've always thought the marriage-bond is overrated, Mr

Drachmann,' she'd said to him one day. 'I know you have been married several times yourself, and now, of course . . . ' She allowed her sentence to trail coyly off.

'Indeed?' said Drachmann, looking at Krøyer, to see how he took it. Krøyer did not catch his eye. He seemed to be looking for the sugar.

'Yes,' Marie persisted. 'Dr Brandes' idea is that marriage is essentially a marketplace.'

'Dear, dear,' said Drachmann, uncomfortably. 'I don't know that it's as – ahem – as crude as that, my dear Mrs – Marie.'

'No? You don't think women sell themselves into marriage? That they give themselves over to their husbands in return for a home and a comfortable standard of living and a certain social status, Mr Drachmann? That, indeed, it is a respectable form of prostitution?'

Drachmann might well have taken this position himself in a beer-hall in Copenhagen, but he couldn't countenance this kind of talk from a young married woman. He owed it to her husband to encourage a more appropriate line of thinking.

'No!' said Drachmann. 'I believe it is something more noble than that, Mrs Krøyer.'

'I see. How is it noble, Mr Drachmann?'

'Well, you know, there is love, Mrs Krøyer, Marie. We do have to think about the love factor.'

'Ah yes, the love factor, Mr Drachmann. So, when two people love each other, marriage is the natural progression, so to speak? The right thing.'

'Assuming they are both free to marry, Marie, yes, I do think that is the ideal. Marriage . . . well, ideally, marriage between two people who love each other, made in heaven, don't you know – it's a very beautiful thing, Marie.'

'Beautiful. Yes, I do see your point, Mr . . . Holger? As I say, I see your point, Holger. But the natural corollary of that . . . is corollary the right word, Søren? You know, when one thing follows from another?'

'Yes,' said Krøyer, polishing his spectacles. 'Yes, yes.'

'The natural corollary, Holger, is that when . . . if . . . love fades, dies, then the bond is dissolved, wouldn't you agree? And the two parties involved should be happy to loose each other and go their separate ways. After all, if they loved each other, they should want each other's happiness, is that not true?'

'Well,' said Drachmann, 'of course that is true, in principle. I suppose the difficulty arises when the two people in question can't agree about when . . . if . . . the bond has been dissolved. That's the problem, you see.'

'Yes, indeed, I see exactly your point,' said Marie, taking a delicate sip from her cup and then setting it down with great precision upon its saucer.

Drachmann knew perfectly well how much Marie was enjoying this, but he took the teasing in good part, because he was grateful to her for the way she made Rita welcome. Perhaps, indeed, there was a kind of connection between this theory of hers and her kindly reception of Rita. In any case, she was the only one who seemed to have no interest in whether or not Drachmann and his consort were married, divorced or living in sin, though she did visibly wince – Drachmann saw it – when she first heard Rita speak. It wasn't snobbery, though. She really couldn't care less that Rita's accent betrayed lowly origins ('earthy', Drachmann called it); it was just that she found the woman's voice grating on her ears.

The main reason that Marie accepted Rita so easily was that she took her own social code so completely for granted that it never occurred to her to expect that Rita might trample all over it, in spite of the evidence of her own eyes. It simply didn't cross her mind to hold her breath – as everyone else seemed to do – in case

Rita might put her knife in her mouth. (She never did. It wasn't a case of etiquette, but she wouldn't dream of endangering her pretty teeth.)

Still, Marie's tolerance was hardly enough upon which to construct a whole summer, and in view of the general opposition to his mistress, Drachmann felt forced to leave Skagen early in the season, taking Rita with him. The whole trip had not been a success, and he never brought her back. They heard later that she had taken up with a German sausage-maker and the next time Holger came to Skagen, he came alone.

Chapter 27

O ne summer's day, the Schillings came. There was a train all the way to Skagen now, no need to travel the final miles by post wagon, and when Mr and Mrs Schilling stepped down from the train, there was a reception party on the platform, singing and cheering. It was their silver wedding.

The Schillings laughed with pleasure. They kissed Anna and hugged Marie.

'You are too thin, my dear,' said Mrs Schilling to Marie. 'It cannot be good for your health.' She took Marie's hands in hers and noticed how easily the wedding ring slid over her knuckle.

Marie had developed the habit of anchoring it with her thumb, and she did it now, unconsciously.

'There's cake today,' she said, as if she was looking forward to tucking in.

Michael Ancher would not stop tooting on his hunting horn, as they escorted the guests to the fragrant 'wedding coach' that was to take them from the station to the Krøyers' house. Søren had covered it in petals and flower heads. He'd had to send to Port Frederick to the florist's, and he had got the driver to plait flowers and silver ribbons through the horses' manes.

He'd gathered flowers from all his friends' gardens too, and made an archway over his own garden gate, and twined it round with blooming roses and honeysuckle and every bright and scented flower he could find to make a triumphal arch. People came from all over the village to see it, and when they found it was so pretty they went back to their own gardens and returned with armfuls of flowers to add to it. It was overflowing with blooms by the time the guests of honour arrived, with Michael still tooting on the horn.

Helga Ancher was in her best summer dress, and she carried a little basket of rose petals and had a toy drum on a string around her neck. She alternated between tattooing on the drum and flinging petals about. She was to be Mrs Schilling's special helper, and her mother said she was to follow her around and make sure she was comfortable at all times. Fetch her drinks, carry her shawl, find her spectacles, whatever was required.

Mrs Schilling cast about looking for little tasks.

'I tell you what, Helga,' she whispered, bending conspiratorially to Helga's ear. 'The very best thing you could do would be to hide that wretched hunting horn of your father's. It is giving me a headache, but I wouldn't tell him so for the world. If we could arrange for him to lose it . . . that would be much the best solution. Don't you agree? Maybe you could put it away somewhere with your drumstick?'

What a lark! And they couldn't possibly complain about a prank a grown-up lady had put her up to. 'Leave it to me,' Helga said. She took the drum from around her neck to free up her movements and shot off on her errand.

After a decent interval – this was how Mr Schilling described a quick wash and a short rest – the special floral carriage made its triumphal progress to the beach, where there was a feast, with oysters and champagne and a precariously tiered cake.

Søren explained that he had wanted twenty-five tiers of cake, one for every year.

'But Søren,' cried Mrs Schilling, 'it couldn't be stable.'

'That's what Old Erik the baker said,' Søren replied. 'He said it would topple over like the Tower of Babel. I told him he might be able to emulate the Leaning Tower of Pisa instead, but that made him very cross.'

People tittered, not sure why, except that they felt it was

required of them. When Krøyer made a speech, people felt the urge to react.

Only Mr Schilling was interested in Erik's problem. 'Why was that?'

'He'd never heard of that tower,' explained Søren with a guffaw, as if it was the funniest thing in the world that a Danish village baker should not have heard of a tower in an ecclesiastical compound in a city hundreds of miles away, in another country, where they spoke another language, worshipped another god, for all he knew. Everyone laughed with him. 'And now he is going to have to read the whole Bible over again to look for it.'

There were five compromise tiers on the cake, and it did look rather like the tower at Pisa, except that it was straight, and sprinkled with rose petals. Everyone said it was all just like old times, which Marie took to mean, like it had been before she had come to Skagen and spoiled everything. Søren said she was just being gloomy; nobody thought anything of the kind.

In the evening, after the feasting was done and most of the guests had left, Marie took a walk with Anna along the water's edge in the long evening light. The sea was blue and silver and the sand was silver and blue. The strolling women in their best party frocks inclined their heads to one another in a gesture of tenderness that excluded the world. Their faces were hidden, but their intimacy was written in the flowing line of their bodies. Mystery hung, like the evening star, in the light, silvery air.

Søren sat with Michael on the beach, amidst the debris of the feast, and watched the slow progress of the two women away from them, still conversing, into the blue.

Søren held his breath. The evening stood still. This was a moment out of time. He would never see anything so magical again. He couldn't let it go. He must recreate it for ever.

He turned his head and saw that Michael was also following the wives with dreamy eyes.

'Let's test that theory of mine, Michael,' he said.

'What?' Michael turned to look at Søren.

'Let's both paint it, and see the differences.'

Michael smiled lazily. 'I have no paints, no canvas.'

'But I have this,' said Søren, and he stood quickly to his camera, which was still set up. They had used it earlier to take a silver wedding portrait of the guests of honour.

Marie and Anna would be out of sight soon. He had to work quickly, but he was used to the machine, and within seconds he had done it. The moment was retrieved. It would be his gift to posterity. It would be the most beautiful painting in the world. This was the definitive image. It was Japanese in its purity. His whole career had been a preparation for this picture. It was for this he had met Marie.

He felt filled right up with satisfaction. His toes, his fingertips, his very lips and earlobes felt heavy with the sensuous weight of the moment.

'Tomorrow,' said Søren to Michael, 'we'll start to paint. We will have to get them to pose again, at the same time of evening, so we can get the light right, but we have it now, the shape of it. I mean, the camera has. It will be wonderful. You'll see.'

'Tomorrow,' said Michael, raising his glass.

A shrill note pierced the air, and the two artists looked around, the moment shattered. Mrs Schilling stood on the dunes, with Michael's hunting horn to her lips.

The wandering wives looked back also and waved and started to retrace their steps.

'Supper's ready,' Mrs Schilling announced, and tooted again. Helga stood beside her and rapped on her tin drum.

'I thought I'd lost it!' said Michael, standing up. He meant the horn.

'Supper!' said Marie. 'But we've only just had lunch.'

'We made it!' called Helga, scattering the last handfuls of her rose petals over the bugler on the dunes. 'Mrs Schilling and I. It is cold ham and meringues and slices of the Pisa cake. Hurry up, everyone.'

Chapter 28

O ne morning, when Søren was away in Copenhagen meeting his art dealer, Marie got up early to take advantage of the light. In spite of all Anna's encouragement, she had never gone back to conventional painting, but she had developed a whole new art form, she claimed, painting directly onto walls and doors and floors, even curtains and soft furnishings. She'd decorated the Skagen bathroom with fish and fishing nets and mermaids and ships and waves and spray; the kitchen and dining room with cornucopias of fruits and vegetables; and the sitting room with animals and flowers and trees. The best part about this kind of art, she said, was that she never had to think how much better Søren might do it, because, of course, Søren would never do it.

She had made a set of stencils for a floral frieze she planned for the guest bedroom, and she wanted to experiment with colours without anyone coming in and fussing and offering opinions.

She rumbled her fingers about unexpectantly in the bread crock, but there was no bread. She'd always found breakfast a nauseous meal, and when there was no one to cluck about it, she could perfectly well do without. She opened the damper on the range and boiled the kettle for a cup of hot water before she started in to work.

Lunchtime came and went. She was totally engrossed in her floral design, and never gave a thought to food, but worked through until dusk made her eyes ache and she thought she should stop and have supper. She went into the kitchen and cast about half-heartedly for something to eat. Bread had not appeared miraculously during the day. There were eggs. Her stomach heaved.

Cheese. No. A piece of cold beef. Not very appetising. In the end, she just made herself a cup of chamomile tea and put a spoon of honey in it – someone had told her once that honey was a marvellous food – and had an early night.

The following day she didn't even consider breakfast. Her head ached, but she worked all day on the design. It was working so beautifully, she thought she might extend it right down the walls and make it look like an enchanted garden in here. She forced herself to stop for a cup of tea at midday. By evening, she was lightheaded, but she put it down to the excitement of her work. Climbing down from the stepladder, brush in hand, she suddenly saw stars shooting before her eyes and remembered she hadn't eaten for two whole days. Søren would be cross. She was supposed to observe a proper regimen of meals.

She checked the time. Too late for the bakery. It would be long closed. She searched the unpromising pantry again, and this time she found some Madeira cake left over from a tea party she'd given the previous week. She forced herself to eat it, but it was dry and ticklish going down and it came right back up.

She dragged herself to bed, hardly stopping to wipe away the mucus that hung in crumby streaks from her nose and mouth, and slept for twenty-four hours. Søren found her sprawled half-dressed and unconscious. He had to call the doctor to help him waken her.

To Søren's relief, the doctor did not seem too alarmed. He twitted her about overworking and took her temperature and her pulse and kneaded her stomach. He looked in her eyes and shook and nodded his head in baffling sequence.

'How have you been tolerating food lately?' he asked.

Tolerating food. She liked the way this man understood that food was something to be tolerated. She smiled wanly and said, 'Not too well.'

He nodded, as if this was just an interesting fact and not a moral issue, an attitude she found refreshing.

'And your energy? Do you tire easily?'

He seemed to be feeling the glands in her neck, which, as far as she knew, were perfectly all right.

She considered the question. She could hardly remember a time when she did not tire easily, but did she tire more easily than usual lately?

'I am permanently exhausted,' she answered, meaning to explain the difficulty of the question, but it came out rather melodramatically.

'Well?' said Søren, hovering in the doorway.

'Hmm,' said the doctor, steepling his fingers under his considerable chin. 'Hmm.'

'Well?' asked Søren again. 'What's the problem? She is not a well woman, doctor. She hardly eats, you know. And she gets headaches. She never fully recovered from that bout of typhoid fever, that's my opinion.'

'No,' said the doctor. 'It's not that. No.'

'Well, what then?' snapped Søren. 'Spit it out, man, for God's sake.'

'I'd say she's nearly three months pregnant,' said the doctor.

Søren leaped up and began prancing about the room. In delight. Or terror.

Marie burst into tears. It was the shock, she kept saying, that was all. She was all right really.

The doctor clucked soothingly. He was cultivating his bedside manner. It was said to be important. He was young.

'Had this possibility really not occurred to you, Mrs Krøyer?' he asked. Women fascinated him.

'No,' she said, snuffling into a clean antiseptic-smelling handkerchief he had produced from his leather bag. She was not good at noticing how her body was behaving, she explained. Mostly, it behaved badly, and she had long ago decided that the best course was to ignore it.

She still had no clue as to whether Søren was thrilled or alarmed. They had given up discussing the subject of children after Søren had taken that last cure in Switzerland and nothing had happened.

The doctor stood up and went to congratulate Søren. To Marie's astonishment, Søren flung his arms about the young man. It was good news, then. She closed her eyes, relieved.

The doctor left a list of instructions with Søren. He hardly listened. He couldn't. But even with her eyes closed, Marie noted most of it. It included a lot of admonishments about eating. Meat seemed to be called for. Not a substance she regarded with any relish.

Søren went on prancing about, running in and out all afternoon with new pronouncements, ideas for names, calculations of expenses, menus for Marie's meals. He declared that the child had been conceived on the night of the silver wedding celebrations, after Marie took that walk by the sea with Anna in the blue summer light that had inspired the beach painting.

'What makes you think that, Søren?' Marie asked, but he had clearly decided to believe it, whether or not it was true.

Instead of answering, he said, 'He's going to be an artist, Marie. He must be, after that start in life.'

'He is going to be born,' was all that Marie was prepared to concede, and that was an alarming enough prospect for the time being. 'Or she,' she added.

Childbirth was much, much worse than Marie could possibly have imagined. It went on all day and all night. During the day, she was able to move about, do small tasks. This isn't too bad, she told herself, though she cried out when the pains came. But as night fell and they took her to bed, everything got suddenly much worse. She passed out briefly on several occasions, but nature wouldn't allow her that respite for long, and she came back to consciousness almost immediately.

Surely one small being squirming to free itself from its warm cave could not possibly create this amount of agony. She felt as if a whole colony of evil engineers were constructing cathedrals, Gothic ones, with very high and pointed steeples, in her abdomen. She was sure her body must be distorted completely by the merciless activities of the building squad within, who stomped around viciously in oversized hobnailed boots, kicking the sides of her abdomen in random rage. Towards dawn, when she thought she must die of pain, the cathedrals all suddenly collapsed into a huge and storm-propelled avalanche and she was in the avalanche and the avalanche was in her and it all came roaring down the mountainside, roaring and tumbling and laying waste everything in its path, steeples and scaffolding and engineers and everything, and burst relentlessly out and she was ripped apart by it and screaming, screaming, and someone was hanging on to her legs, as if forcing them to break apart at the groin and she was like a roasted fowl being set out to be carved, prodded by the carver's fork and forced to crack and yield.

'It's a girl,' someone said.

She had no idea what they were talking about. She pulled her legs together, to try to hold herself in, to prevent everything from spilling out of the gaping hole she knew her body had become. She drew her knees up protectively under her and closed her eyes.

'It's a girl,' said the voice again, and this time, she registered what that meant, but she was too exhausted to open her eyes. She moaned and pushed away whatever hand was trying to attend to her.

Then came Søren's voice. 'A girl?' she heard him say. The words seemed to swim towards her, but it was his voice all right.

She waited for the next comment. None came.

A girl, she thought. Poor thing. And then she slept.

Chapter 29

Vibeke was the prettiest child, blonde and solemn-eyed with a cornflower stare, like a Nordic princess, and everyone adored her. Her grandmother came frequently from Germany, to help with her upbringing, and Vibeke in turn went often to Augsburg to be with her grandparents, while Marie and Søren travelled or took long rest cures in sanitoria and nursing homes of various kinds, in various countries, Marie trying to learn to eat and Søren to draw clear distinctions between fantasy and reality and to keep his increasingly alarming thoughts untangled.

As soon as they felt well enough, they would travel. They roamed all over Europe, visiting galleries in the great cities, looking at Goya and Velázquez, Monet and Manet, Rembrandt and Vermeer, or viewing exhibitions where Søren's paintings were shown. They were often in Paris, more often still in Italy. Sometimes they did not see Vibeke for months on end.

'She's better off,' Søren would say. 'Her grandmother is a better influence than either of us.'

Marie thought this both true and a terrible admission, and her confusion on this matter silenced her objections to leaving Vibeke so often and for so long. She loved her little daughter, but she could not tolerate her company for extended periods of time. The headaches she had been prey to for most of her adult life came at her with a vengeance when the child was around. She didn't even have to shout or cry; it was enough that she was there, and might shout or cry at any moment.

Vibeke grew up knowing that good little girls who care for their mamas are very, very quiet. Marie had made curtains for her bed, to keep out draughts, and Vibeke would crawl in and close the curtains when she wanted to be alone, to practise being good.

Marie found her huddled in there one day when she and Søren came home from a trip.

'There you are, Vips,' Marie said, peeping between the curtains.

'Hello, Mama,' said Vibeke.

'We're home,' said Marie.

Vibeke nodded.

'Were you a good girl while we were away?' asked Marie, climbing in beside the child.

'I think so,' said Vibeke. 'Were you a good mama?'

'I hope so,' said Marie, stroking the blonde head. 'Is this Mitzi?' she asked, picking up Vibeke's doll.

'She used to be called Mitzi,' said Vibeke, 'but I think that sounds like a cat. I call her The Princess Marina now. I think it suits her better.'

'I bet she speaks German, doesn't she?' Marie had had a German-speaking doll herself, she remembered.

'Yes, because she comes from Augsburg, like Oma and Opa, but I am teaching her Danish. Have you been to It-ly? What do they speak there? It-ish?'

'Italian,' said Marie. 'We brought you some cake from there. With almonds. Do you like almonds?'

'You should know what I like,' Vibeke observed.

'I'm sorry, I forget. Do you?'

'I expect so,' said Vibeke. 'Marina doesn't. Marina is a fussy eater, I am afraid.'

Marie suppressed a laugh. 'Come downstairs and kiss your papa. He is having a sandwich in the kitchen with Oma.'

'Why doesn't he come up here to talk to me?' Vibeke asked.

'Because he is very tired after coming all the way from Italy.

You know how he hates trains. But he asked me specially to say to you that he would like you to come and sit with him and have some of the almond cake.'

Vibeke dutifully laid her doll back against the pillows and went with her mother to find her father.

'How is your head today, Mama?' Vibeke asked, as they went.

'Quite well, darling. Because you are so good and quiet.'

Vibeke nodded. She worked hard at staving off her mother's headaches.

'We leave her alone too much, Søren,' Marie said when Vibeke had gone to bed.

'We never leave her alone!'

'You know what I mean. We do not spend enough time with her. I was thinking, this year, maybe . . . maybe I might stay in Skagen for the winter, with Vibeke.'

'What on earth for?'

'I told you, to spend time with her.'

'But in Skagen? What's wrong with Copenhagen?'

'We have a house here, Søren, a home. That's what she needs.'

'But I can't stay up here, I have things to do, people to meet. And I don't like the cold.'

'You can come for Christmas.'

And so it was arranged. Søren appointed an acquaintance of his, a reliable fellow from the village, Tugend his name was, to watch over the little household and make sure they had funds and attend to whatever practical matters there might be, and a girl from the village was taken on to come three days a week to wash and clean and cook. A local jack-of-all-trades agreed to see to the outdoor chores and keep the stoves stoked.

As soon as Søren left for the city, it seemed, the days started to draw in, and Marie had to send for Jørg to bring in wood for the stoves and fetch supplies from the village. Twice a week Mr

Tugend called 'to cluck over the accounts', Marie said to Vibeke, which made them both giggle, for it was true that Tugend had rather hennish ways. As the winter wore on, Vibeke used to like to watch from the window for his arrival, the yellow light of his lantern winking uncertainly as he came towards their little house through the afternoon gloom.

A much better caller, in Vibeke's view, was Mrs Ancher. Anna called at least once most weeks. She came bouncing along and she pounded on the door to be let in and when they opened up she said 'Brrrr!' Then she banged the door shut and stood up against the inside of it as if to make quite sure it was tightly closed and the cold couldn't come in. She rubbed her hands up and down her arms and said 'Brrrr!' again and she wouldn't take her coat off for ages, until she had got used to being indoors.

The best days were when Helga came with Anna, because then they painted together, Vibeke and Helga, even though Helga was much older. Vibeke's father had shown her how to paint as soon as she was old enough to hold a brush, but Marie didn't much like it when Vibeke painted, because of the mess she made. When Helga came, however, Marie always said they might paint, and she spread out newspapers on the kitchen table and gave them pinafores to wear over their dresses.

'Are you going to be a painter when you grow up, Helga?' Marie asked.

'Uh-huh,' Helga said, matter-of-factly, as if she'd asked her if she liked milk in her coffee. 'Like Mama and Papa.'

'And what about you, Vibeke?' Mrs Ancher asked.

'My mama doesn't paint,' Vibeke said. 'She doesn't like mess.'

'Your mama is a very good painter, Vibeke. It's just she's been a bit busy with other things.'

'Mama?' Vibeke turned a surprised gaze on Marie.

Marie sighed.

'Show her the yellow painting, Marie,' Anna urged. 'The one you did in France.'

Marie wished Anna wouldn't keep on about it. She was quite happy not to paint any more. She enjoyed her 'domestic arts' as she called them.

'If you don't, Marie, I shall have to go and look for it myself.'

Marie stood up without a word and went into a bedroom. She came back with a small square painting, showing a market scene.

'Did you paint all this sunshine, Mama?' Vibeke asked, her voice full of astonishment.

'Yes, she did,' said Anna.

'It's very pretty, isn't it, Helga?'

Helga looked over Vibeke's shoulder. She was not terribly impressed, but she said, 'Very nice.'

Anna laughed.

'If you could do half as well, young lady, you would not be content with "very nice".'

Sometimes Anna told the children stories, 'right out of her head', Helga said to Vibeke. But she didn't just tell, she drew the stories. They all sat around the table together, one girl on each side of Anna, and Marie would sit opposite and pour the coffee for the grown-ups and milk for the girls and offer biscuits round and it was 'very festive', as Helga put it. Anna would start the story, and Helga would say after a few moments, 'What did it look like in that place?' and then her mother would draw the place for the children. She didn't paint it, that would take too long, so it was just a sketch and they had to 'imagine-in' the colours. That meant you had to fill in the colours in your imagination, and you had to describe them to the others using your best words. Vibeke loved this. She would say, 'That mountain is mauve and lilac and brown with all the heather growing on it, and the lake is the deepest turquoise, like a jewel from the crown of an Arabian prince, and the roses growing on that rose bush are yellow, like the silk brocade in the Emperor of China's boudoir.'

'Boudoir!' Marie exclaimed with a laugh.

Then it would be the next person's turn to imagine-in the embroidery on the prince's cloak, for example, or the gleaming harness on the hero's trusty steed or whatever it might be.

On days when Anna and Helga didn't come, they would sometimes have stories anyway, from a big illustrated storybook with Vibeke's favourite stories in it, and they read it by the stove and if they were lucky and it was one of Magda's days, she might bring them some hot chocolate. Those were very happy afternoons.

But most days, nobody called, and sometimes the afternoons were very long and dark and boring.

Then Christmas came, and with it came Søren, striding in at the hall door, with tiny snowflakes whirling round his head. He swooshed Vibeke up in the air. He went through the rooms with long steps, singing. Sometimes he carried a glass of wine around with him, and sipped it as he went. He sang all day long, like a person in an opera, Vibeke said, delighted. Sometimes he even sang things like, 'Vibeke, come and have your supper!' or 'I believe it's going to clear up out there.'

The child laughed and laughed at this. 'It's *silly* to sing such ordinary things, Papa!'

At that, he would translate 'Vibeke, come and have your supper!' into Italian or French, to make it more like an opera. She learned the words, and they sang it together: '*Vieni a mangiare!*'

To Marie's consternation, Søren always left the doors standing wide open all over the house.

'I have spent weeks, Søren, weeks, trying to get Vibeke to close the doors and keep the heat in.'

'Yes, Papa,' said Vibeke severely. 'You're making a dreadful draught!'

'Nonsense!' cried Søren. 'If you leave the doors open, the house will heat up to an even temperature all over, and then there won't be that awful blast of icy air when you open a door. It stands to reason. Just so long as we don't leave the outside doors open, of course. That would never do, Vibeke, would it?'

'No, Papa. That would be silly.'

'Not even I would do that, Marie. I am not quite that mad, am I, my dear?'

Everything seemed to be going along nicely, Vibeke thought. She must be doing very well, because her mother hadn't complained of her head for days. Though that might have been because she was mostly in bed. She told Vibeke she was terribly tired, and Vibeke wondered if she and Papa should go back to Copenhagen for a while and leave Mama in peace.

'That's a terrible idea, Vibeke,' Marie said. 'Surely you wouldn't want to leave me all alone in the cold and dark while you and Papa are having a jolly time in Copenhagen?'

Vibeke hadn't meant that at all. She'd only been thinking of how tired her mother seemed, and she said so.

Marie apologised, and got up out of bed, and they all had a lovely Christmas. Vibeke helped to polish apples to hang on the tree to reflect the soft light of the Christmas candles, and to thread coloured string through tangerines to make bright orange splashes, and they made little wooden figures and a big silver star to go on top of the tree. They had a grand time.

Vibeke and Marie stayed in Skagen right through the winter – what an adventure! they reassured each other frequently – and they survived it pretty well. When summer came, Søren joined them once more, to Vibeke's great delight. Marie was pleased to see him too, and they kissed and kissed when he arrived first. But then she started sleeping badly again, and having to resort to sleeping draughts, which meant that when she awoke, her mouth felt like a forest floor and she was muzzy-headed and cranky.

One evening, after many sleepless nights, she had just drifted blessedly off without the help of a draught, when Søren came bounding into the bedroom, calling her to get up and come out into the garden to listen.

'A nightingale!' he cried. 'Marie, you must hear it, what a glorious sound!'

To his astonishment, Marie yelled at him.

'But my dear . . . ' he said, 'I only wanted us to have a beautiful experience together.'

'Søren,' she said, through clenched teeth, 'the only beautiful experience I am interested in having at the moment is a night's sleep. How can you be so thoughtless!'

'I'm sorry, Marie,' he said, 'but now that you're awake, you may as well come and hear it.'

Grumbling, Marie got up and pulled on a dressing gown and went to the window. She drew the line at actually going out into the garden.

In the morning, she announced she had had enough, she could not live with these headaches and these sleepless nights, she was going to have to go to a rest home for a while to get her strength back.

'What about Vibeke?' Søren asked.

'Can't you look after her, Søren? She so loves being with you.'

'Oh, yes, Papa!' Vibeke pleaded. 'Please say yes! We can look after each other.'

But Søren wouldn't countenance it. 'A gentleman can't look after a little girl, Vibeke. He wouldn't know what to do.'

'I can do for *myself*,' Vibeke said. 'I only need help with my boots. I can even butter my own bread and pour my own milk.'

But he said no, she was to go to stay with a family called Mendel, where she'd been before, when her mother had to be away and her father was busy.

'I don't like it at their house, Papa. It is very dull, and Mr Mendel never sings.'

'Now, Vibeke, don't make trouble. You like Tabitha, don't you?'

Tabitha Mendel was Vibeke's age, but they did not always get along.

'She's all right, but she doesn't like me to come living in her house,' Vibeke explained. 'She likes it better with me not there.'

'You play together, I'm sure, Vips,' said her father.

That was true, sometimes quite good games.

'But she takes my doll,' Vibeke said.

Her father said, 'Dear me,' which was not of much help.

Vibeke felt her lips tremble.

'Don't cry, Vibeke,' said Søren. 'You will only make Mama feel worse.'

So Vibeke didn't cry, but then *she* felt worse.

Just as they were packing, Mr Drachmann called by. He was one of the best friends of the family, and when he heard the story of the nightingale, he said Søren was a tyrant.

Vibeke wasn't sure what that meant, but she thought it didn't sound like a kind thing to say.

'Don't exaggerate, Holger,' said Marie, folding her dresses to make them fit in the trunk. 'Things are difficult enough without you coming along and dramatising it all.'

'My dear Marie,' said Holger, 'I wouldn't *dream* of it. I do apologise. And what about this little princess?'

He chucked Vibeke under the chin.

Vibeke knew that Mr Drachmann was Mama's very best old gentleman, and that she loved him very much, next to Papa and Mrs Ancher.

'I am to go to the Mendels' house,' she said.

'Good, good, good,' he said, which just went to show how much he knew.

'Are you still sad about your lady love?' she asked, because her mother had told her that his lady love had left him, even though Vibeke had seen him only a week ago with a lady with her hair all piled up on top of her head, but maybe she was not his lady love. That made her think of a poem, which was right, because he made up poems. That was his job.

'Quite devastated,' he said.

'I think,' said Vibeke, 'that you are old enough to be married, and not be having lady loves.'

'I am sure you are right, princess,' he said. 'But I am waiting for you to grow up, so I can marry you.'

'You are too old for me!' said Vibeke, alarmed, for he was quite whiskery and wobbly.

'That is exactly what your mama says,' said Mr Drachmann.

'Don't mind him, Vips,' Søren said. 'That is just the way old gentlemen carry on. Marie, are you sure you will need that winter shawl? Surely you will be home before it gets that cold?'

'I don't know what I need, Søren,' wailed Marie. 'I cannot decide. I wish I could stay here with you and Vibeke, but I just . . . can't.'

Marie was in floods of tears, even though Vibeke was there and she usually tried not to cry in front of the child.

'I know, dearest,' said Søren, patting her shoulder soothingly. 'I know, I know.'

The carriage was at the door by now, to fetch Marie away.

'You go with her,' said Holger. 'I'll take this little one up to Anna. She'll look to her, until it's time to go to the . . . Mendelsohns? Mendels. Go on, go on.'

So Vibeke and Mr Drachmann stood at the front door and waved Marie and Søren away. As they had done before, and would do many times again.

Chapter 30

Søren and Marie perched briefly in a rented apartment in Copenhagen between summers in Skagen, periods in rest homes and the trips abroad that they undertook with increasing frenzy. One morning, Søren left this Copenhagen apartment to go shopping for some linen shirts and to have a new head fitted to an ebony cane he was fond of.

While he was out, he bought a house.

'You're going to love it, Marie,' he said when he got home with his packages and his news. It was a fabulous villa in a fashionable street. 'I know you love decorating a home, my dear, painting, choosing fabrics, that sort of thing.' He waved an impatient hand to indicate the infinite variety yet essential unimportance of 'that sort of thing'.

She didn't know what to say. She knew what she wanted to say, but she didn't know what to say all the same.

She'd had a royal time doing up the house in Skagen, he went on. Now he'd bought her a veritable palace to decorate. What did she think of that! He twirled the newly mended cane between his fingers as if it were a magic wand and he the magician.

Perhaps it was the way the sun caught his eyeglasses, but there was a glint about Søren at that moment that chilled Marie's blood.

'Aren't you pleased, Marie?' he asked, suddenly aware of her silence, searching her face for signs of disapproval.

She tried not to seem disapproving – Søren did not appreciate lack of enthusiasm for his schemes – but her mouth was dry and she could not seem to get her tongue to enunciate her thoughts.

'Well?' he persisted, pinning her with his gaze. She felt like a butterfly spread-eagled under a collector's glass.

'Of course, Søren – if you are sure we are not overstretching ourselves. It . . . it sounds lovely. I'm sure it is very fine, if you chose it.'

'Overstretching? Marie, what do you know about it? Have you the least grasp on the kind of money I make, the sort of income we have?'

'No, Søren.' She wished she could say that perhaps she should have.

'You see!' he said triumphantly, flinging his pigskin gloves onto a table that stood between them, as if he had proved a point.

Other people laughed when he did this sort of thing, said it was so eccentric, practically congratulated Marie on having landed herself such a playful fellow. They made his spendthrift escapades into dinner-party conversation. It didn't seem odd to them that he hadn't consulted her. She wondered why that was. Was it really not odd at all? Or was it that there was some character flaw in herself that made it acceptable for him to take important decisions like this, which had a direct impact on her life, without consulting her? Or was it simply that Søren was so larger-than-life a character that anything he did, though it might be odd or even reprehensible in another man, was acceptable simply because it was he who did it?

Even Anna, who could normally be relied on to dispense common sense, seemed to be of an opposite opinion to Marie on this matter. Michael Ancher's indecisiveness was legendary. Anna could never plan anything, not even a trip to Port Frederick, for Michael would dither and vacillate and hum and haw, until eventually she would go without him, and then he would be hurt that he had been left behind. Anna had learned to cope by just not going anywhere any more, unless it was absolutely necessary. There was no point in buying tickets for boats or trains. Michael would pay for them one minute, and demand his money back the next, or he would get up in the morning and put on his boots and be all set for a day out, and then he would suddenly decide it was too cold or too hot or too wet, too far or too pointless, and the expedition would have to be put off. This grieved Anna, who loved to travel. She loved Paris, with its sniffy waiters and its people straight out of Zola. She adored Amsterdam with its crooked little houses and its canals and alleyways and its roofs that looked as if they were about to fall in. She was mad about Munich and Vienna and Rome and Barcelona, with their palaces and gated courtyards and stately buildings and fountains, all so different from their own homely capital. But she forwent it all for the sake of Michael's peace of mind. She didn't think it so very great a sacrifice, when you took everything into account.

'What an adventure!' Anna said to Marie. 'Isn't Søren extraordinary? I do admire a man who will just follow his heart like that, and not eat himself up with worry and indecision.' She was remembering a time when Michael had sold a house they'd owned and then the very next day had changed his mind and had tried to evict the new owners, demanding the deeds back. Mortifying.

'I suppose so,' said Marie, though Søren was perfectly capable of eating himself up with worry on other occasions.

Anna's failure to understand Marie's fears about this unexpected turn of events was nothing more than a minor deficiency of imagination, but it had disastrous consequences, for it made Marie doubt her own sanity.

Not immediately. At first, she doubted his. It was from this event that she dated her beginning to entertain the thought that perhaps Søren was mad. And yet, though it was certainly foolhardy and irresponsible, she thought, and the kind of thing people loosely called 'mad', it was hardly madness of the sort that landed one in a lunatic asylum, was it? He couldn't be mad. He didn't think he was

Napoleon or hear voices. It was just a combination of high spirits and artistic eccentricity – wasn't it? Maddening rather than mad.

She felt herself alone in resisting the idea that Søren's endearing irresponsibility was only boyish high spirits. It was all of a piece, in a way, with throwing lavish champagne parties on the beach at Skagen, and no one had ever objected to that. The difference between throwing extravagant parties and buying a mansion they probably couldn't afford to run was only one of degree, but such a very steep difference of degree as this struck Marie as profound. Yet no one else seemed to think anything of it. They, of course, did not have to live with the consequences.

Marie felt lost, adrift, as if she was the only one who had any grasp on reality. But being all alone in one's view of reality, even if one is in the right, makes one uncertain of one's judgement. It felt like being on the deck of a boat in a storm. She knew, ordinarily, how to place her feet so that she could stand up, but no matter where she put her feet in this situation, she felt she was bound to fall over. The disjuncture between her knowledge of how to behave and the unreliability of the circumstances, the swaying deck under her feet, was sickening.

She felt she wanted to cry, but who ever heard of a woman crying because her husband had bought her a beautiful house?

One old friend of Marie's, with whom she had kept in touch since childhood, did share Marie's view of it. She wrote that she thought they were quite mad. This sounded like the voice of sanity, and Marie was filled with relief to find her own uneasiness mirrored in her friend's opinion. But then, she reflected, Agatha had no money at all. She thought people 'quite mad' if they bought a party frock when they had two perfectly serviceable dresses not ten years old in their wardrobe. So her opinion was of limited value in a case like this, and Marie was no farther on. What could she do only accept the situation and hope for the best?

Søren took her and Vibeke to see the house, flinging doors open, exclaiming about the proportions of the rooms, knocking on the panelling to show how sound it was. The rooms were like halls and the halls were like corridors. The ceilings seemed too high and the fireplaces were always too far away. To go from one room to another was to make a journey requiring some planning and perhaps even a map. They drifted from room to room, Marie and Vibeke, hand in hand, their footsteps sounding sharp and determined, much more sharp and determined than Marie felt, in the crisp, brittle air. The smell of new paint was like a taste, a tart yet sweetish burst on the roof of Marie's mouth, releasing sensations both intoxicating and disturbing.

'It's an investment,' Søren said when Marie wondered about the number of rooms.

'I see,' she said.

'You have to spend to gain,' he elaborated, seeing her puzzlement.

'I see,' she said again, running her finger along a dusty groove in the architrave of a door.

She regarded the scum on the pad of her finger and sighed.

'Plaster dust,' Søren said defensively, as if she were inspecting the house for dirt. 'It's because of the refurbishment, that's all. And there's plenty of space for Vibeke to run around in.'

'Run around?' Marie said vaguely. 'You expect her to run around indoors?'

He didn't answer. He had stalked off into another room and was loudly admiring some feature he found there.

She trailed after him, dragging her daughter with her.

'We can make it a haven, Marie,' he said, taking her hand.

'A haven,' she said, without much conviction. 'Yes . . . '

His idea, he explained, was that they could be truly themselves in this place, and truly separate from the world. This was to be a place apart, a place of peace and tranquillity and beauty, hung with exquisite tapestries, furnished with simple good taste, all light and air and comfort, where they reigned supreme, undisturbed by the busyness of the city and the art world and its demands. Eager young art critics might ring on the doorbell, or old friends might drop by with news or solicitous enquiries, or interested patrons might ask to be invited in to discuss some proposed new project or other, but to all they would turn the same polite, cool, refusing gaze and retreat into the newly painted drawing room or the newly tiled dressing room or the newly plumbed bathroom.

Yes, she agreed, yes, that would be nice.

Things went wrong, however, as soon as they moved in. There were floods, leading to buckling floors and blistering walls and ruined rugs and a smell of mushrooms in the downstairs rooms. It made Marie's headaches worse even to think about it. They sent Vibeke to the Mendels again, but that didn't help as much as Marie had hoped it would.

The strain was starting to show on Søren too. He was painting frantically now just to keep ahead of the bailiffs. This was a new experience for him. For years, he had had more money than he knew how to spend. He took on big commissions now, from important patrons who put demands on him, expected him to come and see them at the drop of a hat, take direction from them – what did they know about pictures that they should direct him? It was enough to drive a man wild. But he needed the cash. And Marie wasn't helping. Always moaning about not being able to sleep. Always sick or threatening to be sick or recovering from being sick. Flitting off to rest homes if he so much as looked askance at her. And she wasn't looking after Vibeke properly either, left her with anyone who would have her, and on the brief occasions she was at home, the poor child darted about like an apologetic shadow, scared to be noticed, afraid of being singled out for attention and sent off again somewhere out of the way.

As the house took shape around them, Søren and Marie

seemed to lose shape within it. She drifted about the rooms, often still in her peignoir at lunchtime, wringing her hands distractedly about her inability to sleep, her headaches, Søren's constant absences and trying presences, her own inability to bear Vibeke's company long enough to bring her home from whatever place of refuge she had put her in for the time being. Every now and then she would rouse herself to do something that looked like normal behaviour, as if acting on the magic principle that dramatising a situation in ritual form could bring the situation about in reality. And so she invited people to dinner, to lunch, to coffee-and-cakes, as if to create out of the illusion of conviviality conviviality's very essence, as in the old days, when they had all gathered under leafy canopies on Skagen's shores and eaten and drunk together. But it wasn't the same. It just wasn't the same.

Chapter 31

Vibeke was not always allowed to stay up late on New Year's Eve, but the eve of the new century was an exception. She had special permission. The dining room of the house in Copenhagen was decorated with paper chains and hundreds of candles and swags of ivy from the garden. There was sorbet between courses, and a string trio to entertain the guests.

As midnight approached Søren went out onto the balcony, 'to see the stars', while Marie was opening champagne to toast the new century. She was always making fresh starts, Marie, and this was a golden opportunity for one of those. She wore a dark blue dress that night. It deepened the blue of her eyes and she seemed to sparkle with a particular radiance.

The bells of all the city's churches suddenly burst into joyous peals, a signal that midnight had broken, and at the same moment, the cork flew from the champagne bottle in Marie's hands with a loud report, much louder than expected, ridiculously loud, so that you could feel it in your ribcage. The guests roared with laughter and crowded around to put their glasses under the foaming bottle and catch the precious golden liquid before it gushed to the floor. 'Happy New Year!' They kissed. They sang. They drank.

Marie was taking the foil off the next bottle when there came a loud report again, breaking harshly through the sound of the bells. It couldn't be a champagne cork this time – the cork of the next bottle was still firmly in place. People stared at each other, puzzled, shocked. Then came a loud bang for the third time. It was no longer possible to avoid the conclusion that someone was shooting. The sound was coming from the balcony.

The curtains were closed. Marie drew them wide with a frantic tweak and flung open the French doors and icy night air rushed in. Søren stood, hunched in silhouette, leaning over the railing, with his hunting rifle to his shoulder, firing off apparently at random into the nearby gardens. It was not clear whether he thought he was shooting vermin, or just welcoming in the new century.

'Søren!' Marie called him. 'You can't shoot like that in the city! Come in and close the window.'

Søren ignored her, and shot again.

'Stop shooting,' she cried, panic in her voice now. 'It's illegal, Søren. You'll wake people up; you might hurt someone. Søren! The police will come! You're not allowed to shoot within the city limits. It's dangerous. You might kill someone.'

'Ha! The police!' Søren roared, turning to face the assembled guests, brandishing the rifle in front of him. 'Let them come! Let them arrest me! It's a free country. I'm in my own house. I can shoot if I want to. It won't hold up in court. No judge will convict me on such a paltry charge. And you!' He waved the gun. 'You're all witnesses, that's what you are! Witnesses, you hear? I am on my own property; you can attest to that, can't you?'

He waved the gun again, pointed it first at one person, then the next, his eyes wild in his head, his mouth foaming. Everyone cowered back from him, with terrified gasps. Some people were screaming.

'Can't you?' he yelled ferociously.

'Yes, Søren,' said one of the men.

Vibeke was there in the middle of it, watching wide-eyed from the shelter of some woman's skirts. The little girl turned to see who spoke, holding a bunch of the fabric of the unknown lady's frock in her terrified fist.

It was her Uncle Villem, her father's brother.

'Come in now, brother,' Uncle Villem said quietly, 'and close that door, you are letting in all the cold air, and look at Vibeke, she's shivering, her teeth are chattering.'

Now that Vibeke's chattering teeth had been mentioned, they rattled madly, echoing loud as a train in her head.

Uncle Villem put his hand out, and Vibeke's papa handed him the gun, without his even having to ask for it, as if Villem had simply reached for a book or a newspaper. He seemed to have lost interest in the rifle.

'Villem,' he said wonderingly, grabbing hold of Uncle Villem's lapel and pulling his face down to meet his own. 'I didn't know you were here. They didn't tell me; they tell me nothing, you know, they try to keep information from me, and then they threaten me with the police, that woman there, she's always talking about the police.' He was pointing a manic finger at Marie, who still held the unopened champagne bottle in her hand.

'That's not "that woman",' Villem said gently, passing the gun behind his back to someone, anyone who would take it from him, put it out of harm's way. 'That's not the woman who calls the police. That's just Marie. Your wife.'

'Marie?' said Søren, turning his head slowly from Villem's stare and looking at Marie.

'Oh, Marie!' he cried then and flung himself into her startled arms. She was forced to wave the unopened champagne bottle in the air until someone took it from her. 'Marie! I had to shoot them to get to you. They were threatening me with the police, but I said no, no, I must protect Marie. And the child. The child. Where is the child? What is his name?'

Something made Vibeke respond. Perhaps she sensed his desperation. She stepped forward and said, 'Here I am, Papa.'

'Papa?' he said, looking down at her. 'And your name. Your name is . . . '

'Vibeke, Papa. It's Vibeke,' she said, looking up at him.

His beard was damp. Perhaps it was perspiration, or perhaps the night was wet, though earlier it had been cold and sharp. In any case, his beard was streaked with wet and the hairs formed themselves into dank clumps. It made him look anxious, Vibeke thought, as if he had just hatched and hadn't worked out yet how the world went.

'Ah yes, Vibeke,' he said, a grin breaking over his face. 'They said you were dead, but I knew you hadn't died. I knew it all along. Though, I had thought you were a boy, you know. I am surprised that your name is Vibeke. You didn't go to America with your mother?'

Uncle Villem took Vibeke's hand and placed it in her father's, which was hot and dry. She kept her hand in his and, following Uncle Villem's unspoken directions, she led him from the room and up the stairs to his bedroom, followed by Marie and Villem.

Søren sat on the edge of the bed, staring. Vibeke knelt down and opened her father's shoelaces and took off his shoes. 'Now, Papa,' she said, as if she were talking to The Princess Marina after she had got herself over-excited, 'you lie down and have a little sleep.'

Søren nodded and heaved his feet up onto the bed and stretched out, fixing his eyes on the ceiling. Vibeke pulled an eider-down over him and then looked up at her mother. Her little face was grey.

People didn't exactly laugh off Søren's New Year's outburst, but they put it down to drink, together with the excitement of the occasion. But drink had never made him peculiar before.

'Little girls don't really understand grown-ups,' Marie said in answer to Vibeke's bewildered questions, as if this were a short-coming of little girls' understanding rather than of grown-ups' be-haviour. Vibeke knew from her tone that there was no point in pursuing the matter, and that her best course of action, if she wanted to keep on her parents' right side and not get sent off to share Tabitha Mendel's nursery again and her nasty nanny who smelled of onion water, was to pretend, as they did, that nothing peculiar had happened after all. She was to pretend that it was perfectly unremarkable that her father had thought she was a boy and that she was dead, and that he had shot the neighbours' potted camellias to bits with a hunting rifle fired from their balcony in the middle of the night, leaving shards of smashed terracotta and great swathes of ruined plants and clumps of congealed earth all over their terrace.

Søren went off to Marie's favourite rest home for a few months, and when he came home, Marie had it all planned. They were to go to Sicily, where it was warmer and there were no guns or camellias. She always prescribed Italy when there was a problem, usually for herself, sometimes for Søren, but never before had it been suggested that Vibeke might be included in this epic curative pilgrimage. Perhaps they were starting to like her just a little. Or perhaps – more likely – there was no one they could get to agree at such short notice to take her in. She was not to be allowed to take The Princess Marina with her (she was too large and cumbersome, apparently, and besides, it would be such a disaster if she were to get lost), but Vibeke was not to mind, because she could write postcards to her, which would be something enjoyable to do on wet days or tiresome stretches of the journey.

Mama talked incessantly about Sicily as they packed. She described lemons and oranges growing on the trees, like little golden lanterns lighting up the dark, glossy leaves. She talked about olive groves, which she made sound like some sort of enchanted forest. She described the light and the sea and the heat of the sun and she told Vibeke that everyone ate a substance called macaroni – which sadly had nothing to do with macaroons.

'You will love it, Vibeke,' she said, her eyes shining.

Vibeke was old enough to have read about people's eyes shining, and to know it didn't really mean that their eyes are shining, just that they have an enthusiastic expression. But when she was enthusiastic about something, Vibeke's mother's eyes had a peeled look, and they really did shine. The whites of her eyes gleamed like the whites of hard-boiled eggs and the blue of her irises was the very blue of irises, deep and intense, but, unlike the flowers, with fathomless black centres; and the surfaces of her eyes seemed to be coated in a glittering liquid, like fairy dew. Vibeke's eyes were blue too, but of a more ordinary shade, edging onto grey, like her father's. Nobody on earth had eyes like Vibeke's mama.

The charms of Italy are lost upon children. All Vibeke saw was crumbling old ochre houses with irregular looking roofs that someone ought to patch up. The orange and lemon trees were as delightful as promised, but the magic olive groves turned out to be rather dull stretches of sandy mountainside, with aged olive trees in serried ranks that looked as if they should be put out of their gnarled misery. There were donkeys everywhere, which sounds charming, but up close they were smelly and mangy-looking and flies buzzed about their rheumy old eyes. Vibeke found the marble floors hard on her feet, mosaic pictures of stories from the Bible meant nothing to her, and she hated the gloomy old churches which always appeared to be inhabited by murmurous bundles of rags who turned out to be widow-women with raisin eyes and hairy chins. There never seemed to be any salt herrings or sugar ginger or the sort of thing she was used to eating, though she developed a taste soon enough for the ubiquitous macaroni.

Everyone seemed to be poor, the children barefoot. Of course, the fisherfolks' children in Skagen ran barefoot in the summer, but Vibeke had never before seen children with feet grimy with the dirt of city streets. The barefoot children seemed brutish to her. She felt silly in the pretty summer smocks in pastel colours that her mother dressed her in, in the face of their hunger and filth. They scowled at her with a resentment she knew they disguised from the adults, in the way children everywhere reserve their scorn for other children. She was helpless to enlist the protection of her parents because, as adults, and thus not the objects of this childish disdain, they neither perceived it nor could be persuaded to believe in it. Not that she even tried. She knew from experience that adults do not appreciate children's complaints about other children, and complaints about the stares of urchins would be treated as hubris.

Vibeke was surprised at how little her parents did in Sicily, having gone to so much trouble to get there. She had assumed the journey must have some sort of goal. They set so much store by these Italian trips, she thought they must do something very absorbing while they were there, something that drew them back again and again. But her mother seemed content to sit in the loggia all morning over breakfast, until her father came back from painting. And then they would lie in their darkened room all afternoon. Vibeke hated those siesta hours, the endless lying in hot rooms in semi-darkness, and so she often opened her shutters to see what was happening outside, and was shocked by how white and blinding the light was. After she'd blinked away the ache, she could see that nothing was going on out on the streets. The piazza was deserted. Even the fountain was still. Perhaps the water would have evaporated if it ran through the hottest hours of the day. Dogs lay panting in the shadows of doorways, but otherwise there was no life. It was eerie, and it was the image of Sicily that remained most vivid in her memory: hot, bright and uneventful. Towards evening, when the pavements cooled and the people appeared out of their houses, Vibeke and her parents would take a short stroll around the streets or along the strand or around the harbour. Then they would have a long dinner at their hotel, or at some other eating house Vibeke's father had found, after which her father might go to a concert or to meet someone he knew in a wine cellar, and her mother usually went to bed.

Vibeke's parents behaved impeccably together. There was never the least altercation, not so much as a raised voice. If you didn't know them, you would probably not have noticed how unhappy they were. Vibeke herself could hardly tell how she knew it, but she sensed, in some way that is perhaps accessible only to children, that they were profoundly distressed in each other's company, though they treated one another with courteous solicitousness. Nor were they being merely polite: they were genuinely considerate of each other. They held each other in the highest regard. It was just that they seemed to have lost the connection they once undoubtedly had, and Marie in particular craved that connectedness. It grieved her that it was lacking in her life. She was like an animal whose young had been removed from her, constantly looking for something, but not sure what it was.

Chapter 32

Because Marie loved Holger and Holger loved Marie, with a fraternal, uncorporeal love, she was uniquely permitted to discuss and even poke fun at his complex and ruinous love affairs. She always said that if Rita/Amanda had left Holger for a minor nobleman or a cellist or a professor of mathematical physics or maybe even a high-class garden designer, he might not have minded so much, but to be rejected in favour of a sausage-maker wounded his pride as well as his heart. In Marie's opinion, which she happily made known to Holger, Rita's preference for the sausage-maker revealed her essential unworthiness. She thought perhaps he might come to see that he was better off.

Holger was not, however, convinced, and he continued to grieve for Rita until Marie had an unconscious brainwave. They were sitting together one evening watching the sunset from the window of a room at the top of the Copenhagen house, and she asked him lightly, just by way of conversation, if he ever heard from Emmy these days, how she was, how the children were. She had never really met Emmy or her children; it was just an idle enquiry. To Holger's ears, though, it came as a kind of revelation. He suddenly saw, as the sun went fierily down over the city, illuminating the skies with a party pink, that what he needed was to go back to Emmy.

He had promised her, all those years ago, that he would leave Rita one day and go back to her. It hadn't worked out exactly like that. But that was a minor detail, and not, in any case, any of Emmy's business. Here he was, casting about, lonely, not knowing what to do next with his life, when Marie, bless her, showed him the way. He had a wife. He had a family. They were mostly grown by now of course, and weren't really in need of his care. He hardly remembered their ages. He used to send money a few times a year for Emmy to dole out on birthdays: she knew the dates.

But Emmy was still there. She had not remarried – well, they had never divorced, so she couldn't have. She had always loved him, dear Emmy. It was obvious. He had to go back to her. He owed her that much. They could grow old together, old friends, old comrades, old marriage partners that they were. Yes. It was blindingly obvious, he didn't know why he hadn't thought of it before.

Emmy had moved, when the children had grown and left, from the house they had shared in Copenhagen, and now lived in a small apartment on her own. By the time he arrived at Emmy's, he had forgotten that the whole thing had been Marie's idea – or, rather, sparked by something Marie had randomly dropped into conversation – and had managed to convince himself that this had been the plan all along, that he would eventually free himself of Rita's unworthy grasp and come back like a faithful pet to Emmy, who would welcome him with open arms, as she had done so often in the past, and this time, he would stay. For sure. His philandering days were over. He was ready for a more settled way of life now. That had been the problem in the past. He had been too adventurous, too restless, he had not been capable of the containment that is marriage. But now he thought he could see his way to it. He could see the advantages, where, in the past, he had seen mostly the disadvantages. He would point this out to Emmy. It was a young man's fault, restlessness, but he was no longer a young man, so she could be sure now of his desire for rest and permanence – which, after all, is what women want, is it not?

Emmy had furnished her small apartment in a vaguely oriental style, with rugs and tapestries and brightly coloured drapes and hardly any actual chairs or tables, just a desk with a comfortable writing chair and a lot of bookshelves and cushions. Holger laughed when he saw the appointments. At least, he managed to make it appear that it was the apartment he was laughing at, but the way she dressed these days was what really amused him. She was got up in an orange kimono-like garment, something between a dress and a wrap, and she had wound some sort of a scarf around her head, like a turban. She looked the very caricature of the poetess. He put it down to the turn of the century. That double nought – it unsettled people, made them feel they had to be different from what they were before.

He waved his arms at the room in general and said it was 'all so feminine', by way of explaining his sudden burst of laughter.

Emmy, whose pleasure at seeing him right at that moment was mixed – she was at a difficult point in the novel she was writing – said of course it was feminine, since it was furnished and lived in by a woman. What did he expect?

'You are so sharp, Emmy,' he replied. 'You always were.'

Sharp? She had only been making conversation. It hardly seemed fair to be accused of sharpness merely because she had challenged the triteness of his observation.

'So you are a writer now, Emmy?' he said, sitting into the only chair and leafing idly through the manuscript that lay on the desk in front of him. He put his hat down beside the neat pile of paper.

'Don't touch it, please, Holger. I haven't numbered the pages, and I am anxious not to let it get out of sequence.'

She tried to keep her fury at his casual appropriation of her chair, his uninvited perusal of her work, out of her voice. What was he doing here, anyway? She hadn't heard from him for years. He had broken her heart. And now here he was, bumbling into her life, expecting to be fussed over. She was prepared to entertain him civilly, but she was busy, she had no time for playing games with an ex-husband. Almost ex-. He was probably looking for a divorce.

He had aged, his hair and beard had become grizzled, but he was otherwise unchanged. Still the arrogant, nervous jut of the chin, the languid hand gestures in conversation, the benign look in his eyes that made people forgive him his outrageousness.

She felt a tug of affection for him, as she looked upon him now, but she was relieved to find the old longing had dissipated. She could bear to sit and talk to him and not yearn to be in his arms. That knowledge gave her the strength to be gracious.

'I came back, Emmy,' he said, delighted with himself, she thought. He took off his gloves and dropped them onto the manuscript. As if he lived here.

She sat cross-legged on an upholstered footstool and looked at him, her eyebrows raised, inviting conversation, but he said nothing more for the moment.

'It is good to see you, Holger,' she said as if to encourage him to get to the point.

'I mean,' he said, 'I came back to you as I promised. I always said I would come back to you, Emmy, so here I am.'

'Will you have coffee?' she said, as if she had not heard.

She had heard. Those were words she had craved for so long, she had conjured them up so often that, now they were actually spoken, they sounded like an echo of something she had often heard. But only an echo, a reverberating sound that carried no meaning.

'Thank you,' he said. 'Coffee would be . . . I'll have coffee, yes.'

She poured with an arm that clinked with silver bracelets.

'You never used to wear jewellery,' he said.

'Nobody used to give me any.' He thought her sharp. Well, she could be sharp.

'So, Emmy?'

'So, Holger.' She smiled at him. It was pleasant to sit opposite him and look at him and be glad of his presence and not dread the moment he would stand up to leave.

'What do you say?'

'To what?'

'To my coming back.'

'As I said, I am glad to see you. Are you passing through? Or do you intend to settle in Copenhagen again?'

'I hoped I might settle, yes, as you put it. I thought maybe, you and I, Emmy . . . '

She laughed then. It should have been a sweet moment of victory, to be able to laugh at such a proposal, but her laugh had nothing of retribution in it, only genuine amusement.

'Holger, that is not – it is just not – possible.'

'Why not?' There was no anxiety in his question. He was confident that she was only putting up a symbolic protest. 'I promised you I would return when it was over with Rita. And now it's over.'

What he left out of this roughly accurate account, however, was the passage of years. When he had promised to come back, he had thought the affair would be like the others, short-lived. But since he was prepared to overlook the unforeseen lapse of time since he had made his promise to Emmy, he imagined she would be able to bring herself to do the same. It might take a little persuasion, of course, he was prepared for that, and elaborate contrition on his part. That would present no difficulty. He had had practice.

But he was still reckoning with the old Emmy – that is to say, the young Emmy. He assumed this Emmy, for all her orange kimono and her preposterous manuscript, was essentially the same as the young mother and ardent wife he had left. It did not occur to him that her needs and desires had also changed. He had the self-absorption of a child. He could observe, and laud, change in himself, but he did not expect it to occur to those around him.

'And I am supposed to take you back and we just continue from where we – were interrupted?'

'Yes,' he said. 'I mean, I know it is not as simple as that, but we did have that arrangement, did we not, my dear?'

Suddenly, out of nowhere, it hit her. The anger of years. It had not crossed her mind to refuse him when he wrote, suggesting this meeting. She had been pleased at the prospect of seeing him again. But the cool arrogance of that last sentence released something in her that was so deeply buried she hardly knew it was there. She gritted her teeth against it and resolved not to be engulfed by it.

'No, Holger, we did not have that arrangement. That may have been your understanding, but I certainly never agreed to any such arrangement. I have reared your children without you. I have lived my life without you. I have no desire to return to the anguish in which I lived with you for so long.'

'Anguish?' He had the nerve to sound surprised.

'Yes.' There was no point in elaborating. If he didn't understand, he never would.

She stood up.

He stood too, and opened his arms to her, in a gesture she had never resisted before, but she folded her arms against it now.

'I think it is time to say goodbye, Holger, because if this conversation continues, we will not say goodbye on good terms.'

'Very well, I will go,' he said, sweeping his wide-brimmed hat off the desk, slapping his gloves together. 'But since you won't have me back, will you give me a divorce?'

She thought she had been prepared to negotiate but, after all, she found she could not acquiesce so easily.

'What do you want a divorce for? I thought your little nightingale had left you. Are you planning to marry a parlour-maid?'

That was more than sharp. It was spiteful, and he winced.

'I am not planning to marry anyone. But I may some day wish to marry. You would not deny that comfort to me?'

'I would,' she said, her anger transmuted now into pure resentment.

'How can you be so vengeful?'

'How can you be so arrogant?'

She had been right. They should have parted two minutes ago. Now it was all spoiled, their careful edifice of good fellowship. But she wrote to him shortly afterwards and said he could have his divorce. She still loved him, she told him, and she knew that he had always loved her too:

I know you loved me, Holger, but you also loved your dog. Your love for me was nuzzling, familiar, comforting, though no less real for that. If I weren't there, I knew you would miss me. If I died, you would mourn me. You valued my opinions and enjoyed my company. To you, I was like a favourite armchair, prized and cherished. But to me, you were like an oak tree, mighty and adored and eternally tossed by electric storms. Your love for me was deep and warm; my love for you was violent and overpowering and it consumed me every second of every day that we were married and I hated you for it. It took me years to recover from my love for you, and to learn to love you the way you loved me, with tenderness and regard but without passion. I have achieved that with pain, and I do not wish either to rekindle that pain by having you back, or to put you through even a shadow of the pain through which you have put me, and so I agree, reluctantly, to our divorce. If ever a woman divorced a man for love, it is now. I know now that the most we can ever be to each other is kind, and so I am being as kind as I can. My one consolation is that I did not divorce you sooner, for you surely would have married that Amanda creature, and you would be even unhappier than you are now.

God bless you, Holger, and I wish you joy in whoever it is that you will marry as soon as the ink is dry on our divorce agreement, for I am sure there will be someone. I hope she deserves you – or maybe not.

You know who my solicitor is. Deal with him from now on, if you please.

Your loving Emmy

Chapter 33

As soon as the Krøyers got home from their Sicilian trip, Søren threw himself fretfully into the work he had 'neglected', as he said, while they were away. He worked crazy hours, staying up half the night to do paperwork for some project he was involved in, and getting up as soon as dawn broke to get on with his painting. Marie begged him to take it easy, to rest more, to go to bed at a reasonable hour, but he argued that he lay awake worrying about the work he wasn't getting done and that he felt better when he was up and doing it. At least it gave him some sense of control, he said.

Within a month he was in a lunatic asylum. They told Vibeke it was a rest home, like the other times, but she heard Tabitha Mendel's nanny telling the parlour-maid that he had gone on the rampage and had had to be sent to the loony-bin.

He hadn't exactly gone on the rampage. Vibeke knew, because she'd been there that day. She was playing under the piano in the music room in the Copenhagen house, and she thought she heard her mother calling. She sat still for a moment, and waited for the sounds of the servants' feet on the stairs, running along the hall to the drawing room, but nobody came. Nobody heard. The house was so large, a servant in the kitchen quarters downstairs would never hear a voice from the drawing room. Vibeke sat in the warm and felted shelter of the piano for a little while and wondered what she should do. She poked a finger up on the underside of a piano key, and a muffled note sounded, as if someone had wrapped the sound in flannel. She tried another key, and got the same muffled effect. Then she heard her mother's voice again, and it sounded strange and frightening. She crawled out from under the piano, and dusted herself down. Grasping The Princess Marina by the wrist, she set off for the drawing room.

When she opened the door, she saw her father lying on the floor, crying and moaning, scrabbling at her mother's ankles and begging her to look after him. He was babbling something about the king being dead and his paintings being destroyed by the Russians. Her mother was crying too. She kept trying to get away from him, but every time she moved, he pulled the hem of her dress like a little child and crawled after her and she couldn't make any progress. Vibeke stood as if paralysed by fear and shame in the doorway. She felt as if she had come upon her parents in a moment of intimacy. She should not be witnessing this.

Marie looked up at the sound of the door opening, and saw her daughter, framed by the architrave, with her doll in her hand.

Thank God!

'Vibeke!' she called. 'Oh, darling! Get someone, like a good girl. I need help. Your father . . . I can't manage him on my own. He's gone crazy. Find someone, quick.'

Crazy. Vibeke stared. Her mother had never used a word like that before.

'Please, sweetheart. It will be all right, but just find somebody to help me.'

Vibeke didn't move. She felt as if she had been transformed into a statue, like in that game where you are supposed to freeze and not blink or twitch, even if they tickle you. The brass doorknob felt cold and hard in her hand.

'Vibeke!' Marie wailed, frantic now.

Vibeke concentrated on making her body work. It was like forcing a foot that has gone asleep to bear your weight, pricklish and wobbly.

Marie had meant Vibeke to go downstairs and get one of the

servants, but the child was too terrified to think straight, and as soon as she had worked some movement back into her limbs, she ran along the hall, creaked the hall door open, and ran down the front steps, onto the street, and looked up and down in desperation.

She wished her Uncle Villem would appear, but he had gone to France on business. There was a policeman on the other side of the street, but she knew her father was afraid of the police, and to fetch a policeman might only make things worse for her mother. But how could she run up to a stranger on the street and beg for help for a situation she could not even describe?

Overcome by the impossibility of it all, she sat down on the bottom step and cried, but no one took any notice. She could see their feet and hems and the legs of their trousers as they hurried by. They must have thought she was a spoiled little girl having a tantrum.

After a moment, she blew her nose and decided that she must go and get the policeman after all. She had to get someone. She stood on the kerb, and looked up and down before crossing the road, and saw, coming around the corner towards her, a gentleman she knew. Her heart sang. She couldn't remember his name, but he was a friend of her parents'. It was as if God had parted the clouds and taken a look down and noticed that little Vibeke Krøyer was in trouble, and He had sent her a saviour, though in fact it was not such a great coincidence. Karl Madsen was on his way in any case to visit the Krøyers, and had just appeared at the opportune moment.

The tear-streaked little girl flew to the gentleman she recognised but whose name she could not remember and flung herself at him, grabbing him by his coat-tails, and sobbed, 'Come quickly, come quickly, Papa is . . . I don't know what he is, but Mama is frightened and she needs someone to help her. He is – not himself.'

That was the formula her mother always used when her father went stomping about, drinking and singing or when he sat for hours in his armchair and stroked the backs of his hands and wouldn't talk, which he had taken to doing lately.

Vibeke had left the front door open when she ran into the street, so she and her catch were able to get back into the house without ringing the bell.

By now Marie had got Søren bundled into a chair and she had put a blanket over him and was stroking his hair and murmuring to him to calm him down. He wasn't howling any more, but there were tears coming down his cheeks, and Marie stopped each one tenderly with the tip of a finger.

She looked up when she saw Karl, holding Vibeke's hand, and Vibeke still holding on to the doll.

'Oh, thank God,' she whispered. 'Karl.'

'Why don't you go and fetch the parlour-maid, little miss?' Karl had evidently no more idea of Vibeke's name than she had of his. 'Ask her to bring some smelling salts and a glass of brandy with water.'

When the servant girl came in, trembling, Karl took the things from her and sent her immediately for the doctor. They all sat un-speaking then in the drawing room, like people at a railway station waiting to go on a mystery tour. Vibeke swung her legs, which didn't reach the floor from her chair. The only sound was the tick-ing of the clock and Søren's occasional sobs and Marie's voice mur-muring to him. She'd given him a little of the diluted brandy, on Karl's advice, and he was starting to nod off now, a strange, angu-lar shape under his thin blanket, emitting occasional soft snores.

When the doorbell rang, Marie sprang up.

'The doctor! Oh, Karl! Vibeke, I think maybe you and Marina should go to your room for a little while. I will come and fetch you when the doctor is finished talking to Papa. You have been

284

such a great help, my darling, such a good girl. Go on now, no arguments.'

Of course, her mother never did come for her. She'd evidently forgotten all about her. By the time Vibeke came sneaking downstairs, wondering what was happening about supper, her father had gone to the 'rest home' and the gentleman her mother called Karl had left. Marie's eyes were red. Even her nose was red.

Vibeke expected a lecture about having come downstairs, but instead, Marie put her arm around Vibeke's shoulders and rested her chin on the top of Vibeke's head. They sat there for a while and then Mama said Vibeke might choose what they would have for supper and she said scrambled eggs, which she always chose. Her mother hated eggs, but she said, 'Very well' and they had a surprisingly snug evening by the fire, eating toast and scrambled eggs and drinking milky tea, like they do in England.

Vibeke felt strangely light and free, as if there had been a giant sitting on the roof and squashing the family in the house, and now he had gone and there was headroom again. She felt guilty for feeling like this, because she knew the giant she was glad had gone away was really her papa.

As if to make up for being glad he had gone, she missed him terribly, and she worried about him being in that place, because she knew by now it wasn't really a rest home, but something more like what Tabitha Mendel's nurse had said. She was staying with the Mendels again. This time she hadn't raised any objections, but when her mother came to visit, she begged her to take her to see her father, so, one day, they dressed up in their best coats and hats and set off.

Marie hated going to this place, and she hated even more that Vibeke should see it, but the child was so distraught, she was afraid she might think her father was dead, and, in any case, the only way to assuage her fears was to make her face up to them. That was

Karl's advice. (He had been so kind.) Anna thought so too, and of course Anna knew a bit more about bringing up a girl than Karl did.

It was a large grey house with a long stony driveway. It reminded Marie of The Dolls' House that Søren's mother had described to her all those years before, a memory that made her shudder now. When they knocked on the door, there were scufflings and shouts from inside, as if they were putting away the evidence before people from the outside world could be admitted. Eventually, the door was opened, and a small crooked person, so bent that he seemed to be talking to his own feet, enquired as to their business.

Marie gave Søren's name, and they were shown into a room like a pencil box turned on its end. It was brown on the inside, with a tall narrow wooden door, and very small, just room for two chairs and a battered table, but extremely high. The ceiling was so far away, Vibeke could hardly see it, and way up high, near the ceiling, was a small barred window. The room smelled of something awful. Clean, but awful, as if the place had been scoured with a dreadful caustic bleach to keep some kind of vermin down.

They were left there for the longest time in that depressing, bleach-rank room. In the end, Vibeke opened the door to see if anyone was coming or if they had forgotten about her and her mother. As soon as the door was opened, the noise of the house came in, and Marie put her hands to her ears. So complex and refractive were the echoes that it was impossible to distinguish human from mechanical sounds: everything made the same harsh, hollow, screeching noises, and the din was constant. A patient was being wheeled by, bundled up in grey blankets in a bath chair, and when she saw Vibeke, she started screaming as if she was being tortured, but the attendant shouted over the screams to Vibeke, with a hoarse laugh, not to mind, she was just putting on a show for the visitors. Vibeke didn't answer. She closed the door again quickly, her heart pounding and her hands shaking, and sat back on the wooden chair. She tried to shuffle her chair closer to the table so that she could rest her arms on it, but the chair would not move. It was bolted to the floor. For some reason, that was the most frightening thing of all, the unmovable chair, like an object in a nightmare that won't respond to your most desperate exertions.

At last they brought Søren in, also in a bath chair. The room was so small that they couldn't close the door now. He wasn't screaming. He seemed half-asleep, his head nodding onto his chest, as if he had no neck, only a piece of thick rope attaching his head to his body.

'Papa?' said Vibeke, and he lifted his head. His face seemed longer than before, and grey, and his eyes looked as if they were made of some opaque resin, like a doll's eyes.

He said something, his voice thick and muffled, like the notes Vibeke had sounded from underneath the piano that day he had been taken ill.

Vibeke said, because nobody else seemed to know what to say, 'How are you, Papa?' but she thought maybe he didn't hear, because he didn't answer. His head lolled forward again, and he made a gurgling noise, like a drain.

They took him away again after a few moments, and Vibeke and Marie went home. Vibeke's mother said that she mustn't mind, that Papa would get better presently, and then he could come home and they could all be together.

Vibeke didn't say anything. She didn't want this horrid, grey, bath-chair Papa to come home, but she thought she should not say that, so instead she said nothing.

When he finally did come home, his neck was able to support his head and his eyes looked real, but he was awfully old. Vibeke had not remembered him being so old. Some of his teeth had fallen out, and when she hugged him, his body felt like a bundle of sticks in a sack. A sour smell hung about him, as if he carried the odour of that place in his pockets and among the folds of his clothing, which had somehow got too big for him.

His hands shook, except when he was painting.

As soon as he was fit to travel, they decamped to Skagen for the summer but, within weeks, Marie was fretful and restless. She needed to go to Sicily again, she announced.

'Excellent idea,' said Søren cheerfully. He had found his cheerful self again by now, and he talked sense, though he was still old and thin. 'This country is so damned cold, even in the summer it never gets really hot. We need to toast our bones. Don't we, Vibeke?'

Vibeke smiled up at him. She missed the jolly, rambunctious father she used to have, and she treasured this old and sad father's every small attempt at playfulness.

Marie stood firm.

'No, Søren,' she said. 'Not all of us, not this time. I mean to go alone. I need to get away. I need . . . some . . . freedom, some time . . . to reflect.'

She was searching for words, trying to present her motivation as personal to her, not related to him and his illness. It was like trying not to be afraid of a dog, knowing the dog would smell her fear. At all costs, she must not let him know how desperate she was to get away. She must make it appear like ordinary selfishness.

'I have spoken to Anna, and she has agreed to look after Vibeke. Helga will help out.'

'I can look after Vibeke,' Søren protested.

Vibeke wondered how that could be. When she had wanted him to look after her before, he had said something about how she couldn't even button her own boots. But she had been younger then. Perhaps that was what made the difference.

'My dear Søren, that is a lovely idea, but you know it would be a strain on you. And you know what would happen. You'd be so taken up with your work, you'd forget to feed her. Poor little mite, she gets passed around like a parcel, I know, but at least we do make sure she is properly looked after, and you know she will love being at Anna's. You can see her every day, of course, it's not as if she is going off to the Mendels.'

Søren sulked all through the packing and readying period, but Marie just went on making her preparations. It was clear that she was going to see this through. She kept up a cheery front, chattering about the route, the hotels, the trains, the porters, the temperature, the clothes she would need, the number of trunks, the food; the medicaments against heartburn, stomach ache, fever, diarrhoea, constipation, mosquito bites, seasickness, sunstroke. She made it sound like a military campaign. In a way, it was just as desperate — a defensive action for her own sanity, as she saw it.

She could not possibly travel all that way alone, Søren said, but she did not propose to, she assured him. She had thought of that objection and had an answer to it. She'd agreed to meet someone's cousin's sister-in-law in Copenhagen, who also wanted to go to the south of Italy. They would chaperone each other, she said gaily, as if she were a young girl, setting her parents' anxieties at rest.

'There is no need for you to worry about me, Søren. You know I am perfectly capable. You just concentrate on getting your health back and laying down some fat for the winter.'

That was their expression for enjoying the summer. She dropped it into the conversation now, to remind him of their intimacy, their shared life, the little turns of phrase they used together, as a token of their closeness. But he knew what she was playing at, and he turned away from her, so she should not see how disappointed he was.

'I will be back, Søren,' she assured him.

He did not find that information at all reassuring. The very least he expected was that she should be back. Even to mention it was to suggest there might be a doubt about it.

'I hate leaving you behind, Vibeke, darling,' she said to her daughter on the last night before she left.

'I hate it too,' said Vibeke, dutifully, though she was so pleased not to be going to those Mendels but to the Anchers' house that she really wasn't all that very put out. 'Will you bring me back some almond cake?'

'Certainly, I will. Do you like almonds?'

Vibeke shrugged. 'I will like whatever you bring me, Mama,' she said.

The pathos of that struck Marie, and she enfolded the child in an embrace.

'Be good to Papa,' she whispered.

'For Papa,' Vibeke corrected.

'That too,' said Marie.

Chapter 34

Marie always felt battered and grimy after the journey south; her bones ached from sleeping – trying to sleep – in confined spaces, the congealed dust of railway carriages lodged under her fingernails and the stink of soot hung in her hair. But there came a morning – she knew it would come – when she woke refreshed and when the bathwater finally ran clean and she emerged, pearly and soap-scented, and put on a soft, fresh-smelling summer gown from which the creases had mostly fallen. She felt human again, she assured her reflection as she brushed her hair, and she could almost relish the idea of a bowl of hot, milky coffee.

Her only regret was having left Vibeke behind. She could have brought her. She was older now, no trouble, actually good company. But her whole point to Søren was her need to be alone, and if she'd said she would take Vibeke with her, that argument would have been exposed as false. She would send her a postcard directly. In fact, she might send her a postcard every day.

She took her breakfast by an open window. The morning was young enough still to have that luminous rinsed quality about it, and the air was filled with birdsong and the scent of lavender. She longed to walk in the garden, before the heat of the day had burned the dew from the flowers.

The hotel owner's wife, who was experienced in reading the moods of guests, appeared by her breakfast table just as she finished, and asked if Mrs Krøyer would care to cut some roses from the terrace to fill the vases that stood about in the public areas of the hotel.

Mrs Krøyer would be delighted. What a charming idea!

The hotelier, who understood that guests liked to potter in the garden, instantly produced a flat-bottomed basket, a pair of secateurs and a pretty cotton apron, which served the dual purpose of looking sweet and keeping a guest's gown clean. Guests were not really interested in gardening, but they were glad of an excuse to linger among the sweet-smelling rose bushes and it was best if they could look romantic while they did it.

Exclaiming at her hostess's solicitousness, Marie wrapped the pretty apron around her pretty waist, hung the basket prettily on her arm and wandered out to the terrace, which was overhung with roses. She hummed as she worked in the morning sunshine, which drew a heavy fragrance from the blossoms. She fingered her way carefully along the stalks, watching out for thorns, aiming to cut the longest stems she could, so that the signora would have maximum scope for arranging them later in their vases.

She was pleased to have a small, pleasant task that she could do in the sun, a thousand miles from her worries. She would write to Søren as soon as she had finished, and tell him she had arrived safely. Better, she would telegraph him this news, and follow it up with a letter. By wiring, she could buy herself three or four blessed days, she calculated, before she needed to write a breezy, reassuring letter, enquiring about their health and the weather and whether the pointer bitch really was pregnant and whether Vibeke was being kind to Papa and whether Søren was joining Vibeke at the hotel for lunch and whether the Brøndums' cook had invented any new desserts. In fact, since she had resolved to send daily postcards to Vibeke, she wouldn't need to write to Søren very often at all. That would give her a breathing space.

She heard a soft step behind her, but did not look around, expecting it was just some guest crossing the terrace to go down into the garden. The person – or perhaps it was a dog, the step had been muffled – did not move, though, and after a moment she thought whoever it was might be waiting for her to turn around. Perhaps it was someone with a message for her, someone who did not know how to address her, or what language to use, and was waiting to be spotted before making his or her approach. She had enough roses now anyway.

She slotted the last bloom into place in her basket and turned casually to see what was going on. It was not a servant with a message or waiting to sweep the terrace or anything like that. It was a slight, dark man, probably a fellow-guest, she thought, wearing a startlingly bright white collarless shirt and pale trousers, with no jacket and – she noted with surprise, her eye travelling half-consciously down to see what kind of footwear had made such a soft footfall – no shoes or socks. His feet were neat and almost hairless, the toes pink and clean and arranged as regularly as a menorah. She didn't think she'd ever seen a man's feet before, except for Søren's, of course, which were splayed and yellow and bony.

'Mrs Krøyer?' said the man with the good-looking feet.

That voice! It was like dark honey, warmed by the sun, trickling slowly over something rich and sweet – chocolate cake, perhaps. Its resonance echoed in her breast and she felt her heart lift at the sound. The corners of her mouth lifted also, and she looked him in the eyes. Like his voice, his eyes were dark and deep and honeyed. Her whole body seemed to drift towards those eyes, as if she were made of . . . not even air, something even more ethereal – musical notes. It was a ridiculous idea, she knew, but she felt as if she had been transformed into a melody played by this man's voice.

She didn't answer. She couldn't open her mouth. She didn't have anything as mundane as a mouth. She was incorporeal, a flutey sound hovering in the air on a level with his dreamy dark eyes.

She wondered if she should know him, since he appeared to recognise her. His face was dark, unbearded but with the blue, bruised look that meant he needed a shave. No, she didn't know him, she'd never seen him before. She'd remember if she had. Was he real? Perhaps he was a projection of her own weariness with her life and her own desire for something much more enticing. But no. Whatever about the depths of his brown eyes and the blue-black of his flop of hair, she could never have imagined those perfect feet. She could not be falling in love with a man's feet! The very idea was absurd. It made her want to laugh with pleasure.

In love with? Where had *that* thought come from? She shook herself lightly, and finally – it seemed as if minutes had passed, but it had probably been less than a second – she said, 'Yes. I am Marie Krøyer.'

Even from the two words he had spoken, she knew he was not a Dane. Italian then. He could certainly pass for Italian, as far as looks went. Perhaps he was some sort of servant after all, though she thought it unlikely that the staff would be allowed to go around barefoot, even on the terrace. She wished he would say something more, so she could hear that wonderful voice again.

'Forgive me,' she said pleasantly, still half-expecting a message from the proprietress or some indication about the rules of the hotel with regard to the cutting of roses that had unfortunately not been drawn to her attention earlier. 'I am afraid I don't appear to know you.'

'No,' he said. 'But I know you. I have seen you before.'

A Swede, she realised now. Definitely a guest then, not a member of the hotel staff.

'Only in real life, you are even more beautiful.'

In real life! She was not in real life. This was a dream, an enchanting dream, one she was hoping not to wake up from for some time.

'In real life?' she said. 'Do I have a false life that you are privy to, Signor . . . '

'Alfvén,' he said. 'Hugo Alfvén. Yes, I think you do have a false life, Mrs Kr . . . Marie. Your false life is as Mrs Krøyer. You married the wrong man, Marie. A dreadful mistake, but it can be rectified.'

Marie laughed. The effrontery of it! It must be the effect of being in Sicily. His gallantry was audacious enough for an Italian – though it was not, she supposed, all that very gallant to tell her she had married unwisely. Even if she had.

She was none the wiser for hearing his name.

He grasped her hand in both of his, and held her gaze with his sultry look. She thought she would faint with the deliciousness of his touch. It was the kind of thing Venetian boatmen did, she knew, and was rarely sincere, but just at this charmed moment, she didn't give a fig for sincerity. She laughed again, a little uncertainly.

'And you are . . . a guest here?' she asked, as she withdrew her hand.

'Arrived last evening. Exhausted, I have to say. I have been look-ing for you for years, you know. Thought I should never track you down. Not true!' He put a hand up. 'I knew I would find you even-tually, but I had moments of despair, you know.'

She didn't know what he was talking about.

'You seem to know me, Mr Alfvén,' she said interrogatively, 'and yet, I think we have not met.'

'I have seen your portrait.'

It had happened before that she had been recognised from Søren's pictures.

'Which one?'

'The one on the beach,' he said.

'Which one on the beach?' she asked.

He hadn't known there was more than one.

'Dozens,' she said, exaggerating. 'We live practically on the beach, mainly because it makes such a good setting.'

This was not quite true; she was being *witty*. She had not felt the urge to sparkle for . . . years.

'Well, in this one, you are half-turned towards the viewer, you look as if you are inviting him to supper, you have a hat in your hand, and your knee is crooked against the inside of your dress.'

'My knee?' she said, blushing prettily.

He noted how she coloured, but he did not excuse himself. Instead he added, 'And if I am not mistaken, there is a dog. Rather spoils it, if you ask me.'

The nerve of him! But she only laughed again.

'And I've been looking for you ever since. I have trailed you all over Europe, and at last I've found you. Some people would say it is fate. But I assure you, it is sheer will-power on my part.'

He was speaking in riddles, but as far as she was concerned, he could go on riddling all morning. She was perfectly happy to listen.

'I fell in love as soon as I saw it,' Mr Alfvén said.

'With the picture?' She was laughing freely now, her head thrown back. It was a sensation she had almost forgotten, a good, clear laugh.

'No,' he said. 'Don't be silly, my dear. With you.'

She stopped laughing and said, 'It is you who are being silly, Mr Alfvén, not I. You can't fall in love with a woman in a picture.'

But even as she denied it, the idea thrilled her. The idea of being loved by this man ran around her nervous system like a delicious shock. The fact that his love was based on a picture, an image of her – her beauty, in other words – was irrelevant, though she had spent all her life trying to dissociate herself from her looks.

'That's what Dirk said. My friend, who was with me that day we saw the painting. He said it was not possible. But, you see, it is. I told him I would find you one day, and marry you, my painted lady.'

She shook her head, laughter still sparkling out of her. If men wanted to fall in love with her, they could do her the courtesy of falling in love with all of her, she said, but she said it so lightly, he hardly took it in; not with her image, she expanded. She was more than an artist's model. She was a breathing woman with her own thoughts and dreams.

'Breathing,' he said, stepping closer to her. 'Exactly. I want to feel your breath on my face.'

Instinctively, she inclined her head towards him, even as she said, 'Out of the question.'

He took her hand again.

She freed her hand, still laughing, and instantly regretted letting his hand go. But all the same, she knew this was a game. He was playing a role. It was a scene from a comic opera – he was the barefoot gypsy prince, she the comely village maiden with her basket of flowers. Laughter was the appropriate response. Perhaps he would burst into a tenor aria. The kind of thing that Søren did. Søren. She stopped laughing.

'My dear Mr Alfvén,' she said, 'you are most gallant, but you know I am married already, and I take my marriage seriously.'

'So I hear,' said Hugo, 'but you've been married to him for ages. Don't you think it's time for a change? I am younger, better-looking, just as talented, though possibly not as rich . . . but let's not worry about that.'

He was being purposely outrageous. It would only be feeding his nonsense to be offended by it.

Marie moved a step away from him and then started to walk back across the terrace to go in at the French doors to the dining room. She spoke back over her shoulder, 'I am afraid there is no contest, Mr Alfvén. I do not believe in changing husbands on a whim.'

'It's ten years since I saw that portrait,' he said. 'I don't call that a whim.'

She stopped by the door.

'And you have doubtless been prowling Europe in pursuit of me all this time,' she said.

She did not care to puncture the light-hearted spirit of their exchange by pointing out that he had not done the obvious thing, if he really wanted to find her, and come to Skagen.

'Yes!' he said, flinging out his arms theatrically and bending one knee slightly, as if to suggest he was about to sink to the ground before her. 'And then I thought, ah, Sicily, she is sure to come to Sicily. I shall go there, find where the Scandinavians stay, and wait for her. She'll come eventually, and, when she is ready, she will come alone.'

That logic was uncannily accurate, she had to admit – but only to herself.

'What a fibber you are, Mr Alfvén! It is the purest coincidence, our meeting here.'

'It is not!' He had followed her across the terrace and stood now at her side.

'Of course it is. You have just arrived. If you had been lying in wait for me, as you suggest, you would have been here before me.'

'That does not follow. Lying in wait has to have a starting point. I have just been lucky that my starting point is also my moment of victory.'

'Well,' she said, 'if being refused is your idea of victory, you may call it what you like, but I have an appointment shortly with my travelling companion. Goodbye for the present, Mr Alfvén.'

He noted the 'for the present'. Good.

She gave him her hand. It was unnecessary, but she couldn't resist it. Instead of shaking it in farewell, he raised it to his lips, like an eastern European count.

Again she laughed as his lips touched her fingers, and her body was licked by a pulse of flame.

He lingered over her hand, and finally dropped it with theatrical reluctance. He stood aside to let her into the dining room.

'You will marry me,' he said to her receding back.

She turned a laughing face to him. She had never been flirted with so persistently in her life. He *must* have Italian blood.

'It is impossible,' she said. 'I told you, I am married already.'

And to that argument he gave the same reply that he had given in Copenhagen ten years earlier: 'Divorce, my dear lady; it is for cases like this that it exists.'

She shook her head and went out of the dining room by the far door, taking her roses out to the foyer. Her hands shook as she handed over her basket to the hotelier's wife.

She was thinking about the picture he had described, the portrait on the beach, with the dog. Her knee was not crooked against her dress, she was sure of it. He'd said it to be provocative. A dangerous man.

A young woman was coming down the stairs as Marie stood at the reception desk. Marie wished her a good morning, in Danish. She replied in Swedish.

Marie hated to admit it, but her heart sank. She watched as the girl crossed through the dining room to the door of the terrace and called, 'Hugo? Have you had breakfast yet?'

His 'sister', he would certainly inform her the next time they met. So much for all his claims of faithful pursuit down the length of a continent! Well, at least they would be sure to meet. It was a small hotel.

She sat down at a small table in the foyer to compose her telegram home. First, though, she had to compose herself.

Chapter 35

Holger had been coming to Skagen for years, lodging here or there, staying at the hotel, renting various cottages. Now he'd finally bought a place of his own, a cottage on the edge of the village, with apple trees in the garden. He had the place refurbished, installed a tremendous new stove in the kitchen, big enough to provide hot water for a large family – Emmy would have been delighted with it when the children were small – and acquired a dining table so large it had to be disassembled to get it through the doorway. Reassembled, it was wedged into an alcove under the window, with built-in benches around it, able to accommodate a dozen guests, as long as they did not mind all having to stand every time one person needed to leave the table. He built on an airy living-room-cum-studio, with a capacious fireplace. He furnished it with bookcases and his easel and desk, and, as a final flourish, he asked Søren to come and paint his portrait there.

Søren traded insults with his old sparring partner as he set up his easel. He had painted him several times, but now Holger wanted to pose, as Søren put it, as the Grand Old Poet at Home, surrounded by his books and paintings, his fire blazing at his feet and – vain as ever – a red fez on his white head.

The painting was to be a wedding present for his wife, Drachmann explained. His bride. The fourth Mrs Drachmann.

Søren laid down his brush. 'Holger! A new wife. At your age!' Drachmann was sixty if he was a day. 'Well, congratulations! This calls for . . . well, let me think . . .'

In the old days, they'd have had a champagne party on the beach, but it was autumn already, too chilly for their old bones, and a beach party seemed too ... obvious. A dinner party might be better, Søren thought. And Holger had a fine dining table.

'Tell you what, old man,' he said, 'when Marie gets home from Sicily – she's bound to be home any day now, her last letter said she was packing already – she and Anna will surely get together to arrange it. Well, well, a wedding! I can't remember the last wedding I was at. God damn you, Holger, you are a dark horse.'

Holger munched his teeth with pleasure and patted his pockets for a cigar. He did not feel the need to say anything. It was enough to let Søren patter on. He'd stop soon enough and then the questions would start.

'And when are we to meet the lady?' Søren asked, arranging a ruby-red rug over Holger's lap, to pick up the colour of the fez and reflect the firelight. 'Do we know her? A widow, perhaps?'

'No,' said Holger. 'Divorced.'

'Ah,' said Søren, 'I see.'

'Or at least, she will be shortly.'

'Holger! Don't tell me you have snatched her from under her husband's nose!'

Drachmann leaned forward and lit a spill of paper at the fire. Then he sat back and concentrated on puffing at his cigar, till it glowed as red as his knee-rug. He looked like some despotic eastern potentate.

'I suppose a crude person might put it like that,' he conceded. 'But I would call it a rescue operation. Frightful old bore; don't know how she came to marry him in the first place, probably co-erced into it, I shouldn't wonder. An engineer, you know. Can't think of a worse occupation for a fellow. All measuring things and bossing people about. Dreadful way to spend your life.'

'I think there is a bit more to it than that,' said Søren, smiling. Holger was renowned for the making of sweeping statements. 'So the lady is still married?'

'In theory,' said Holger, as if a marriage, even a dissolving one, could be hypothetical. 'She will have her divorce papers by next week, however, and we have arranged to be married directly in Copenhagen. We'll be back to Skagen by next month, though, before the winter sets in. Make this place as cosy as we can before then.'

'Children?' asked Søren, as he daubed out the outline of the painting.

'Well, we haven't thought about that yet.'

'No, no,' said Søren, 'I mean, has she got children? Will she be bringing them with her?'

'Oh no, no children. She wasn't married long.'

'I see,' said Søren. The old reprobate. Breaking up a recent marriage. Really and truly, he was incorrigible. 'A youngish lady, then?'

'Twenty-five,' said Holger, giving his cigar a satisfied twirl.

'Holger! Twenty-five! She is only a child!'

'Don't be absurd, Søren. I told you, she is a married woman.'

'Yes, but you are . . . forty years older.'

'I am not!' said Holger.

'You old goat!' Søren said on a shout of laughter. 'Holger, what will we do with you?'

'Well,' said Holger, pleased with the reaction his little story was provoking in Søren Krøyer, who was not exactly the world's most famous example of chastity – it was rumoured he was seeing a local girl in the afternoons while Marie was away – 'that little dinner party you mentioned sounds like just the thing. We could have it here, of course, but I don't think Sophie . . . '

'Of course not,' said Søren. 'We can't expect her to cook her own wedding banquet. Don't worry, I will speak to Anna. Anna will come up with a plan. You just name the date, and we will handle the rest. Holger! I can hardly believe it. It is like old times. Does Emmy know?'

Drachmann smirked. Søren had always had a soft spot for Emmy. After all these years, his interest in her still came to the surface.

'Yes. And no.'

Søren raised his eyebrows.

'Well, when she agreed to our divorce, she predicted I would be married within six months. But I would not say she has actual information. I will write to her, of course, to apprise her. As a courtesy.'

Søren would not write to apprise Marie, though. She would probably be under way already, and it would be an interesting surprise for her when she got home. He was looking forward to seeing her, and already starting to secrete little items of news, theatre programmes from Copenhagen, reviews of exhibitions from the newspaper, some sketches he had been working on and wanted to discuss with her. It was a strange thing about their relationship. They wore each other out when they were together, pawed and scraped at each other's wounds, could not resist picking each other to pieces, but as soon as they were apart, he missed her bitterly, and as her return approached, he began to long for her with a youthful ardour.

He came home through the village from Holger's. A crisp dusk was closing in, and there was wood smoke on the air. He stopped into the grocer's to see if there was anything festive he might buy to welcome Marie, though he knew it was a pointless exercise, since she was coming from a country where fruit grew outside one's window and sweetmeats abounded. Disappointed, but unsurprised, he bought some ordinary provisions, and moved on to the haberdasher's, where he got several yards of satin ribbon. He would make the ribbon into bows and pin them around her bedroom door. And he would finish a painting he had started of Vibeke, and hang it opposite her bed. He must remember to air the bedclothes with the copper warming pans that had stood in the scullery since before she'd left.

Making these boyish welcome plans, he arrived home to find that Marie was there ahead of him, her trunks blocking the hallway, her travelling cloak thrown over the rocking chair in the sitting room, the scent of her on the stairs.

He put his bags of groceries on the kitchen table, took the stairs two at a time, and flung open the bedroom door.

She was asleep. The sheets must surely be damp, but she was probably too tired to notice.

'Marie! What a lovely surprise!' He opened his paper bag of ribbon and scattered it over her sleeping body like long bright loops of confetti.

She woke querulously and scrabbled the coils of satin off her face and chest.

'Søren,' she said, through a yawn. 'I caught an earlier ferry.'

He kissed her nose, and patted her hair.

'I will make tea,' he said, 'if you will come downstairs. Unless you would prefer coffee?'

'Oh, Søren, I just want to sleep. If you knew the journey I have had!'

'Please, Marie, I am dying to talk to you.'

'Is there anything in particular? Anything wrong?' She sat up, clutching the fatuous lengths of ribbon to her, as if they were a peignoir that had been worn to pieces.

'No,' he said. 'I just want to . . . bask in you.'

'You could come to bed,' she suggested, patting the mattress beside her. 'We can talk here.'

To hell with the damp sheets. He took off his shoes and his outer layer of clothing and stretched himself delightedly beside her, elbowing under her head, so that she lay on his upper arm. They did not talk. They just sighed into the warmth of each other's bodies, and drifted together with an old tenderness into a sleep that lasted right through the darkening afternoon and into the evening.

They woke when the moon rose. Søren got up to close the shutters and tiptoed away to his own room.

Marie broke her astonishing news over breakfast.

'*What*!'

Søren meant the barked word to convey only incredulous grief. There was no doubt that he had heard her.

He clawed at his face with his hands, and then he made frantic swimming movements in the air, as if to save himself from drowning.

'*What*!' he said again, and bent over in his chair, bringing his knees up almost to his chin.

'I told you, Søren,' Marie said, as patiently as she could. She owed him at least her patience. 'I was on the terrace of the hotel, cutting ro – '

'Stop!' he cried. 'Spare me the roses.'

He was batting the air now with his palms, as if to smack her into withdrawing what she had just said. It couldn't be true. It was only twelve hours since they had slept a sweet homecoming sleep in each other's arms. It could not be that they would never do so again, and yet that was the import of what Marie was saying.

She stopped speaking.

'Marie! You can't . . . ' His voice was strangled, gasping.

She could, of course. She was going to. She had, in fact.

She kept silent, letting him right himself, orient himself in this new reality that only a moment before he had not even suspected of existing.

'It's . . . ridiculous. You can't expect me to take it seriously.'

'I do, Søren. I am not sure you have ever taken me really seriously, but this time I am deadly serious. I can't explain it or justify it. All I can do is tell you.'

'It is the most preposterous story I have ever heard. It's a *joke*. A man can't fall in love with a painted woman – not even if I have painted her. It's absurd.'

'Oh, Søren,' said Marie. She sank onto the floor beside his chair, and put her forehead to his knees.

She would have said the same. She would even have said that a man should not fall for the *living* image of a woman either. It was something she had fought all her life, but she couldn't change the nature of men.

He pushed her head away, stood up, strode about, left the room, came back in, strode about some more, and finally said, 'All right, tell me again. I don't want the details, I just want you to tell me *exactly* how things are, precisely what it is that you are asking of me.'

She had come home directly to Skagen as soon as the situation between herself and Hugo had reached a point where she realised she was going to have to divorce Søren in order to marry Hugo. She would not carry on behind his back, she said. He was a reasonable man, she told Hugo. He understood about love. What she was asking for was a divorce.

'A *fiddler*!' Søren screeched, when she had finished her story. He was striding up and down the room again, tearing pointlessly at his clothing. 'A *Swedish* fiddler. You can sit there and tell me you have fallen in love with a Swedish fiddler that you met in Sicily, and that you want to *leave* me, Søren Krøyer, for this . . . this upstart.'

She was glad of his anger. It was easier to face than grief.

'He is not precisely that, Søren,' Marie said quietly.

She had gained a new composure since she had been away. He might have known. She'd put on a little weight, her skin was luminous, her hair shone, her eyes were bright. The fretful hypochondriac who dashed about the house like a nervous chicken had disappeared, and the shade of the lovely young woman who had looked out at Søren all those years ago through that Parisian café window looked at him now again,

He knew he had lost her. All that was left to him was to rail at it.

'Oh, so how would *you* describe him?' he asked sarcastically. 'And don't dream of telling me how *fine* he is, how beautiful his *mind.* I warn you, I will not put up with starry-eyed nonsense. Say one single thing that makes him more than a philandering adventurer, and I might be prepared to consider the idea.'

He sounded like an outraged father whose daughter has taken up with some sort of riff-raff rather than a wronged husband, but she had promised herself she would not let him needle her, no matter what he said, and she tried hard to see things from his point of view. He was, after all, the offended party. She had behaved shamefully, and the fact that she had come home and was looking for his blessing didn't excuse her or make her conduct any more acceptable. She tried to remember all that when he infuriated her.

'Well,' she said calmly, 'he directs the national orchestra of Sweden.'

'I see,' said Søren, deflated. He could hardly quibble with that.

She thought briefly of Holger and Rita's sausage-maker and was glad she was at least not bringing such ignominy to Søren. It would matter to him.

'He is something high up in the Conservatory, I can't exactly remember the title, Søren, and he is a composer of some . . . ' Marie searched for a word that would encompass both Hugo's high status and his celebrity. 'Renown,' she finished.

'Hmph,' said Søren, mollified in spite of himself.

It came to her that she was describing the Swedish musical equivalent of Søren himself. As he was the grand old man of Danish painting, so Hugo was the . . . well, he was not old, but he was certainly grand . . .

'And what does his wife think?' Søren asked.

'He is not married.'

Marie did not feel it necessary to explain about the young woman who had been accompanying Hugo when they met. It had been tricky and expensive to despatch her. Marie had watched with some amusement as Hugo achieved it. At the same time, he had been laying siege to Marie, scattering posies wrapped in love notes in her path, posting pieces of manuscript music he claimed she had inspired under her door, sending glasses of champagne to her table at every meal. As long as the girl was there, Marie had been able to refuse to take him seriously.

Even after he had sent his girlfriend packing, the fact that she had been there stood as evidence, in Marie's eyes, to Hugo's deep unseriousness – that and his ridiculous story of falling in love with her picture. Her own initial reaction to that fairy tale had been just as incredulous as Søren's was now.

Hugo had claimed the girl was not the obstacle, and that if he had only been wearing shoes at their first meeting, he would have conquered Marie more easily. He'd got off, he said, on the wrong footing, and then he had yelped with laughter at his own un-intended humour.

Insincerity was, to Marie, a sure defence against any kind of ro-mantic involvement, and so convinced had she been that Hugo was merely play-acting that she'd hardly noticed that she was actu-ally falling in love with him. It had all been such a joke, it could not at the same time have been real. That faulty logic had been her un-doing, and by the time she'd realised it, it had been too late.

After Miss What'shername had finally left, in a trail of tears and threats – the surest guarantee of his love for Marie, in Hugo's own estimation – he'd turned with open arms to her, and all unexpect-edly to herself, she'd fallen gratefully into his embrace. There fol-lowed long days and weeks of bliss. They walked and talked and sang and played and painted in the bougainvillea-splashed gardens of their small hotel. They wandered along the sands by the turquoise sea, like people in a poem, Marie said, though she would not have been able to identify the poem if she had been challenged – it just seemed a poetic kind of thing. Eventually there had come a day, when Hugo drew her into the shadow of a rock by the shore, and in the circle of his arms she felt the world spinning around her and knew now for sure that she was lost. He kissed the dip beneath her throat, and she floated out of her body and lodged in his heart. While she was absent, her body did as it pleased, which was to accompany Hugo up the back stairs to his shutter-darkened room and to open herself silkily, deliciously and finally with total drunken abandon.

From that moment, there was no question but that she was caught in the nets of his passion. It was not just how her sense of honour worked. It was that she had sunk her whole self into loving him, and nothing could rescue her now. But she was not a woman to have affairs, and if she wanted Hugo, her only option was to marry him. Nothing less even occurred to her.

'Not married?' Søren was spitting incredulously. 'What age is this . . . prodigy?'

'He is about the age you were when you married me,' she said. It was a sly riposte, but she had to make him see that even if Hugo was bound to be Søren's sworn enemy, he was not after all so very different. They were men with the same . . . appetites. That made *her* sound like some kind of a prize cheese, but the truth of the situation was that Hugo was their sort of person and, in any other circumstances, he would have been welcomed into their circle.

Søren and Marie were both, in theory, believers in sexual freedom. At least, Søren had had a lot of this kind of freedom in his past, something Marie would not be so mean-spirited as to point out; but that fact gave her the courage to claim a share of it now for herself. He would not have acknowledged the parallel, had she called upon it to bolster her case – he was a man, after all, it wasn't the same – but fortunately she did not call in that debt, or she would have been dismayed at the impatience with which he would undoubtedly have set all her painfully constructed tolerance at nought.

She was not proud of the situation; she would not for the world have brought it about on purpose; she had certainly not set out to hurt Søren and if there was anything she could do, short of giving Hugo up to assuage his grief, she would do it; but it did not seem unreasonable all the same, for her to claim her right now to this love. She felt entitled. And it was not as if she wanted to *elope* with her lover. She had done the honourable thing by coming straight home to Søren and asking for her freedom.

That was the killer, of course. What she saw as the only honourable course was to him humiliation of the worst kind. She wanted him to acquiesce in her leaving him. A less insistently ethical person might just have sloped off quietly and spared him this confrontation, left him the dignity of his wounds. What sort of sainthood did she require of him?

'Very well,' he said, eventually, sitting down heavily and pulling his tartan rug over his thin knees, 'bring him here. Let's get a look at him.'

He had hardly thought of what he was saying, but the effect was gratifying. Marie was shaken by his suggestion, as if he had knocked her sideways, unbalancing her carefully created composure. He had been about to say how his heart was breaking, how he could not see his way forward without her, how his world would disintegrate if she left. But perhaps he did not need to say these things. Perhaps what he needed to do was to destabilise this improbable relationship from underneath. He didn't need to try to knock it down with the combined force of his grief and her guilt. It might be much better to chip away at its foundations so that it crumpled from within.

'Bring him here, Søren? To Skagen? What on earth for?'

He thought quickly.

'Because this is your home, Marie. This is where you belong. The people who love you need to see this . . . new friend of yours.'

'I see,' she said.

'By all means, my dear, if you must take a lover . . . ' He made it sound as if she were some figure from history, 'taking' a lover, like a queen.

'If you must . . . well, it is not for us . . . ' – who was this 'us', what did he mean by this use of the plural? – 'it is not, apparently, for us to object, but let us at least be civil about it. Let us have him here. Invite him to stay. We'll have him to lunch. To dinner. For Christmas. See the cut of his jib. And then . . . well, who knows? We shall see.'

His thinking was that by domesticating the situation, by inviting this interloper into their family, he might be able to defuse the sexual element in the whole affair, put the younger man right off, in fact, with the vision of familial life that would be unfolded before him, shame him, even, into withdrawing from a husband's rightful territory. But it would have to be carefully handled, and he wasn't, he realised, with a sudden flash of self-awareness, very good at handling situations carefully. He was much better at the more dramatic response. He was quite possibly going to make a fool of himself. But he had that right, she could hardly object.

'Very well, Søren,' she said. 'I will invite him here. For Christmas. Thank you, dearest.'

'He can stay at the hotel,' Søren went on. He had not really expected that she would agree so readily, and now that she had, he needed to set limits to his magnanimous invitation.

'Very well, Søren,' she said again, meekly. 'I will arrange a room for him. And, Søren, he paints.'

She offered this as some sort of emollient, but it had the opposite effect from the one she intended.

'He *what?*'

'He paints. He's only an amateur, of course. But he's quite good. '

'An amateur painter. Pshaw!'

'Yes, the same way as you play and sing. For fun.'

'*Fun!*' he spat. 'Another damned Drachmann! Thinks painting is some sort of play. Good God, woman!'

'But . . . oh, Søren, just think. He put a brush into my hand, there in Taormina. Just handed it to me, and pointed at a canvas. I hadn't painted for *years*. But somehow, it all came flooding back, and I sat to that easel, and . . . '

'Was it any damned good, though?' asked Søren, contemptuously.

Marie didn't answer. She just patted the back of his hand and left the room.

She began to think that maybe this 'civilised' arrangement that Søren suggested might work. Perhaps the two men might develop a gruff kind of comradeship, go shooting together, sit in the Brøndums' bar over a beer in the evenings, agree to differ about Marie, and Søren could become a sort of avuncular figure to the younger lovers, a valued old friend they visited frequently and loved sincerely, the way she loved Holger.

Chapter 36

Holger's Sophie was a pretty little thing. Well, of course she was. That was his speciality. But within a few months, she was starting to chafe at the marriage. Perhaps she had expected that Holger would paint her, and she would become famous as a model, like that Marie Krøyer.

But Holger didn't paint portraits. He never had. He certainly never represented himself or his intentions in such a way. If she expected to be an artist's wife in that sense, it was a fantasy entirely of her own devising. The best he could offer was to put her in a poem. It didn't do.

'She gets up in the night,' Holger whispered to Marie, when she came visiting.

'Perhaps she's pregnant,' said Marie, practically. After all, she was awfully young, probably very fertile. 'It puts pressure on . . . you know, the *bladder*.'

'Oh, I don't mean *that*,' said Holger. 'I mean, she gets up and *leaves the house*.'

Marie looked out the windows. There was nothing to see, except occasional scrubby trees and, in the distance, the roll of the dunes, the heave of the sea.

'Where does she go?' she asked.

'I don't know,' he said. 'The beach, I suppose. She comes home wet.'

'My God, Holger! How wet? I mean, from rain? The sea spray?'

'No, it is sea*water*. I think she walks into the sea.'

'She goes swimming, you mean?'

'No, she *walks* in, in her nightgown, Marie. And her overcoat.'

'Holger!' said Marie, taking his hand.

He'd married her on a whim, almost as a lark, to show he could still do it, and now it appeared she was . . . well, that was not normal behaviour, was it?

'She doesn't cook, of course,' Holger said, waving towards the kitchen.

There was a glass-fronted dresser between the dining room and the kitchen, with enormous numbers of plates and cups.

'Matching crockery, Holger,' said Marie looking towards it now. 'You always swore we were all "too married" just because our cups fitted our saucers.'

But Holger was not in the mood for teasing.

'And she doesn't eat, unless I cook and put it in front of her and make her.'

'Holger,' Marie said, 'she sounds like a very unhappy woman. Is there anything . . . I mean, I am sure you love her, but you know, are there . . . problems?'

'Of course there are problems. A woman who walks into the sea at night like a *mermaid*, leaving me shivering in my bed. And who cries all day and won't eat unless I force her.'

'Oh, my dear Holger,' Marie said. 'You can't live with that sort of thing going on.'

'You should know, Marie,' said Holger. 'What's this I hear about a younger man? Coming to Skagen, I believe.'

Marie hadn't realised the story was out. She'd only been home a few days. But she was relieved now, that she could talk about it.

'He's not younger,' she said.

'Not than you, of course,' Holger said. 'Than Søren, I meant.'

'But he is beautiful,' she went on, as if Holger hadn't spoken. She didn't want to discuss Søren. 'And so talented. He writes me sonatinas, Holger! He adores me.'

'Adores you, Marie? I thought I heard you say once that you . . .'

'Yes, yes, I did. But that was before I had been adored. Oh, Holger, I've never felt like this before. Never. I mean, I love Søren, that goes without saying and, in the beginning, I was of course totally infatuated. But this is different. This is like breathing another air. He lets me paint.'

'Good heavens, Marie, surely . . . '

'Oh, I don't mean that Søren ever prevented me. I just mean . . . it's a kind of freedom, Holger.'

'And are you planning to marry this man, my dear?'

'If Søren will release me. Don't you think that is the right course, Holger?'

'I do, Marie. You know Søren and I are old sparring partners, but we are friends, and I don't relish the idea of his being hurt. But I have watched you fading away for years in that man's shadow. I don't blame him, he can't help it. But if you have a chance now to come out into the light, I think you should jump at it, my little Marie.'

Marie stood up as if to go.

'What about Vibeke?' asked Holger.

'I can't think about Vibeke,' said Marie. 'Every time I think about her, my heart turns over. What that poor child has been through! But tell me, Holger, where is Sophie? Am I not to meet her?'

'Oh, she's been called away to England, to her sister. She's ill.'

'And are you missing her?'

Holger gave a sly grin. 'Well, let us say that I will be glad when she comes home, but for the moment, I am enjoying the peace.'

Alfvén arrived in Skagen shortly before Christmas, and Søren tolerated him ostentatiously. He treated him like an upper servant who had fallen on hard times and was invited to join the family at Christmas dinner out of charity. He explained things to him that did not need explaining, pointing out which cutlery went with which dish, asking him if he had ever eaten this or that perfectly common food.

Marie was mortified. That was, of course, the intention. Søren treated his wife's lover more or less civilly when they met at table or about the streets, but he would not acknowledge his claim on Marie, and he feigned surprise every time Hugo appeared. Or perhaps he genuinely was surprised: perhaps he really did expect the whole business would just wither away if he over-watered it with husbandly solicitude.

Hugo bore it pretty well, and Søren's strategy of wearing him down backfired in the end, for it was Søren himself who ended up eroded away by attrition.

Hugo went back to Sweden in the new year and Marie was alone with Søren and Vibeke. She felt as if she was losing her reason, but by now she had learned that the panicky feeling that overcame her and made her fuss fretfully about the house was an indication not of illness in herself but in Søren. The more panicky she got, the more she ran around the rooms wringing her hands and crying, terrified that the walls were going to close in on top of her, the more convinced she became that he was spiralling into madness.

This time, he did not scream or roll on the floor. He whooped about the house drinking vermouth and flinging the windows open onto the winter air, announcing that he had decided to become an opera singer and abandon painting, only that there might be a problem, because he had it on good authority that they were thinking of making him king of Denmark, but of course it was being kept very quiet for fear of upsetting the reigning king.

Once the king came into it, Marie knew for sure that he had lost his grip, and she sent for Anna and Michael.

Anna had never seen Søren like this, but she seemed to have an instinct about how to handle him. She sat by his chair and spoke quietly to him, as if he were a nervous child.

At first, he stared past her, as if he didn't know her, couldn't take her presence into account.

She kissed him and said his name, and he seemed to wake up. He looked at her and said 'Anna,' very faintly.

'Yes, Søren, it's Anna. How are you?' As if he just had a touch of bronchitis.

'Not well, Anna. Not well enough to be king.' He pawed at her with a hand that seemed out of his control, and he started to sob. 'Tell them I should not be king. Please, Anna. It is too much. I just can't. I have a painting to finish first.'

'You shan't be king, Søren,' Anna said, and held his hand. He kissed her fingers and his tears trickled over the backs of her hands.

'You need to pack your things now, Søren,' Anna said. 'Michael is here. He will help you.'

'Yes, yes, yes, indeed, oh, yes!' said Michael, and he put out his hand to Søren, who was calm now.

Together they went upstairs, Søren and Michael, holding hands. One of them would step ahead and then pause on the step, waiting for the other; then the other would join the first on the step and they would stop and smile at each other, and then one or other of them would shuffle ahead again, and so they made slow progress upstairs to Søren's room, to pack.

Afterwards, they all went out to Søren's studio and he showed them the evidence in his paintings for his latent talent as a sculptor, and they agreed with him that he should certainly try sculpting when he came home.

'Home?' he said. 'Am I not already at home?'

'Yes, of course, Søren, dearest,' said Anna. 'You are at home, now, and all the people who love you are here, me and Michael and Marie and Vips. But you are not well, you know that. You need to rest and get well again.'

Marie was sitting on a stool by the studio door, looking out onto the rain.

Anna took Søren's hand when the carriage came, and told him where he was going and then he started to cry again, but she said it was not the same place he had been before, not the dreadful echoey place. She knew of a bright, modern clinic not far away, where they had new kinds of treatment and the patients were regarded as honoured guests. She kissed him and said she would go with him, they all would go with him, but he said he wanted only Marie.

'Of course you do, dear,' said Anna. 'But think what will happen when you get there, Søren. You will need to stay for a little while, till you are well again, but Marie will have to come back home to be with Vibeke, won't she?'

'Yes,' said Søren.

'And you wouldn't want her to have to make that journey home all alone, would you? Think how she would be feeling, after saying goodbye to you.'

Søren looked doubtfully at Marie, who would not meet his eye, but only because she was so exhausted, she was afraid the least thing might push her over the edge and into tears.

'No,' Søren said. 'No, I do not wish to upset Marie. I love Marie, Anna. Will you tell her that?'

'I will,' said Anna. And then, with a logic that was almost cheerful, she went on, 'So you see, Søren, if we go too, Michael and I, we can be company for Marie on the way home. What do you think of that for an idea? Is it not an admirable arrangement?'

'Hugo is not to come,' said Søren. 'I will not have that scoundrel about the place.'

'Of course not, Søren,' said Anna. 'Hugo is in Uppsala. Or Gøteborg. One of those places. He has a concert. He is far too busy to come bothering you.'

Søren nodded, and stood up, to indicate that he was ready to go.

Anna sent Vibeke to Helga, and said she was to ask Helga's grandma to give her something to eat later, and she was not to worry about her papa, he would be fine quite soon, she would see.

'It is the best place,' Anna said to Marie as they came home again, having left Søren in the care of the clinic. 'And just think, when he is up and about, which will be very soon, he will have Sophie to talk to.'

'Who?'

'Sophie Drachmann,' said Anna.

'Anna!' Michael's voice was shocked. 'You are not to be trusted.'

Anna clapped her hand over her mouth. 'Oh, Marie, he is right. I have broken a confidence. It was to be a great secret, and I have let it out.'

'Anna, what are you saying? You have to tell me now you have got this far, or I shall imagine all sorts of things.'

Michael sighed.

'I put you on your honour, Marie,' said Anna, 'not to breathe a word to Holger.'

'You have a secret from Holger? Oh, Anna!'

'Well,' said Anna, 'you remember that Sophie was supposed to be going to England? That was just a cover story. Michael and I met her off the train at Port Frederick and took her to the clinic. It was all arranged on the quiet, so as not to "upset" Holger, though, if you ask me, Holger would have been delighted to think she was being looked after. The poor girl is mad as a hatter. She makes Søren seem like a slightly distracted rabbit.'

In spite of everything that had happened, Marie could not help giving a nervous giggle, though she did not know if she was laughing at the idea of Sophie keeping her whereabouts a secret from Holger – pretending, poor girl, that she was not mad, as if the whole village did not know it – or at the prospect of Søren and Sophie providing companionship for each other as they convalesced or whatever it was, but it all struck her as mighty funny. Anna laughed with her, as they rattled along in the carriage back to Skagen.

Michael said they were a disgrace.

Chapter 37

Hugo rented a cottage that summer, about a mile from the Krøyers. Søren was home from the clinic by then, and quite well, but he had given up entertaining Hugo. He was prepared to tolerate him, he said, as long as he did not have to meet the fellow at breakfast.

He had never had to meet him at breakfast – they would not be so crass – but in view of this new mood of his, Marie thought it wise to keep Hugo at a distance, and so Hugo's being there became a kind of absent presence in the Krøyers' house. They all lived a known but unacknowledged double life: Søren and Vibeke tiptoed around the absent Hugo, pretending he wasn't a mile down the road waiting for Marie to slip away and join him for the afternoon; and, for her part, she was always home in time to cook supper.

Marie found it all a dreadful strain, but Søren affected hardly to notice. He was in high good spirits as midsummer approached, and the sun lingered later and later in the sky so that the evenings, stretching out long, tenuous hands, almost touched the dawn, with hardly any night in between, only a long, blue twilight. It seemed to him as if he had painted the beach in Skagen all his life: the morning sun on the sea, children splashing on the shore, their slippery bodies glistening with seawater; the afternoon sun, even and still on calm summer days; the evening sun tinting fishing boats with rosy warmth and slanting on fishermen casting their nets; blue moonlight on bathing boys. But now he wanted to paint the midnight, and his friends in the light of the midsummer bonfire.

It was to be his grandest project yet. His eyesight was failing –

new spectacles made not a jot of difference, he said, though he constantly took them off and polished them vigorously – and he was going to harvest what light was left to him for this painting.

In honour of its being his last big work, he was going to paint *everybody* – all his friends, his whole circle. He, the greatest thrower of parties that Skagen had ever known – perhaps that Jutland had ever known – was going to give the greatest, most splendid party of his life. They were going to have the best St John's Eve bonfire that Skagen's beach had ever seen on the lightest night of the year. Drachmann was working on a poem, some sort of anthem, he believed, and Alfvén could doubtless be relied upon to come up with a tune. He threw out the last idea carelessly, as if Alfvén were a regular supplier of goods to the household, a tradesman one could depend upon but could not be expected to have to deal with personally. And as for Degn Brøndum, the hotelier, he was to lay in stocks of food and wines for the feast.

Weeks before the big night, he made everyone stand around an imaginary fire on the beach in a huge circle and he sketched them in, adults and children, artists and their wives, local dignitaries, townspeople and friends, uncles and visitors and relations, everyone except strangers who happened by, sitting and standing, chatting together or watching the imaginary fire. He spent feverish days in his studio transferring his sketched-out plan onto canvas, and calling people in, one at a time, to fill in their individual portraits. At night, he would go down to the beach to study the sky and the sand and the sea and come home with small canvases on which he had painted the colours that he saw. He lit brazier after brazier on the beach and made his friends go with him to the shore in the middle of the night to sit or stand by his blaze, to see what effect the firelight had on their shadows and their skin tone.

Marie kept out of his way. She knew from experience that when he got like this, he could easily become febrile, brittle, and confrontation could be disastrous. Things had come to a pitch where she needed to force a final confrontation, but she didn't want to ruin this important painting of his, and she resolved to hold her fire until after midsummer.

But he noticed how she skulked about, and the way her cheeks had collapsed inwards and her forehead had developed spidery lines of worry and weariness. He couldn't bear to think he was keeping her like some bird that could not thrive in captivity. But neither could he bear to let her go, because, if he did, she would soar right away, and he would never ever see her lovely face again. It was a problem without a solution; at least, it was a problem whose solution would leave him with a problem, which came to the same thing. Either way lay heartbreak.

One evening, he went out without saying where he was going, and when he came home, Hugo was with him. Marie sprang out of her chair when they came in and fluttered around the room. She plumped a cushion. She drew the curtains. She opened the curtains again, to let the moonlight in. She offered Hugo a glass of wine. She offered Søren a glass of wine. She plumped the same cushion again.

'No wine, no wine!' said Søren impatiently. 'Not yet. I want you to come to the beach with us, Marie. For my painting. I want you and Hugo to pose for me. There's an upturned boat that I've got nicely in position. It will make a good backdrop for you. Will you do that?'

'What do you mean, Søren? You want to paint me and Hugo *together*?'

'Yes, yes, of course. That's what I mean.'

She fluttered about agitatedly looking for her shawl.

'It's on that sofa,' Søren said. 'Your shawl.'

'Søren,' she said, taking his arm as they walked to the beach, 'Søren, what is it?'

'I have to paint it as it is,' he said. 'It's not just a pretty picture. It is how things *are*. It has to show that.'

'I see,' she said.

'I know,' he said.

'What?'

'I know, Marie,' he said again. 'About . . . you know. Hugo has spoken to me. We'll work out the details, but you can have your divorce, though it breaks my heart to lose you.'

She kissed his cheek, and she rested her face against his upper arm, and walked like that, half-slumped against him, all the way to the beach. Hugo kept several paces behind them.

'Anna will help me to look after Vips,' he said. This is her home. She stays here, Marie.'

Marie felt as if the air had been sucked out of her lungs. She couldn't answer him.

When they arrived at the sea, Søren showed them where he wanted them to stand, and then he stood back and looked at them for several long minutes, drinking in his Marie, standing there in the blue midnight, awkward as a girl.

She was silent, sullen, eaten up by what he had said.

'You're going to be at the centre of the painting, my dear,' he said to her, 'but far back, at a distance, hardly recognisable.'

She nodded mutely.

She stood with Hugo, as Søren directed them, like a newly engaged girl with her fiancé, having her betrothal picture taken. Søren told them how he wanted them to stand, half-leaning against the boat. He pulled their elbows this way and that, till he got the effect he wanted.

'Good, good, good!' he muttered, as he sketched them in, shy and anxious, half-turned to each other, embarrassment hanging in their angled arms. 'That's perfect. Perfect. That is exactly what I want. The situation, you see, as it is. Thank you, my dear.'

Marie and Hugo looked askance at one another, not knowing what to make of this performance.

'Good!' Søren called again, and captured their very askanceness in his sketch. 'Well done, Alfvén.'

When the real St John's brazier was finally ablaze, everyone stood and sat for one last time, like an opera chorus, in the places Krøyer had allocated to them, and he made swift amendments with his paintbrush, catching here a glance, there a play of firelight on a curl, and then he enlisted help to lift the giant canvas back to his studio, where he would continue to work on it over the following months. It was far from finished, but he was happy that he had got the shape and the mood of it, the portraits were all prepared, the colours were planned and the fall of the light was clear to him.

The village children had sat patiently around, evening after evening, while Krøyer painted them. He told them that they might order whatever they wanted for the real Eve of St John, when the real fire was lighting. Whatever they wanted to eat, Mr Brøndum was to get it and they were to have it on the night, and he would pay for it. They ordered crabs' legs and barley sugar and candied fruits and cinnamon drops and persimmons – Degn baulked at persimmons – and lemonade and goose and mashed potatoes and toffee apples and ginger cake and cheese soufflé and liquorice sticks. For the adults, there were jellied eels and beef in aspic and soft white bread rolls and piles of salad and raisin pudding and any amount of champagne and seltzer water to wash it all down.

Once the painting was safely stowed in the studio, the guests fell upon the feast. Drachmann conducted several rousing renditions of his new song. Someone produced a concertina, and there was dancing at the water's edge, where the sand was most compacted, though the dancers' feet still sank up to their ankles and they laughed till they cried as they clumped about on sandy feet, trying to catch up with the music. It reminded Anna of the days when

Helen used to play for them in the hotel and they would spill, laughing, out onto the beach, waving champagne bottles and calling to each other across the sands. When they were young courting couples and newlyweds, before any of these children chasing each other up and down and into the waves had even been thought of.

It was almost breakfast time before Søren carried Vibeke's half-sleeping body home in the grey light of dawn, and put her to bed, still in her party frock, damp and sandy about the hem. The child slept through the clatter of her mother's departure, the trundling out of trunks, even the wailing that rose from her father's studio as the carriage went rumbling off to the station. When she woke, she found a thick square envelope propped against her mirror. Her name was on it, in her mother's handwriting.

Vibeke took off her still damp frock and changed into an everyday dress, washed her face and hands and brushed her hair. When she was good and ready, she sat on the edge of her bed, and read her mother's lavender-scented letter:

Dearest Vips,

I came in to kiss you this morning, but you were so deeply asleep after all the excitement, I did not care to wake you.

Papa will explain to you why I have had to leave. He is good at explaining things, isn't he? But I will just tell you the main thing for now: I am going to have a baby, and Mr Alfvén is the baby's papa. Mr Alfvén and I will be married shortly in Stockholm. We will stay there then, for a little while, until the baby comes, and then we will go to Mr Alfvén's house in the country.

Then you must come and visit your new brother or sister, for of course it will be your brother or sister, even though it has a different papa.

Be kind to your own dear papa, Vibeke. You know I love him

very much, but I love Mr Alfvén too, and since I can't be married to both of them, I have had to choose one of them. I have chosen Mr Alfvén, not because I love him better, but because this new baby needs to have his or her papa, as you have yours.

When you come to visit after the baby is born, you can decide then if you would like to live here with us, or if you would prefer to stay with Papa. You would have to learn Swedish, of course, if you want to stay with us, but that is not so hard. Whatever you choose, you can always visit me in Sweden or Papa in Skagen. It is up to you.

You don't need to decide now, my darling. For now, just be very kind to Papa and help him not to be so sad. I will miss you both most dreadfully, as I know you will miss me.

> Your own
> Mama

Vibeke read the letter twice. Then she folded it over, tore it in two, tore it again, and again, until she had made the tiniest pieces of it, and then she scattered it, like confetti, all over the floor, and went downstairs to get something to eat.